The Royal Cricket of Japan   *by James Lash*

Marlin the Magnificent   *by James Abrell*

The Shoes That Were Danced to Pieces
                    by Dorothy Beck Webb

The Golden Mask   *by Edward Kessell*

Huck Finn   *by Paul Brady*

The Strolling Players
                    by Darwin Reid Payne and Christian Moe

6

NEW PLAYS

FOR

CHILDREN

Edited by

Christian Moe *and* Darwin Reid Payne

Preface by

Jane Dinsmoor Triplett

SOUTHERN ILLINOIS UNIVERSITY PRESS

Carbondale and Edwardsville

FEFFER & SIMONS, INC.

London and Amsterdam

All rights reserved
Printed in the United States of America
Designed by Andor Braun
International Standard Book Number 0–8093–0453–8
Library of Congress Catalog Card Number 70–112391

*To those playwrights, directors, and actors
of children's theatre whose work admits no
compromise with high standards when meeting
an audience of children; and to that children's
audience who represents the real hope of the
American theatre.*

Contents

Preface   ix

Introduction   xiii

A Note on the Production of the Plays   xix

The Royal Cricket of Japan   1
   Original Fantasy *by James Lash*

Marlin the Magnificent   45
   Original Fantasy *by James Abrell*

The Shoes That Were Danced to Pieces   89
   Adaptation of a Grimms' Fairy Tale
    by Dorothy Beck Webb

The Golden Mask   139
   Mystery *by Edward Kessell*

Huck Finn   195
   Adaptation of Mark Twain's Classic Novel
    by Paul Brady

The Strolling Players   239
   Based on the Characters of the *Commedia dell'Arte*
    by Darwin Reid Payne and Christian Moe

Preface

ONE of the most urgent needs in children's theatre today is for bodies of dramatic literature which are easily available for study. A producer of plays for children should have knowledge of many plays in order to select those which fill the needs of his particular audience and which are within the capabilities of his particular organization.

That collections of plays written for children do not exist is not surprising since the total number of such dramas is small compared to the number written for adults, since almost all of these have appeared within this century, and since productions have been sporadic as well as poorly reported. But this void must be filled before the quality of children's theatre can improve. Too much time and effort is required to obtain every play from scraps of evidence discovered in the catalogues of publishers, in professional journals, in brochures from other theatres, and among the woefully small number of scripts on the shelves of most public, high school, and college libraries. The use of such sources is not to be discarded as it represents the only method for discovering new plays, but it is time consuming, may be expensive, and is frequently disappointing.

The publication of this collection of plays is, therefore, an important step forward. It is hoped that many more volumes will be forthcoming. Such anthologies make it possible for the producer and/or director to spend his time reading and comparing plays. Once secure in the knowledge of the literature in the field of children's theatre, he can apply it to his audience.

Few plays will hold equally the interest of children from all levels, primary through junior high school, and then only if the play is directed and produced to that end. Maturation and learning level are the important factors. Actual age and school grade offer only the barest clues. Less mature children with shorter attention spans cannot be expected to follow subplots or to sit for more than an hour. They are less verbal and almost continuous action is required to enable them to understand the content of the play. More mature children enjoy a fairly complex plot structure and are able to remain involved for a longer period of time without intermission. They are more able to follow changes in locale and time. They are intrigued by disguises and mistaken identities which only confuse children on more primary learning levels. All levels of maturity express their delight in period plays as well as in fantasy, from fairy tale to science fiction. A play laid in the present day may seem easier to do, but it must be magnificently written and produced to hold a child audience.

Any real study of the interests of children for the purpose of selecting plays for them begins with classroom teachers and school librarians. Ask these specialists what is included in the curriculums at the various levels (particularly in social studies and in language arts). What books and/or stories are the children reading and when? What do they wish to talk about? What ideas already presented to them can drama successfully deal with? What new ideas can theatre supply based on what the children already know?

Sit in the classrooms of successful teachers. How long can the children deal with one subject? How extensive are their vocabularies? What experiences do they have in common? How do they react to the actions of their peers as well as those of adults? What are their responses to tones of voice, music, noise, color, texture?

The producers of theatre for children may go to the schools to learn about children, but the plays they produce must not be fiercely educational. Theatre fails when it tries to teach facts for facts' sake. Plays may be based on fact, but they must deal with concepts expressed through the actions and reactions of characters. Theatre is entertainment, entertainment with an idea, acted by skillful performers assisted by a fine scheme of production to present a unified whole.

Good teachers are always skillful performers. Their rooms always represent settings which contribute to their teaching. Much can be obtained by studying their methods. In their classes there is no evidence of an adult condescending to a child. Each teacher feels that the knowledge he wishes to impart is important but not to the exclusion of the responses of the children to that knowledge. In his own peculiar style, every good teacher is looking for experiences that he and his students may share. These qualities are part of every good theatre production. Actors, directors, and production staff must be convinced of the importance of what they are doing and the equal importance of the response of their audience not to spectacle for spectacle's sake, which is the worst form of condescension, but to spectacle for art's sake.

The producer should study plays with a fine eye to their possibilities for spectacle as well as to the honesty with which their characters are developed and their ideas and story lines presented. Children's theatres are just now beginning to replace highly romanticized and pictorially presented dramas with plays of ideas in which the characters are neither good as gold nor bad as brass. This change should not be made at the expense of the essential theatricality, the color and action, which distinguishes drama from other art forms.

Few children prefer neutral colors. The question they put most often to a storyteller is, "And then what happened?" Something must be happening, too, in their play and in the movies or television they watch. This "something" may be sad or comic, quiet or exciting; but it must have meaning for them. The producer of plays for children should observe children in these situations. What makes them comfortable? What makes them uneasy? What are their standards of fair play? What clues make them reject one person and ensure the acceptance of another? How do they distinguish between a hero and a villian? What will hold their gaze for minutes at a time and what do they turn away from immediately in boredom or incomprehension?

Holding the interest of a child audience and presenting material which is comprehensible to that audience is not enough. Theatre for children like theatre for adults is an art form and can be dealt with only as such. Study of the child will indicate to producer and playwright the direction in which this form must move and the method by which this movement must be obtained. If, however, the producer has no play to produce and the playwright has no one to produce his play the potentials of both go unrealized. The increased availability of scripts such as this volume represents makes more possible the combination of their two efforts. Only then can the goal of children's theatre, the creation of art, become a realization.

Jane Dinsmoor Triplett

January 1971
Evanston, Illinois

Introduction

THIS anthology of new plays for children seeks to provide one answer to a current and rather desperate dilemma. The growing number of producing groups—women's clubs, junior leagues, college and university theatres, community theatres, established children's theatres, and professional companies—interested and involved in presenting effective theatre for children do not have adequate opportunity to encounter fresh new dramas of tested quality and theatrical effectiveness. Unless such groups have qualified playwrights in their own ranks, and most do not, they are forced to turn to a handful of commercial publishing houses that specialize in children's drama. And here they encounter a dearth of new plays. To be sure, there are reasons for this. The standards of such publishers, with a few exceptions, often lag behind the growing advances being made in the educational level of the children for whom the plays were written. The same tired, twenty-year old fairy-tale plays and mystery-comedies (television has surfeited our children with the latter) are offered; and the largest portion of them are neither particularly well written nor stageworthy. (Incidentally, we hold no prejudice against dramatized fairy tales as long as they are new tales or old tales presented in fresh playscripts.)

Children's tastes are becoming more sophisticated. Since plays are one valuable means through which children learn about people in the world around them, the importance is obvious of introducing the audience of youngsters to new plays whose writers reflect the world of today.

Another reason why commercial publishers lack enough new plays is that they normally possess a large backlog of published old scripts which they earnestly wish to sell. They are reluctant to gamble an investment on a new playscript, and therefore tend to be extremely timid about encouraging the new writer since in reality they publish so little of his work. And this leads us to another point.

Talented new writers of children's drama have few open avenues to reach prospective producers and audiences. They encounter difficulty in getting their scripts published. If they are not fortunate enough to be associated with a producing group, or win a playwriting contest whose sponsors promise production, their work never reaches *any* audience. If a group does stage their play, it is usually for a brief run and then is forgotten. Such work, when deserving, should be accessible on a nationwide scale to those persons interested in reading and producing children's plays. Here we have the playwright and the producer both wanting to reach each other, and yet both are unable to do so. The writer who has written an effective play for children deserves to have it published; the producer searching for a good children's play should be able to acquire it easily. To give an example of this situation, the Children's Theatre Conference of the American Educational Theatre Association recently has attempted to present an unpublished script display at every one of its regional meetings so that producing groups in attendance may read new scripts by new writers. Admittedly this is a stop-gap measure whose success cannot be estimated at the time of this writing. It reveals, however, that the problem is not an isolated one.

As we see it, this twofold problem of qualified new writers needing a larger outlet for their work and producers needing greater access to new plays for children, only can be met now through the publication of new playscripts. This will furnish a direct practical means by which the producers can meet the work of the new playwright. Ideally such new drama should be of proven quality by first having been tested and judged effective in performance.

The following collection is composed of new plays for children written and produced at Southern Illinois University over the last decade. Because producers frequently welcome advice on the production of new works, each playscript is accompanied by one or more sketches for suggested settings, a property list, and notes of unusual production demands when present. Most of the plays have relatively small casts and are suitable for touring. In point of fact, at least half the plays have been taken on tour. The average performance time for each play is approximately one hour.

The plays represent some variety in subject-matter appeal and authors. James Lash's *The Royal Cricket of Japan* and James

Abrell's *Marlin the Magnificent* are original fairy tales. Dorothy Beck Webb's *The Shoes That Were Danced to Pieces* is a play based on a fairy tale by the Grimms. In the mystery category stands *The Golden Mask* by Edward Kessell. Paul Brady's *Huck Finn* is adapted from Mark Twain's famous novel. And *The Strolling Players* by Darwin Payne and Christian Moe turns to the traditional comic characters and antics of the *commedia dell' arte* to let children experience an exciting theatre of the past within the framework of a drama for young audiences.

A brief description of each play may prove helpful.

Directed toward younger children from prenursery-school age to sixth grade, *The Royal Cricket of Japan* is set in an ancient and mythical Japan. The Emperor's royal cricket is found missing from its cage kept in the custody of the royal cricket keeper. The unfortunate keeper is threatened with death by the cruel Royal Executioner who dominates the will of the timid Emperor. Given only until dawn to find the tiny insect, the young son of the cricket keeper and his companion, an acrobat, temporarily turn themselves—with the help of the audience—into cricket-size creatures and explore the palace garden encountering the royal executioner's pet spider and a clue to the cricket's whereabouts. In a final act, the children return to life size and with some help unravel the mystery of the missing royal mascot. A storyteller acts as a dramatic frame for the plot and guides audience participation in controlling the action. Over the past ten years of touring children's theatre at Southern Illinois University, no children's play has been so enthusiastically received by young audiences, principals, parents, and teachers. The chief reason for this may lie in its appeal to the younger children (preschool to sixth grade) who seem to take delight in being able to directly participate in the story. There are three acts, two simple settings, and seven characters: five men, two women.

Response to the touring production of James Abrell's *Marlin the Magnificent* indicated that the story held the attention of children ranging from first grade through tenth. Unknowingly trespassing in a kingdom ruled by an irascible queen, an unsure young magician named Marlin and two pixielike companions discover an unhappy princess with blue hair. The unusual color of her hair seemingly has caused her stepmother, the queen, to treat her harshly and forbid her marriage to a royal prince. The group is captured by the queen who commands Marlin to do a magic trick. Feeling that his magical powers rest not within himself but entirely on his magician paraphanalia, Marlin foolishly relies on a broken magic wand to summon up ten thousand Easter eggs only to find they are rotten. When he discovers—while fleeing the fury of the queen—that he needs no equipment to produce magic, he ends the princess's unhappiness and the queen's bad temper by bestowing the gift of blue hair upon the head of the secretly bald monarch. The play makes a timely comment on self-reliance and prejudice. There are three acts, one interior and one exterior setting, an deight characters: four men, four women. The play is suitable for touring.

Adapted from a fairy tale by the Grimms, Dorothy Beck Webb's *The Shoes That Were Danced to Pieces* treats elements of make-believe that stimulate children's imagination, particularly those of preschool age through the sixth grade. Neglected by a kind but forgetful father and treated strictly by their aunt who acts as a stepmother, the three daughters of the king deceptively steal away every night through a magic door to dance their shoes to pieces in a magic land under the sea. Since the three princesses are locked in their room every evening, the king and his sister cannot discover why the girls' shoes are so worn. Therefore, they proclaim that a suitor may win the hand of any one of the princesses if he discovers the secret while guarding them for three nights. If he fails in this charge, the penalty is death. Thanks to a sleeping potion, two volunteers do fail. But the young palace cobbler, wishing to win the youngest sister, learns the secret whose disclosure causes the princesses to confess their deceit and restores a happy equilibrium to the royal household. There are three acts, one setting, and nine characters: four men, five women.

A children's whodunit in a land of make-believe setting, Edward Kessell's *The Golden Mask* traces the efforts of a young sorcerer's apprentice to retrieve a golden mask possessing great power which has been stolen from his mistress. The apprentice's search takes him to the royal palace of the kingdom to solicit the king's aid but he is refused admittance. Winning the friendship and help of a young princess, the boy gains entrance to the castle where he encounters a host of suspicious characters, and several narrow escapes from death. After many adventures intensified by strange riddles, disguises, and mistaken identities, the mask and its thief are discovered. There are two acts, four settings, and fourteen characters:

nine men, five women. The play holds appeal for children from the first grade through the eighth.

Mark Twain's well-known *The Adventures of Huckleberry Finn* furnishes the base for Paul Brady's *Huck Finn*. Three of Huck's adventures have been dramatized into a story taking only an hour and twenty minutes to perform. Befriending the runaway slave Jim, Huck runs away from home to escape the wrath of his ne'er-do-well father. The two companions meet two colorful reprobates, the King and the Duke, who join their company and persuade them to raise some money by putting on a dramatic performance in a nearby town. The performance is not a success and Jim is captured by townspeople and held by a local farmer for safekeeping until his lawful master is notified. In act 2 the King and the Duke pose as two English uncles in order to steal the inheritance left two orphan girls by their deceased father. Having a bothersome conscience, Huck protects the girls and averts the theft of their money by exposing the imposters. Act 3 discloses Huck's successful efforts with the aid of Tom Sawyer to free Jim. At the end of the drama Huck is left in the care of the friendly Phelps family who intend to civilize him. There are three acts, three settings, and twelve speaking characters: nine men, three women. The play is most effective with audiences in the nine to sixteen age range.

The Strolling Players by Darwin Payne and Christian Moe brings child audiences back to the days of the Renaissance when colorful troupes of comic actors toured the European countryside performing short comedies from town to town. In *The Strolling Players* such a troupe of actors present a play calling upon the traditional antics and characters of the *commedia dell' arte*: the wily servants Arlecchino and Columbina, the foolish old Pantalone, the garrulous Il Dottore, and the vain and boastful Il Capitano. The play-within-a-play recounts the attempt of the unhappy old Pantalone to find a particular apple tree whose fruit, when eaten, will make anyone happy. Confirming the location of such a tree by means of an ancient but unclear map, Pantalone's friend, the Doctor, persuades him to set out in search of it. After a boastful but cowardly Captain is hired as a military escort for protection, Pantalone and the Doctor set out on their journey also taking with them the mischievous young servant Arlecchino. A second youthful servant, a girl named Columbina, joins the group on the highroad in the disguise of a boy since earlier she has been forbidden to go on the trip by virtue of her being "just a woman." During the trip, the Doctor and his map leads the company around in circles while the fun-loving servants trick the three older men into several strange adventures including a tree that walks and talks, and an invisible army of "robbers." Finally at the journey's end, the apple tree is discovered—in a surprising place—and causes a happy if sobering conclusion for the major characters. There are three acts, one setting, and eight characters: six men, two women. The play is directed to audiences from third grade through junior high school.

The six new plays in this collection spring from the children's theatre program of Southern Illinois University's Theatre Department, a program which over the past ten years has produced a substantial store of original plays tested in performance. In operation since 1953 the children's theatre program has produced approximately forty-five plays for children; at the time of this writing fourteen of those forty-five plays have been new works—a rather respectable percentage. With the exception of three plays written by Theatre Department faculty members, the fourteen new plays of the program have been written by university graduate students now pursuing active careers in theatre.

The successful production of *The Shoes that Were Danced to Pieces* in the fall of 1958 stirred the Theatre Department as a matter of policy to encourage the writing and production of deserving new plays for child audiences. The results have been good. The majority of these new plays are of sufficient quality, we feel, to be offered to a wider audience. The six plays here have been selected with a view to representing a variety of types and authors.

The child audience represents the real hope of the American theatre and always deserves the best in play and production. If the promising playwright with his new play effectively produced can have fuller opportunity to reach this wide audience, a large and important step will be made to insure the healthy, upward growth of children's theatre in this country.

Christian Moe

Darwin Reid Payne

Southern Illinois University
January 1971

A NOTE ON THE PRODUCTION OF THE PLAYS

WITH each play a property list, a suggested floor plan and a sketch of each scene is included. Since it is always the duty of a producing group to evolve its own particular production, these simple drawings represent only the bare scenic requirements for the performance of the play, and, in some cases, the productions can be more simply designed than shown. While children's audiences are intrigued by elaborate and colorful productions—as most audiences are, regardless of age—it should never be forgotten that all audiences are more interested in what is happening rather than where the action is taking place. This is especially true of children, to whom action is the most important feature of any play. But this does not mean that a production will be drab if it is simply produced. Often when children's imaginations are challenged, they take a more active interest in the play. And when time or money is a question of concern for a producing group, those things that most directly affect the actor, his costume and his props, should receive the greatest attention. Since the actor's costume and his relationships to objects help him to reveal his character, it is evident that the whole narrative of the play will be strengthened when these departments are carefully considered. When unique problems arise or special effects are required, the authors have often included suggestions in their own notes, which are given along with the texts of the plays. These do not represent the only solutions to these problems, however, and all producing groups are encouraged to experiment with new approaches to these scripts.

The Royal Cricket
of Japan

AN ORIGINAL FANTASY

BY

James Lash

Cast of Characters

ROYAL STORYTELLER

ROYAL CRICKET KEEPER

OSEE, *son of Cricket Keeper*

AHPOO, *the Royal Acrobat*
 (TUMBLEBUG *in Act 2*)

KUDA, *the Royal Executioner*
 (BIG SPIDER *in Act 2*)

OOPS, *his assistant*
 (POOPS *in Act 2*)

EMPEROR

BUTTERFLY

TUMBLE, *a Tumblebug*

BIG SPIDER

POOPS

Synopsis of Scenes

Act One   Royal Cricket Keeper's cottage

Act Two   A clearing in a forest of grass, later the same day

Act Three   Royal Cricket Keeper's cottage, at sundown

PROPERTY LIST

Act One

Low table
Tall stand with covered cricket
    cage
Large storage chest
Fish-shaped kite
Sheet of gold paper
Paint
Glue pot and brush
A bowl
A tumble bug

Act Two

A net

Act Three

Black paint and brush in chest
Water
Ax

Act One

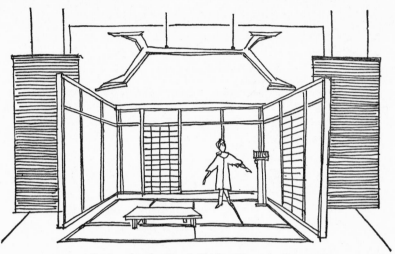

Setting for the Royal Cricket Keeper's Cottage

PROLOGUE

STORYTELLER [*coming before curtain and bowing*]:
Pretty ladies, noble gentlemen. I am Royal Storyteller of the land of
Japan. Is my Honorable duty to tell you story of Royal Cricket of
Japan.

You know where is land of Japan? Is far-off islands in blue Pacific
Ocean. They are very small islands, but most pretty, all green, with
tall mountain Fujiyama, mountain that spits smoke and fire, and
has many laughing streams.

Once, long ago, in land of Japan, there was Royal Cricket. You
could tell he was Royal Cricket because he had a golden spot on his
head in shape of crown. This Royal Cricket was prize possession of
Emperor, for whoever possessed Royal Cricket, possessed power of
Emperor. You know what Emperor is? Emperor is like king only
much more powerful.

Because of this, this special cricket had special keeper call Royal
Cricket Keeper. He had son, named OSEE, a boy almost your age.
And now, sit back, watch, and listen as we go back long years ago,
to day Emperor came to house of Royal Cricket Keeper.

> *As the last words are spoken, the curtain opens, and the*
> STORYTELLER *bows and exits.*

SCENE: *The cottage of the Royal Cricket Keeper. A simply, almost starkly furnished room. The walls are rice paper shojii bordered with dark wood. There is a double-width door open UC leading to the garden and here is the main road. DR is a smaller door leading to the rest of the cottage. A low table is C, a tall stand with the Royal Cricket Cage is against the UR wall, and a large storage chest against the back wall in UL.*

AT RISE: *OSEE is kneeling upstage of table putting the finishing touches on a fish-shaped kite. There is a sheet of gold paper, paint, and a glue pot on the table. OSEE picks up glue brush, fastens a last bit of paper on kite and tries to put brush back in glue. It sticks to his fingers, and he has some trouble getting it back in the pot.*

O S E E : Sticky old glue!

He frees himself as the ROYAL CRICKET KEEPER enters from DR and crosses to table.

K E E P E R : Good morning, young son.

O S E E : A happy day, Honorable Father.

K E E P E R : In truth, this is a happy day. The Emperor will be coming today to view the Royal Cricket. [*Indicating the cage.*] We must hasten to make our humble cottage worthy of his Royal presence. Hurry, Osee, and clean up the scraps of your kite-making, while I see that the Royal Cricket is in good health. [*Crosses upstage to cage.*]

O S E E [*picking up paper and kite*]: Why is this the Royal Cricket, Father? What makes him different from the other crickets?

K E E P E R : Because whoever possesses him has the power of the Emperor and rules all Japan. This cricket is different from the common black ones because of the golden spot in the shape of a crown that is on his head. Look, Osee, you can see it.

O S E E [*moving to cage*]: On his head, Father? I see nothing on his head.

K E E P E R : Look, there on the very top of his head is—yii! There is no mark! This is not the Royal Cricket!

O S E E : Are you sure, Father? Let me look closer. [*They look closely.*] It is true. This is not the Royal Cricket!

K E E P E R : Someone has taken the Royal Cricket and left this one in its place! Dishonor! Oh, that this should happen to me!

OSEE : Maybe he got out. He might be around the room. Hunt for him, Father. I'll help you.

KEEPER : But where can he be?

OSEE : Look there, Father, running away from the cage!

KEEPER : Quick, quick, catch him!

OSEE [*picks up bowl from table and claps it over bug on floor*]: I've got him. I've got him!

KEEPER : Gently, Osee. We must not harm the Royal Cricket. Put your hand under the bowl and pick him up.

OSEE [*lifting bowl and reaching under it*]: There—oops— hummmmm, I've got him—ug! It's a spider!

KEEPER : Did he bite you?

OSEE : No, he didn't get a chance. But he frightened me. There he goes! I'll step on him!

KEEPER : No. Do not do that. He may be one of the Royal Executioner's pet spiders.

OSEE [*shuddering*]: Oh, I can't understand why Kuda would want to keep hairy, wiggly crawly spiders for pets! [*Another shudder.*] I'd hate to get caught in one of their webs.

KEEPER : Never mind now. We must find the Royal Cricket. You look over there. I'll hunt here.

OSEE [*searching* UL *by door*]: Here, cricket, cricket, cricket. Come cricky, cricky, cricky.

> AHPOO *somersaults in from* UC *door and runs into* OSEE. *They end in a heap at* C.

OSEE : Oooops!

AHPOO : No, I'm Ahpoo. Oops is the assistant executioner.

KEEPER : Executioner!

AHPOO : *Hai,* I'm the new Royal Acrobat.
   Ahpoo is my name.
   With twirling spins and many leaps,
   I ever increase my fame.

   In many and many long years ago
   When all was dark and murking,
   In the forests and the glades
   Mean animals were lurking.

   Toads with lumps and bumps and warts
   Wanted us for their food.

And frogs with spots and glistening eyes,
Were just as mean and rude.

Salamanders, spiders, too,
Decided on us to sup.
All the slimy creatures round
Wanted to eat us up.

For acrobats were Tumblebugs.
We got our names, you see,
From being quick and brave and strong
And never wanting to flee.

We'd somersault into trouble,
Then tumble on our way.
No matter what the trouble was,
We'd make of it child's play.

So if you're ever in trouble
And don't know what to do.
Just ask my uncles and my aunts
And all my cousins, too.

Ask any of the Tumblebugs,
They're all relatives of mine.
They'll come and give you all their help,
And things will turn out fine.

Hai, I'm the Royal Acrobat.
Ahpoo is my name.
I come from a line of Tumblebugs.
From them I get my fame.

[*Ends with a low bow.*]

KEEPER : If you are the *Royal* Acrobat, why are you here?

AHPOO : Well . . . [*Looking around.*] I'll tell you why
I'm *here*—if you will tell me where here is?

OSEE : This is the cottage of the Royal Cricket Keeper.

AHPOO : Oh dear, it's happened again! Whenever I start doing
somersaults, I enjoy it so much, I just keep going and going.

KEEPER : Where were you doing these somersaults?

AHPOO : I was on the road with the Emperor on the way to your cottage when suddenly I had an urge to somersault. So I started. [*He does one.*] And then [*another*] I just [*another*] couldn't [*another*]

O S E E : STOP!

> OSEE *and* KEEPER *catch him by the feet as he starts another somersault, stopping him while he is standing on his head.*

A H P O O : That's right, I just couldn't stop. Thank you, you can let me go now.

> KEEPER *and* OSEE *let go and* AHPOO *stands up.*

A H P O O : It's even worse when I'm frightened. Then I do backward somersaults.

O S E E : I'm glad you weren't frightened.

K E E P E R : So am I.

A H P O O : Royal Cricket Keeper, may I ask you a favor?

K E E P E R : You have only to ask, and if it is in my power, I will grant it.

A H P O O : May I see the Royal Cricket, up close? I've never seen the golden crown.

K E E P E R : Of course you—the Royal Cricket? [*In fear.*] Oh no, no you can't see him.

A H P O O : Oh, please, won't you let me see him? It is said that if you look at the golden crown of the Royal Cricket, you will always have good luck.

K E E P E R : But I can't let you see the Royal Cricket.

O S E E : He's gone!!

A H P O O [*starting backward somersault*]: Gone!

O S E E : Stop him, Father. We frightened him.

> *They stop him.*

Yes, he's gone.

K E E P E R : When I went to bed last night, he was safe in his cage, but now look!

A H P O O [*moves to cage*]: There's a cricket in the cage. [*Closer.*] Are you sure it's not the Royal Cricket?

O S E E : Look at his head.

A H P O O [*looking closely*]: No golden crown!

K E E P E R : And with the Emperor on his way here to see the Royal Cricket. What shall we do?

AHPOO: Quick, hunt for him. He may be in this room. Hurry, you look there; Osee, you help me here.

They search frantically.

OSEE: He's not here!
AHPOO: Keep looking!
KEEPER: We must find him!

There is the sound of someone in the garden.

OSEE: Someone's coming!
KEEPER: Cover the cage!
AHPOO: The Emperor!

AHPOO *starts a backward somersault.* OOPS *enters* UC. AHPOO *stops when he sees him.*

OOPS [*trying to be mean and forceful, but not doing a very good job of it*]: What's going on here!
AHPOO: Oh, stop being so gruff, Oops!
OOPS [*starts crying*]: Ooooooohh! Everytime I try to be mean and make people afraid of me, someone shouts at me! How can I ever become Chief Executioner if no one will respect me he-he-he-he.
KEEPER: People won't respect you if they are afraid of you.
OSEE: Now don't cry. I'm sure Ahpoo is sorry he shouted at you.
AHPOO: Of course, I am, Oops. Now do stop that sniffling!
OOPS [*with a wail*]: There, you did it again! You don't like me!
AHPOO: Yes I do.
OOPS: No you du-du-du-don't!
KEEPER: He said he did.
OOPS: He didn't mean it.
OSEE: Yes he did, didn't you, Ahpoo?
AHPOO: I do like you, and I'm sorry I shouted at you.
OOPS [*sniffling*]: You are?
AHPOO: Yes. Now please stop snif—crying.
OSEE: We all like you and respect you.
OOPS: You don't—respect? [*All crying stops.*] Well, respect. Humm! [*Smiling.*] Since you all respect me, would you mind telling me what you were doing when I arrived—please?
KEEPER: Doing? Oh yes, doing, ah doing. Well, you see——

o s e e : We were cleaning the cottage in preparation for the arrival of the Emperor!

o o p s : Then you had better hurry. He'll be here any minute. I was sent ahead by Kuda, the Royal Executioner, to see that everything is ready. Is it?

a h p o o : Is what?

o o p s : Is everything ready?

o s e e : Oh yes. Everything is ready.

o o p s : Good. [*Starts out, then stops.*] Royal Cricket Keeper, my fortune has been running bad. I wonder if I might look at the crown of the Royal Cricket? It would bring me good luck.

k e e p e r : See the Royal Cricket? Of course you can. [*Realizing his mistake.*] I mean, CAN'T.

a h p o o : No. Oops, you can't see the Royal Cricket until the Emperor has seen it.

o o p s : Why not?

a h p o o : Why not? Well, ah you see, as, I——

o s e e : That's the law!

o o p s : Oh, please, can't I take just one little peek?

o s e e : We'd like to let you but——

k e e p e r : It's no use. Tell him the truth. You can't see the Royal Cricket because we don't have the Royal Cricket!

o o p s : Don't have him?!

k e e p e r : No, somehow he got out of the cage last night. We were looking for him when you came in.

o o p s [*runs up to the cage and takes off cover*]: But there's a cricket in the cage.

o s e e : Look at it closely.

a h p o o : No golden crown!

o o p s : Ah sooo! [*Starting to whimper.*] Oh, this is terrible! Now I'll have to cut off your head because you lost the Royal Cricket. And I don't want to cut off anyone's head!

k u d a [*voice from the garden*]: Make way, make way for the Emperor!

o o p s [*wail*]: Oh, ohoh, ohoh, oh OH!

k e e p e r : The Emperor is coming!

o s e e : What can we do?

a h p o o [*very efficiently*]: Oops, stop that blubbering and go out and hold them up for a little bit. Tell them the cricket doesn't feel well or something.

OOPS [*through the tears*]: I wouldn't——

AHPOO: Yes you would! Now do as I say.

OOPS: How can I stop them from coming? Kuda's with the Emperor and you know how mean Kuda is.

OSEE: Please help us, Oops.

OOPS: I don't think I can, but I'll try. [*Still standing by door.*]

AHPOO: Go on, Oops.

He doesn't move.

SCAT!!

OOPS *runs out.*

KEEPER: What good will that do? We've hunted high and low, and the Royal Cricket can't be found.
cricket in the cage.

OSEE [*running up and getting cage*]: What are you going to do?

AHPOO: I have a plan. I'll take a small bit of this gold paper and some of this glue and paste a gold crown on the head of the cricket in the cage.

KEEPER: But that's not honest. We can't do that.

AHPOO: Oh brother! This will give you enough time to find the real cricket.

OSEE: Yes, Father, we must do it.

KEEPER: I won't let you deceive the Emperor! [*He snatches the cricket from the cage.*]

OSEE: It's the only way to save your life. Hurry!

OOPS [*offstage*]: Make way for the Emperor!

KEEPER *lets the cricket free when he hears* OOP's *voice.*

AHPOO [*grabbing cricket*]: Got it!

> AHPOO *runs to the table and takes the glue brush and dabs a bit of glue on the head of the cricket. He tries to put the brush down, but the handle is sticky and he has trouble getting rid of it. He gets rid of the brush and picks up the gold paper, tears off a piece and puts it on the head of the cricket. Now the big sheet of paper is stuck to his fingers. In trying to get rid of it, the cricket escapes.*

OSEE: Don't let him get away! [*Dives for cricket.*]

AHPOO: There he goes, Get him!

KEEPER [*chasing cricket*]: This way!

OOPS *peeks around the corner of* UC *door.*

OOPS: Is everything ready?

All spring up. AHPOO *hides the paper behind his back.*

OSEE: Almost.

OOPS: Hurry. The Emperor and Kuda are in the garden. [*Looking offstage.*]

AHPOO [*grabbing cricket*]: Where's the cage?

KEEPER: I won't let you do this.

AHPOO [*cricket is being put back in cage*]: There!

OSEE: Get the paper off your hand!

OSEE *and* AHPOO *struggle with paper, each gets stuck on it.* AHPOO *finally gets it and hides it in chest as* OOPS, KUDA, *and* EMPEROR *enter.*

OOPS: All is ready

KUDA [*to* OOPS]: It had better be. [*to* EMPEROR.] All is ready.

EMPEROR: All is ready? That's nice. Ready for what?

KUDA: Ready for you to view the Royal Cricket.

EMPEROR: View the—? Oh yes, the Royal Cricket. Where is my little darling?

KUDA [*to* OOPS]: Where is his little darling?

OOPS: Where is his little darling?

AHPOO: His little what?

KUDA: The cricket, you fool!

AHPOO [*back somersault*]: Right there.

KEEPER: Most Glorious Emperor, there is something I must say.

KUDA: Silence, old man! No one may speak to the Emperor but the Royal Executioner! Besides, he can't hear you. He hears only my voice.

KEEPER: But——

KUDA: SILENCE!!! Now bring the Royal Cricket into view.

OSEE *rushes over and takes the cover off the cage.*

OSEE: The Royal Cricket.

OOPS: The Royal Cricket.

KUDA: The Royal Cricket.

EMPEROR: I heard you the first time, Kuda. [*Goes to cage.*] Yes, there's my little darling. Ah cricky, cricky, cricky.

KUDA [*surprised to see cricket*]: Is it the Royal Cricket?

KEEPER: That's what I was——

KUDA: SILENCE!

AHPOO: Of course it's the Royal Cricket. See the gold crown on his head.

KUDA [*looks at cricket*]: Hum. [*Looks closer.*] Humm. [*Still closer.*] Hummm AH!

OOPS OSEE AHPOO KEEPER [*in unison*]: Ah?

KUDA: Royal Emperor, this is not the Royal Cricket.

EMPEROR: Cricky, cricky, nonsense, Kuda. It has the golden crown; don't you, my pet?

AHPOO: Only the Royal Cricket has the golden crown.

KUDA: Quiet, fool, or I'll have Oops chop you up for food for the Royal Goldfish!

OOPS [*begins to whimper*]: Who, me?

KUDA: SILENCE!

EMPEROR: Now tell me, Kuda, what is this talk about this not being the Royal Cricket?

KUDA: Watch, Royal One. [*Takes cricket from cage and removes gold paper.*] Not a gold crown, but a bit of gold paper stuck on with glue! [*Puts cricket back in cage.*]

EMPEROR: It's not my little darling? Oh dear, oh dear, oh dear!

KUDA [*to* KEEPER]: What have you done with the Royal Cricket!

KEEPER: I tried to tell you when you first asked for him. When I looked in the cage this morning, this cricket was there and the Royal Cricket was gone.

KUDA: Liar! If that were true, why did you try to hide the fact that he was gone. Why did you paste the gold paper on the head of that cricket? Answer me, or I'll throw you to my pet spiders!

OSEE: It wasn't my father's fault. I was the one that did it. He didn't want me to, but I did it anyway.

KUDA: Quiet, bean sprout, or I'll feed you to the ducks! [*To* KEEPER.] So, you let your son deceive the Emperor. A poor father as well as a careless cricket keeper. Oops, off with his head!

OOPS [*trying to be mean*]: Off with his head! [*Realizing what he is supposed to do.*] Chop off his head? [*Starts to cry.*]

KUDA: At once! Or my spiders will feast on your sniveling carcass today.

A H P O O : Wait! The only one who can give the sentence of death to Royal servants is the Emperor. Are you trying to take over the power of the Emperor, Kuda?

K U D A : I'll fix you, you tumblebug, mark my words!

O S E E : Please, Emperor, give my father a chance.

A H P O O : It's no use. Only Kuda can talk to him.

O S E E [*to* KUDA]: Oh please, sir, ask the Emperor to give my father a chance.

K U D A : What does he think he can do, find the Royal Cricket?

K E E P E R : I know I can if you will ask the Emperor to be kind and give me the time.

K U D A : Very well, I will ask him. [*To* EMPEROR.] These miserable beings wish a chance to find the Royal Cricket.

E M P E R O R : Do you think they can find him?

K U D A : Of course they can't. They just want the extra time to give the cricket keeper a chance to escape!

E M P E R O R : But there might be a chance. It is so lonely without him. He was the only one besides you that I could talk to.

K U D A : Off with his head, I say!

E M P E R O R : No, Kuda. Better to find the Royal Cricket than to lose the Royal Cricket Keeper for his mistake. If you only knew how lonely it is, not to be able to hear any voice except yours. And your voice is never happy. The chirping of the Royal Cricket was the only happy sound I ever heard.

K U D A : I never smile! I hate to smile! Why should an executioner smile?

E M P E R O R : Give the Royal Cricket Keeper all he needs in time to find the Royal Cricket.

K U D A : Royal One. Give him no more than the setting of the sun to find the cricket. If you give him more time, he can escape.

E M P E R O R : You know best. Hear me. You have until the last ray of the sun leaves this room to find the Royal Cricket. If you find him, I will grant anything you desire. If you fail, Kuda may do whatever he wishes with you. [*In a pleading voice.*] And please find him. It is so lonely without him.

K U D A : You heard the Emperor, until the last ray of the sun is gone. If you fail, off with your head! [KUDA *growls and his shoulders shake.*]

EMPEROR *and* KUDA *exit.*

OSEE : What was he doing?

AHPOO : Laughing.

OOPS : Please find the Royal Cricket, or—— [*Starts to cry*] I'll have to chop off your head!

KEEPER : Until the last ray of the sun is gone from the room! So little time to look, and I don't even know where to begin! He could be any place!

AHPOO : I say look in Kuda's garden.

OSEE : Why would he want to steal the Royal Cricket?

AHPOO : He wants to be Emperor. If he were to find the Royal Cricket the Emperor would do anything he asked. He's so lonely that he would even make Kuda Emperor, just so he could be able to talk to people.

KEEPER : But I couldn't get into Kuda's garden.

AHPOO : Yes you could, if I were with you. Come on, I'll help you.

KEEPER : Search the cottage and garden, my son. I'll go to the garden of Kuda and try to find the Royal Cricket. And hurry. The time is short!

AHPOO *and* KEEPER *exit.*

OSEE : Where can he be? [*Starts hunting.*] What was that? [*Looks toward the chest.*] Something moved under the chest. [*Walks slowly to chest, catches something under it.*] I've got him! Father, Ahpoo, I've caught the Royal Cricket! They're gone. [*Opens his hand.*] Only a tumblebug. Poor little tumblebug. Just like Ahpoo. When you are frightened, you somersault away. Don't be afraid. I won't hurt you. [*Puts tumblebug on table.*] If you could only tell me where the Royal Cricket is. [*There is heard a high piping sound.*] You're talking! Oh, tumblebug, can you help me? [*More piping.*] You will? That's wonderful! [*More piping.*] But how can we hunt for him? I'm so big, I might step on him. [*More piping.*] You can make me as small as you are? How? [*More piping.*] You will say a magic word to make me small? All right, I'm ready. You say the magic word. [*More piping.*] You can't remember the word! Hurry, try to remember! I have only until the sun is gone to find the Royal Cricket. Think, Tumblebug! Try to remember the magic word! Try! Try!

CURTAIN

Act Two

Setting for a Clearing in a Forest of Grass

PROLOGUE

STORYTELLER [*entering before the curtain and bows*]: So! This is most unhappy thing, most unhappy! Unusual tumblebug cannot remember magic word to make Osee small. Time is short, haste is necessary. Is most fortunate that I also know magic word. Shall I help them? Very well. First magic word to make him small. Is *okii*. You must help me say. All of you say. *Okii*. Oh, much louder. *OKII!*

A large crash from behind the curtain.

Itai! I remember! *Okii* is magic word to make one big! Osee must be big as cottage. Ah, I remember. Magic word to make him small is *chissai*. All of you help me say *Chissai*. Ah, most fine, very good. But we must make him very small, so say very softly. *Chissai.* Good. Now he is small.

Osee and Tumblebug hunt and hunt for Royal Cricket, but they cannot find him. At last they come to small clearing, in grass, grass that is now as big as trees to little Osee.

STORYTELLER *bows and exits as curtain opens.*

SCENE: *A forest of giant stems of grass circling a clearing. There are two entrances on each side of the stage:* RC *and*

UR, LC *and* DL. *There is a broken bowl hiding the* LC *entrance. In center stage is a large rock cutout, big enough to hide all but the head of the Tumblebug.* DR *is a clump of grass large enough to hide behind.*

AT RISE: OSEE *and* TUMBLEBUG [*who looks like* AHPOO] *enter from* UR *and cross below the rock. They look around, then* TUMBLE *sinks down by rock in exhaustion.*

T U M B L E : Oof! I'm so tired I don't think I could move another step. I think we've looked in every corner of the whole country for the Royal Cricket.

O S E E : We can't stop now. The sun is almost gone. We have to find the Royal Cricket before the last ray of sun is gone or my father will die. Get up, Ahpoo. We have to keep going.

T U M B L E : My name isn't Ahpoo. I'm Tumble, the tumblebug.

O S E E : I'm sorry, Tumble. You look so much like Ahpoo, the Royal Acrobat, that I forget sometimes.

T U M B L E : That's all right. It's a natural mistake. Ahpoo and I are distant cousins.

O S E E : Don't sit down now. We have to keep looking for the Royal Cricket.

T U M B L E : Where can we look? We've asked every insect we met if they had seen him, but none of them could help us. Please, Osee, can't we sit and rest for just a minute? [*He looks around the clearing.*] It seems so strange to see the grass look as big as the tallest tree. [*Pointing to distance.*] Tumble, what is that? It looks like a paint brush.

T U M B L E [*looking off*]: That's what it is.

O S E E : But it's so big. Who could ever use a brush that big?

T U M B L E : You. I saw you drop that brush when you were still a big person.

O S E E [*crossing to downstage of rock and sitting next to* TUMBLE]: It hasn't helped to make me small. We still haven't found the Royal Cricket. If there was only someone who could tell us where the Royal Cricket is. Someone must know.

T U M B L E [*who has been looking around the clearing*]: I don't like this place. It's so spooky.

O S E E : There's nothing wrong. Stop being so jittery. We've got to think.

T U M B L E : I can't help it. I'm s-s-s-scared!

O S E E : Now stop that, Tumble!

T U M B L E [*holding up hand*]: Listen!

O S E E [*listening*]: I don't hear anything.

T U M B L E : That's just it. When you can't hear anything in the grass, look out. That means there is something bad around.

O S E E : What kind of something bad?

T U M B L E : Something that is looking for dinner, like a toad or a spider.

O S E E : If there was a spider or a toad coming, we could hear him.

T U M B L E : He wouldn't be coming, he'd be right here, hiding, and waiting for us. He might be hiding right now over there by that broken bowl.

O S E E [*a bit frightened*]: By the bowl? [*Looks around rock at bowl.*] I don't see anything there. [*More bravely.*] I'll go up and see. [*Crossing to bowl.*]

T U M B L E : Don't Osee. Don't go near there!

O S E E [*below bowl*]: There's nothing to be afraid of, Tumble.

T U M B L E : Please, Osee, don't go any closer!

O S E E [*looking behind bowl*]: There's nothing here, nothing but an old spider web.

T U M B L E : Well, there could have been.

O S E E : Spider web. [*Thinking.*] That reminds me of something, but I can't remember what it is.

T U M B L E : You mark my words, where there's a spider web, there's a spider. [*Looking around.*] He could be anyplace around here, waiting to jump out at us.

O S E E : SPIDER!

T U M B L E [*back somersault*]: Run!

O S E E [*stopping him*]: No, no, Tumble. I didn't mean I *saw* a spider, I just remembered *about* a spider. There was one by the Royal Cricket cage this morning. Maybe he knows where the Royal Cricket is. We can find him and ask him.

T U M B L E : You can't ask a spider anything. They're just plain mean and nasty! All they want to do is eat you.

> *There is movement* UL *behind bowl, then a face peeks from above the bowl.*

O S E E : Aren't there some spiders who are nice?

T U M B L E : None!

The face vanishes.

OSEE : Now that's not a fair thing to say. You don't know all the spiders in the world, do you?

TUMBLE : No, but I have met one, and that was enough! [*Moves near LC entrance.*] He caught me by jumping out from behind some grass and I almost got eaten up.

BUTTERFLY *jumps out from LC.*

TUMBLE : Spider! [*Does a back somersault.*]

OSEE : Look out! [*Starts to run, then sees BUTTERFLY and stops.*] Come back, Tumble. It's only a butterfly. [TUMBLE *stops and looks.*]

BUTTERFLY : Only a butterfly! Well I like that! In all my travels, flitting around the world, I've never been so insulted!

TUMBLE : It's your own fault. You shouldn't have frightened us like that.

BUTTERFLY : Frightened! Oh, now this is too much! I've a good mind to leave right now. [*Spreads wings to go.*]

OSEE : Please don't go. We didn't mean to be unkind.

BUTTERFLY : Well, maybe you didn't, but that foolish tumble-bug did.

TUMBLE : Who are you calling foolish, you painted caterpillar!

BUTTERFLY : You! [*Turns back on them and preens herself.*]

OSEE [*to TUMBLE*]: Don't argue with her, Tumble. Didn't you hear her say she had been everywhere? She may have seen the Royal Cricket.

TUMBLE : That butterfly is too vain to have seen anything but her own reflection in a dew drop!

OSEE : But we've got to ask her. It's almost dark and we still haven't found the Royal Cricket.

TUMBLE : Very well, but I don't think she knows anything.

OSEE : Miss Butterfly, we are very sorry that we insulted you. I hope you'll forgive us. You see, we are worried. The Royal Cricket is missing, and we must find him.

BUTTERFLY : So?

TUMBLE : We need your help.

OSEE : You've been everyplace, Butterfly. Have you met anyone who has seen or heard of the Royal Cricket?

BUTTERFLY : I might have.

OSEE : Who? Tell us!

BUTTERFLY : No.

TUMBLE : No? Why not?

BUTTERFLY : Because you were rude to me. You said I was only a butterfly and I looked a fright.

OSEE : That isn't what we said, or at least, not what we meant.

BUTTERFLY : I don't care. You hurt my feelings. [*Pouts.*]

TUMBLE [*attempting to placate her*]: Your wings are pretty.

BUTTERFLY : Pretty! Only pretty?

OSEE : What Tumble meant to say was that your wings are beautiful.

> OSEE *nudges* TUMBLE, *unfortunately in the stomach, knocking part of the wind out of him.*

TUMBLE : Oof!

BUTTERFLY : What did you say?

TUMBLE : I did say that they are beautiful. [*Gives* OSEE *a dirty look.*]

BUTTERFLY : Yes they are, aren't they? [*Spreads wings and preens.*]

OSEE : I don't think I've ever seen such beautiful colors.

BUTTERFLY [*very pleased*]: I'm glad to see there's one of you who appreciates the finer things in life.

TUMBLE : Such a beautiful butterfly must meet many interesting people.

BUTTERFLY [*being coy*]: Well——

OSEE [*catching the idea*]: And you must learn such interesting things, too.

BUTTERFLY : Indeed I do. Why, only the other day I was talking to a queen bee—

TUMBLE [*keeping her on the track*]: You see, Osee, I knew we could count on the butterfly.

OSEE : I'll bet she even knows where the Royal Cricket is.

BUTTERFLY : Of course I do.

TUMBLE   OSEE [*in unison*]: You do?

OSEE : Where is he? Tell me, quickly. There isn't much time left. The sun has almost set!

BUTTERFLY : Why should I?

TUMBLE : Why shouldn't you! Because Osee's father will be put to death if you don't.

BUTTERFLY : I don't care a fig for his father. I don't even know him.

OSEE : Oh please, please tell us.

BUTTERFLY : I don't think I will. You were only being nice to me because you wanted something.

TUMBLE : If you don't tell us, I'll tell all the insects that you paint your wings, that they're really an ugly gray.

BUTTERFLY : You wouldn't dare!

TUMBLE : Yes, I would, if you won't tell us where the Royal Cricket is.

BUTTERFLY [*stamping her foot*]: That's mean!

OSEE : He won't do it if you tell us.

BUTTERFLY : Very well, I'll tell you where the cricket is.

OSEE : Where, where!

BUTTERFLY [*with a wicked gleam*]:
    If you paint with color black,
    The thing you seek will not come back.
    But
    If you paint with water clear,
    The thing you seek will reappear.

TUMBLE : So you're a poet! Now where is the Royal Cricket?

BUTTERFLY : You're so smart! You find him.

OSEE : But you haven't told us where he is.

BUTTERFLY : Yes. I have. Solve the riddle, and you will have the Royal Cricket.

TUMBLE : "If you paint with color black," paint what? What does the riddle mean?

BUTTERFLY : That's for you to discover.

OSEE : Won't you tell us what it means? Please, Butterfly, help us!

BUTTERFLY : No. If you want help, get it from the Royal Executioner's pet spider. [*Sarcastically.*] I'm sure he will be glad to see you! [BUTTERFLY *exits laughing.*]

OSEE [*running after her*]: Butterfly, butterfly, come back! She's gone. Now we'll never know where the cricket is.

TUMBLE : Cheer up, Osee. All we have to do is solve the riddle. Come on, think. If that flutter-brained butterfly can make it up, we can figure it out.

o s e e : "If you paint with color black, The thing you seek will not come back." If you paint what?

t u m b l e : Let's see. "The thing you seek. . . . ." That must be the Royal Cricket.

> *A small spider, POOPS, appears UC by bowl, sees TUMBLE and OSEE, and runs quickly to RC and hides.*

o s e e : What was that? I thought I saw something move.

t u m b l e : I didn't see anything. It must have been a leaf.

o s e e : I'm sure I saw something black move. [*Jumps up.*] Maybe it was the cricket.

> *Both run up and look behind the bowl. Spider runs DR and hides.*

t u m b l e : There's nothing here.

o s e e : I thought I saw it run over there.

> *They exit to RC entrance. Spider crosses to DC below rock.*

Nothing here, either. I guess I imagined it.

t u m b l e : Maybe what ever it was ran off that way. [*Pointing off R.*]

o s e e : You search here, and I'll look off there. [*Exits R.*]

t u m b l e : Search here? [*Looks around.*] Nothing here.

> *Spider peeks from behind rock, sees TUMBLE and ducks back out of sight.*

What was that? [*Crosses DR to stone.*] I thought I saw something move!

> *TUMBLE starts around stone L, spider moves with him. The action is repeated in the other direction. They stop with spider on L of stone, TUMBLE on R.*

I don't like this, not one bit at all.

> *TUMBLE starts backing downstage of stone, spider does the same. They bump into each other, turn and look.*

A spider! [*TUMBLE does a somersault to URC.*]

p o o p s : Help!

> *He hides behind stone. OSEE enters and runs into TUMBLE. They end in a heap DR.*

OSEE: Oof! [*Gets up and helps* TUMBLE.] What's wrong, Tumble? I heard you call for help.

TUMBLE: A sp-sp-spider! I saw a spider!

OSEE: Where?

TUMBLE [*pointing*]: Over there.

OSEE: Quick, let's find him.

TUMBLE: Yes, we must—[*fearfully*] *find him!*

OSEE: He may be the spider I saw by the cricket cage. He could tell us where the Royal Cricket is. Come on!

TUMBLE: You go ahead. [*Hiding* DR.] I'll stay here. [*Hides head.*]

> OSEE *goes* L *around stone, the spider goes in same direction. This is repeated with spider ending above the stone.*

OSEE: Come on, Tumble, help me. You go one way, and I'll go the other.

> *Then he shoves* TUMBLE *to stone.* OSEE *goes around stone from* R, TUMBLE *from* L, *backing up with one hand over his eyes, the other groping behind him. The spider comes from behind the stone, backing in the direction he is going, with his hand behind him. The two hands meet. Both stop frozen. They slowly grope behind them, feeling out the thing they just touched. They slowly turn and face each other.*

POOPS: Gulp!

> *Falls down and covers head.* OSEE *comes from behind rock and sees the situation.*

OSEE: Good work, Tumble. You've caught him!

TUMBLE [*lifting one hand and peeking out*]: I have?

OSEE: Yes, you're lying on him.

TUMBLE [*lifting both hands and looking*]: I'm lying [*with realization*] on top of him! [*Jumps up.*]

OSEE [*crossing to spider*]: Help me get him up, Tumble. [*To spider.*] I hope we didn't hurt you.

POOPS [*uncovering his eyes, looks at* OSEE *and* TUMBLE, *then starts to cry*]: Ooooho, ho-ho-ho.

OSEE: Where does it hurt?

P O O P S [*between sobs*] It doesn't hurt. It's just that I'm a failure! I try to catch someone, and they catch me!

T U M B L E : See? I told you he was up to no good!

P O O P S : Of course I wasn't. I'm supposed to catch things. That's what spiders are for.

O S E E : Then why didn't you spin a web around us and catch us?

P O O P S : Because every time I spin a web, I'm the one who gets caught in it; I just haven't learned the web spinning part of being a spider.

T U M B L E : Ha ha ha ha!

> *Unable to control himself he falls on the ground and rolls around in a fit of laughter.*

Ho ho ho, he he he!

P O O P S [*hurt*]: What are you laughing at?

T U M B L E [*between gulps for breath*]: A . . . spider who . . . can't . . . [*giggle*] spin a web!

O S E E : That's not kind, Tumble.

P O O P S : It's awful! How would you like it if you couldn't tumble?

T U M B L E : I wouldn't. [*Stops laughing.*] I'm sorry.

O S E E [*looking at spider*]: You look just like Oops, the Assistant Royal Executioner, and you act just like him!

P O O P S : How?

O S E E : Well, he's not a very good executioner, either.

P O O P S [*looking at both a bit fearfully*]: Now that you have caught me, what are you going to do with me?

O S E E : We aren't going to do anything with you. We only want to ask you something.

P O O P S [*much relieved*]: Oh, is that all? What do you want to know?

T U M B L E : Have you seen the Royal Cricket?

P O O P S [*frightened*]: The Royal Cricket? Oh dear, oh dear, oh dear, oh dear!

O S E E : What's wrong?

P O O P S : I can't tell you.

T U M B L E : Why not? What are you afraid of?

P O O P S : The Royal Executioner's pet spider!

O S E E : Why are you afraid of him?

POOPS: If I tell you anything about the Royal Cricket, he will spin me in a web and never let me go!

TUMBLE: Was he the one that took the Royal Cricket?

POOPS: I can't tell you!

OSEE: Please help us. If we don't find the Royal Cricket before sundown, Kuda will put my father to death.

POOPS: That's awful. I wish I could help you, but I don't dare.

TUMBLE: You've got to. You can't let Osee's father die!

POOPS: But I'm afraid!

OSEE: Please.

TUMBLE: Won't you please help us?

POOPS: Even if I did tell you where the Royal Cricket is, you wouldn't be able to get to him.

TUMBLE: Why couldn't we?

POOPS: Kuda's pet spider is guarding him. He would get you and gobble you up.

OSEE: We have to try. I can't let my father die!

POOPS: The Big Spider might find out I told you where to find the cricket.

OSEE: You can't be afraid all your life. If you do, you'll always be a failure.

POOPS [*looks at them, then looks around the clearing*]: All right, I'll tell you.

OSEE: Hurry, the sun is almost gone!

POOPS [*bringing both to* DR]: Kuda wanted the Royal Cricket so that he could become Emperor. Last night he sent his pet spider to see that no one was awake at the house of your father. Then Kuda came and took the Royal Cricket from the cage and——

BIG SPIDER [*offstage*]: Poops, you miserable excuse for a spider! Where are you?

POOPS: The Executioner's spider!

TUMBLE: Another spider! [*Starts back somersault.*]

OSEE: Stop it, Tumble! Quick, Poops, tell us where the Royal Cricket is!

POOPS: Not now. There isn't time. Quick, hide!

TUMBLE: Where?

OSEE: Behind the rock. Come on, Tumble, hurry!

TUMBLE: I can't. I'm so frightened, I can't move!

OSEE: Help us, Poops.

They grab TUMBLE *and drag him behind the rock.*

POOPS [*moving downstage of rock*]: Duck down, Tumble. I can see you!

TUMBLE *starts to duck, but hears the* BIG SPIDER'S *voice and straightens up.*

BIG SPIDER [*still offstage, but closer*]: Poops, answer me, or I'll feed you to the toads!

OSEE : Duck down, Tumble.

TUMBLE : I can't. I'm scared stiff!

OSEE : Stop being so frightened and bend!

TUMBLE *disappears behind the rock as* BIG SPIDER *enters* LC.

BIG SPIDER : Poops, you sniveling substitute for a spider, there you are! Where have you been?

POOPS : Here.

BIG SPIDER : I heard voices! Who was with you?

POOP : With me?

BIG SPIDER : Stop repeating everything I say. What were you doing?

POOPS : I was . . . . I was . . .

BIG SPIDER : Bah! You'll never learn! [*Starts toward upstage of rock.*] I thought I saw someone behind this rock.

POOPS [*getting between* BIG SPIDER *and the rock*]: Behind the rock? There's nothing behind the rock. [*Waving* OSEE *and* TUMBLE *to other side of rock.*]

BIG SPIDER [*pushing* POOPS *aside*]: Out of my way. [*Crosses upstage of rock.*] No one!

POOPS [*hiding* TUMBLE *and* OSEE DR]: I told you there wasn't.

BIG SPIDER : SILENCE! I'm sure someone was here.

POOPS : If there was, they aren't here now.

BIG SPIDER : I know that, you weed head! Oh, that I should be cursed with an assistant like you. [*Starting to leave.*] Come along. We're going to the cottage of the Royal Cricket Keeper.

POOPS : What will we do there?

BIG SPIDER : Make sure they don't find where the Royal Cricket is hidden. Come with me! [BIG SPIDER *and* POOPS *exist* LC.]

OSEE [*coming from* DR]: Did you hear that, Tumble? The Royal Cricket is hidden in my father's cottage.

TUMBLE: But where? You've searched every inch of it.

OSEE: Then we must hunt again. Kuda's pet spider said it was there. Hurry! There's not much time left.

TUMBLE: Which way is your house? I'm all twisted around.

OSEE [*pointing off* L]: It must be that way. Poops and Kuda's spider went that way. Come on!

As they start out L, BIG SPIDER *jumps out before them.*

BIG SPIDER: Aha! I knew there was someone here. So, my inquisitive friends, you want to find the Royal Cricket, do you? I'll be glad to show him to you!!

OSEE: You will?

BIG SPIDER: Of course. [*Hastily.*] Just as soon as my master, Kuda, becomes Emperor. [*Starts toward* OSEE *and* TUMBLE.]

POOPS [*who has been cowering behind* BIG SPIDER]: Run, Osee, run!

OSEE *and* TUMBLE *start below rock to* DR. TUMBLE *trips and falls and* BIG SPIDER *catches him in a web.* OSEE *turns to help him and in turn is caught. Both end up* DR *of rock.*

BIG SPIDER: Ha! All trussed up like flies for my supper. And that's what you'll be as soon as I get back!

POOPS *peeks out from behind* UL *corner of rock. During the following lines, he tries to cast a web over* BIG SPIDER.

OSEE [*seeing* POOPS]: Please, Mr. Spider, since we are going to die, won't you tell us where Kuda hid the Royal Cricket? We know he's in my father's cottage, but we don't know here. It can't matter now.

BIG SPIDER [*crossing below stone to go*]: I haven't time for that.

TUMBLE: Wait!

BIG SPIDER *stops and turns to* TUMBLE.

You have no reason to keep it from us. Why won't you at least do that for us? Before, before——

During the above speech, POOPS *sneaks up behind* BIG SPIDER *and at end of speech, casts web about him. They*

spin around and disappear from view behind the rock.
There is no sound of a struggle, then sudden silence.
Slowly the head of the BIG SPIDER *comes into view above*
rock, then POOPS *comes* DL *dragging* BIG SPIDER, *wrapped*
in a spider web.

POOPS : That will only hold him for a short time. I'm still not
very good at web spinning yet.

OSEE : That was wonderful, Poops!

TUMBLE : You bet! Now help us get out.

As POOPS *is helping* TUMBLE, BIG SPIDER *is slowly freeing*
himself. Both get free at the same time.

BIG SPIDER [*with a sneer*]: Thought you could get the best
of me, did you!

BIG SPIDER starts toward POOPS *and* TUMBLE. OSEE *trips*
him and he falls.

OSEE : Run, Poops, run, Tumble! Find the cricket and save my
father's life!

The two friends hesitate a moment, then see they can't
help OSEE *and exit.*

BIG SPIDER [*getting up*]: You meddling child! Even if they
have gotten away, they can't save your father. See, the last ray
of the sun is almost gone. Before they can find the cricket, your
father will be dead. And then Kuda will be Emperor. [OSEE
struggles to free himself.] Struggle all you wish, my little morsel.
It will only tangle you more. I'm going to your cottage to watch
your father die, and then I'll come back and feast on you!

BIG SPIDER exits as OSEE *struggles fruitlessly to free him-*
self.

CURTAIN

Act Three

STORYTELLER [*entering before the curtain and bowing*]: *Itai!* Such a terrible thing has happened to our little friend, Osee. With his friends Poops and Tumble on their way to cottage, there is no one to help him get free! We will help him. If we don't, his father will die, Osee will be supper for Kuda's pet spider. But how? How can we help him?

Wait! I have wonderful idea! Word of magic. With one we made him small, with other, we can make him so big that spider webs that now bind him like strong ropes, will be no stronger than threads.

Yiii! What was word to make him big? *Chissai* made him small, but that is not what we desire. Oh my most unworthy head cannot remember word. Was it *oabo?* No, no, that is wrong. *Kobi? Tobi?* No, no, no. Wait! That is right. *Okii.* We all must say, *okii.* Very much louder, for he is very small, and we must make him very big. Ready? *Okii!*

Now let us see if magic worked.

> STORYTELLER *leaves as the curtain opens.*
>
> SCENE: *The cottage of the Royal Cricket Keeper. It is the same as Act I except the time is late afternoon. A single ray of sunlight shines through the garden doors, falling on the wall above the cricket stand.*
>
> AT RISE: *The stage is empty. Then* OSEE *comes in from the garden, brushing himself off.*

OSEE: I'm back home again! [*Brushing his face.*] Ug, spider webs on my face! Tumble and I were in my garden all the time. Someone must have said the magic word to make me big again. [*Looks around the room, then crosses to* DR *door.*] Father! He must be in the other part of the cottage. [*Exits* DR *door.*] Father!

> KUDA *peeks around the* UC *door, sees no one in the room and goes to cricket cage, takes out the cricket and looks at it closely.*

K U D A : Well, Royal Cricket, is the black paint I put on your head to cover the golden crown still there? Some of it has worn off!

> KUDA *moves to chest, takes out black paint and brush, moves to table and carefully paints the head of the cricket.*

First I'll paint with color black,
And the thing they seek will not come back.
Then I'll paint with water clear,
And the golden crown will reappear.

No one will ever guess that you are the Royal Cricket.

O S E E [*offstage*]: Father. Is that you?

K U D A : Ah! That brat is back! He must not catch me here!

> *He puts cricket back in cage and rushes out* L *just as* OSEE *enters from* R.

O S E E : Father? He and Ahpoo must not be back from Kuda's garden. I wish they would hurry. Maybe they can solve the riddle. Wait a moment. That spider said that the cricket was in the cottage. I wonder where it could be? [*Walks to table.*] What's this? Where did this paint brush and black paint come from? I must have left it out when I was cleaning up my kite-making.

> AHPOO *and* KEEPER *enter from garden.*

O S E E : Oh, Father! I've failed! I didn't find the Royal Cricket.

K E E P E R : Do not blame yourself, my son. Ahpoo and I searched every corner of Kuda's garden, and we found no trace of the cricket.

A H P O O : All is lost. The only thing you can do now is to run away. If you stay here, you will die.

O S E E : No, Ahpoo, there is still a chance. I learned that Kuda took the Royal Cricket and hid him in the cottage. All we have to do is solve a riddle, and we will have found the Royal Cricket.

A H P O O : Kuda took the Royal Cricket!? Then you can tell the Emperor this when he comes, and he will make Kuda tell where he hid it.

K E E P E R : We can't do that. You saw how the Emperor can hear no one but Kuda. We would never get the chance to tell the truth.

AHPOO: You're right. The only thing left is for us to solve the riddle. What is it, Osee.

OSEE: Listen carefully and see if you can solve it.

> "If you paint with color black,
> The thing you seek will not come back.
> But
> If you paint with water clear,
> The thing you seek will reappear."

That's the riddle.

KEEPER: "If you paint with color black." What is it you must not paint black?

AHPOO: "The thing you seek . . . ."—that must mean the Royal Cricket.

OSEE: I think I have part of it!

AHPOO: What is it?

KEEPER: What is it, my son?

OSEE: "If you paint with color black," that means that if you paint something black, the Royal Cricket will be gone forever. Now the second half of the riddle. "If you paint with water clear, the thing you seek will reappear." That means that when you paint something with water, the Royal Cricket will be back in his cage.

KEEPER: I think you have solved the riddle, Osee.

AHPOO [running to chest and getting brushes and paint and water]: Quick, what is it we paint? There is no time left. The last ray of sun is almost gone.

OSEE: That's just it, I don't know what to paint!

AHPOO [running to C door]: Maybe we have to paint the door?

KEEPER: No, that wouldn't be it.

OSEE: What about the floor of the room?

AHPOO: What if we have to paint the whole cottage!

KEEPER: No, no, no. If the painting is to bring back the Royal Cricket, we must have to paint something that belongs to the cricket.

OSEE: Would it be the table that holds the cage?

AHPOO [running to cage and taking out cricket]: No, that isn't it. Why should a common cricket be able to make the Royal Cricket reappear?

AHPOO [*puts cricket back in cage and moves to table*]: If the Royal Cricket is to reappear in his cage, then maybe it's the cricket cage that is to be painted.

KEEPER [*getting cage and bringing it to table*]: Here is the cage. Wait, I'll let this other cricket go. He doesn't belong in the Royal cage. [KEEPER *reaches in and puts cricket on table.*]

OSEE: Quick, Ahpoo, paint the cage with the water! [AHPOO *starts painting cage with water.*]

KEEPER: Hurry, my tumbling friend. With each stroke of the brush, the last ray of sun grows dimmer.

OSEE: Is it working yet?

AHPOO: I haven't got it all painted. Heavens! I've run out of water.

OSEE [*taking water pot*]: I'll go into the garden and get more. [*Exits.*]

KEEPER: Go fast, my son, before the water already painted on the cage dries.

AHPOO: Suppose this isn't right? Suppose the cricket doesn't reappear? What will you do then?

KEEPER: There will be nothing for us to do but pack our few meager belongings and leave.

OSEE [*entering with water*]: Here is more water. Finish painting the cage.

AHPOO *starts painting.*

OSEE [*running to door and looking out*]: Hurry, Ahpoo, hurry! The Emperor may be here any minute!

AHPOO: There! It's finished!

All rush to cage.

KEEPER: Nothing is happening.

AHPOO: Maybe it takes time for it to work.

OSEE: We haven't got any time.

KEEPER: It's no use! Painting the cage with water isn't the answer to the riddle!

AHPOO: Let's try painting something else. I've got it! The cover of the cage.

OSEE: Yes, try the cover.

KEEPER: There's not time! We must pack our belongings and leave before Kuda and the Emperor arrive.

AHPOO : But where will you go? This is your home.

KEEPER : We will wander over the world. We can never stay long in one place or we will be captured.

OSEE : Can we never come back here, Father?

KEEPER : No, my son. This is the cottage of the Royal Cricket Keeper. I have lost the Royal Cricket; I can no longer stay here.

AHPOO : What will you do? How will you get food? You have never been anything but a Royal Cricket Keeper. What else can you do?

KEEPER : I don't know. My father, and his father, all their fathers before were Royal Cricket Keepers. The only thing we can do is beg for our food.

OSEE : I'll help, Father. I'm very strong, and I can work hard. I'll get a job running errands.

KEEPER : I had always hoped that someday you would become Royal Cricket Keeper, but now all that is gone. My son must grow up to be a beggar. [*With resolve.*] No! I won't let that happen. I would rather go to my death, than have my son become a wanderer.

OSEE : No, Father. We'll pack our things and leave before Kuda gets here.

AHPOO [*at door*]: Hurry, I hear someone *coming!*

KEEPER : No, I will stay!

OSEE : No, no, Father! [*Pushing him to door.*] We must run and hide!

KEEPER : But we can't leave with just the clothes on our backs.

OSEE [*pulling him to* DR *door*]: Go out the back door. I'll stay here until they leave. Then I'll make a bundle of our belongings and meet you at the well by the road.

AHPOO [*still at door*]: Quickly, they are at the garden gate!

OSEE : Hide, Father! [KEEPER *exits.*] And remember, the well by the road!

AHPOO [*running to* OSEE]: Here they come! Cover the cage.

OSEE [*covers cage*]: What good will that do?

AHPOO : We may be able to convince them that the cricket is there but isn't well.

OSEE : That won't work!

AHPOO : We can try.

OOPS *and* KUDA *enter* UC.

K U D A : SILENCE!

O O P S : Yes, silence!

K U D A : Well, brat, has your bumbling father found the Royal Cricket yet?

O S E E : Why, ah . . . . you see . . .

K U D A : Stop that stuttering and answer me! Has the Royal Cricket been found?

A H P O O : Yes.

K U D A : I didn't think . . . . it HAS!

O O P S : It has? Oh wonderful! Now I won't have to chop off anyone's head.

K U D A : Silence! So, you have found the Royal Cricket, have you?

O S E E : Yes, we did.

K U D A : Where is it?

O S E E : In the Royal Cricket cage.

K U D A : Where did you find him?

A H P O O : He was in the garden, by the fish pond.

K U D A : In the garden, was he?

O S E E : Yes.

K U D A : By the fish pond?

A H P O O : Right by the fish pond.

K U D A : Let me see him. [*Starts toward cage.*]

A H P O O [*coming between* KUDA *and cage*]: You can't! The excitement of being lost has upset the Royal Cricket. He's not well.

K U D A : Bah! Out of my way. [*Pushes* AHPOO *aside and starts to remove cage cover.*]

O O P S : Perhaps we had better wait for the Emperor, Kuda. After all, he is supposed to see the Royal Cricket first.

K U D A : Quiet, you jattering idiot. When I want you to say something, I'll tell you.

O S E E : Oops is right. The Royal Law says that only the Emperor or the Royal Cricket Keeper may take the cover off the Royal cage.

A H P O O : And you wouldn't want to break the law, would you, Kuda.

K U D A [*sees he is stopped*]: Toadstools! Very well, we will, ah, have the Royal Cricket Keeper remove the cover. [*Looking around.*] Where is he? [*No one answers.*] Answer me!

O S E E : He's gone.

K U D A : Where!

A H P O O : To get some special leaves to feed the Royal Cricket to make him well again.

K U D A : Liars! He's run away so he wouldn't be punished! Oops, go after him. Find him and bring him back. If you don't, I'll feed you to my spiders.

O O P S : Oh dear!

K U D A : Now GO!

OOPS *exits* UC.

O S E E : Why should my father run away if we have found the Royal Cricket?

K U D A : Because you are lying. You haven't found him!

A H P O O : How do you know we haven't?

K U D A : Because I didn't hide him by the fish pond.

A H P O O : So you did take him!

K U D A [*startled, then recovering*]: What if I did? It won't do you any good to know that.

O S E E : I'll tell the Emperor that you took him, and he will make you tell where you hid him.

K U D A : Fool! You know the Emperor can only understand the words I say to him. He won't even hear your voice!

A H P O O : That's not true! He can understand us when we talk. You've just made him think that he can't hear us.

K U D A : So, you've learned my secret, have you? Well, it won't do you any good! [*Rushes up to door where* OOPS *has left the Royal ax.*] I'll put you to death right now!

A H P O O : You can't. I'm the Royal Acrobat and Osee is the son of the Royal Cricket Keeper. We can't be put to death except by order of the Emperor.

K U D A : Very well. I shall go and get the Emperor. When I return, both of you shall die! [*To* AHPOO.] You for stealing the Royal Cricket, [*to* OSEE] and you! Since your father is not here, you shall take his place! [*Exits laughing.*]

O S E E : Oh Ahpoo! I'm so sorry! Now you must leave, too.

A H P O O : We both must hurry!

K E E P E R [*entering from* DR]: None of us can leave.

O S E E : Father! I thought you had gone to the well to wait for me.

K E E P E R : I couldn't let you face the Emperor alone.

A H P O O : Come, we must go away from here before Kuda returns with the Emperor!

KEEPER: I can't leave. If poor Oops doesn't find me, Kuda will feed him to the spiders. I can't let that happen.

OSEE: What can we do?

KEEPER: You, my son, and Ahpoo must run away.

OSEE: No, Father. I won't leave you.

KEEPER: You can't help me by staying. You'll only lose your life.

AHPOO: Yes, we can. We can tell the Emperor the truth.

OSEE: But he won't hear us!

AHPOO: We must make him hear us!

KEEPER: I won't let you take the chance.

There is a noise of someone outside.

Quickly, run away. Go, my son, before harm comes to you!

OSEE [*holding on to* KEEPER]: No, Father, I won't leave you. Please don't make me go!

KEEPER [*pushing him into* AHPOO's *arms*]: Take him, my tumbling friend, take him far from this place where he will be safe. Guard and protect him, and guide him to manhood.

OSEE: No, Father, no!

KEEPER: Goodbye, my son.

AHPOO *and* OSEE *start out* UC. OOPS *comes in.*

OOPS: The Emperor is almost here!

OSEE [*running to* KEEPER]: You see, Father, I can't leave now.

OOPS: Why should you want to leave? Everything is all right. You have the Royal Cricket. [*Looks at them.*] You do have him, don't you?

All shake their heads "no."

You don't? Oh dear! Oh dear OH DEAR! That means I'll have to [*starts crying*] chop off your head!

AHPOO: There's still a chance! The riddle. We've got to find the answer to the riddle!

OOPS [*in the middle of a sob*]: Riddle? I'm very good at riddles. What is it?

OSEE: If we find the answer, we will find the Royal Cricket.

OOPS: Wonderful!

OSEE: It goes like this?

"If you paint with color black,
The thing you seek will not come back."

O O P S : Slowly, not so fast.

O S E E :   "But
              If you paint with water clear,
              The thing you seek will reappear."

There, that's the riddle. Can you solve it?

O O P S : Don't rush me. Let me think for a moment. "If you paint—— [*Starts mumbling to himself.*]

A H P O O : Hurry, Oops. Kuda will soon be here.

O O P S : Now stop that. You made me forget what I was thinking about.

K E E P E R : Yes, Ahpoo, be quiet and let Oops think. Go to the door and watch for the Emperor and Kuda. Let us know as soon as you see them coming over the hill.

A H P O O [*crossing to door*]: I'll do that.

O O P S : Now let me think. What is it that you must *not* paint black, but must paint with clear water?

> OOPS *is* C *upstage of the table,* KEEPER *is* R *of it and* OSEE *is left.* OOPS *screws up his face in the effort of thought, and closes his eyes. Slowly he sinks down into a squatting, then stitting position. He leans on his back and his feet slowly rise straight in the air.* OSEE *and* KEEPER *look on in amazement.* AHPOO *is only slightly interested.*

O S E E [*in a frightened whisper*]: Is anything the matter with him?

A H P O O : No, he always does that when he starts to think. He says that when he raises his feet, all the blood rushes to his head and helps him think.

> OOPS's *feet kick once and then lower slowly. He sits up and leans forward, resting his elbows on the table, chin in his hands. His face relaxes and his eyes open in a blank stare.*

K E E P E R [*to* AHPOO]: What is he doing now?

> AHPOO *moves to* OOPS, *passes hand in front of his face.* OOPS *gives no reaction.*

A H P O O : This is his mulling stage. He's saying the riddle backward to see if he can make more sense of it that way. [*Moves back to door.*]

O O P S [*still in blank stare*]:
> "If you paint with water clear,
> The thing you hunt will then be here.
> But
> If you paint with color black
> The thing you seek——"

> OOPS *springs up, looks around, crosses to chest and gets paints, brushes, and jar of water; moves to table and puts them down. Paints thumb during line.*

If you paint with color black——

O S E E : What are you doing?

O O P S : SHHH! [*Takes another brush and paints same thumb with water.*] If you paint with water clear. [*He looks at thumb, takes cloth and wipes off thumb.*] Ah yes! [*Shakes himself like a dog coming out of the water.*] I've solved it!

A H P O O : You have?

K E E P E R : You did?

O S E E : What is it?

O O P S : It was easy. If you paint something black, the thing you seek will not come back. What is it we are looking for.

K E E P E R : The Royal Cricket.

O O P S : How do you tell the Royal Cricket from any other cricket?

A H P O O : The golden spot on his head.

O O P S : See? That's the answer.

O S E E : What is?

O O P S : Don't you see? [*They all shake their heads.*] What do you wash your hands and face with?

K E E P E R : Soap.

A H P O O : And——

O S E E : WATER!

K E E P E R A H P O O [*in unison*]: What?

O S E E : Kuda painted over the golden crown on the head of the Royal Cricket with black paint. The cricket is black, so the paint hid the crown and made him look like a common cricket.

O O P S : All you have to do is get the Royal Cricket and paint his head with plain water, and the black will come off.

KEEPER [*his hopes falling*]: But that makes it even harder! The Royal Cricket looks just like millions of other crickets now. How are we to find him?

OSEE: The spider said that Kuda hid the Royal Cricket in the cottage. It should be easy to find.

AHPOO: Wait! Where would be the safest place to hide the Royal Cricket? In the Royal Cricket cage!

KEEPER: Of course! The common cricket that was in the cage this morning was the Royal Cricket with the crown painted over with black.

OOPS: Did you say "was?"

AHPOO: That's right! You took it out when I painted the cage with water.

OOPS: Where did you put it?

KEEPER: On the table, next to the cage.

OSEE [*rushes to table*]: It's not there!

AHPOO: Look under the table.

OSEE *does so.*

KEEPER: Careful where you walk. Don't step on it.

All start looking on the floor for the cricket. OOPS *in* UR *corner working toward center door.* KUDA *slowly appears in door and stands watching.* OOPS *works his way to door, sees the feet and slowly looks up.*

OOPS [*in feeble voice*]: Make way for the Emperor?

KUDA: SILENCE!

All look up in fear at KUDA.

So, the Royal Cricket Keeper is back. Good. [*Points to* R *wall.*] Look! The last ray of sun has left the room. Your time is up. Show me the Royal Cricket or die!

KEEPER: He is in this room. We know he is. Give us a few more minutes to find him.

KUDA [*glancing at covered cage*]: Yes, I would think he's in the room. You get no more time! Make way for the Emperor!

All bow as EMPEROR *enters.*

EMPEROR: Well, Kuda, have they found the Royal Cricket?

KUDA: They haven't, Royal One, and the day is gone. Time is up.

E M P E R O R : Do they have any idea where he is, any at all?

O S E E : Yes!

K U D A : SILENCE! Of course they didn't find the Royal Cricket, Emperor. I found out from one of my spies that that one [*points to* AHPOO] stole him with the help of the Royal Cricket Keeper and his son!

O S E E : That's not true!

K U D A: They stole it so that he [*pointing at* AHPOO] could become Emperor!

K E E P E R : No! It is you who want to become Emperor. You are the one that took it. Make him tell the truth, Royal One.

EMPEROR *does not hear.*

K U D A : Emperor, with my cleverness, I found out where those traitors hid the Royal Cricket.

E M P E R O R : You did? Bring him back to me and you can have anything you wish.

K U D A : Anything?

E M P E R O R : Whatever you want. Only bring him back to me.

K U D A : The thing I wish for is to bring happiness to my Emperor. I know that you are lonely, therefore, to rid you of this loneliness, I will become Emperor, so that you can again enjoy the sound of people's voices.

E M P E R O R [*startled*]: What? You be Emperor? [*Remembering his loneliness.*] Very well. But first show me the Royal Cricket.

K U D A : At once, Royal One. [KUDA *crosses to cricket cage and removes cover.*] There, Emperor, is the Royal Cricket, his golden crown hidden by black paint!

E M P E R O R [*goes to cage*]: Where, Kuda, where? There is nothing in the cage.

K U D A : What? ! [*Looks at cage.*]

O O P S : The cage is empty!

K U D A : The Royal Cricket is gone!

E M P E R O R : Of course the Royal Cricket is gone. What do you think all the fuss was about all day long.

K U D A [*in rage to* KEEPER]: What have you done with him? Answer, or I'll feed you to my spiders!

K E E P E R : I told you. He's in the room.

K U D A : Find him! Find him at once! Oops!

O O P S [*whimpering*]: Yes sir?

K U D A : Search the whole cottage. Find the Royal Cricket! I'll look in the garden. Don't stand there staring, you fool, FIND HIM!

KUDA *and* OOPS *exit.*

A H P O O : Quickly, while Kuda is gone, tell the Emperor the truth.

K E E P E R : Will he be able to hear us?

O S E E : We can try. We must try. It's our only chance.

K E E P E R [*crosses to* EMPEROR *and bows*]: Royal One, hear the words that I speak to you.

E M P E R O R : I do wish Kuda were here. I know the Royal Cricket Keeper is talking to me, but I have to have Kuda to tell me what he is saying.

O S E E [*crosses to* EMPEROR]: No, Royal One, you don't need Kuda. Listen, and you can hear and understand us.

E M P E R O R : Another one talking. I wish Kuda would hurry.

A H P O O : It's no use. He won't listen.

K E E P E R : Maybe if we all shout together he'll hear us.

O S E E : Yes, Father, that might work.

A H P O O : We can try.

K E E P E R : All together now.

A L L : EMPEROR!

E M P E R O R [*jumps*]: Oh my! Who called me?

K U D A [*in door*]: I did, Royal One. [*To the others.*] Spoiled your plan, didn't I. [*To* EMPEROR.] There is no time to waste. We must put these three to death at once, before they do more harm.

E M P E R O R : But we have not found the Royal Cricket.

K U D A : We will, as soon as they are dead.

E M P E R O R : Very well, do as you wish, only please find the Royal Cricket.

K U D A : Oops!

OOPS *hurries in.*

Get the Royal Ax.

O O P S : The Royal Ax? [*Starts crying.*]

K U D A : Quiet, you numbskull! Do as I say.

OOPS *crosses to door for ax.*

You, Cricket Keeper, will be the first to lose your head.

O S E E : No, you can't Oh, Ahpoo, stop him!

A H P O O : There's nothing we can do.

O O P S [*starting downstage with ax*]: I can't do it.

K U D A : SILENCE! The old one first. Quickly, or I'll make you a feast for my spiders.

> OOPS *raises the ax slowly over the head of the* KEEPER, *suddenly he drops it and begins jumping around, laughing.*

K U D A : What's wrong? Get on with the execution.

O O P S [*between laughs and gyrations*]: I can't. Something is tickling me!

K U D A : Pick up that ax and do as I order! ! At ONCE!

> OOPS *picks up the ax, but just as he raises it, another fit of laughter hits him, causing him to swing around, the ax almost taking* KUDA *in the neck. He then turns in the other direction, almost getting the* EMPEROR.

K U D A : Look out!

E M P R O R [*ducking*]: Oh dear.

K U D A : Put down that ax!

A H P O O [*moving to* OOPS]: Here, I'll help you.

O O P S : There's something down my back.

A H P O O [*reaching down* OOP's *back*]: Hold still. There, I've got it. See, a cricket.

O S E E : A cricket!

A H P O O : Quick, where is the water and paint brush? [*Gets them.*]

K E E P E R : Paint his head.

A H P O O : Watch, Emperor. [*In front of* EMPEROR.] See, the golden crown was covered with black paint.

E M P E R O R : The Royal Cricket! [*Takes cricket from* AHPOO.] There you are my little darling. Did those mean people hurt you?

K U D A : Oops, at once. Off with his head! [*To* KEEPER.]

O O P S   A H P O O   O S E E [*in unison*]: No!

E M P E R O R [*looking up from cricket*]: No what?

K U D A : SILENCE!

E M P E R O R : I wasn't saying anything. You were the one who said "no."

KUDA : I didn't say it. Those fools did.

EMPEROR : Oh, I see, they said—— [*With realization.*] They said it? I hear what they said! I can understand them!

KUDA : Oh no, Emperor——

EMPEROR : Be quiet, Kuda.

KUDA : But Royal One——

EMPEROR : SILENCE! Boy, come here. Now, say something to me.

OSEE : What shall I say, Sir?

EMPEROR [*happily*]: I did! I understand what they say.

AHPOO : Of course you do, Emperor. It was Kuda's evil plan to make you lonely. He is the one who took the Royal Cricket so he could become Emperor.

KUDA : I–I–I——

EMPEROR : QUIET! Very well. You shall become Emperor, the emperor of fools. Come before me, Kuda.

> KUDA *kneels before* EMPEROR.

EMPEROR : You have been evil and cruel, always frowning and scowling on all you met. People have always feared you. We will change that now. Smile.

KUDA : Oh no, don't make me smile. Please don't make me do that.

EMPEROR : Smile! [*He attempts a smile. It looks more of a grimace.*] Bigger [KUDA *strains more, and bares his teeth.*] Now go, and make people laugh. If you ever fail, you shall be fed to your own spiders. [KUDA *slinks out.*] Oops!

OOPS [*frightened*]: Y-yes Sir?

EMPEROR : To you I give the position of Royal Executioner. [OOPS *starts to cry.*] What is wrong? This should make you happy?

OOPS : Oh please, Sir, don't give me the job. I don't want to cut off anyone's head.

EMPEROR : I know. That is why you are to be Executioner. There will be no more executions. [*To* KEEPER.] You have a very clever son. But he is more than clever. He has a warm and gentle heart.

KEEPER : Thank you, Royal One. I am very proud of him.

EMPEROR : And I shall give you more reason to be proud. For bringing me happiness and taking away my loneliness, I pro-

claim Osee, son of the Royal Cricket Keeper, Prince of Japan,
and heir to the Royal Throne. Let all the people know it is a
time of celebration, a time to honor new royalty: Osee, the
Prince of Japan!

CURTAIN

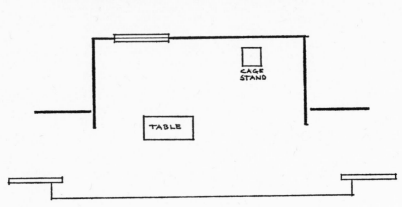

Floor Plan for the Royal Cricket Keeper's Cottage

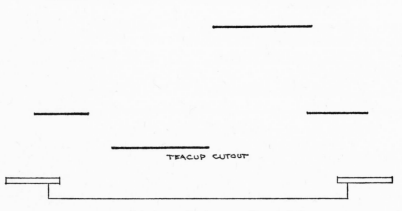

Floor Plan for a Clearing in a Forest of Grass

Marlin
the Magnificent

AN ORIGINAL FANTASY

BY

James C. Abrell

Cast of Characters

PRINCESS	HEAD GUARD
PIXIE	OTHER GUARD
HELPER	QUEEN
MARLIN	PRINCE

Synopsis of Scenes

Act One   In a forest clearing.

Act Two   In the Queen's throne room.

Act Three   Back in the forest clearing.

PROPERTY LIST

Act One

Bucksaw
Suitcase
Two maps
Magic wand
Glass of water
Flower (edible)
Small salt shaker
Bunch of wildflowers
Two pikes (GUARDS)
Fan
Sack of cookies
Cookbook
Watch
Two colored eggs (breakaway)

Act Two

Magic wand
Small salt shaker
Flowers (edible)
Cookbook
Fan
Scepter
Basket of colored eggs
Two colored eggs (breakaway)

Act Three

Little map
Scepter
One flower

Act One

Setting for a Forest Clearing

SCENE: *As the curtain opens, we see a beautiful young* PRINCESS *in a forest clearing. She is cutting firewood with a bucksaw. Also, she is sobbing bitterly. Then, gradually the sobbing subsides and the drudgelike sawing slowly ceases. All is quiet. She takes a tiny lace handkerchief from her pocket, sniffs two sniffs, and dries her eyes. She sighs deeply, a long heartfelt sigh, then looks off stage left. The memory of what lies there reawakens her sorrow and she bursts into a fresh flood of tears.*

Then, voices are heard off right. Someone is coming. Quickly she gets up and, after a moment of indecision, hides behind a large bush, up right.

Enter the PIXIE, *the* HELPER [*carrying a large suitcase which is rather heavy*], *and* MARLIN. *The last holds a map.*

MARLIN: Well, I give up. I don't know where we are!

PIXIE [*helpfully*]: We're lost.

MARLIN: I know we're lost!

HELPER: Now, now. Let's not argue. Let's all look at the map.

MARLIN: Map my foot. I've looked at that map till I'm blue in the face.

PIXIE : If you hadn't taken that short cut, none of this would have happened.

MARLIN : Me! You were the one got us lost in the first place. Had to go chase that stupid rabbit.

PIXIE : I wasn't chasing the rabbit. I was following it. There's a difference you know.

HELPER : Let's all look at the map.

MARLIN : If he hadn't sat on my magic wand, I could wish us back to Magic Land. But, now . . .

PIXIE : I said I was sorry.

HELPER : Marlin, the Fairy Godmothers are having a special banquet this evening. Now, I've got to be there! I promised!

MARLIN : How can I do anything with a broken magic wand. Look at that!

> *He shows her, for the nineteenth time, the broken wand. It is bent, and taped in a rather unprofessional manner, in the middle. Disgustedly, he puts the wand on the suitcase.*

HELPER : Marlin, you don't need a magic wand.

MARLIN : I do too!

HELPER : And you don't need that silly costume, either! [*She points at suitcase.*]

MARLIN : I need every bit of that equipment!

HELPER : If you'd only try a trick without it!

MARLIN : I can't do tricks without my wand and all my equipment. Now that's all there is to it!

> *The* HELPER *sighs and once again they all return to their map-reading. Then,* MARLIN *speaks, but, to no one in particular . . .*

MARLIN : Boy, I'm thirsty. I wish I had a glass of water.

> *There is a four-second pause and "the sound," then a puff of smoke to the left of the* PIXIE's *left foot. He hears "the sound" but has no idea where it came from.* MARLIN *and the* HELPER [*at the* PIXIE's *right*] *hear nothing and continue their inspection of the worthless map. The* PIXIE *grows suddenly weary of trying to read anyway. He looks about him, casually, and there, to his amazement,*

sits a glass of water. He stoops, picks up the glass, and hands it to MARLIN *who takes it and drinks half of it.*

MARLIN [*wonderingly*]: Where did you get this?

PIXE [*pointing*]: I found it on the ground.

MARLIN: You found it on the ground!

PIXIE: You said you wanted a glass of water and I just looked . . .

MARLIN: How do you know where it came from, or what's in it!

PIXIE: You said you wanted a glass . . .

MARLIN: It might be dirty. How long has it been there. I might be poisoned!

PIXIE: Well, you said you . . .

MARLIN [*to* HELPER]: Do you see what he just did to me?

HELPER [*lowering map*]: Honestly! I don't see how you two can argue *all* the time. [*She takes the glass and inspects its contents.*]

MARLIN [*clutching his chest*]: Germs could be multiplying inside my body.

HELPER: It looks fairly clean. I wouldn't worry. [*She hands him back the glass.*]

MARLIN: Fairly clean.

HELPER [*continues speaking*]: Now, that looks like a path over there. You two stay here and I'll go look. And try not to argue. [HELPER *exits left.*]

PIXIE: Hey! There's a wild flower!

He walks briskly to it, down left, and plucks it. After inspecting it, smilingly, he inhales its beauty, and then, he eats it. His joy changes to mild concern as he munches reflectively.

Needs salt. Hey! There's another.

This is a real gold mine. He stoops, picks the flower, takes salt shaker from his pocket, salts the flower, and eats it. This one is perfect.

By golly, these are good! [*He spies another up left.*] They're all *over* the place!

Joy reigns supreme. With a tremendous effort of will, MARLIN *says nothing. Instead, he spreads the map and tries to figure their position. The* PIXIE, *being friendly, plucks an exceptionally fine example of flowerhood and takes it to his good buddy.*

Here's a real good young tender one. Try it. [*He salts it liberally over the map.*]

MARLIN : Will you get that weed out of my face! How can you eat junk like that?

PIXIE : It's delicious. If you'd only try one.

MARLIN : Thank you . . . no.

PIXIE : Okay. But you don't know what you're missing. [*All is quiet.*] HEY LOOK!

MARLIN *jumps.*

Flowers! [PIXIE *points stage right.*] A million of them. How'd I miss all those? [*And he rushes off, right, out of sight.*]

MARLIN *is left all alone on stage. He sighs, audibly, and looks at the suitcase on which rests his wand.*

MARLIN : If I could find my way back to Magic Land, I could get a new magic wand.

He returns, with regret, back to his map reading, but after a few moments he wads it up in a ball and says . . .

This map is terrible! Doesn't tell me anything. It's too old. I wish there were a new map around here, somewhere.

He straightens out the old map. As he does, there is a light "gong" sound, and there appears a little map. [It can unroll like a scroll.] MARLIN *gets his wrinkled map straightened out, then says* . . .

What a shame I can't do tricks without a magic wand.

Now, the PRINCESS, *who has remained hidden all this time, peeks out from behind her bush. She looks to the right and to the left, and, seeing only* MARLIN, *summons up enough courage to step out. Silently, hesitantly, [he does not see her] she approaches him. She stands by his side, not knowing quite what to do. He is still completely unaware of her presence. Finally, she taps his shoulder.*

MARLIN : YAAAHHHH! [*He jumps nine feet straight up.*]

PRINCESS : I'm so sorry. I didn't mean to frighten you.

MARLIN : Oh, you didn't frighten me.

PRINCESS : I couldn't help hearing what they said.

MARLIN : What who said?

PRINCESS : Your two friends.

MARLIN : You mean the Helper and the Pixie?

PRINCESS : Yes, I guess. What's a Helper?

MARLIN : Why, she helps. She's a very good one too. And, in only six more weeks, she gets her certificate, and then she'll be, "A Registered Fairy Godmother!"

PRINCESS [not understanding, but friendly]: I'm glad.

MARLIN : That's what this picnic was all about. We were celebrating, and that nutty Pixie had to go chase a rabbit, and we followed him, and then he sat on my magic wand, and then . . .

PRINCESS : That's what I want to talk to you about.

MARLIN : What?

PRINCESS : About your magic wand. I need some help. [A sniffle.] I'm so sad, and I have such a problem. I don't think I'll ever be happy again. [She appeals to him.] Can you help me?

MARLIN : I'll try.

PRINCESS : Oh, good! Now, is that really a magic wand?

MARLIN : Well, it was a magic wand.

PRINCESS : Could it still do magic tricks?

MARLIN : That's hard to say.

PRINCESS : Well, will it or won't it?

MARLIN : Uh, mmmm, errr . . .

PRINCESS : Could the Pixie do a trick with it?

MARLIN : The Pixie! I'm the magic man! I do the tricks with it!

PRINCESS : Well, would you? Would you do a trick with it, for me?

MARLIN : Oh, dear.

PRINCESS : Uh huh. HUH!

MARLIN : I beg your pardon?

PRINCESS : HUH!

MARLIN : What do you mean, HUH!

PRINCESS : Just what I said. You're no magic man at all.

MARLIN : But, I am! It's only that my wand is broken. If I try to do a magic trick with that, I don't know what will happen.

PRINCESS : Oh, excuses, excuses. You men are all alike. [The flood.] You can't do any tricks at all and you were my last hope and now nobody in the world can help me! [*She sobs, bitterly.*]

MARLIN: Oh, good Heavens. [*He's completely at a loss.*] Please don't do that. Good grief. I hate to see a woman cry. [*Jokingly.*] You'll get a tummy-ache. [*An even louder burst of tears greets this attempt at humor.*]

HELPER [*enters from left*]: There's a big castle, right over there. [*She points over her shoulder, then sees the girl.*] Who's that. Marlin, what have you done? [*She rushes to the* PRINCESS.]

MARLIN: I haven't done anything!

HELPER [*to the* PRINCESS]: There, there, there . . . [*She mothers her, comfortingly.*]

PIXIE [*enters from stage left carrying a huge armload of local flora*]: There're wild flowers all *over* the place! [*He gestures wildly, spilling a few flowers.*]

MARLIN: Shh . . . Not so loud. [MARLIN *looks about.*] Say, how did you get over there?

PIXIE: I followed another rabbit. [*He points left.*] And there's a big castle right over there!

MARLIN: I already know that.

PIXIE: Oh, were you over there? I didn't see you over there. Were you in it? Who lives there? HEY! Who's she? What's she doing here? What's the matter with her? Why is she crying? Did you make her cry?

MARLIN: Will you sit down and be quiet!

> He does . . . *on* MARLIN's *wand!* MARLIN, *although facing front, hears the wand snap and reacts. So does the* PIXIE *who is surprised and freezes.* MARLIN's *expression is one of unbearable pain as he stares straight ahead. The* PIXIE *reaches under himself and cautiously extracts the now twice mutilated wand. He stands up, and views the thing sheepishly. He looks at* MARLIN, *then back at the wand. He wiggles it sadly. The wand is quite wiggley. He wiggles it again. It looks rather funny. He smiles and wiggles it once more, then, again and again! It works like a lasso! He whirls it vigorously, round and round his head.*
>
> MARLIN, *wondering at the delay, turns and sees what is happening. He strides to the* PIXIE *and grabs his wand back.*

MARLIN: Give me that!

HELPER: Marlin?

MARLIN: What?

HELPER: Can you come here a minute please?

MARLIN [*he does*]: What is it! [*He's still sore.*]

HELPER: Do you know who this girl is?

MARLIN: I haven't the faintest idea!

HELPER: She won't tell me either. She just sits here and cries.

PIXIE: Maybe she's lost something . . . [*he joins them*] like a rabbit?

MARLIN: No, it's not that. She said she had a problem.

PIXIE: Rabbits can be a problem.

HELPER: Maybe she can't find her way home. That's certainly a problem. We know that, don't we!

MARLIN: Do you think we can help her?

PIXIE: Maybe she's hungry.

HELPER: Are you hungry? Do you want a sandwich?

MARLIN: Would you like my handkerchief?

PIXIE: You want half a glass of dirty water?

PRINCESS: You're all very kind, and thank you, but no one can help me. My problem is the biggest problem that ever was.

HELPER: What is your problem, and who are you?

PRINCESS: I'm an orphan Princess, and I can't marry my Prince Charming.

HELPER: How terrible.

PRINCESS: My wicked stepmother is the Queen, and she won't let me.

MARLIN: Who's your Prince Charming?

PRINCESS: Her nephew. His name is Earl. And he's a real Prince!

HELPER: Why can't you marry him?

PRINCESS: The Queen won't let me! I've done everything to please her. I've washed, and dusted, and chopped firewood, and pulled up crabgrass. Look at these hands!

HELPER: But, why is the Queen against the marriage?

PRINCESS: Oh, I can't tell you that. It's too horrible! [*She cries anew.*]

HELPER: But, you must tell us, don't you see, or else how can we help you?

PIXIE: Don't cry Princess. It makes my throat hurt.

MARLIN: Just dry your eyes and tell us—why won't the Queen let you marry the Prince?

PRINCESS: All right. You asked for it. [*She stands.*] Here's why I can't marry him! [*Recklessly, she snatches the scarf from her head. Out tumbles a wealth of bright blue hair.*] Well?

PIXIE [*casually takes a bite from his flower*]: Well?

PRINCESS [*to* HELPER]: Well!

HELPER [*trying to understand so she can "help"*]: Well?

PRINCESS [*to* MARLIN]: Well, look!

MARLIN [*smiling vacuously*]: I'm looking.

PRINCESS: My hair!

MARLIN: Your hair . . .

PRINCESS: It's BLUE!

MARLIN: It's blue . . .

PRINCESS [*to* HELPER]: I have blue hair.

HELPER: Yes dear, it's lovely.

PRINCESS: You don't think that's just a little strange?

MARLIN: No.

PRINCESS: You don't?

MARLIN: No. See it all the time, where we come from.

PRINCESS: Well, the people around here sure think it's odd.

MARLIN: That's because this is a very tiny little kingdom.

PRINCESS: True. But, I've still got to live in it. The Queen is the worst of all. She HATES my blue hair, but she won't tell me why.

MARLIN: Is that your problem then? You want to get rid of your blue hair?

PRINCESS: Yes. If I weren't blue-haired than maybe the Queen would love me.

MARLIN: Why not dye your hair or get a wig?

PRINCESS: I tried that. But she still knows I was born with blue hair. Only a magician can help me. Will you?

HELPER: Of course he will. He'll help you all he can, won't you Marlin?

MARLIN: No. [*They glare at him.*] I can't! My magic wand is broken!

HELPER: Marlin, I just know that if you really tried, you could do a trick without that wand. If you only had more confidence.

MARLIN: The answer is no! I'm sorry. My problem right now is how to get us back to Magic Land. I'd help you if I could, but

I can't. [*Gets map.*] Now, do you know the territory around here?

PRINCESS: No.

MARLIN: Well, I wish I could find somebody who did.

> *From off left we hear a voice. It belongs to the* HEAD GUARD.

HEAD GUARD: Halooooo. What's going on around here?

PRINCESS: You're in trouble now. That's the Queen's Head Guard.

MARLIN: What a coincidence. Just the man I'm looking for. Now, maybe somebody can tell us how to get back home.

HEAD GUARD [*enters from left*]: What are you people doing here?

MARLIN [*on hands and knees with his map*]: Be with you in just a minute, fellah. [*Ponders.*] Mmmmmm, which way is north?

HEAD GUARD: What?

MARLIN: Which way is north!

HEAD GUARD [*completely taken aback, he points up center*]: That way.

> MARLIN *sheepishly turns map completely around, grins at the* HELPER, *then once more takes command.*

MARLIN: All righty . . . [*Studies map.*] Where are we now?

HEAD GUARD [*asserts fully his official authority*]: You're on private property!

MARLIN: Thank you. [*Hunts for it on map.*] Private property . . . [*He looks up.*] Private property?

HEAD GUARD: That's right. This is the Queen's Private Forest!

MARLIN: AH! [*That's more like it.*] Thank you. [*Back to the map.*] Queen's Private Forest . . . Queen's Private Forest . . . [*Without looking up.*] Is that with one "r" or two?

HELPER: Here it is, Marlin! Oh, no. That's Queen's River Drive . . .

HEAD GUARD: I don't know anything about that. All I know is you're not supposed to be here. That road you came down on, that's a private road. You're not allowed to walk on it. Nor, you're not allowed to stand on this grass, either. Nor sit on it.

Nor kneel on it, like you're all doing. [*They keep hunting.*] Do you understand?

MARLIN [*reads along margin*]: "Beyond here, there be Dragons."

[*To* HELPER.] Say, how old is this map?

HEAD GUARD: Did you hear what I just said?

MARLIN: What? [*Looks up and smiles engagingly.*] Oh, I'm sorry. What was that?

HEAD GUARD: I said . . . ! You're not allowed to be here! You . . . and her . . . and that fellah there . . . in the green underwear!

MARLIN: Look buddy, we're lost, okay?

HEAD GUARD: Well, you'll have to get lost someplace else.

MARLIN: How can we get lost someplace else?

HEAD GUARD: That's your problem. Don't bother me with it!

MARLIN: Everybody gets lost once in a while.

HEAD GUARD: Maybe. But there're some places where you can't do some things, and this is one of them. You can't stay here!

MARLIN: I think that's a very hard-headed attitude to take. If you're here why can't *we* be here?

HELPER: Please, Marlin . . .

MARLIN: Well, we're not hurting his old grass.

HEAD GUARD: All I know is, if the Queen finds you here, she'll have you arrested for trespassin'. Or maybe worse!

MARLIN: Oh, she will, will she? I wish she'd try. I just wish she'd try.

> OTHER GUARD *enters from left, hurriedly. He is extremely agitated.*

OTHER GUARD: The Queen's coming, the Queen's coming! And the Prince, too! [*He gestures wildly.*] Clean up the forest!

MARLIN: Clean up the forest?

OTHER GUARD [*screams in horror*]: Look at that! [*Points to* MARLIN'S *suitcase.*] Get that junky trash out of here! [*He starts kicking it toward the stage right.*]

MARLIN: That's my magic costume! [*He hangs on to it, protectively.*]

OTHER GUARD [*another frenzied yell as he points at the floor*]: SAWDUST! Get that sawdust up! Get it up. UP, UP, UP!

HEAD GUARD: [*frantically, on hands and knees*]: I'm trying, I'm trying. What'll I do with it?

OTHER GUARD [*sees flowers on floor, goes into hysterics*]: YAAAHHH!! Those flowers; the queen will kill us all! Get them out of the way. Out, out, out!

> *They now all have their hands full of flowers, sawdust, and they begin hiding it quickly.*

HEAD GUARD [*assumes dignified posture, bellows out*]: Her Royal Majesty! The Queen! All bow down!

> *There is a mad scramble for "places" and they all bow down. All except the* PIXIE, *who remains upright looking off right.*

PIXIE: Boy, is she ugly!

> *They pull him down. Then, enter the* QUEEN, *a large, militant creature. She is wearing a large black hat. The* PRINCESS *hides again, fast!*

QUEEN: Earl! Get in here!

HEAD GUARD: The Queen's Royal Nephew! His Majestic Highness. The Prince!

> *The* PRINCE *enters. He is engrossed in a volume entitled* [*in big print*] COOKBOOK. *From time to time, he helps himself from his bag of goodies.*

QUEEN: You may all rise. [*To* HEAD GUARD.] Have you seen my lazy, good-for-nothing stepdaughter?

OTHER GUARD: I saw her, I saw her. She was here a minute ago, but she sneaked away!

PRINCE: Tattle-tale, tattle-tale!

> *The* QUEEN *bangs him on the head with her fan.*

Ouch ouch ouch ouch . . .

> *He covers his head with his hands. When she turns, he doubles up his fist and shakes it at her posterior. She turns back to him, he assumes an angelic expression, and smiles, straight front.*

> *The* QUEEN *spies the trio.*

QUEEN : What are these people doing on my private property?

HEAD GUARD : They say they got lost, Your Majesty.

QUEEN : And just what . . . [*she has spied the* PIXIE] are you?

PIXIE : I'm a Pixie.

QUEEN : You look more like a grasshopper. [*To* HELPER.] Who are you?

HELPER : I help, Your Highness. I'm a Helper. But, in just six weeks I get my certificate, and then I'll be, "A Registered Fairy Godmother."

QUEEN : I don't believe in Fairy Godmothers.

HELPER : Oh. I'm so sorry.

QUEEN : And who, may I ask, are you?

MARLIN : My name is Marlin, and I'm from Magic Land!

QUEEN : Why are you here?

MARLIN : We got lost.

QUEEN [*to* HELPER]: Is that right?

HELPER : We did get lost, Your Majesty. We're very sorry, really.

QUEEN [*to* PIXIE]: Did you get lost, too?

PIXIE : Why don't you like blue hair?

> The QUEEN *throws her arms in the air and explodes in violence!*

QUEEN : AAAGGGHHH! Blue hair! Don't you ever mention that again! How I hate it. Hate! Hate! Hate! If I ever hear you say that word again, do you know what I'll do?
> The PIXIE *shakes his head.*
I'll cut you up in so many green slices, you'll look like you got run over by a lawn mower! Is that clear?

PIXIE : Yeah. Wow! Why are you so mad?

PRINCE [*in a sing-song voice*]: I know why she's mad . . . I know a secret . . .

QUEEN [*hits him on head again with fan*]: If you ever tell that secret, I'll skin you alive, do you hear? [*Calm descends.*] Now then, back to you. You say your name is Marlin.

MARLIN : That is correct. I am Marlin, a magician.

QUEEN : A magician, eh?

MARLIN : That's right. A magician.

QUEEN : Do a trick.

MARLIN : How's that?

QUEEN : Do a trick.

MARLIN : Well, you see . . .

QUEEN : I command you. If you're a magician, prove it! Do a trick!

MARLIN [to HELPER]: Why is it when you're not sure of yourself, you always wind up having to prove something?

QUEEN : Bah! You're no magic man at all!

MARLIN : But, I am!

HELPER PIXIE [in unison]: He is, really. He's a magician.

QUEEN : Silence! I'll settle this once and for all this afternoon. You three are under arrest for trespassing . . . or maybe worse! [To HEAD GUARD.] Bring them to my castle in one hour. [To MARLIN.] And you'd better have a trick then, Mr. Marlin, the magician . . . or . . . you'll be sorry. [To HEAD GUARD.] Announce that I'm leaving.

HEAD GUARD : Her Royal Majestic Highness, the Queen, is now leaving. All bow down. [Everyone bows down.]

QUEEN [to the PRINCE]: Not you! You're the Prince! [She whacks him on the head again as they leave.] And stop eating all the time.

PRINCE : I have a nervous stomach.

They exit.

ALL : WHEW!

OTHER GUARD : Mister, unless you can do a trick for the Queen in one hour, you're in real trouble!

MARLIN : But my wand is broken. Surely she can understand that!

OTHER GUARD : She doesn't have to understand anything. She runs our government.

PRINCESS [runs out from her place of hiding]: Did you see him? Did you see him?

MARLIN : See who?

HELPER : See "whom" . . .

PRINCESS : The Prince! The Prince! Oooh . . . [She almost swoons.]

MARLIN : That was "Prince Charming"? [She nods, dreamily.] He's nothing but a big baby.

PRINCESS : Maybe that's why he appeals to me. I've always wanted to be a kindergarten teacher.

HELPER : Then you should teach kindergarten. [To MARLIN.]

We could use her in Magic Land. [*To* PRINCESS.] There's a teacher shortage, you know.

PRINCESS : But it's every girl's dream to marry a prince. And I want to marry Earl. Will you help me? . . . Please?

MARLIN : Help *you!* My wand is broken! I can't even help *me!*

HELPER : You'd better figure out something quickly Marlin, because in just . . . [*Looks at her watch.*] fifty-five minutes you've got to do a trick before the Queen!

PRINCESS : Why don't you try a trick *with* your wand?

MARLIN : Because, it's broken!

PRINCESS : It still might work. Lots of things do, even though they are broken.

MARLIN : Name one thing that works as well after it's broken!

PRINCESS : An ice cube.

MARLIN : Mmmmm . . .

HELPER : If Marlin tries to do a trick with that wand, it won't work.

PRINCESS : Why not?

HELPER : Because Marlin has no confidence in himself. We learned all about his kind at Fairy Godmother School.

MARLIN : "His kind"! What do you mean, "his kind"! You're always so sure of yourself. They don't know everything at that school, you know.

HELPER : They know a great deal, Marlin. You'd be surprised.

MARLIN : They do, do they? Well, I'm going to do a trick with this wand, broken or not!

PRINCESS : Oh, goody, goody, goody!

HELPER : You're making a big mistake.

MARLIN : I've got to do a trick for the Queen, and I'd rather experiment now with a broken magic wand, than with none at all. Give me my magic wand.

HELPER : Won't you try it without the wand, please?

MARLIN : Come, come . . .

HELPER : Oh, Marlin . . .

MARLIN : Come, come, come . . .

HELPER : Please be careful, Marlin. Just do an eensy-teensy trick first . . . please . . . for me?

MARLIN : All right. Before I try anything, big, I'll do a little bitty trick. What would you like?

PRINCESS : Could you make two hard-boiled Easter Eggs?

[*Everyone stares at her.*] I'm starved! I haven't had any lunch.

H E L P E R : It's as good as anything, Marlin.

M A R L I N : Well, why not. As a wand-warmer-upper then, I shall manufacture two, big, brightly colored Easter Eggs. Stand back. [*He assumes the position.*]

O T H E R   G U A R D [*enters from left*]: All right, let's go!

M A R L I N : Just a minute, fellah, I'm doing a trick.

O T H E R   G U A R D : It'll have to wait! We don't have time. Let's go!

M A R L I N : Look Buster, don't get smart with me or I'll turn you into a statue.

> OTHER GUARD *starts to make a particularly nasty response, then reconsiders. He looks at the* HELPER.

O T H E R   G U A R D : Could he do that to me?

H E L P E R : I've often seen him turn people into statues.

O T H E R   G U A R D : Well, all right, but hurry it up.

M A R L I N : One . . . two . . . three!

> MARLIN *makes the grand gesture and a puff of smoke appears behind him.* [*This can be accompanied by "the sound."*] *The* PIXIE *walks to where the smoke appeared and reaching down, picks up two eggs, as specified.*

P R I N C E S S [*she has a new idol in her life*]: You really are a magician!

M A R L I N : Certainly I'm a magician . . . and . . . [*To the* HELPER.] My wand still works. [*He begins handing the* HELPER *his costume.*]

P R I N C E S S : I think you're wonderful!

> *The* PIXIE *gives her the eggs.*

Thank you so much!

M A R L I N : Nothing really. [*To* HELPER.] Well?

H E L P E R : I never would have believed it.

P R I N C E S S : Mr. Marlin?

M A R L I N : Yes?

P R I N C E S S : Your wand works, right?

M A R L I N : That's right.

P R I N C E S S : Well, aren't you going to help me?

M A R L I N : Certainly I am. But first, I'm going to find out why the Queen hates your blue hair. Once I find that out, then maybe I can change her mind.

PRINCESS : And I could *keep* my blue hair. Oh, good!

MARLIN : Are you coming with us to the castle?

PRINCESS : If I do, she'll just put me to work again. I'm going to stay here and eat these eggs. I'm starved!

OTHER GUARD : I hate to interrupt you, sir, but, really we've got to be going.

MARLIN : Oh, all right.

The trio and the two GUARDS *exit.*

See you later.

Then the PIXIE *comes back.*

PIXIE : Here's some salt. [*Shakes salt into napkin through following.*]

PRINCESS : Oh, Pixie, your friends are so nice. They don't seem to mind that I have blue hair.

PIXIE : It doesn't matter whether or not you have blue hair. The really important thing is that you're a very nice person.

PRINCESS : Thank you.

PIXIE : Boy, I hope nothing goes wrong this afternoon.

PRINCESS : Don't worry, his wand works fine. Nothing can go wrong. Can it?

PIXIE : Hah! You don't know Marlin. He can get into more trouble!

PRINCESS : Do you think he will this afternoon?

PIXIE : I hope not. But, you never can tell about Marlin.

PRINCESS : Oh, my! Pixie, will you do me a favor?

PIXIE : Sure. What?

PRINCESS : If anything goes wrong at the castle this afternoon, will you and the Helper and Mr. Marlin meet back here?

PIXIE : Sure. But why? Is this a good place to hide?

PRINCESS : Oh, yes. This is a wonderful place to hide.

PIXIE : But, all those people. And this place is so out in the open.

PRINCESS : That's why it's such a good place to hide. That's the first time they've been out in the open for years.

HEAD GUARD [*sticks head in from left*]: Will you please come on, please!! I'll lose my job!

The PIXIE *exits left. The* PRINCESS *is now alone on stage. She seats herself and spreads a little napkin before her. Then, with a happy smile, she cracks one egg against the other. They are not hard-boiled. In fact, they are two of the rottenest, gooiest, stinkingest eggs that ever existed. After the shock of what has happened leaves her, a terrible thought comes.*

PRINCESS : The magic wand! Mr. Marlin's magic wand! It really doesn't work at all! Oh, I must tell him before it's too late! [*She rushes off, stage left.*]

CURTAIN

Act Two

Setting for the Queen's Throne Room

SCENE: *The curtain opens slowly on the Queen's throne room. After a moment, the* PRINCESS *enters, hesitantly. She wants to find* MARLIN *but she doesn't want the* QUEEN *or the* GUARDS *to find her. Thus, she calls with a tinge of worry, her eyes frightened wide.*

PRINCESS: Marlin . . . [*No answer.*] Mr. Marlin . . . [*All is still. Then a noise off left. Quickly, she hides behind the throne.*]

PRINCE [*enters reading from his* COOKBOOK]: "One cup sugar, two pints whipping cream, half-cup chopped walnuts . . ." Oh, I'd give anything in the world if I could have my own kitchen!

PRINCESS [*steps out, smiles*]: Hello, Earl.

PRINCE: Oh, it's you. Hi.

PRINCESS: Have you seen Mr. Marlin?

PRINCE: I haven't seen anybody. The Queen doesn't know it, but I've been in her kitchen again.

PRINCESS: I've got to find Mr. Marlin and tell him something terribly important. It's about his magic wand.

PRINCE: Oh, tell me, tell me. What is it? I can keep a secret.

PRINCESS: No, you can't.

PRINCE: I can so! I've never told a secret in my life!

PRINCESS: Yes, you have. You tell everything you know. Oh, Earl, why can't things be different.

PRINCE: Yeah. Then I could have my own kitchen.

PRINCESS: That's not what I mean. Why can't you be like a storybook prince? I'm in distress, Earl. Why can't you come to my rescue and be a real Prince Charming and dash up on a White Charger!

PRINCE: A white whater?

PRINCESS: A White Charger! [*No reaction.*] A horse.

PRINCE: Oh! I don't like horses. They're all slobbery. They go BLUBLUBLUBLU.

PRINCESS: Earl? Does it bother you that I have blue hair? Is that it?

PRINCE: No.

PRINCESS: Then, why don't we ever . . . get together?

PRINCE: Oh, do you cook, too?

PRINCESS: That's not what I mean. Oh, Earl . . . Why can't we run off together and get married!

PRINCE: What?

PRINCESS: I'll never feel like a Princess till I'm married to a Prince, and you're the only Prince I've ever known. But, why do you let the Queen order you around and hit you on the head like she does? Why can't you stand on your own two feet and be a real man!

PRINCE: I know, I know. And I will . . . some day . . . when I'm older . . . when I grow up.

PRINCESS: When you grow up?

PRINCE: Yes.

PRINCESS: But Earl, you're twenty-seven now!

PRINCE: Yeah, Yeah. I guess I'm just sort of a late grower-upper.

PRINCESS: Earl, I don't know what to do. I'm just miserable. And the Queen hates me so much.

PRINCE: OH! Yes! And guess what! I know why! I found out just this morning.

PRINCESS: You know why the Queen hates my blue hair?

PRINCE: I certainly do! But it's a secret and I can't tell you . . . cause I promised. [*Earl pantomimes the "cross my heart and hope to die" routine.*]

PRINCESS : Oh, Earl. You must tell me! I won't tell a soul!

PRINCE : Well . . . [*He looks about him.*] I really shouldn't . . . [*It's too good to keep.*] But! [*He whispers in her ear.*]

PRINCESS : Really? [*Whisper, whisper.*] No! [*More whispering.*] Can you imagine that!

PRINCE : And I just found it out this morning!

PRINCESS : Oh good heavens! Now I must find Mr. Marlin. If he tries a trick before the Queen. Oh, I must find him in time, before it's too late!

PRINCE : Time! Late! I just remembered. I've got a pie in the oven. It'll be burned to a cinder! [EARL *rushes off left.*]

PRINCESS : You're supposed to help me. I'm in distress. I'm a maiden. Darn it. Oh dear. And if Mr. Marlin tries the trick with that broken magic wand, everything will be ruined! Mr. Marlin? [*She goes off right.*] Yoohoo . . . Mr. Marlin.

> *All is still on stage. Then, from stage left, we hear the sound of marching feet. The sound grows louder, and in marches* MARLIN, *the* PIXIE, *and the* HELPER. *They are followed by the two* GUARDS. *They halt.*

MARLIN : Are we under arrest?

HEAD GUARD : The Queen says you are under escort.

MARLIN : What's the difference?

OTHER GUARD : If she doesn't like your trick this afternoon, you'll find out. [*Exit* GUARD.]

HELPER : Marlin, I'm still worried.

MARLIN : Why? My wand works.

HELPER : It seems to work on eggs, but will it work on anything else. Would you try another little trick?

MARLIN : Well . . . can't hurt anything, I guess. But, I'm confident that this wand is in perfect working condition. And, as you know, I am hardly ever wrong.

> *This last is too much for the* PIXIE. *He walks upstage. There he stands, quietly watching the* QUEEN's *flowers.*

HELPER : The Queen may want a fancy trick.

MARLIN : Yeah, you're right. What fancy trick could I give her?

> *The* PIXIE *takes his first bite.*

HELPER : What about red roses on a small snow bank?

MARLIN : No, the snow would melt and get the floor all wet.
HELPER : Yes, you're right. I never thought of that.

> PIXIE *eats another flower . . . with salt.*

What about that trick you did with all the butterflies?
MARLIN : Yeah, yeah, yeah . . . or what about the one with the cherry blossoms and the bluebirds?
HELPER : Oh yes . . . or the one with the puppy.

> *The* PIXIE *eats a third flower.*

MARLIN : No, last time I did it, it got the floor all . . .
HELPER [*sees what the* PIXIE *is doing*]: Oh, Marlin! LOOK!!
MARLIN [*rushes to* PIXIE, *grabs flower*]: Don't do that. We're in enough trouble as it is!
HELPER [*points off left*]: Oh, Marlin, here comes somebody!

> MARLIN *is confused.*

Quickly Marlin, somebody's coming!

> MARLIN *tries to give flower back to the* PIXIE, *but the* PIXIE *won't take it.*

It's the guards. Marlin . . . *do* something!

> MARLIN *eats the flower.*

PRINCE [*enters with two* GUARDS]: But, I'm a Prince, and I shouldn't get run out of the royal kitchen.
HEAD GUARD : It was the Queen's orders, Your Majesty. She says you always make a big mess and never clean it up.
PRINCE : But, I thought royalty could get away with that sort of thing.
HEAD GUARD : Not any more, Your Majesty.
PRINCE : Oh, darn.

> GUARDS *exit.*

I wish I had my own kitchen. [*Sees* MARLIN.] Hi there. [*Examines him more closely.*] Mmmm. You don't look so good.
MARLIN : I'll be all right in a minute.
PRINCE : Probably something you ate.
MARLIN : I'm sure of it.
PRINCE : You gonna do a magic trick for the Queen?

MARLIN : Yes. I am.

PRINCE : I know a secret about her. But I promised I wouldn't tell.

MARLIN : Ahaaa! You know why the Queen hates blue hair?

PRINCE : I found out this morning. But, it's a secret.

MARLIN : Would you tell me, please?

PRINCE : Well . . .

HELPER : If you'd tell Marlin, maybe we could fix it so you could have your own private kitchen.

PRINCE : My own kitchen?

HELPER : He is a magician, you know.

PRINCE : Oh . . . if she found out I told you, she'd be furious!

MARLIN : I wouldn't tell her.

PRINCE : You wouldn't, huh?

MARLIN : Cross my heart.

PRINCE : Well . . . [*Looks right and left.*] She didn't know I was upstairs . . .

MARLIN : Yeah . . .

PRINCE [*gets close to* MARLIN]: And . . . [*Whispers in his ear.*]

MARLIN : Yeah . . . [*Whisper-whisper.*] Yeah . . . yeah . . . NO!

The PRINCE *rocks on his heels, smugly.*

HELPER : What, Marlin? What, what, what . . .

MARLIN [*to* PRINCE]: Can I tell her?

PRINCE : All right. But, keep it quiet.

MARLIN *whispers in her ear.*

HELPER [*listening*]: Yes . . . yes . . . well! I never!

MARLIN : It's a fact.

HELPER : Can you imagine that!

PIXIE [*tugging at her sleeve*]: Imagine what . . . imagine what?

HELPER [*to* MARLIN]: Is it all right if I . . . [*She points over to* PIXIE.]

MARLIN [*to* PRINCE]: Is it all right if she . . . [*He indicates the* PIXIE.]

PRINCE: Oh, sure. But, whisper it, cause it's a secret.

HELPER *whispers to* PIXIE.

If the Queen found out I told, she'd *skin me alive!*

PIXIE [*loud, surprised voice*]: You mean, the Queen is *BALD!*

The PRINCE *throws his hands in the air and nearly dies!* MARLIN *and the* HELPER *smother the* PIXIE *with hands, arms. Then, they all look around to see if anybody has heard. Everything seems safe.*

PRINCE: Not so loud!

MARLIN: Can't you keep anything to yourself? [*This last to the* PIXIE.]

PIXIE: All I said was   .   .   .

But they stop him. Then they all conspire.

HELPER: Doesn't she have any hair at all?

PRINCE: Not one! She's as bald as a goldfish bowl!

HELPER: Marlin! That's why she hates the Princess! She's really jealous! She's jealous of all that beautiful long blue hair.

PIXIE [*fascinated*]: Doesn't she have *any* hair?

PRINCE [*confidentially*]: I've seen more hair on a cake pan.

MARLIN: Really bald, huh.

PRINCE: Slick as glass.

They all shake their heads and go "tsk, tsk, tsk."

MARLIN [*to the world in general*]: Well, the answer is simple then.

PRINCE [*to the* HELPER]: What was the question?

MARLIN [*to the* HELPER]: In order to make the Queen like the Princess, I'll give the Queen long blue hair. That way she won't be jealous.

HELPER: That's an awfully big trick, Marlin.

PRINCE: Well, good luck. [PRINCE *sits at foot of throne.*]

HELPER: Giving blue hair to somebody is much more difficult than just making two big Easter Eggs.

MARLIN: Yes, it is. I ought to try it out first. I wish I could try the trick out on somebody. [*And then he sees the back of the* PRINCE'S *head!*] Mmmmm   .   .   .

HELPER [*sees what* MARLIN *has in mind*]: Oh, Marlin . . .

> *But* MARLIN *shushes her and is in the process of giving the* PRINCE *blue hair. The* PIXIE *hiccups. The* PRINCE *looks up and around.* MARLIN *hides his wand.*

PRINCE : Did you say something?

MARLIN : It was nothing, nothing at all. Go right on back to your reading.

> *He does and again* MARLIN *prepares . . . and again the* PIXIE *hiccups.*

PRINCE : He has the hiccups, doesn't he?

MARLIN : Yes. He does.

PRINCE : He should hold his breath.

MARLIN : For a week.

PRINCE : Or maybe he just needs a good scare.

MARLIN : He needs something.

PRINCE : He needs somebody to say, "BOO." That always frightens me.

MARLIN : An excellent suggestion! Why don't *you* do it?

PRINCE : Who, me? Oh, no really. I'm not much good at that sort of . . .

MARLIN : Nonsense. You'd scare a lot of people. Pix, come here. Not another word now, Prince. Just you stand here, and Pix, you stand over here, and I'll stand . . . here.

> *The* PRINCE *now faces the* PIXIE *and* MARLIN *is behind the* PRINCE. *Thus with the* PRINCE's *attention fixed on the* PIXIE, MARLIN *will be able to work magic wonder on the* PRINCE's *hair.*
>
> *The* PRINCE *gets ready to say "boo" in his most frightening manner, however, each time* MARLIN *gets his wand in the air, the* PIXIE, *feeling that he stands in the "line of fire" [which he does] dodges out of the way.* PRINCE *is thus caused to move and* MARLIN, *so as not to be seen by the* PRINCE, *must also move. This happens a couple of times.*

MARLIN [*to the* PIXIE]: Will you hold still.

PRINCE [*to* MARLIN]: He keeps moving. [*To* PIXIE.] Don't worry. I won't hurt you.

PIXIE: You're not the one I'm worried about.

MARLIN [to HELPER]: Will you give me a hand?

HELPER: Marlin . . .

MARLIN: Please!

HELPER: I'll probably be sorry for this, but I am your helper. [She walks over and holds the PIXIE.]

MARLIN: Okay, Prince, scare him again.

PRINCE: He looks pretty scared already. [The PRINCE gets his hands in the air.] BOOOOOO!

> PIXIE hiccups, MARLIN gestures, again nothing happens. MARLIN does everything but throw the wand at the PRINCE's head, but that hair will not turn blue.

PRINCE [again to MARLIN, who hides wand]: It doesn't seem to be working very well.

MARLIN [inspecting the top of the PRINCE's head]: Doesn't seem to be working at all.

PRINCE [looking at the PIXIE]: I wonder why?

MARLIN [looking at his wand]: I don't know. It worked all right with eggs.

PRINCE: Yes. [Turns.] With eggs?

OTHER GUARD [enters from left]: Your Royal Majesty, the Queen says you have her royal crown, and she wants it back. Right now!

PRINCE: Oh, all right. It's in the kitchen. I was using it as a cookie cutter. [As he exits.] That's about all they're good for anymore.

HELPER: What happened Marlin, what happened!

MARLIN: I don't know! I tried and tried to give him blue hair, but I couldn't. And if I can't give it to him, I can't give it to the Queen either, can I?

HELPER: No, you can't. Oh, Marlin, I'm worried.

MARLIN: What'll I do? I don't trust this wand any farther than I could throw an elephant.

HELPER: Are you sure you can still make eggs?

MARLIN: I don't know.

HELPER: Marlin? Make two in my hat. [The HELPER removes her hat. She has blue hair.]

MARLIN [seeing it]: ARGGGGG . . .

HELPER: Marlin, what's the matter?

MARLIN *can't talk. He just points and makes little gagging sounds in his throat.*

I have never seen you act so silly.

MARLIN [*regaining his voice*]: Put on your hat!

HELPER: Why should I put on my hat?

OTHER GUARD [*enters from left*]: Her Royal Majestic Highness, the Queen! All bow down!

MARLIN: Please, don't argue. Just put on your hat.

She does.

PIXIE [*still standing*]: Hey! My hiccups are all gone!

They pull him down as the PRINCE and the QUEEN enter. OTHER GUARD exits. The PRINCE walks in front of the QUEEN, gets to the throne before she does, sits on the corner of the throne platform, and opens his COOK-BOOK. The QUEEN strides to the throne, sees that he is seated, and whacks him on the head.

QUEEN: Will you get up!

He does.

And now . . . [*she seats herself, majestically*] you all may rise.

They all rise. The PRINCE remains standing.

Sit down, Earl.

PRINCE: But you just said . . .

QUEEN [*whacks him again*]: Sit down!

He does.

Now, then, if I remember correctly, we had a little trick planned for this afternoon . . . [*she visually nails MARLIN*] and you were to do it!

MARLIN: Yeah, how about that.

QUEEN: Have you a trick ready to perform?

MARLIN: If I tried a trick and it didn't work . . .

QUEEN: I would be *furious!*

MARLIN: Yeah, well, in that case I'll do a trick . . . with Big Easter Eggs.

QUEEN: Wonderful! I just love to eat Easter Eggs.

MARLIN: How many eggs would you like?

QUEEN: Ten thousand.

MARLIN: Ten thousand? Gee! That's an awful lot of eggs.

QUEEN: Can you do it or can't you!

MARLIN: Certainly I can do it! [to HELPER.] I did it with two
. . . I can do it with ten thousand.

> MARLIN *assumes the position, but is interrupted by the
> entrance of the two* GUARDS. *They bring in a struggling*
> PRINCESS.

QUEEN: What is the meaning of this! Where did you find her?

HEAD GUARD: She was snooping outside, your Majesty.

QUEEN: Why aren't you out working?

PRINCESS [*runs to the* QUEEN, *kneels by throne*]: Oh, Your
Majesty, hear me out. I've worked and I've worked! I've done
everything for you. And now you can do something for me.
Please let me marry the Prince, and please don't make Mr. Marlin do a magic trick!

QUEEN: I've put up with about enough from you. Tomorrow
I'm going to double your work load, cut your food rations in
half . . . and also I think I'll just cut off all that ugly blue
hair! Then you will be as bald as . . . as . . . well,
never mind.

> PRINCESS *moves off and cries.*

HELPER: That wasn't very nice!

QUEEN: I don't like her.

HELPER: If you're going to act mean, Your Majesty, then after
Marlin does his trick we'll just go straight back to Magic Land!

QUEEN: What do I care.

HELPER: Oh, I just thought you'd enjoy having a magician
around, that's all. He can do ever so many clever things. He
can make flowers, and zebras, and purple polar bears, and
. . . hair . . . and big friendly dragons, and . . .

QUEEN: What was that! What was that? He can make what?

HELPER: I said he can make flowers and zebras . . .

QUEEN: No, no. Not that! You said something else!

HELPER: Purple polar bears.

QUEEN: No, no. That "other" you said.

HELPER: What other?

QUEEN [*in a "just between us girls" manner*]: Uhh . . .
[*Looks around nervously.*] You said he can make . . . [*she
says the word softly*] hair?

HELPER: Oh yes. Marlin's been making hair now for years, haven't you, Marlin?

MARLIN: What? Oh! Yes, yes . . . years now. All lengths, all colors . . . green, pink . . . blue . . . polka dot . . .

QUEEN: Blue, eh?

HELPER: Uh huh. One of his favorite colors.

QUEEN: I don't suppose you could do that trick . . . now?

MARLIN: Not with this particular wand. Now, if I could go back to Magic Land, and get *another* wand . . .

HELPER: Your Majesty?

QUEEN: Hmmmmm?

HELPER: If Marlin can prove to you that he's really a magician, will you be nice to the Princess, and let us go back to Magic Land?

QUEEN: If I did, would you come back with the right kind of wand? One that would make . . . uh . . . hair?

MARLIN: We certainly would!

HELPER: Word of honor!

QUEEN: Cause, you see . . . [*she holds her hat*] I've got this . . . well . . . sort of . . . problem. I can't tell you what it is. Nobody knows about it. It's a secret.

PIXIE: HAH!

MARLIN *kicks the* PIXIE *in the shins!*

QUEEN: All right, then. It's all settled. Prove to me first, however, that you're a good magician.

MARLIN: Oh, I'm sure I can do that, Your Majesty.

QUEEN: See? I'm not so hard to get along with. You can ask anybody. [*To* EARL.] Am I so hard to get along with?

PRINCE: Yes.

QUEEN [*she hits him with her fan*]: Now, let's have the trick.

MARLIN: Right! [*To* PRINCESS.] All your worries are over.

PRINCESS: What trick are you going to do?

MARLIN: I'm going to give the Queen ten thousand Easter Eggs!

The PRINCESS *bursts into more tears!*

QUEEN [*to* PRINCESS]: Please, no demonstrations.

MARLIN: All right, Your Majesty, here we go! Ten thousand,

brightly colored, delicious-tasting, Easter Eggs! And may I say that I believe you're in for quite a surprise. [*He assumes the position.*] The eggs shall appear on the count of three! One!— Two!——

PRINCESS : STOP!

MARLIN : What?

QUEEN [*rising*]: How dare you! What is the meaning of this?

PRINCESS [*thinking fast*]: Well, Your Majesty . . . ten thousand eggs . . . right here in this room . . . don't you think they might crowd us a little?

QUEEN : Mmmmmm. Yes, you're right. They might indeed. And we certainly wouldn't want to step on one, would we?

PRINCESS : We certainly wouldn't!

QUEEN [*to* MARLIN]: See that little door there? [*Points left.*] Through that door and to the left, there's a little balcony. Under that balcony is the main dining room. You may put them there.

MARLIN : I'll go see if there's enough room. [*Exit left.*]

> *The* PRINCESS *takes this opportunity to slink away from the* QUEEN's *area. She whispers her secret to the* HELPER *as she pantomimes it.*

HELPER : Oh, NO!

> *The* PRINCESS *nods emphatically.*

Both of them?

> PRINCESS *nods again.*

PIXIE : Both of what . . . both of what . . . what are you talking about?

> *The* HELPER *whispers the secret and pantomimes it.*

ROTTEN!

> *They both shush him, and look guiltily at the* QUEEN, *but she is reading.*

Both of them?

> PRINCESS *and* HELPER *both nod.*

MARLIN [*enters, pleased as punch*]: The room will be just fine.

QUEEN : Wonderful! This is all so exciting!

HELPER : Marlin . . .

QUEEN : QUIET!

MARLIN : One—Two—*Three!* [*Sound effects and smoke from off left!*] You'll find your ballroom is now full of eggs.

QUEEN : Oh, wonderful, wonderful. I must go look. [*She exits.* MARLIN *swaggers over to his friends.*]

HELPER [*with a deadpan expression*]: Marlin?

MARLIN [*all smiles*]: Yes?

HELPER : They're rotten.

MARLIN : What's rotten?

HELPER : Those eggs you just made for the Queen. They're all rotten.

MARLIN : What are you talking about?

HELPER [*to* PRINCESS]: You tell him.

PRINCESS : Your magic wand. It doesn't work at all. Those eggs you made for me back in the forest! They were both rotten!

MARLIN : You mean . . .   [*He points.*] All those eggs for the Queen . . .

> *They nod.*

> Oh, NO!

QUEEN [*returns with basket of eggs*]: Well, here we are, back again!

MARLIN : Yes, so you are. It is getting late, and we really should be going . . .

QUEEN : Nonsense! You stay right here. [*Happily.*] I never saw so many eggs in all my life! [*To the* PIXIE.] Here. Would you like to eat one?

PIXIE : NO!

QUEEN : You're sure?

PIXIE : I'm *real* sure!

QUEEN : Very well. I'll eat it myself. [*She starts to break it.*]

MARLIN : No!

QUEEN : What?

MARLIN : Uhh . . .   What I mean is . . .   uhh . . .   don't be impolite Pix . . .   Take the egg!

PIXIE : Are you kidding?

MARLIN : *Take the egg!*

PIXIE : Oh! Yeah! Yeah! Gimme the egg, gimme the egg!

> *She does.*

QUEEN [*to* MARLIN]: Would you like an egg too?

MARLIN : Yes, yes. Maybe even . . .   two?

QUEEN [*gives* MARLIN *two eggs, says to* PRINCESS *and* HELPER]: How about you two. Would you like some eggs?

> *The* HELPER *and the* PRINCESS *walk quickly to the* QUEEN *and take two eggs each.*

PRINCE : Can I have some?

> QUEEN *gives him her last two.*

QUEEN : Imagine that. They're all gone.

MARLIN : Yes, so they are. Well, we've certainly had an interesting afternoon, but it is time we were going. You see, we've got this . . .

QUEEN : Stay where you are! I'll go get some more eggs. [*She exits.*]

HELPER : Quickly, Marlin, break open one . . . see if it's any good!

> *He does. It isn't. The* QUEEN *reenters.*

QUEEN : Well, here we are, back again. I have a basket *full* this time! Anybody want any more? I have ten thousand, you know.

> *They rush forward and help themselves as the* QUEEN *seats herself on the throne. After the rush, she looks at her basket.*

All gone again.

MARLIN : Yes. Looks as if you're out of eggs. That's the way it goes.

QUEEN : Yes. That's the way, all right. [*She laughs. They all laugh with her, nervously.*] But, I already have my two. [*She takes two eggs out of her pockets.*] Now then! It's Easter Egg Eating Time! Let's all eat eggs! [*She whacks the two together.*] They're not hard-boiled. [*The aroma gets to her.*] They're ROTTEN! [*She stands.*] Seize them!

> *The* GUARDS *rush forward as she yells to the* PRINCESS.

I'll throw you all in the dungeon and you'll never marry the PRINCE if you live to be a thousand!

> *However, the group doesn't want to be captured. Eggs are thrown, flower pots fly through the air, a suitcase is ruined, the* QUEEN's *hat gets knocked off in the fight, the place is bedlam.*

CURTAIN

Act Three

SCENE: *Same as Act 1, back in that same forest. After a moment, the* PIXIE *scurries on from stage left, limping a little bit.*

PIXIE: Marlin . . . [*No answer.*] Hey, Marlin? [*He looks around. There's nobody.*] If you're hiding, please don't . . . Helper? [*Only silence.*] Helper?

> *Then, a noise off left. He hears it, too, and hides behind the large bush.*

PRINCESS [*enters cautiously from left*]: Is anybody here?
PIXIE [*runs out*]: Are Marlin and the Helper with you?
PRINCESS: No. What happened. The lights went out and I just ran.
PIXIE: That's all I did, too. I couldn't see anybody, or find Marlin, and I just ran, and I fell and hurt my knee . . . and I'm worried! Marlin's not here and the Helper's not here. I'm scared.
PRINCESS: Look, you stay here. I'll go hunt around and see if I can find them.
PIXIE: Okay. But, please be careful. There are guards all over the place!

> *The* PRINCESS *exits right. The* PIXIE *walks left and looks off. He sees something! Quickly, he runs back to his bush and hides. Enter, two* GUARDS, *evilly.*

HEAD GUARD: I guess the other guards back at the castle have that phoney magician and his helper. All we need now is that little green Pixie, and the blue-haired Princess.
OTHER GUARD: Who was it that fell off the balcony and into all those rotten eggs? Was that the Prince?
HEAD GUARD: It sounded more like the Queen. Boy, what language!
OTHER GUARD [*pointing off right*]: Listen! [*They both listen.*] Did you hear something?
HEAD GUARD: I didn't hear anything. [*Studies the shrubbery.*] I wonder if anything's behind this bush?

The HEAD GUARD *starts upstage around the right side of the bush, leaving the* OTHER GUARD *about a foot down right of the bush, in an attentive position, still trying to hear something off right. After a moment, we see the rear end of the* PIXIE, *slowly backing downstage, from the left side of the bush. He backs and backs, not seeing where he is backing to. The* OTHER GUARD *is also bent over, facing right, listening in an attentive position. The two posteriors bump!*

OTHER GUARD [*waves hand without turning*]: Watch it, will you? I think there's something over there.

The PIXIE *turns and is struck numb with terror. After a moment, he regains the use of his limbs, and starts again, upstage, around the left side of the bush, but the* HEAD GUARD *is coming that same way, backing down toward the* PIXIE. *Panic stricken, the* PIXIE *grabs a flower, crouches in front of the bush and "hides."*

HEAD GUARD [*not seeing the* PIXIE *at his feet*]: See anything?
OTHER GUARD [*still looking off right*]: I'm not sure. Let's go look.

The GUARDS *exit down right. After a moment, the* PRINCESS *enters up right, creeps down to the bush, and spies the* PIXIE.

PRINCESS: Are you all right?
PIXIE: Did you hear what they said?
PRINCESS: Shhhhh!
PIXIE: I never wanted to be home so much in all my life!
PRINCESS: This is all my fault. I should have done it all myself!
PIXIE: Maybe Marlin's dead.
PRINCESS: I should have tried a march on the throne room.
PIXIE: Maybe the Helper's dead, too.
PRINCESS: I should have joined a national association . . .
PIXIE: Magic Land won't be any fun without them!
PRINCESS: For the advancement of certain princesses.
PIXIE: This not knowing's no good. I'm going back to the castle!
PRINCESS: Wait here just another two or three minutes. Maybe they got away.

PIXIE: What if they're wounded . . . or dead . . . or maybe worse!

PRINCESS: That's not what the Guard said.

PIXIE: He said they were captured.

PRINCESS: He said he thought they were captured! But, he didn't know. He wasn't even sure who fell in all the eggs.

PIXIE: I hope it was the Queen. I don't like her! [*Sniffs the air.*] Do you smell something?

PRINCESS: Yes, and I'll tell you what it is. It's those broken eggs back in the castle.

PIXIE: Yeah. That's what it smells like. Phew! It's getting stronger! Pheeewwwww!

PRINCESS: Good heavens! That's terrible.

HELPER [*enters from left*]: Well . . . guess who fell in the eggs!

> *Enter,* MARLIN. *He is covered with yellow egg goo. He seems in a trance. The* PRINCESS *and the* PIXIE *clap their hands and generally there is much joy onstage. Then, carefully, (for he doesn't smell good), they lead him downstage . . . while they talk.*

PIXIE AND PRINCESS [*in unison*]: How did you get away . . . were you frightened . . . are you all right . . . you smell just awful . . .

PRINCESS [*to* HELPER]: How could he possibly have fallen into all those eggs?

HELPER: He was on the balcony and tried to fly.

PIXIE: Why won't he talk?

HELPER: Oh, he thinks it's the end of the world, that's why! When he fell off that balcony, he lost his magic wand in all those rotten eggs.

PRINCESS: But, it didn't work anyway.

HELPER: That's what I keep telling him.

MARLIN [*in a stunned voice*]: It's gone . . .

HELPER: Marlin . . . now this is ridiculous!

MARLIN: Gone . . . gone . . .

HELPER: *You're* the magician. You don't *need* a magic wand!

PRINCESS: Where's all the rest of his equipment? His hat, and his scarf . . .

MARLIN: All gone . . . lost forever . . . [*He stares straight ahead, vacantly.*]

H E L P E R : Oh, this is so silly! I wish there were some way I could prove to you . . . Marlin, will you do me a favor?

M A R L IN : Nothing left . . . all gone forever . . .

H E L P E R : Marlin, now listen to me!

M A R L I N : No hope . . .

H E L P E R : All your equipment is back at the castle, right?

M A R L I N : I see nothing but darkness before me.

H E L P E R : Will you do me a favor?

M A R L IN : What!

H E L P E R : Will you just make a wish?

M A R L IN [*bitterly*]: HAH!

H E L P E R : Will you, Marlin? Will you just make a wish? Right now. For me. Please? Just say, "I wish . . ." and then wish for something.

M A R L I N : Yeah! I'll wish for something. I wish I had a decent map so that I could get out of all this! [*And the little map falls in his arms.*]

> *Everyone is so amazed that they are almost terrified. All except the* HELPER. *She exudes smugness!*

H E L P E R : Well?

> MARLIN, *again, can't talk. He just stares at the map and makes little funny noises in his throat.*

Well, Marlin? What did I tell you?

M A R L I N : I'm a magician!

H E L P E R : You're a magician.

M A R L I N : I *am* a magician!

H E L P E R : Yes, Marlin.

M A R L I N : *I* am a magician!

P I X I E : I hear something! [*He runs stage right, then points and yells.*] The British are coming.

M A R L I N : The British?

H E L P E R : Marlin, it's the Guards!

> *Everyone on stage is petrified with fear. But not* MAR- LIN. *Melodramatically, he holds up both hands and says* . . .

M A R L I N : Fear not! [*He rolls up his sleeves.*] Stand back and give me room.

The PIXIE, who has been halfway across the stage, watching the approach of the enemy, off right, now starts to run. We immediately see why. The HEAD GUARD runs on stage and, ignoring all the others, begins to pursue the PIXIE around the stage, counterclockwise. On the second time around, MARLIN makes the grand gesture. There is "that sound" and the GUARD is turned into a statue. But, the PIXIE keeps on running. He makes a complete circuit around the stage. Then, seeing the back of the GUARD, he jumps up, turns around and heads the other way. He makes the full circle and again, he sees the GUARD. Terrified, he turns and starts to run away again, but, the HELPER and MARLIN each grab an arm, and lift him from the ground. The PIXIE, suspended, stays in the same position, but his little legs keep running. He notices, then, that he isn't going anywhere. He stops trying, turns his head, and says . . .

PIXIE [*looking off right*]: Here comes another one!

The OTHER GUARD rushes on stage. He sees MARLIN and rushes toward him in a menacing manner. MARLIN gives him the old double whammy! The GUARD is frozen in mid-stride and turned into a statue, also.

MARLIN [*gleefully*]: Let 'em come! I'll take on the whole army!
HELPER [*looking off left*]: Oh, Marlin. Here comes the Queen!

The QUEEN flies on stage. She sees MARLIN, rushes toward him, and with all her might, slashes down with her huge scepter. MARLIN gestures. The clublike weapon stops an inch from his head. She, too, is now a statue.

PRINCESS: I never saw anything like that in my whole life!
PIXIE: What a magician!
HELPER: You were wonderful, Marlin.
PRINCESS: What a talent.
PIXIE: My pal!
MARLIN [*holds up hands for silence*]: Wait!

They hang upon his every word.

You haven't seen anything yet!

PRINCESS: We haven't?

MARLIN: I'm now going to do a trick that will amaze and astound you!

ALL: What . . . what . . . what . . .

MARLIN: I'm going to give the Queen the longest, bluest hair you ever saw!

ALL: Goody goody . . . wonderful . . . what a magician!

MARLIN: Quiet, please. I must have absolute silence. [*He looks about him.*] First of all, I wish that the Guards would go back to the castle and clean up all those eggs.

> *He makes the gesture. There is "the sound" and both* GUARDS *march offstage like little wooden soldiers.*

And now, that that's done . . .

> *He goes to the frozen* QUEEN *and surveys her. He takes the scepter from her hands.*

I wish that this scepter would turn into a hand mirror.

> *There is "the sound." He adjusts the "scepter-mirror" so that she is now "looking" at her own reflection. Then, he steps away and prepares for the final grand trick of the day.*

And now, I wish the Queen had long . . . blue . . . hair!

> *The gesture, "the sound," and it seems that nothing happens, but* MARLIN *is confident. He walks over to the* QUEEN, *reaches up, and gently removes her hat. Out tumble tons of bright hair.*

And now, Your Majesty, awaken!

> *He claps his hands twice, and gestures. There is "the sound," and the* QUEEN *comes back to normal. Furiously, she raises the mirror and rushes toward* MARLIN. *Then, the double take, as she stops, a confused look on her face. Cautiously she turns toward the audience and, with much hesitancy, lifts the mirror into view. She stares at herself in amazement.*

QUEEN: Hair! I've got long blue hair. I'm not bald anymore. [*To the gods.*] I've got beautiful long hair . . . hair . . . hair . . . hair! [*She spies* MARLIN.] And . . . you must have done it!

> *She shrieks with laughter as she lunges forward and hugs him with boundless enthusiasm.*

MARLIN [*with embarrassment*]: Madame, please, control yourself . . .

> *Bearlike, however, she embraces him and plants a big, wet kiss, right on his forehead.*

Good grief! [*At last he extricates himself.*]

QUEEN: I'm so happy. I'm SO happy, oh! [*To the* PRINCESS.] From now on I'll be the best stepmother in the whole world. And we won't ever cut our hair, will we?

PRINCESS: No.

QUEEN: And you won't have to work . . . and you can eat all you want. And, while I'm in the mood . . . [*She puts her arm around the* PRINCESS's *shoulder.*] You know all that trouble we had about the Prince? Well look, I know you want to marry him, right . . .

PRINCESS: Wrong!

QUEEN: So here's what I've decided. He's still pretty much of a kid. We both know that. What do you mean, "wrong"!

PRINCESS: I'd rather go to Magic Land with them.

MARLIN: You'd what!

PRINCESS: I've been thinking. I'm not in love with Earl. I was just in love with the idea of marrying a Prince.

HELPER: If you weren't a Princess, you'd have married him.

QUEEN: Are you saying you don't want to marry Earl?

HELPER: Wonderful!

HELPER [*she's so pleased*]: Then you can teach kindergarten in Magic Land!

PIXIE: Hot dog!

HELPER: Marlin, we can use her at Fairy Godmother School. [*To* PRINCESS.] Did you ever teach a cherub?

PRINCESS: No, but I could learn!

HELPER [*suddenly remembers*]: Oh, Marlin, I've got a Fairy

Godmother's meeting . . . [*She looks at wristwatch.*] In fifteen minutes.

QUEEN: Wait a minute. I've been running things around here for years! What if I don't want this to happen!

MARLIN: Fifteen minutes! Holy Smoke! Where's that map. Pix, where's the map?

The Magic Land trio begin hunting frantically for the map. They look everywhere through all the following conversation.

QUEEN: I represent an old established kingdom. Listen to me!

PRINCESS: Please say you don't mind . . . please? [*The* QUEEN *weakens.*] And give Earl his own little kitchen. He'll never be much of a Prince, but he could be an awfully good cook.

QUEEN: Oh, why not. There's not much I can do anyway. Besides, I've got long, blue hair! [*She holds it lovingly.*]

MARLIN: I put the map right here. [*To* PIXIE.] And you are sure you haven't seen it?

PIXIE: You lose everything, don't you. Now you've lost the map. [*The* PIXIE *laughs.*]

MARLIN: Why don't you try to help me look . . .

HELPER: I wish we could just fly back to Magic Land.

PIXIE: Yeah, on the back of a big, friendly dragon!

MARLIN [*without thinking*]: Yeah, I wish we could!

For the last time we hear "the sound" and out onstage tromps the biggest, friendliest dragon that ever walked on six legs. The gang panics. The Magic Land trio, the QUEEN *run off left. The friendly dragon turns toward the audience, grins, and runs after them.*

CURTAIN

NOTES

General Comments

Although *Marlin the Magnificent* is a fantasy, everything that happens onstage must seem to be true. The actors must believe in the reality of each situation, for only in this way will anything be accepted as true by the audience. The actors should not be condescending toward the younger children, but rather, should play to the older ones. If this play is performed with the intention of pleasing those of junior high-school age and above, it will entertain all. If it is acted out primarily to please first graders it will probably please no one.

Characters

The characters in this play can be understood from the play itself. The playwright appends the following only as personal opinions which may prove helpful to the actor.

MARLIN is energetic, impractical, impatient, and a bluffer—if he can get away with it. He is unconsciously in love with the Helper. Her good common sense and maturity aggravate him.

THE HELPER is young, pretty, and unconsciously in love with Marlin. She has a tendency to "mother" him.

THE PIXIE is a truant dressed in green, utterly irresponsible, and always hungry. To him Marlin seems like an older brother who is highly gifted, but accident-prone. To achieve the proper voice quality, a girl should play the Pixie; but on stage she should not *look* like a girl. She does not have to look like a boy either. (Pixies are neuter.)

THE QUEEN, though sensitive herself, fails to respect the sensitivity of others. She does not approve of Earl's way of life, but tolerates him because he is her only living blood relation.

THE PRINCE loves to suffer. He smokes pastel-colored cigarettes secretly in the kitchen.

THE PRINCESS was spoiled by her parents before they died. Now she is persecuted by the Queen. The result is confusion. She has extremely good manners and is in desperate need of guidance.

Set

In this realistic fairy tale the set can be kept quite simple.

In acts 1 and 3 the forest can be suggested with painted flats, a few ground rows with attachments, and a tree with two or three removable limbs.

In act 2 the flats can be reversed, suggesting a throne room, and the throne can be made by reversing the especially constructed ground rows and fitting them onto a chair.

Costumes

The costumes should be gaudy, ornate, and complicated. The style can best be specified by the writer as "Medieval German."

Special Effects

Because much dramatic appeal lies in the special effects, the following suggestions are offered.

The flash powder needed for the puffs of smoke in act 1 can be ignited by running six volts of electricity through a fine wire placed in the powder. One hundred and twenty volts can be cut to six by using a child's ordinary train transformer. These same results can be achieved without wires by using dry cell batteries triggered on stage by the Pixie, and built into one of the ground rows.

The map in act 1 can be tied to a black string and tossed over one of the upstage flats. In act 3 Marlin may receive the map by having someone offstage throw it at him. (Try to hit him in the head.) It is advisable to accompany all tricks with a sound. A gong is suggested.

The flowers must be edible, for the children will greatly enjoy watching the Pixie actually eat them. Stage flowers may be made of red cabbage, attached to a wire stem, and "planted" wherever necessary.

Not too many eggs need be hurled at the end of act 2, and they need not be hurled downstage in full view of the audience. But the ones broken by the Princess, Marlin, and the Queen should approach real life counterparts. "Breakaway" eggs, made of styrofoam and painted, can be used.

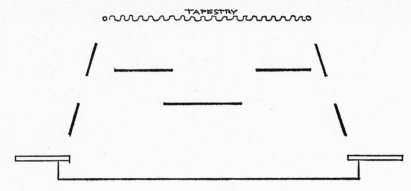

Floor Plan for a Forest Clearing

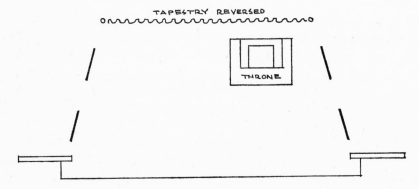

Floor plan for the Queen's Throne Room

The Shoes
That Were Danced
to Pieces

AN ADAPTATION

BY

Dorothy Beck Webb

ORIGINAL MUSIC BY

Lowell V. Hanbeck

Cast of Characters

KING, *the father*
AUNT, *sister of the King*
KATHLEEN, *oldest daughter*
COLEEN, *middle daughter*
JULEEN, *youngest daughter*
NURSE

COBBLER'S SON
PRINCE HEGERT
FIRST DANCING PRINCE
SECOND DANCING PRINCE
THIRD DANCING PRINCE

Synopsis of Scenes

Act One Scene 1: Early afternoon.
        Scene 2: Late afternoon.

Act Two Scene 1: Early the following morning.
        Scene 2: Later the same day; and the next morning.

Act Three Scene 1: Afternoon. Nine days later.
         Scene 2: Night.
         Scene 3: Early the following morning.

With the exception of act 3, scene 1, which takes place in the Land of the Sapphire Sea, all other scenes take place in the sitting room adjoining the Princesses' bedroom.

PROPERTY LIST

Act One

SCENE 1

Woman's shoes with a hole in the toe part of the sole

SCENE 2

A key
A picture
A vase of wilted flowers
A rug
Three glasses of milk
A key ring with many keys

Act Two

SCENE 1

Fresh flowers
A key

Six shoes (Girls) with holes in soles

SCENE 2

A vase of flowers and ferns
A key
A jug of milk and four glasses
 —one colored blue
Three pairs of worn women's shoes
Several scrolls

Act Three

Ten scrolls
A wastebasket
A jug of milk and four glasses
Pillows
A silver branch
A jeweled leaf

Act One

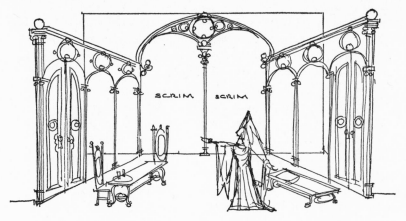

Setting for a Sitting Room Adjoining the Princesses' Bedroom

Scene 1

SCENE: *The sitting room adjoining the* PRINCESSES' *bedroom. The regality of the room gives it an obvious coldness. The people of this play lived in an unrecorded time in a land that may have later become Ireland.*

AT RISE: *The* KING *enters looking for his three daughters.*

K I N G [*calling*]: Kathleen! Where are my daughters? Coleen—Juleen! They're not here—perhaps they're in the garden. [*He starts to exit.*]

A U N T [*entering*]: Here you are! I've looked all over the palace for you.

K I N G : For me?

A U N T : Have you forgotten we were supposed to meet in the throne room half an hour ago?

K I N G [*stammering*]: Meet? Why—eh—w-h-y, of course. Eh—eh—is it afternoon already?

A U N T : You know very well that it is afternoon. You forgot again.

K I N G : I never forget!

A U N T : I'll vow you've even forgotten why we were meeting.

K I N G : We were meeting to discuss—ah—to discuss—why the girls,

The AUNT *gives an icy stare; the* KING *corrects himself.*

the Princesses, have not been eating their royal breakfasts again?

AUNT: We were not discussing their breakfasts, and how many times have I told you that you must refer to your daughters as the Royal Princesses! Breakfasts indeed! We were to discuss these bills!

KING: Bills? We discussed those bills last week.

AUNT: Last week we discussed the bills for the Princesses' new dresses; and the week before that we discussed the bills for the new jewels. But this week, we must discuss the bills for new shoes.

KING: New shoes? But we agreed the girls, the Princesses, must have new things.

AUNT: You agreed, not I! If I do not need new dresses and shoes——

KING: If you are in need of new clothes——

AUNT: That is not what I was going to say. The Queen, God rest her soul, left the girls, the Princesses, in my care.

KING: You have done your job well.

AUNT: That is why I shall not allow such wasteful spending on shoes.

KING: But the girls, the Royal Princesses, cannot go without shoes as the country milkmaids do.

AUNT: I am not suggesting they go barefoot like milkmaids——

KING: The entire kingdom expects to see them dressed like princesses.

AUNT: The entire kingdom does not wish to pay taxes for the Princesses to throw away!

KING: The Princesses are still young: they will learn to save as they grow older.

AUNT: How will they learn to save when they are allowed to throw money away on shoes?

KING: But one pair of shoes is not a great waste.

AUNT: One pair perhaps; but what of twenty-one pairs?

KING: Twenty-one pairs! You jest; what would the Princesses do with twenty-one pairs of shoes? There is some mistake!

AUNT: The Royal Treasurer assures me there is no mistake. Last week the Palace Cobbler was ordered to make twenty-one pairs of shoes.

KING: Who gave such an order?

AUNT: The Nurse!

KING : The Nurse?

AUNT : Yes, Nurse always orders their clothes.

KING : Then I shall ring for her; she can explain this mistake.

AUNT : She could not explain the mistake of the new dresses last week, nor the new jewels the week before that.

KING : The Princesses had outgrown their old dresses, and the new jewels——

AUNT : The Princesses twist old Nurse around their finger until she gets them anything they want. That's why they care more for her, than they do for me, their own Aunt!

KING : It is true that Nurse has been with them since they were born and that she has cared for them when they are sick, and told them bedtime stories, and sung to them about their mother; but you are their Aunt. There is room in their hearts for both of you.

NURSE *enters.*

NURSE : You rang, Your Majesty?

AUNT : Explain the——

KING [*interrupting*]: Please explain the mistake the Royal Treasurer has made.

NURSE : What mistake?

AUNT : Your mistake of ordering all those new shoes for the Princesses.

NURSE : Oh, that was no mistake your Ladyship! [*To the* KING.] I did order the Cobbler to make the new shoes.

AUNT : What did I tell you!

KING : Why? Surely my daughters, The Royal Princesses, don't need new shoes everyday!

NURSE : Oh, but they do! It is strange, but the Princesses wear a pair of shoes one day and they are full of holes.

AUNT AND KING [*at the same time*]: Impossible! But why?

AUNT : The Princesses could not walk that much.

NURSE : Sometimes they walk in the garden.

KING : If they had walked over every inch of the palace grounds, they couldn't have walked holes in their shoes in one day.

AUNT : They shouldn't be on the palace grounds at all!

NURSE : Perhaps the shoes are not made as strong as they once were.

AUNT : What kind of excuse is this?

NURSE: Perhaps the new Palace Cobbler does not do such fine work as the old one did.

KING: Bring him and we shall find out; and bring back one of the worn-out slippers.

NURSE *exits*.

KING: Do we have a new cobbler?

AUNT: Was there ever such an absentminded King! First you forget our meeting; and now you forget the new cobbler!

KING: I have many things to remember.

AUNT: Surely then, you remember the old cobbler was sick last week.

KING: He was? How is he?

AUNT: He's all right; but he's retired.

KING: Then who's making shoes now?

AUNT: That's what I'm trying to tell you!

KING: What is?

AUNT: The old cobbler asked that his son take his place. Surely you remember!

KING: Of course, I remember! And the old man asked that his son take his place.

AUNT: And make shoes that wear out in one day!

NURSE *and* COBBLER *enter*.

COBBLER: Your Majesty.

KING: Nurse tells us you were ordered to make the Princesses new shoes every day last week.

COBBLER: Yes sir; a new pair every day for each of the Princesses. There are seven days in the week and there are three princesses; 3 times 7 is—20; so I made 20 pairs of shoes last week.

AUNT: Twenty-one, young man!

KING: Didn't it seem strange to you that the Princesses should have a new pair of shoes every day?

COBBLER: No sir; they are princesses and everyone knows princesses must have many fine clothes.

KING: Do you need a new pair of shoes every day?

COBBLER: Oh no, sir! I'm only a cobbler's son. I have no need for fine clothes. I need only the clothes I work in.

AUNT : Let us see one of the *fine* shoes which he made the Princesses!

KING [*to* NURSE]: Did you bring the slipper?

NURSE : Yes, Your Majesty.

> *The* NURSE *gives the slipper to the* KING *who examines it.* AUNT *takes the shoe, puts her finger through a hole in the sole and holds it up.*

AUNT : Is this an example of your fine shoes!

COBBLER : I don't understand.

AUNT : What is there to understand about a hole in the sole of a shoe?

KING : Perhaps the boy has not had materials good enough to make shoes of fine quality.

COBBLER : But Your Highness; the leather which I used to make these slippers came from the skin of your strongest deer, stalked by the finest hunters in the kingdom. Their arrows are molded of the lightest silver with points of such sharp diamonds they can pierce the heart in such a way that the deer feels no pain. When the skin is removed from the deer, it is dried by the sun's early morning rays. To make the leather strong, we bathe it in the fragrant oil from the olive trees and then stretch it into shape under the shade of the rose arbors.
Sir, my leather has been of the finest quality; as strong as iron, as soft as velvet, and as fragrant as the honeydew. It cannot be the leather.

AUNT : Then perhaps it is the workmanship. Perhaps you did not make the shoes correctly.

COBBLER : Your pardon, my lady, but I learned to make shoes from my father when I was only this high. [*He indicates the height of a young boy.*]

KING : Yes, we know; that is why you were given the job.

AUNT [*disgusted with the* KING's *sentimentality*]: Ha! Evidently you did not learn your trade well!

COBBLER : Oh Madam! [*To the* KING.] Your Highness, please do not misunderstand me. I am not as skillful as my father but I know my shoes will last longer than one day!

AUNT : Then how do you explain these holes? [*She hands him the shoes.*] If it is not the leather, and if it is not his workmanship, then perhaps he will tell us the holes came there by magic.

COBBLER [*examining the shoe*]: Not by magic. The only way these holes could have been made is by–dancing!

ALL : Dancing?

NURSE : The Princesses have not been dancing.

KING : There was a ball at Prince Hegert's!

AUNT : That was many months ago. The Princesses have not been dancing.

NURSE : There's not been a dance in the whole kingdom since the one at Prince Hegert's.

KING : Then the holes must not have been made by dancing. What makes you so sure it was dancing that made the holes?

COBBLER : See how the hole was made.

KING : Why do you say this hole was made from dancing and not from walking or running?

COBBLER : Dancing shoes have scratches on the soles which go in circles. When you dance you turn on your toes many, many times. Each time the scratches become deeper and deeper; soon there are holes–round holes near the very toes of the slippers.

KING : I see.

AUNT : Well, I do not. Anyone who walks will have scratches on his shoes and the more he walks the deeper the scratches become and there will soon be holes–from *walking*.

COBBLER : People don't walk on their toes; and holes made from walking would be in the middle of the shoe.

AUNT : Impossible! There is no dancing in the palace!

COBBLER : There's dancing down by the mill.

NURSE : The Princesses would never go without permission.

AUNT : I forbade them to go beyond the garden wall.

KING : Surely the Princesses will explain.

NURSE : I will bring them.

AUNT : Tell them nothing that has been said.

NURSE *exits.*

Our discovery may be quite a surprise to the young Princesses.

COBBLER : I hope I have not spoken out of turn.

KING : If what you say is true, there will be some explanation; I must know what it is.

AUNT : And if what you say is not true, we must know that too; for if what you say is a lie, you will be put to death!

COBBLER : I do not lie. Anyone who makes shoes knows that what I say is true.

NURSE *enters and holds the door as the* PRINCESSES *enter one by one.*

KING : Good morning Princess Kathleen.
How are you Princess Coleen;
And Princess Juleen.
COLEEN : Did we do something wrong again?
AUNT [*to* NURSE]: You did tell them after all!
JULEEN : Nurse only said you wanted to see us.
KATHLEEN : You never want to see us unless we have done something wrong.
AUNT : Something is wrong!
KING [*to* AUNT]: We aren't sure. [*To* PRINCESSES.] I'm certain there's some explanation.
JULEEN : Explanation of what?
AUNT : Of this! [*She holds the worn-out shoe.*]
KING : Nurse and Cobbler tell us you have a new pair of shoes every day.
AUNT : A pair of new shoes every day; for each of you!
COLEEN : Nurse surely told you why we needed the new shoes.
KATHLEEN : They wore out; they do not last!
COLEEN : They were filled with holes after one day's wearing.
KING : We know all this!
JULEEN : Then what can we explain?
AUNT : Explain why the shoes do not last!

The PRINCESSES *are surprised by the* AUNT'S *insight.*

COLEEN : Ask the Palace Cobbler. He makes the shoes!
KATHLEEN : It's his fault! Ask him.
KING : We have—he tells us the shoes were—danced to pieces.

The PRINCESSES *register surprise.*

KATHLEEN : There has been no dance in the kingdom since Prince Hegert's.
COLEEN : That was long before these shoes were made!
KATHLEEN : How could we have worn the slippers dancing when there have been no dances?
COBBLER : There are dances down by the mill, each night in the spring.
JULEEN [*to* COBBLER]: I can hear the music from our window.

COLEEN [*to* KING]: Nurse knows we never leave our room.

COBBLER [*to* JULEEN]: Everyone in the village dances there.

KATHLEEN: We would never go to the mill.

COBBLER [*to* JULEEN]: We have so much fun.

JULEEN: I know; I hear you laughing.

COLEEN: We would not want to dance there!

KATHLEEN: Aunt would not approve!

KING: Juleen, come here. You are my youngest; I've never known you to tell me anything that was not true.

JULEEN: I could not lie to you.

KATHLEEN *and* COLEEN *exchange anxious looks.*

KING: Then tell me—have you been dancing at the mill?

JULEEN [*pause*]: We have not been to the mill.

KING [*to* COBBLER]: This can mean only one thing!

AUNT: Just a minute. [*To* JULEEN.] Do you dance in the garden?

JULEEN: No!

AUNT: In your room?

JULEEN: It isn't large enough.

AUNT: In this sitting room then.

KING: But you have been dancing? [*No answer.*] The Cobbler tells us these holes are made by dancing!

AUNT: If he has lied, he will be put to death.

COBBLER: I do not lie! [*To* JULEEN.] Princess, tell the truth!

KING [*to* JULEEN]: It is up to you. Has he lied, Princess Juleen?

JULEEN [*struggling between her loyalty to her sisters and her conscience*]: He did not lie; we did wear the shoes dancing!

The two other PRINCESSES *groan;* AUNT *and* NURSE *gasp; the* COBBLER *smiles knowingly.*

KING: Where? You said you didn't go to the mill.

AUNT: Nor the garden; your room was too small!

KING: If you don't dance here, then where?

JULEEN: Do not ask. I won't lie, but I can't tell where!

KING: Don't you realize for your safety I must know where you go?

AUNT: Why didn't you ask my permission!

JULEEN: You always refuse.

AUNT [*to* KING]: They must be punished!

KING: I cannot punish them for the truth Juleen has told; but unless I know where you go, I cannot allow you to continue dancing.

The PRINCESSES *are silent.*

K I N G : Very well. From this night forth you shall not leave the palace. Nurse shall turn this key in that lock on your door and bring the key to me; then I shall know you have not left your room. [*Exits.*]

> *The door he refers to is not the bedroom door but the outside door leading to the rest of the palace.*

A U N T : This shall put an end to the shoes that are danced to pieces!

The lights fade out.

Scene 2

SCENE : *same room as scene 1; late afternoon.*

K A T H L E E N : I knew we'd be found out.

C O L E E N : To be locked in our rooms; that's what he said!

K A T H L E E N : If the Royal Treasurer had not sent the bill.

C O L E E N : If the Cobbler had never told Father the holes were made by dancing.

K A T H L E E N : If Aunt had not made Father question us!

C O L E E N : Or if Nurse had only stood up for us!

C O L E E N K A T H L E E N [*both get the same idea*]: Or if you had not told!

J U L E E N : I cannot lie. They knew the holes were made from dancing.

K A T H L E E N : They were only guessing.

J U L E E N : If I had not told the truth the young Cobbler would have been put to death.

C O L E E N : What is this sudden concern for the Cobbler?

K A T H L E E N : Perhaps she would like to be dancing down by the mill!

J U L E E N [*dreamily*]: If only we could! But it is wrong to deceive Father as we have. He worries about us.

K A T H L E E N : If he finds out, our magic key will melt away.

COLEEN: Without the magic key there is no way of opening the secret panel.

> COLEEN *takes the key from its hiding place behind a picture. She gives the audience the idea of location of secret panel.*

KATHLEEN [*to* JULEEN]: You'd never see the Land of the Sapphire Sea again!

COLEEN: Remember the good times we've had there!

KATHLEEN: And that winding path of glimmering gold.

COLEEN: The trees all shiney and silver, with leaves of sparkling jewels!

KATHLEEN: You'd never taste the juice of the wild, red strawberries.

COLEEN: Or hear the soft music of the violins. Or feel the warm evening breezes.

JULEEN: I know; I know.

COLEEN: Then promise you'll never tell.

JULEEN: It's wrong to deceive!

COLEEN: It may be wrong, but there's no fun here in the palace.

KATHLEEN: I couldn't bear to be shut in these dark old rooms if it weren't for our trips to the Land of the Sapphire Sea.

COLEEN: It's not wrong to want to dance and to be with friends.

KATHLEEN: You've heard Nurse tell how Mother and Father once danced at the mill and how all the people of the kingdom loved them for it.

COLEEN: If it were not for Aunt, perhaps we could——

JULEEN: We mustn't find fault. Aunt is strict, but she does what she thinks is right; she does not intend to make us unhappy.

COLEEN: And we need not be unhappy. We still have the key and no one knows where we go dancing.

KATHLEEN [*referring to the door to the palace*]: And locking that door will not keep us here, for we have our own magic door——

> *Footsteps are heard approaching the room.*

KATHLEEN: Quick hide the key; someone is coming.

COLEEN: It's Nurse bringing our warm milk. [*To* JULEEN.] Promise not to tell.

KATHLEEN : Hurry, she's almost here!

COLEEN *tries to hide the key behind the picture.*

COLEEN : It won't stay.

Steps get louder.

KATHLEEN : Give it to me; I'll put it in this vase of flowers.

COLEEN : No! She's sure to take those flowers away tonight.

She puts the key under the edge of the rug just as the NURSE *enters.*

NURSE : Where are my Princesses? I've brought your warm milk.

The PRINCESSES *attempt to act natural.*

COLEEN : Oh, Nurse has brought us our milk.

KATHLEEN : How good it will taste.

JULEEN : Every night for as long as I can remember you have brought us warm milk.

Girls drink milk as the NURSE *scurries around the room, putting it in order. She sees the picture where the key was hidden is hanging crooked; she straightens it.* KATHLEEN *and* COLEEN *exchange looks of relief. Next* NURSE *crosses to the table and runs her finger across the surface; blows dust from it.*

NURSE : How wilted these flowers are. I'll bring you fresh ones in the morning.

Girls exchange looks again.

And this rug! It will not take me long to shake it—— [*She starts to pick it up.*]

As KATHLEEN *speaks,* NURSE *straightens up.*

KATHLEEN : That rug was dusted only yesterday; it can't be dirty already.

NURSE : I don't care if it was shaken this morning, it's dusty now. [*She bends to pick it up once more.*]

COLEEN : You must be very tired after such a long day.

NURSE *straightens up.*

KATHLEEN : The cleaning can wait till tomorrow.

NURSE : Very well, in the morning. But this room must be tidied before your father comes. Aunt would not approve of all this dust.

COLEEN : Aunt never approves of what we do!

NURSE : If you would only tell them where you go dancing, I am sure they would allow you to continue to go.

KATHLEEN : They are even having us locked in.

NURSE : I do not like to lock my Princesses' door, but you heard your father; and it is for your own good.

JULEEN : We are in no harm.

NURSE : But your Father doesn't know that; if you would only tell.

KATHLEEN : We cannot tell!

JULEEN : But we know you must do as our Father ordered.

> NURSE *takes key from a large key ring at her waist. As she does, the key ring breaks and all the keys fall on the little scatter rug, where the magic key is hidden. In the scramble to pick up the keys,* NURSE *also picks up the magic key which has been uncovered. She begins putting the keys back on the ring counting them as she goes.*

NURSE : Here is the key to the garden gate——
And here is the key to the palace pantry——
And here is the key to my room——
And here is the key to your room——
And here is——

> [*She holds up the magic key.*]

Why where does this key belong? I can't remember this key. It has been so long since I used these, I can't remember them all. It's such a pretty key——

KATHLEEN : It doesn't matter—you have the key to our door, that is the only important one.

NURSE : You are right.

COLEEN : It doesn't matter at all.

NURSE : Perhaps the King would remember; I'll go ask him.

> *She starts to go; the* PRINCESSES *move to stop her.*

JULEEN : Don't go yet.

NURSE : But I must take him the key to your room, anyway.

KATHLEEN [*taking charge of the situation*]: Dear Nurse, after all this excitement, I'm not at all ready to go to bed. Perhaps some more warm milk would make us sleepy again.

NURSE : It's almost bedtime—but a little more milk will not take much time. I will not be long and then off to bed you go! [*She exits.*]

COLEEN [*angry*]: Why did you send her to bring more warm milk?

JULEEN : You will need all the time you have to get the key back!

COLEEN : Why don't you think of me.

KATHLEEN : How would you suggest getting the key back?

JULEEN : It is true that Nurse was ready to lock the door.

COLEEN : And take the magic key to Father, who would know it is no ordinary key.

JULEEN : What is your plan?

KATHLEEN : When Nurse returns we must ask her to tell us a story.

COLEEN : A story?

JULEEN : Why?

KATHLEEN : You know how sleepy she always gets when she tells us a story.

COLEEN : I see—when she goes to sleep we will take the key from her belt.

JULEEN : But won't she miss it when she goes to Father?

KATHLEEN : She will think it has all been a dream——

Footsteps are heard.

I hear her coming. We must plan quickly. As soon as she is asleep, you Juleen remove the key. Your fingers are the smallest and you will be the fastest. And you Coleen, have the deepest pockets; you put the key in your pocket.

JULEEN : When the palace clock strikes the hour, she will surely waken.

KATHLEEN : Then you must move quickly.

COLEEN : She's almost here. She must not guess we have been talking.

KATHLEEN : I'll arrange the flowers.

JULEEN : And I'll straighten the rug.

COLEEN : And I'll open the door.

NURSE *enters.*

N U R S E : Why thank you. Here is your warm milk. I hope it will make you as sleepy as all the walking back and forth from the kitchen has made me.

During this time she has set the milk down and picked up the flowers.

I'll take these withered flowers with me.

K A T H L E E N : The flowers can wait until morning when you do the cleaning.

C O L E E N : Come sit here by me and tell us a story.

N U R S E : Tell a story to naughty girls who would not tell their father where they slip off to dance.

J U L E E N : Or sing us a song of our Mother.

N U R S E [*laughing good-naturedly*]: You know all my stories—— [*She gathers the girls around her.*] Which one would you like to hear?

K A T H L E E N : The one about the party that Mother gave for all the people of the kingdom.

N U R S E [*laughing*]: You know that story as well as I, but very well.

It was shortly after your Mother and Father were married and your Mother had come to the palace to be Queen that she decided to have a party for all the people in the kingdom. It was a big party that took weeks and weeks of planning.
    [*Yawns.*]
The cooks in the kitchen cooked all the food in the palace pantries. There were pies as big as wheels filled with the reddest, juiciest cherries in the orchard. And the cakes were so tall that you had to stand on a chair to cut them.
    [*Yawns.*]
So many people were coming that your Mother decided to have the party in the palace garden. The flowers were never more beautiful; and just in honor of the occasion, the roses all bloomed at once.
    [*NURSE shows more signs of sleepiness.*]
But just before the party, big dark clouds began to form and it looked as if the whole thing would have to be called off. The people of the kingdom were so disappointed; but then your

Mother had the guards open the great gates to the palace and she invited all the people inside. It was the first time the people of the kingdom had ever been inside the palace and they have loved your Mother ever since for not letting the rain spoil their party.
[*Yawns.*]
They danced and da-nc-ed and d—a—n—c—e—d.
[*She falls asleep.*]

After some prompting JULEEN *reaches for the key.*

NURSE [*stirring*]: And d-a-n-c-e-d, and d—a—n——
[*Her head drops in sleep.*]

JULEEN *takes the key and* COLEEN *puts it in her pocket just as the clock chimes.*

NURSE [*awakens*]: My goodness, did I fall asleep? It is getting late; I must lock the door and take the key to the King. [*She looks at her keys.*] I had the strangest dream while I was asleep. I dreamed I had found the prettiest key—but it was only a dream. Good night. [*Exits.*]
GIRLS [*standing at the palace door*]: Good night—good night. [*Closing door.*]

They sing song number 1, and exit through the magic door as the lights fade.

CURTAIN

Act Two

Scene 1

SCENE: *The clock chimes the morning hour as the curtain opens on an empty stage.*

AT RISE: *The* GIRLS *are heard offstage, returning from the Land of the Sapphire Sea.*

K A T H L E E N [*offstage*]: Hurry! Hurry!

C O L E E N : Where's the key?

J U L E E N [*from far away*]: I have it!

> *Running footsteps are heard. Magic door opens,* KATHLEEN *appears. She looks back and calls.*

K A T H L E E N : Hurry, Coleen!

C O L E E N : I'm coming. [*Enters.*] I'm coming!

K A T H L E E N : Sh-h-h! Not so loud.

C O L E E N : You took so long!

K A T H L E E N [*starting for bedroom door*]: There's no time to argue; come on.

J U L E E N : I can't get the door shut.

> *Footsteps are heard approaching off* R.

C O L E E N : Someone is coming!

J U L E E N : It's stuck; help me!

K A T H L E E N : If we pull together—One, Two, Three, pull.

J U L E E N : It's moving.

C O L E E N : Watch your fingers.

J U L E E N : It's closed.

> *She turns the key in lock as the other two girls cross to bedroom.*

K A T H L E E N : Hurry or we'll be caught.

> KATHLEEN *and* COLEEN *enter bedroom. Just as* JULEEN *starts up the bedroom steps,* COLEEN *reappears.*

C O L E E N : The key! You left the key!

J U L E E N : I'll get it—go on get into bed and close your eyes.

JULEEN returns to get key and, in rush to get to the bedroom, drops one of the worn-out slippers she has been carrying. She has just closed the bedroom door, when NURSE enters from the other door. She is carrying fresh flowers, and the key which she used to unlock the door.

N U R S E : The door was still locked; there was no dancing last night. How untidy this room is, and the King will be here any minute. [*She begins to tidy the room.*] What is this! One of Juleen's slippers—and full of holes! If the King sees this he will be angry, and Aunt will punish the Princesses.

Approaching footsteps of KING and AUNT are heard as she frantically searches for a place to hide the slipper.

K I N G [*offstage*]: Perhaps I have been too strict!
A U N T : Nonsense! You're not strict enough.
N U R S E : What shall I do!

As the lock rattles, she slips the slipper in apron pocket. The KING and AUNT enter.

K I N G : Good morning, Nurse.
A U N T : Are the Princesses awake?
N U R S E : I will see, your Ladyship. [*Exits.*]
A U N T : Now, perhaps the Princesses will tell where they go dancing.
K I N G : I don't like locking them in.
A U N T : It is for their own good.
K I N G : This way I know the Princesses are safe!
A U N T : And there will be no more worn-out shoes!

NURSE and PRINCESSES enter. The girls are in dressing gowns.

K I N G : Good morning——
A U N T [*sarcastically*]: Did you sleep well last night?
G I R L S : Good morning, Father; good morning, Aunt.
A U N T : How does it feel to be locked in?
K I N G : After a night of being locked here, won't you tell me where you wore out so many slippers?
J U L E E N : I—I can't.
A U N T : Do you want to be locked in these two rooms for the rest of your lives?

JULEEN : I gave my word; I cannot tell.

KING [*to* AUNT]: Then my plan has failed.

AUNT : Are you sure your plan was followed?

KING : What do you mean?

AUNT : Did it ever occur to you that the Princesses may have gone dancing last night, after all.

Girls exchange looks.

KING : Impossible.

NURSE : I locked the door last night.

AUNT [*suspiciously*]: Are you sure?

KING : She brought me the key last night.

AUNT : But how do you know the key had been used; that the door was even locked?

KING : She gave me her word.

AUNT : Her word!

KING : She would have no reason to lie.

AUNT : Let us see the Princesses' slippers, Juleen——

JULEEN *exits.*

They will prove who is right.

NURSE : The slippers can prove nothing.

KING : If there are no holes in the shoes, we shall know the door was locked and the Princesses did not leave.

AUNT : But, if the shoes are full of holes, we shall know that you did not lock the door and that the Princesses went dancing again!

KING : The shoes will prove you tell the truth.

AUNT : Or lie.

COLEEN : She doesn't lie!

KATHLEEN : She locked the door!

COLEEN : Nurse did as she was told.

JULEEN [*appearing with five shoes*]: It is not her fault!

AUNT : Look at these shoes. [*To* NURSE.] And you tell us you locked the door!

NURSE : I did; believe me I did!

AUNT : You lie!

KING : The window! [*To* PRINCESSES.] Did you leave through the window?

AUNT : How would they have gotten through a window covered with an iron guard?

KING : There is no other door which leads from these rooms. But surely there is some mistake——

AUNT : The only mistake is trusting this old woman to look after such deceitful Princesses.

KING : She has never deceived me before.

AUNT : Humph!

KING : She's always taken good care of my daughters.

AUNT [*correcting him*]: The Royal Princesses.

KING [*impatiently relenting halfway*]: The Princesses. She has always taken good care of THE PRINCESSES!

AUNT : How can you look at these shoes and say that? Here are Coleen's shoes with a hole in each toe, and Kathleen's slippers danced to pieces, and Juleen's—— [*She holds the one remaining shoe.*] Where is the mate to this shoe?

JULEEN : I—I—I could not find it.

AUNT [*sternly*]: Where is it?

JULEEN : I—I don't remember.

AUNT : Don't remember! Ha! A day without food will help you remember.

NURSE : Do not blame her; I have the shoe.

KING : You!

GIRLS : You?

AUNT : What did I tell you!

KING : Where did *you* get the shoe?

NURSE : I found it lying here when I came in; I knew you would be angry if you saw it and——

AUNT : So your daughters trick you and their Nurse lies to you. I'll wager she taught them to sneak away and deceive you.

KATHLEEN : She doesn't know where we go.

COLEEN : She is not to blame.

NURSE : The Princesses are good girls, they only want——

AUNT : See how they stand up for each other. They can get anything they want from the old woman.

KING : Maybe Nurse has grown too old to care for the Princesses.

AUNT : Then stop this disobedience! Send her away.

JULEEN : Don't punish her for what we do.

COLEEN : Who will care for us?

KATHLEEN : Who will bring our warm milk?

JULEEN : It is not her fault.

KATHLEEN : Do not send her away.

JULEEN: She has no other home.

COLEEN: Please, Father——

KING: Very well!——I'll not send Nurse away, but someone else must be in charge of the key.

AUNT [*thinking*]: These clever young ladies could not trick someone younger.

KING: There are no young people in the palace.

AUNT: Then choose someone from the kingdom—someone of Royal Blood who can outwit these girls.

KING [*thinks for a moment*]: Very well—I shall send out a proclamation that any prince in my kingdom may spend one night in the palace to discover where the Princesses dance. If he fails, he shall be locked in my darkest dungeon; but if he succeeds, he shall have his choice of my daughters for his bride! [*Exits.*]

JULEEN: What have we done?

KATHLEEN: Oh no!

COLEEN: Oh, oh, oh!

AUNT: He shall not only stand guard over this lock, [*Referring to the palace door lock.*] But he shall stay in this very room, that he may also watch that door. [*Referring to the bedroom door.*]

AUNT *and* NURSE *exit.*

JULEEN: Ooooh!

COLEEN: In this room!

KATHLEEN: What will we do?
The Lights Fade.

Scene 2

SCENE: *The clock strikes six as lights come up. It is late afternoon. The girls, dressed in day wear, are nervously discussing their plight.*

JULEEN: There must be some way of talking Father out of this proclamation.

COLEEN: That's impossible! The palace guards rode away hours ago.

KATHLEEN: By now everyone has heard the proclamation!

COLEEN : Every prince in the kingdom will be coming.

KATHLEEN : Then we will just have to deal with each of them.

COLEEN [*dejectedly*]: As we did with dear old Nurse?

JULEEN : Haven't we caused enough trouble?

KATHLEEN : If anyone finds out, we'll never be able to unlock the magic door again!

COLEEN : And one of us will have to marry the prince who discovers our secret.

JULEEN : One lie leads to another. We should never have started to deceive in the first place.

KATHLEEN : But we did start it and now it's too late to turn back.

JULEEN : Very well; very well.

COLEEN : We must think of some plan.

KATHLEEN : Aunt said the prince will stand guard in this very room.

JULEEN : He'll see our magic door.

KATHLEEN : Unless he falls asleep too!

COLEEN : No young prince is going to fall asleep.

KATHLEEN : Then we must put him to sleep!

COLEEN [*looking around her and picking up a vase*]: I'll hit him on the head with this.

JULEEN : Oh no! We could never do that.

KATHLEEN : I could sing him to sleep.

COLEEN : We couldn't be sure he wasn't pretending to be asleep.

JULEEN : He could always waken and follow us.

They all think.

COLEEN : I know! I know—The Royal Medicine Chest.

KATHLEEN JULEEN [*together*]: The medicine chest?

COLEEN : Remember last winter when Father couldn't sleep?

JULEEN : Yes——

KATHLEEN [*impatiently*]: What has that got to do with——

COLEEN : And the palace physician prescribed a sleeping potion!

JULEEN : Ooooh, yes! Father slept so soundly he didn't even hear the palace clock chime.

COLEEN : There must be many sleeping potions left.

KATHLEEN : I'll get them.

COLEEN : Wait! Let Juleen go. Her legs are swifter.

JULEEN: But won't the prince know?

COLEEN: We'll put it in his milk, of course. Now go quickly.

JULEEN: He won't know; he won't have a chance.

KATHLEEN: Don't argue, go! Father will be here soon.

JULEEN: Very well, if I must.

COLEEN: Don't tarry.

KATHLEEN: Take care no one sees you.

They close the door and move back into the room.

COLEEN: What if someone finds out?

KATHLEEN: No one would ever suspect Juleen of doing anything wrong.

COLEEN: But if they see her——

KATHLEEN: No one will see her; she moves like lightning.

COLEEN: But she might tell.

KATHLEEN: She promised not to tell and she never breaks a promise.

COLEEN: I suppose you're right; but I can't help feeling something will go wrong.

KATHLEEN: What could possibly go wrong, once the prince is asleep?

COLEEN [*suddenly*]: The door!

KATHLEEN: He can't possibly see our magic door when he's sound asleep.

COLEEN: I don't mean the magic door; I mean this one. [*Referring to palace door.*] It'll still be locked in the morning!

KATHLEEN: What difference does that make?

COLEEN: Don't you see? If it's still locked, they'll know we left some other way! They'll look until they find our magic door.

KATHLEEN: They mustn't. When the prince is asleep, you slip the key away from him and unlock that door.

COLEEN: Then no one will suspect our magic door.

A horse is heard galloping into the palace yards.

KATHLEEN: What is that?

COLEEN [*at window*]: The first prince came to stand guard.

KATHLEEN: I hope it's not Prince Michael—I should hate to see him put in the dungeon.

COLEEN [*coyly*]: Would you rather tell our secret and give up our magic key. And let the prince have his choice for a bride?

KATHLEEN: We–ll, if it were Prince Michael.

COLEEN: But if it were Prince Hegert!

KATHLEEN: Oh no! Never–only Prince Michael.

COLEEN: I thought so! You're blushing.

KATHLEEN: No more than you when—— [*She is interrupted by the chimes of the clock.*] It is growing late; Father will be here soon.

COLEEN: I wish Juleen would hurry. Suppose she couldn't get to the medicine chest.

KATHLEEN: There's no one to stop her.

COLEEN: If Aunt knew she was out of these rooms——

KATHLEEN: No one will see her; you're worrying over nothing.

COLEEN: Listen!

Approaching footsteps are heard.

KATHLEEN: What did I tell you; that's Juleen. [*She starts to open the door.*]

COLEEN: Wait! There are two sets of footsteps.

KATHLEEN [*peeks out the door*]: It's Father and the prince! What will we do, Juleen will be caught.

COLEEN: I'll lock the door and put this table in front of it.

KATHLEEN: No, no; Father would know we are trying to hide something.

COLEEN: We'll have to do something; make some excuse!

KATHLEEN: But what? They're almost here.

COLEEN: Act as if nothing is wrong.

Enter KING *and* PRINCE HEGERT.

KING: My dear daughters, this is your last chance–won't you tell? [*Silence.*] Very well! Prince Hegert here will be the first to try. Prince Hegert my daughters: Princess Kathleen, Princess Coleen and Princess Ju— Where is Juleen; why is she not here?

COLEEN: She'll return soon.

KATHLEEN: I think I hear her now.

KING: Where has she gone?

KATHLEEN: Only to another part of the palace.

COLEEN [*quickly*]: Father, did you see the lovely flowers Nurse brought us——

KING: Yes, yes; they're very nice, but why did——

KATHLEEN [*to* PRINCE]: Did you have a long ride?

KING: Will you please tell——

COLEEN [*to* PRINCE]: Are you very tired, Prince Hegert?

KING: Will you please answer——

JULEEN *enters.*

JULEEN: I hurried as fast as I—— [*She does not see the King at first; girls motion her to be quiet.*] Father! I– I– I didn't know we had a guest.

KING: Where have you been?

COLEEN: Juleen, this is Prince Hegert. Prince Hegert, our youngest sister, Princess Juleen.

KING: Will you please answer——

KATHLEEN: Prince Hegert was just telling us about his long ride.

KING [*exasperated*]: Princess Juleen. You know you are not to leave this room.

JULEEN: I am so tired of being locked in.

KING: If you would only tell me where you go dancing, there would be no need for the lock.

PRINCE: Ah, but my good King; that is for me to discover tonight.

KING: If you fail, you shall be sent to the dungeon forever.

PRINCE: But if I succeed, as I shall, I'll have my choice of a bride. Have no fears—Prince Hegert always succeeds.

KING: Here is the key—guard them well. Good night, dear daughters. [*He crosses to the door, but turns back.*] If you would only tell——

The girls are silent. The KING *starts to go when* JULEEN *speaks.*

JULEEN: Father, I'll tell—— [*Sisters glare at her.*] Remind Nurse to bring an extra glass with the warm milk.

KING *exits.*

PRINCE: Did you say warm milk? [*Laughs scornfully.*]

COLEEN: It may be a long night and the milk will be nourishing.

PRINCE: Just long enough for me to decide which of you will be my Queen.

KATHLEEN: You wouldn't want any one of us for your Queen!

PRINCE : Let me decide that!

COLEEN : We wouldn't know how to care for your palace.

PRINCE : I have servants to do all the work.

KATHLEEN : I can't cook.

PRINCE : There are cooks in my kitchen.

JULEEN : I know no one in the kingdom.

PRINCE : My Queen will associate only with people of royal blood.

JULEEN : But a Queen should be able to help her King.

PRINCE : I have built the most beautiful palace in the whole kingdom. I need no help.

COLEEN : Is your palace very large?

PRINCE : Large enough.—But when I've won your Father's bargain, the whole kingdom will be mine!

NURSE *enters with milk.*

KATHLEEN : Good Nurse, you have brought our milk.

NURSE : As I have every night since you were born.

JULEEN : Stay and tell us a story.

NURSE : I can't; your Aunt bade me return immediately. Good night. [*Exits.*]

JULEEN *starts to pour milk.*

PRINCE : Here, let me do that.

COLEEN [*intercepting him*]: Prince Hegert, have you ever heard the stories of wee little elves that slip through the night doing good for people.

PRINCE : I've heard the stories, Princess Coleen. [*He starts back to* JULEEN.]

KATHLEEN : But have you ever heard it said that these little elves have the power of magic.

PRINCE : Surely you don't believe in magic.

COLEEN : We know there's magic.

A Sleeping Potion is put into the milk. Everyone but the PRINCE *sees this "magic."*

PRINCE : Is it by magic you slip away dancing each night.

KATHLEEN : Enough talk of magic. Here is your glass Coleen and yours Juleen and one for you Prince Hegert. [*He takes the wrong glass.*]

COLEEN: Here Prince Hegert. The blue glass is for special guests. [*He takes it.*]

PRINCE: Is it magic? [*To himself.*] How can such sweet, simple girls have a reputation for being so clever? [*Laughs at his own joke.*]

KATHLEEN: Drink your milk before it grows cold.

PRINCE: Is it magic milk only while it is warm. Ha—ha—ha—ha! Whoever heard of magic milk?

COLEEN: One never knows where he will find magic!

PRINCE: [*to his glass*]: Magic milk give me my choice of a bride in the morning. [*He drinks the milk: the* PRINCESSES *exchange knowing glances.*] And to be sure you are all still here in the morning, I must not forget to turn the key in this lock.

> *Girls react to their success while his back is turned. Clock strikes eight times.*

JULEEN: Eight o'clock—already!

PRINCE: That is not late for young girls who are used to dancing all night.

KATHLEEN: We must say goodnight. [*She starts to go.*]

PRINCE: I see I shall have no trouble tonight.

GIRLS: Goodnight—goodnight. [JULEEN *starts to say something, but is stopped by* KATHLEEN.]

PRINCE: Princess Juleen—I have heard you have the loveliest voice in the whole kingdom—can you not sing me a song before you go?

> KATHLEEN *nods for her to stay.* KATHLEEN *and* COLEEN *exit to bedroom.*

Well, what are you going to sing?

JULEEN: I know a magic song.

PRINCE: Magic! Is magic all you think of.

> *She starts to go.*

Wait! —I'll hear your magic song.

JULEEN: Very well—but take care that my magic song doesn't put you to sleep.

> *Sings song number 2. During this song the* PRINCE *gradually goes to sleep. At the end he is snoring comfortably. The other two* PRINCESSES *enter from bedroom, dressed for the dance.*

J U L E E N : Sh-h-h-h. He's asleep!

COLEEN *cautions* KATHLEEN *who is now entering.*

K A T H L E E N : Now do you believe in magic milk? [*Motions* JULEEN *to the bedroom to get dressed.*] Get the key, Coleen.

COLEEN *reaches for the key, but slips. The jolt causes the* PRINCE *to stir; he puts his hand over the key hook on his belt. After some thought,* KATHLEEN *pulls a fern from the vase of flowers and gently tickles his nose. Still asleep, the* PRINCE *moves his hand from the keys to scratch his nose.* COLEEN *snatches the key, runs to the palace door and unlocks it.*

C O L E E N : Now they'll think we went this way.
K A T H L E E N [*in a whisper*]: Hurry, Juleen.

COLEEN *and* KATHLEEN *cross to magic door and begin to unlock it.*

K A T H L E E N : I have the magic key.

As she opens the door, it creaks. The PRINCE *moans and almost awakens. The* PRINCESSES *react, but he goes back to snoring. They sing song number 1.* JULEEN *appears on the third part of the chorus; the other two exit. At the close, she follows.*

The lights fade out. Clock strikes four and the early morning lights come up. The PRINCESSES *enter one by one. They assure themselves the* PRINCE *is still asleep, laugh quietly and exit to their bedroom. As they do, the* KING *and* AUNT *are heard offstage.*

A U N T [*in the hall*]: The door is wide open!
K I N G [*taking key from the palace door*]: Here is the key!
A U N T [*entering*]: And here is the Prince, fast asleep!
K I N G : Wake up! —Wake up!
A U N T : So this is the way you guard the Princesses!
P R I N C E : I—I must have dozed off for a moment——
K I N G : A moment? —Long enough for the Princesses to slip away?
P R I N C E : But I locked the door.
K I N G : With this key?

PRINCE [*looks to his key hook*]: But how—it was on my—It's as if . . . as if. . . .

AUNT [*scornfully*]: As if it were magic!

KING: Princesses Kathleen, Juleen, Princess Coleen, come quickly.

AUNT *exits into bedroom.*

PRINCE: The Princesses are safe and sound, I assure you!

KING: How can you be so sure?

PRINCE: If a mouse had tiptoed across this room, I would have heard him.

KING: Still you can't tell me where the Princesses have been dancing.

PRINCE: How can I tell you where——

PRINCESSES *enter.*

When they did not leave their room.

AUNT [*holding up a worn-out slipper*]: Then how did they dance their shoes to pieces? [*She hands him the shoe.*]

PRINCE: Why—it's magic!

KING: You have failed!

PRINCE [*to* JULEEN]: Princess Juleen, it was your magic song. Help me!

JULEEN *turns to her sisters.*

COLEEN: But you have built the most beautiful palace in the whole kingdom. Last night you said you needed no help.

KATHLEEN: Was the night long enough for you to decide on a Queen.

PRINCE: The milk—the magic milk you gave me!

KING: Enough talk of magic. Remember the proclamation. You have failed; to the dungeon.

They exit.

KATHLEEN [*to sisters*]: With Prince Hegert failing, no one else will try.

COLEEN: Who would have the nerve?

KATHLEEN: No one would dare!

AUNT: Guess again my dear nieces. Here are only a few who would dare. [*She picks up the scrolls.*]

GIRLS : Oh, no!

AUNT [*unrolls first scroll*]: Tonight, Prince Shawn of Kary
Castle. And if he should fail, Prince Michael and Prince Dennis
and——

GIRLS : Oh no!

CURTAIN

Act Three

Setting for the Land of the Sapphire Sea

SCENE: *It is ten days later in the* PRINCESSES' *sitting room. Their sneaking away has left them completely exhausted. The two older girls are discussing the princes who have stood guard; the youngest,* JULEEN, *hears nothing of what is said as she sits daydreaming.*

KATHLEEN [*drops the last of ten scrolls into a large wastebasket already filled to overflowing*]: The last one!

COLEEN : No more Prince Patricks or Prince Michaels or Prince Shawns——

KATHLEEN [*determined*]: And no more Prince Hegert's bragging how he'll win Father's proclamation!

COLEEN : And choose one of us for his Queen. Still I'm sorry for the others in the dungeons.

KATHLEEN : We had no choice; besides they knew the consequences.

COLEEN : There's not a single prince in the kingdom who hasn't tried——

KATHLEEN : And failed!

COLEEN : Lucky for us too; there's only one sleeping potion left.

KATHLEEN : We won't even need it—there are no more princes in the kingdom.

COLEEN : I'm sorry for what we've done.

KATHLEEN : It was the only way we could keep the magic key.

COLEEN : Even Aunt doesn't seem so bad now.

KATHLEEN : We had no choice.

COLEEN [*finally beginning to agree with her*]: We couldn't give up our trips to the Sapphire Sea.

KATHLEEN : I am ashamed of deceiving Father, though.

COLEEN : It was our only chance to have any fun.

KATHLEEN : If Aunt would have only let us dance here in the palace!

COLEEN [*reminding her*]: We would never have seen the Land of the Sapphire Sea.

KATHLEEN : Dancing would be more fun if we did not have to deceive Father——

COLEEN : Or trick people to sleep.

COLEEN : I shall never sing to another prince as long as I live. [*She notices* JULEEN *daydreaming and creeps up behind her.*] I shall never sing to another prince as long as I live!

JULEEN [*shaken from her daydream*]: What—what did you say?

COLEEN : You're as bad as Father.

KATHLEEN : All you do is sit and daydream.

COLEEN [*to* KATHLEEN]: Maybe she's dreaming of her prince from the Sapphire Sea!

JULEEN : I was not dreaming—and I——

KATHLEEN [*teasingly*]: Could it be the one she danced with last night?

COLEEN : The handsome one in blue?

KATHLEEN : Or the tall, dark fellow who——

JULEEN : It's none of them; it's—— [*She stops.*]

COLEEN : Who? Tell us!

JULEEN : It's no one.

KATHLEEN : Remember, it's wrong to tell a lie. Now which one is it?

JULEEN : It's neither of them, believe me.

COLEEN : What difference does it make? We still have our magic key and she can see either of them anytime she wants to.

KATHLEEN : Then the Sapphire Sea is worth all we have done. [*She holds the magic key up for all to see.*]

Approaching footsteps are heard in the hall.

COLEEN: The key; hide it quickly!

> KATHLEEN *darts around the room trying to find a place to hide the key. She starts to put it under the rug.*

COLEEN: No, not there; give it to me.

> *She puts it in her pocket, just as the* KING *and* AUNT *enter.*

AUNT: What a disgrace; look at all these scrolls!

KING: Every prince in the kingdom has tried——

AUNT: And failed!

KING: My dungeons are filled with princes!

AUNT: What shall become of this fellow if he fails?

KING: I hadn't thought of that. [*He thinks for a moment.*] Perhaps he will succeed.

AUNT: But if he doesn't, he must be put to death!

JULEEN: Who will be put to death?

KING [*to* AUNT]: That is harsh punishment; but the dungeons are filled!

KATHLEEN: Is someone else trying?

COLEEN: Every prince in the kingdom has been here.

AUNT [*taking note of the* PRINCESSES' *alarm*]: Surely you would not be responsible for someone's death!

KATHLEEN [*to* AUNT]: He must know he is risking his life.

KING: Princess Juleen, put an end to all this, tell me where you dance.

JULEEN [*to the other two* PRINCESSES]: Sisters—I must——

COLEEN: You promised! We can't give up now, after all we've done.

KATHLEEN: Besides, this prince knows what the terms of the proclamation are!

JULEEN: He surely doesn't realize that failure will cost him his life.

COLEEN: If we only knew who he is.

KING: Who he is doesn't matter, one life is just as important as another. Please tell——

AUNT [*to* KING]: Do not beg them to tell. [*To* PRINCESSES.] It will serve you right if this fellow succeeds and chooses one of you for his bride.

KING: I must be sure he knows the terms of his bargain! [*Exits.*]

AUNT : And I'll send Nurse to clear all this away! [*Exits.*]

COLEEN : She's up to some trick.

JULEEN : Who could he be? Even Father wouldn't tell.

KATHLEEN : What does it matter? There's still one sleeping potion left.

COLEEN : That's right; there's no need to worry.

JULEEN : But we can't use it!

COLEEN : Why not?

JULEEN : Father said if he failed he would be put to death.

KATHLEEN : Father would never do that; he's too kindhearted.

JULEEN : But there's no more room in the dungeons!

COLEEN : What difference does it make?

JULEEN : It was wrong to trick the others to sleep when we knew they'd be put in a dungeon, but to be responsible for someone's life!

KATHLEEN : If he wants to risk his life trying to find out where we dance, why should we care?

COLEEN [*puzzling*]: I wonder who it is?

KATHLEEN : He can't be anyone from the kingdom; we know every prince has tried.

COLEEN : Are you sure we counted them all? We must have left someone out.

KATHLEEN : Their names are all here. [*She picks the scrolls from the wastebasket.*]

COLEEN : There must be some mistake!

KATHLEEN [*counting the scrolls*]: One—two—three—four—five—six—seven—eight—nine—ten! No, they're all here.

COLEEN : Then who can it be?

NURSE *enters.*

NURSE : Her Highness sent me to tidy the room.

JULEEN : Please tell us!

NURSE [*acting as if she didn't know what they were talking about*]: Tell you what?

COLEEN : Tell us who it is!

KATHLEEN : We've tried to think of everyone.

JULEEN : Do you know who is to stand guard tonight?

COLEEN : Every prince in the kingdom has been here.

KATHLEEN : I've counted all the names. Is there a prince we don't know?

N U R S E : You know all the princes of the kingdom.

K A T H L E E N : Then who is it?

N U R S E : Perhaps I do not know!

K A T H L E E N : But you must.

C O L E E N : Aunt said he might succeed; and if he chose one of us for his bride, it would serve us right!

K A T H L E E N : He must be very cruel.

C O L E E N : He's seven feet tall, with a long black beard and carries a club.

K A T H L E E N : And roars like a lion——

C O L E E N : And kills little children——

K A T H L E E N : And beats his wife——

J U L E E N : We're imagining all this. We don't even know who it is.

C O L E E N : He's the meanest prince that ever lived!

N U R S E : He's not a prince and he's not mean.

J U L E E N : Then you do know!

K A T H L E E N : Please tell us.

J U L E E N : Did you say he wasn't a prince?

N U R S E : I have said too much.

K A T H L E E N : You haven't said who he is.

N U R S E : Your Royal Aunt ordered me not to tell.

C O L E E N : We've always known before; why the secret?

K A T H L E E N [*trying another approach*]: What difference does it make. He will fail like all the others.

N U R S E : If he fails, he will be put to death!

K A T H L E E N : Then tell us who it is.

J U L E E N [*looking at her sisters*]: Perhaps something will happen this time.

The other two react.

N U R S E : Very well—but you must promise to act surprised when you see him. Your Aunt would never forgive me——

K A T H L E E N : We promise—now tell us.

N U R S E : I'll tell, but only because I pray you'll find more mercy in your hearts for this lad, than you did for the others.

K A T H L E E N [*impatienty*]: Go on—Aunt will be here soon.

N U R S E : Well, he isn't seven feet tall and he doesn't have a beard or carry a club.

K A T H L E E N : Never mind all that; who is he?

N U R S E : And he doesn't kill little children or beat his wife——
A U N T [*offstage*]: Nurse! Nurse!
C O L E E N : Tell us.
N U R S E : He's the kindest, gentlest person in the palace.
J U L E E N : In the palace?
A U N T [*offstage*]: Nurse.
N U R S E : I must go. [*She moves to the palace door.*]
K A T H L E E N [*stepping between her and the door*]: Not before you tell us who it is.
N U R S E : It's the——
A U N T [*offstage*]: Nurse!
N U R S E : Cobbler's son. [*Exits.*]
K A T H L E E N : The cobbler's son.
C O L E E N : We were afraid of him! [*Laughs.*]
K A T H L E E N [*laughing*]: A black beard! Ha-ha-ha-ha-ha. Roar like a lion. Ha-ha-ha.
J U L E E N [*to herself*]: He has a kind and gentle voice.
C O L E E N [*to* KATHLEEN]: Does he expect to succeed where all the princes of the kingdom have failed?
K A T H L E E N : Aunt meant it would serve us right if we had to marry anyone like a cobbler's son.
C O L E E N : I am surprised he has the courage to try.
J U L E E N : He is braver than all the others.

Two older PRINCESSES *begin to catch on.*

K A T H L E E N : Brave! He was so scared he begged you to tell Father how we wore out our shoes.
J U L E E N : He only asked me to tell the truth.
C O L E E N : You told the truth. You announced to everyone that we go dancing.
K A T H L E E N : If you had not been so truthful, we would never have had all this trouble.
C O L E E N : No one would have ever known how we wear our shoes out, if the cobbler's son had not told. He explained to Father, just how the holes were made.
J U L E E N : He did not know, besides he trusts us. We cannot deceive anyone who trusts us!
C O L E E N : She's defending him!
K A T H L E E N : Perhaps you would like to be the bride of a cobbler!

COLEEN: And help make the shoes!

JULEEN: You don't understand——

KATHLEEN: We understand that you are content to sit here daydreaming of your cobbler.

COLEEN: You've forgotten about us. Forgotten how lonely we were before our trips to the Land of the Sapphire Sea.

JULEEN: Believe me, I have not forgotten, but he will lose his life!

KATHLEEN: Father would never do that; why, who would make our shoes.

COLEEN: Have you ever known Father to do anything that was cruel?

JULEEN: No—o-o.

KATHLEEN: He's probably forgotten about it already.

COLEEN: There's nothing to worry about.

JULEEN: It isn't right——

KATHLEEN [*pretending to be crying*]: It would be terrible never to see the Land of the Sapphire Sea again.

COLEEN [*also pretending*]: Always to be locked in this cold, dark dungeon of a palace.

JULEEN: I don't want you to be unhappy——

KATHLEEN [*recovering quickly*]: Then take the sleeping potion.

COLEEN: He will drink the milk as quickly and sleep as soundly as did all the rest.

KATHLEEN: He'll never suspect you are deceiving him. [*Approaching footsteps are heard.*]

COLEEN: They're coming! [*Puts sleeping potion in* JULEEN's *hand.*]

JULEEN: I—I can't!

COLEEN [*at the end of her patience*]: If you don't, we'll tell Father this all has been your idea!

KATHLEEN: It's too late to go back now—you must do it.

JULEEN: It's wrong——

Enter KING *and* COBBLER.

KING: Here is the last person to stand watch.

KATHLEEN   COLEEN [*together*]: The cobbler's son!

KING: Daughters, tell me; if you only knew how worried I am. [*Silence.*]

K I N G : Very well. [*To the* COBBLER.] Here is the key which locks the only door from these rooms—do not let it from your sight. Stay here and guard the door well; take care not to fall asleep.

C O B B L E R : I shall do my best!

K I N G : If you succeed you may choose any one of my daughters for your bride and I shall crown you Prince of my kingdom. But, remember, if you fail, you shall be put to death! Do you understand the terms of the bargain?

C O B B L E R : I do Your Majesty!

K I N G : For your own sake then, guard them well. [*Exits.*]

K A T H L E E N : Do you hope to succeed where every Royal Prince of the kingdom has failed?

C O B B L E R : I am only a cobbler's son, but I shall try.

J U L E E N : It is not important who you are, but what you are.

C O L E E N [*warning*]: JULEEN!

NURSE *enters with warm milk and four glasses.*

N U R S E : Here is your milk! [*To girls.*] Be merciful to the lad. [*Exits.*]

The three girls are grouped around the tray as the COB-BLER *watches what he considers a happy family ritual.*

C O B BL E R : It must be wonderful.

C O L E E N [*mistaking his meaning*]: What's so wonderful about milk?

K A T H L E E N : We have it every night.

C O B B L E R : Not the milk——

J U L E E N : Then why did you say wonderful?

C O B B L E R : One of the wonderful things about being a family is the chance to share. Your milk is something the three of you share.

J U L E E N : Have you no family with which to share?

C O B B L E R : No.

J U L E E N : No brothers or sisters?

C O B B L E R : There's only my father.

J U L E E N : Your mother?

C O B B L E R : She died when I was very young; I hardly remember her.

J U L E E N : I can barely remember my mother, either, but I can recall her gentleness.

COBBLER: I have heard the servants of the palace praise her truthfulness.

JULEEN: I wish I could remember more about her.

COBBLER: I have heard Nurse say she could sing as sweetly as a nightingale.

COLEEN [*interrupting*]: Princess Juleen sings too; perhaps she will sing to you before she goes to sleep.

KATHLEEN: Enough talk of singing; the milk grows cold. [*To* JULEEN.] The cobbler's son will share our milk with us tonight.

COBBLER: I am only a cobbler's son—I shouldn't——

COLEEN: Of course you should—Juleen pour the milk.

KATHLEEN: Nurse brought glasses for us all, why do you hesitate?

COBBLER: How generous you are!

JULEEN [*to the* COBBLER]: Are you sure——

KATHLEEN: Is this the way to treat a guest?

> *She crosses to* JULEEN, *and makes her put the sleeping potion in the milk.*

Where are your manners, the milk will soon be cold.

> JULEEN *reluctantly takes the milk to the* COBBLER.

COBBLER: How kind you are. [COLEEN *and* KATHLEEN *drink their milk.*] Now you are sharing with me.

KATHLEEN: You only have the chance to share; you won't be sharing until you drink your milk.

COBBLER [*laughing*]: I almost hate to drink it, for then the sharing will be over.

COLEEN: But then there will be Juleen's song. [JULEEN *reacts to this as the Palace Clock chimes.*]

KATHLEEN: It is past our bedtime. [*They start to leave.*] Drink your milk and listen to Juleen sing. [KATHLEEN *exits.*]

COLEEN: Good night cobbler's son. Sing sweetly, sister Juleen. [*Exits.*]

COBBLER: Is it your voice I've heard every night, floating on the warm spring air?

JULEEN: You've heard me?

COBBLER: Yes, but you sing such sad songs.

JULEEN: I do not mean to be sad—it is only—only—— [*She looks to bedroom.*]

COBBLER: Only that a Princess can have so little fun in a palace?

JULEEN: I have so much to be thankful for, it shouldn't matter.

COBBLER: I am thankful to you for telling your father the truth about the shoes and saving my life.

JULEEN: You don't value your life very highly or you would not risk it by coming here tonight.

COBBLER: It is worth my life to see the smile I remember so well.

JULEEN: Your life is a high price to pay for a smile!

COBBLER: Not so high, for I have not only the smile, but the promise of a song and the chance to share.

> *He starts to drink the milk, but* JULEEN *snatches the glass from him, pours the milk back into the pitcher and gives him back the glass. The bedroom door opens just as* JULEEN *speaks.*

JULEEN: Pretend to be drinking.

> PRINCESS KATHLEEN *nods her approval and closes the door.*

COBBLER: Why did you do that?

JULEEN: Please don't ask me.

COBBLER [*looking in his glass as if he could see some of the potion*]: I don't have to; you've saved my life again.

JULEEN: My sisters must never know.

COBBLER: How brave you are.

JULEEN: You call me kind, generous, considerate and now brave. If you only knew.

COBBLER: I know all I need to know about you.

JULEEN: You still don't know where we go.

COBBLER: I know neither where you go, nor how to follow you.

JULEEN: Then you'll be put to death in the morning.

COBBLER: Don't worry about me! Sing your song, your happy song.

JULEEN: There's no happiness left in it now.

COBBLER [*misunderstanding that she is referring to him*]: Don't be unhappy! You haven't betrayed your sisters!

JULEEN: You don't understand—I'm unhappy because of yo——

The bedroom door opens and KATHLEEN *appears.*

KATHLEEN : Your song, Juleen. We haven't heard the song you promised the cobbler's son.

With his back to PRINCESS KATHLEEN, *he stretches and then sits down.*

COBBLER : Sing to me, Princess Juleen.

Satisfied, KATHLEEN *moves to bedroom door.*

JULEEN [*whispers*]: You must pretend to sleep. [*Singing.*]
Magic song I will sing to you

KATHLEEN *exits.*

[*To the* COBBLER.]:
I will not deceive you.
Follow me for the secret
That has baffled the kingdom.
See the Silver Trumpets,
Jeweled leaves and green meadows
Sapphire Sea is awaiting you.
[*She hands him the key.*]
Here's the way to follow.
[*Door opens.*]
Sleep, sleep—lul—lul—lul—lullaby.
[*Door closes.*]
Here's the way to follow.
[*Door opens.*]
Sleep, sleep—lul—lul—lul—lullaby,
This is my magic song.

At the end of the song, the other two come from the bedroom. The COBBLER *pretends to be asleep.*

KATHLEEN [*to* JULEEN]: Hurry! You took too long.

JULEEN *exits to get dressed.*

COLEEN : Unlock the door; it's almost time.

KATHLEEN *takes the key from the* COBBLER's *belt and runs to the Palace door. A trumpet sound; the girls are startled.*

KATHLEEN : The magic key—where is it?

COLEEN : Juleen has it. [*Goes to the bedroom door.*] Juleen—
hurry, give me the key! [*As she goes to the magic door, she sings.*]
Come, come, come with me, I'm off to the Land of the Sapphire
Sea.

> JULEEN *appears;* KATHLEEN *motions her to hurry.*

JULEEN [*calling after her*]: I'm coming, I'm coming!

> She starts to go, but returns for one last look at the COB-
> BLER. *Again she starts to leave, but returns once more.*

I can't, I can't.

> She puts the magic key in the "sleeping COBBLER's" hand.

[*Sings.*] Come, come, come with me I'm off to the Land of the
Sapphire Sea.

> She exits. The COBBLER sits up.

COBBLER : Sapphire Sea! Is this the magic key? But where is
the door. [*He searches; going to palace door.*] It couldn't be this
one. [*He takes his key out of the lock and puts it back on his
belt.*] Could it fit here? [*He tries the bedroom door.*] Then
where? [*He searches along the wall.*] Is this it? It fits; this is the
magic door. [*Comes back to his audience.*] Should I follow? But
what if they should return before I do? But if I don't go I'll never
see Princess Juleen's smile again. [*He covers the pillows on the
couch to make it look as if he is still lying there.*] No one will
guess that's not me.

> He crosses to the door, and sings, "Come, come, come
> with me I'm off to the Land of the Sapphire Sea."
>
> The lights fade.
>
> As the lights fade on the sitting-room scene, they come
> up behind the scrim disclosing the Land of the Sapphire
> Sea. No words are spoken during this scene.
>
> The three PRINCESSES are seen tripping down the "glim-
> mering path" where they are met by the three princes de-
> scribed in their daydreams.
>
> They dance to the same waltz music as that of the lulla-
> bies. During the dance the COBBLER is seen hiding

behind the silver trees. He breaks off a silver branch and hides it in his cloak. The noise startles the PRINCESSES. *He picks a jeweled leaf. The apprehension of the* PRINCESSES *grows.*

At the sound of the trumpet the PRINCESSES *quit dancing and hurry up the glimmering path. This is followed by Pinto's Run, Run! from* Memories of Childhood; *the* PRINCESSES *are out of sight, supposedly running back to the palace. The* COBBLER'S SON *is then seen hurrying from the green meadow.* Run, Run! *goes into Pinto's* Sleeping Time. *On the fourth clock-striking, the light in the Land of the Sapphire Sea fades and the lights on the palace sitting room come up. The* PRINCESSES *are heard offstage.*

KATHLEEN : Hurry, hurry; it's almost morn.

Door opens.

COLEEN [*entering*]: This night has been different from the others.
KATHLEEN : It's as though someone were watching us . . .
COLEEN : Such strange noises and shadows . . .

JULEEN *enters.*

KATHLEEN : It's as if someone were following us.
JULEEN : It's just our imagination!

Door is heard closing offstage, indicating that AUNT *is on her way.*

Aunt will be here soon. Hurry!
KATHLEEN : First I want to check our sleeping cobbler!

She starts to couch, but is intercepted by JULEEN.

JULEEN : There's no time—we must get to bed before Aunt comes.

They exit to bedroom. Just as JULEEN *is leaning over to look at the* COBBLER, *the footsteps of the* AUNT *are heard; she exits to bedroom. The* COBBLER *enters, pushes pillows aside and lies down.*

COLEEN [*offstage*]: The key. Where is the magic key?

JULEEN : Stay here, I'll get it.

COLEEN : You're so careless!

> JULEEN *rushes to the magic door, but the key isn't there;*
> *she turns to the* COBBLER *who is pretending to be asleep.*
> *She sees the key which he has put in his hand just as she*
> *left it.*

JULEEN : Why didn't you follow us? Now you'll be killed.

> *The* AUNT *is almost to the palace door;* JULEEN *turns*
> *away, crossing to the bedroom door. The* COBBLER *raises*
> *up to call to her, but the* AUNT *is heard.* JULEEN *quickly*
> *goes into bedroom and closes the door.*

AUNT [*offstage; rattling the palace door*]: It's still locked. [COB-
BLER *rises.*]

KING : I have another key. [*Unlocks the door and enters.*]

AUNT : You are awake!

KING : You have succeeded where all others have failed!

COBBLER : Your Majesty——

AUNT : Where do the Princesses dance?

KING : And how do they get there? [COBBLER *hesitates.*]

AUNT : Why do you hesitate? Speak up; tell us.

COBBLER : I—I—I can't.

AUNT : What do you mean, you can't?

KING : You're awake, surely you must know.

COBBLER : The noise of your key awakened me.

> *The* PRINCESSES *enter still dressed in their party dresses.*

KING [*dejected*]: You too have failed!

AUNT : How could we expect a cobbler's son to do what all the
princes of the kingdom have failed to do?

COBBLER [*to* KING *and* AUNT]: I'm sorry. [*To* JULEEN.] I am
sorry.

KING : Sorry! It does no good to be sorry.

AUNT : This will mean your death!

JULEEN : No! He——

KATHLEEN : Juleen!

COLEEN : Remember your promise.

COBBLER [*to* JULEEN]: I shall always dream of your smile.

JULEEN: You will never dream again; I will never smile again! [*She sobs.*]

COBBLER: I had a most beautiful dream last night.

AUNT: We're not interested in a cobbler's dream.

JULEEN [*hopefully*]: No, let him tell us of his dream.

COBBLER [*to* JULEEN]: Are you sure?

JULEEN: Yes, oh yes!

COBBLER [*to all*]: I dreamed I walked up a glimmering path shaded on every side by silver trees, covered with sparkling leaves.

KING: Glimmering path?

AUNT: Silver trees—sparkling leaves—Ha!

COBBLER: And saw three beautiful princesses dancing in a land by the Sapphire Sea!

AUNT: What nonsense!

KING: I have no time for such foolishness.

AUNT [*mimicking*]: Where I saw silver trees with jeweled leaves!

COBBLER [*taking proofs from under his cloak*]: Just like these.

JULEEN: Where he followed us by turning this magic key.

AUNT: Is this true?

KATHLEEN: Yes, it's true.

COLEEN: I'm sorry we have deceived you. I'm glad you know the truth.

KING: Why did you deceive me?

COLEEN: If anyone knew, our magic key lost its power. Now that Juleen has told, we will never be able to dance again.

KATHLEEN: But I'm glad she told.

COLEEN: We'll never go to the Sapphire Sea again.

KING: But you can dance here; there is no need for the Sapphire Sea.

KATHLEEN: We could never dance here.

COLEEN: Aunt would not let us.

AUNT: Well!

She starts to go, but the KING *stops her.*

KING: One moment my Royal Sister! Perhaps we both are to blame; perhaps you were too strict and I too forgetful.

AUNT: I only wanted to do my duty.

JULEEN: We have all been wrong; but now that we know we can make this kingdom our Land of the Sapphire Sea.

AUNT [*to* KING]: We no longer have a cobbler.

KING : But we have a new Prince. [*He crowns* COBBLER.] I crown you Prince of my Kingdom. Who will be your bride?

COBBLER : For her gentle smile and truthful ways, I ask Princess Juleen to be my bride.

AUNT : What will be your first wish?

COBBLER : All my fondest dreams have come true. [*To* JULEEN.] But what will you have?

JULEEN [*to sisters*]:

> May all our lying and deceiving be undone
> To make this kingdom a place of fun.

[*to* AUNT *and* KING]:

> Through love and understanding may this land
> Come to know true happiness first hand.

[*to* COBBLER]:

> May we make this, our home,
> One from where we never roam.

ALL : Come, come, come with me I'm off to the Land of the Sapphire Sea.

CURTAIN

SONG I

Come, Come, Come With Me

MUSIC BY LOWELL V. HANBACK

Prince Hegert's Song

MUSIC BY LOWELL V. HANBACK

The Cobbler's Song

MUSIC BY LOWELL V. HANBACK

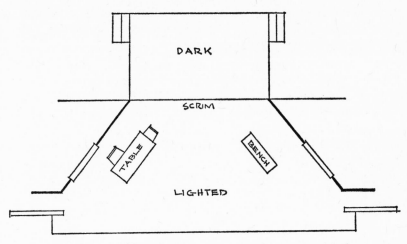

Floor Plan for a Sitting Room Adjoining the Princesses' Bedroom

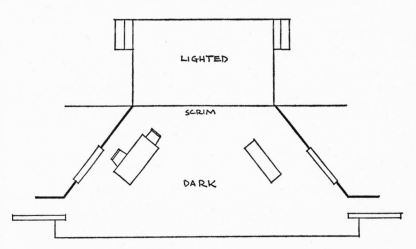

Floor Plan for the Land of the Sapphire Sea

The Golden Mask

A MYSTERY

BY

Edward Kessell

Cast of Characters

THE SORCERESS

ETHAN, *the Sorceress's apprentice*

THE ROYAL GATEKEEPER

LADY ALISON, *Lady-in-waiting to the Princess*

KATHLEEN, *the Princess*

CECIL, *the royal tax collector*

HILDA, *one of his sisters*

MATILDA, *his other sister*

THE PRIME MINISTER

KING JUSTIN III

LESTOR, *a palace guard*

LEROY, *another palace guard*

THE ROYAL COOK

THE OLD WOMAN, *Lady Alison in disguise*

PEDDLER, *the thief in disguise*

Synopsis of Scenes

Act One   Scene 1:   The Cave of the Sorceress. Evening.

              * Scene 2:   Before the Palace. Next morning.

              Scene 3:   Throne Room of the Palace. Later the same morning.

              * Scene 4:   Before the Palace Gate. A few hours later.

Act Two   Scene 1:   Throne Room of the Palace. Several days later.

              * Scene 2:   A Chamber in the Palace. A few moments later.

              Scene 3:   Throne Room of the Palace. The next morning.

              Scene 4:   Throne Room of the Palace. That evening.

* Can be played on the apron.

PROPERTY LIST

Act One

SCENE 1

A golden mask
A lantern
A ring

SCENE 2

Sign "ROYAL GATE"
A staff
Three pieces of paper (Gate passes)
Large spectacles
Peddler's wares (Pots and pans)

SCENE 3

Six shields and swords in scabbards hanging on walls
A ring
Pillows

SCENE 4

A gate pass
A coin
A mask
A dagger
A slingshot
A handle part of a key

Act Two

SCENE 1

A small table
A rolled notice-reward for finding Royal Record Book
A long piece of paper (To drag behind King as he reads to taxpayers)
A large book with some loose sheets
A Royal Record Book
A large cloth sack

SCENE 2

A rope in two pieces
A small bag
A chair
A 3 ft. by 5 ft. rug
A small table

SCENE 3

A piece of paper
Same long list of taxpayers as in scene 1
A plate with a large piece of cake with lots of icing
A spear
A ring
A pot
A note

SCENE 4

Six pots and pans
A lantern
A length of sturdy dark-colored twine
A small knife
A document
The golden mask
A crutch

Act One

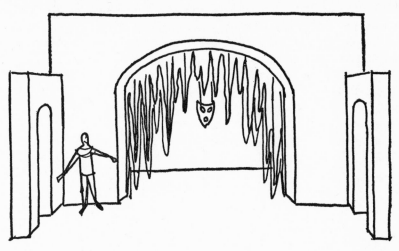

Setting for the Cave of the Sorceress

Scene 1

SCENE: *The cave of the* SORCERESS. *The curtains open to reveal a stage shrouded in almost total darkness. Upstage, exactly center, hangs an imposing looking golden mask. The only light on stage seems to emanate from this object. Enough illumination is afforded to enable the audience to see, in silhouette, the slow entrance of a figure at stage right. This figure stealthily approaches the mask. However, it is not able to avoid disturbing some object lying on the floor; a slight noise results. The figure freezes momentarily, then proceeds. It removes the mask from the wall and starts to leave.*
AT RISE: *At this moment another figure appears from the other side of the stage.*

SECOND FIGURE [*watching first figure*]: You, there! Stop! [*Rushing to intercept the first figure.*] The mask! You must not take the mask!

> *There is a scuffle amid the shadows of the cave, then one figure falls to the floor and the other rushes off. There is a moment of silence and darkness. Then a moan comes*

*from the prone figure. Seconds later, this is followed by
the faint glow of a light stage left. The light grows
brighter until a head with a hand holding a lantern peers
cautiously from the wings.*

ETHAN : Is—is anyone there? [*Silence. Now a 16-year-old lad,
comes hesitantly on stage and looks around. To himself.*] Funny!
I thought I heard a noise in here. [*Shrugging.*] I must have been
having a nightmare. [*Yawning.*] Oh, well, I might as well go
back to bed. [*Turning to leave; the figure's moan causes him to
turn back.*] Who's that?

> *He moves toward the noise, sees the figure, halts and
> then crosses rapidly and kneels beside it. He turns the
> figure over; it is an elderly woman clothed in full robes.*

Mistress, what's happened? It's Ethan! What's happened? Are
you hurt?

SORCERESS [*weakly*]: Ethan—The mask, the mask——[*Points
a feeble finger in the direction of the mask's former location.*]

ETHAN [*turning in the direction indicated*]: It's gone! Who took
it? [*The woman struggles to stand up.*] Here, let me help you
to your room.

SORCERESS : There's no time. Just help me sit up. [*Sits, back
to rock or bench that is present.*] Ethan my boy, someone has
taken the mask. Do you know the tremendous magic it possesses?

ETHAN : No—no, Mistress.

SORCERESS : All my power as a mighty sorceress comes from
that *mask*. As my assistant, someday you will be given that power.
But without the mask you and I are helpless. The present owner,
thief that he is, has unlimited ability to do evil.

ETHAN [*hopefully*]: Can't you use a crystal ball to look for the
thief?

SORCERESS : No, the mask's power will prevent it.

ETHAN [*less hopefully*]: Or magic spells?

SORCERESS : Or magic spells.

ETHAN [*downright discouraged*]: Or magic brews?

SORCERESS : Or magic brews. All magic is powerless against
the strength of the mask. There is only one way to get it back.
You must find the thief. I am too old to undertake this task. As

my apprentice, you must find the mask before it can be used to destroy us all.

E T H A N : I'll try. I've never had to do a thing like this before. I— I hope I won't fail you.

S O R C E R E S S [*taking boy's hand*]: You've done every other task I've ever put before you; you'll succeed in this one too.

E T H A N : How shall I begin?

S O R C E R E S S : Enter the city, go to the palace, and ask for the King. He will help you.

E T H A N : Will he believe me?

S O R C E R E S S [*taking off a ring*]: Give him this ring; he knows it is mine. Mind you, give it to no one but the King. It's very valuable and others would not hesitate to steal it from you. Now you must be on your way.

E T H A N : I'll help you to your room first, then I'll go.

S O R C E R E S S : No. Just let me rest here. Leave your lantern for me, that's all. Now, Ethan, you must go.

E T H A N : Yes, my Mistress. [*Rises and exits stage right.*]

S O R C E R E S S [*to herself; shaking her head*]: Is it fair of me to have sent this boy to do what even an army might not be able to do?

> *She sits, deeply immersed in thought, as the curtain slowly closes.*

Act One

Setting for the Front of Palace Gate

Scene 2

SCENE: *The scene occurs in front of the palace gate, which can be set up at the far right of the stage before the play begins. If it is painted a neutral color, it will not attract attention during the first scene. It may seem advisable to have it so arranged that the onstage side of the gate be quickly swung downstage in the blackout following scene 1. However, since the first scene is dimly lighted, it may be possible to set the gate in place before scene 1 opens and move into the second scene without a pause.*

AT RISE: *The lights come up on the apron as the GATEKEEPER enters. He carries a sign upon which is written "Royal Gate." He places the sign down and begins to pace. He is an average man of undetermined age. He is dressed in a colorful, guard's costume and carries a staff, a symbol of his lofty office. He wears large spectacles which indicate that his eyes are quite bad. After pacing back and forth a few times he halts at sign.*

GATEKEEPER [*peering upward, trying to read sign*]: R-o-y-a-l
G-a-t-e. Tch! Tch! Would you look at the dirt on my glasses.
[*Removes them and immediately squints as he tries to see.*] I'll
just give them a good cleaning. [*Leans his staff against his shoulder and reaches for a cloth. It is not in one pocket, so he must
search in the other, but knocks his staff over in the process.*]
Ooop! [*Scrambling to regain his staff before it falls all the way,
and dropping the glasses.*] Oh, my, now I've dropped both of
them. [*Kneels and cautiously feels around for his glasses.*] Now
where are those things? How can I okay gate passes! [*Angrily.*]
I have a duty to perform! [*Stops his search to recall.*] The King
said to me, "You are officially appointed the Royal Gatekeeper.
You must see that everyone has a pass." "Oh, yes, Your Highness," I said. "I'll see to it. Just leave everything to me." [*Remembers his plight.*] And I can't even see the passes, let alone
okay them!

> *Starts to search, but stops almost immediately as the* OLD
> WOMAN *shuffles on.*

Someone is coming! I must find my glasses!

> *Searches frantically as the woman shuffles steadily to-
> ward the gate; finally finds the glasses, puts them on and
> rises in one scrambling movement.*

Stop there, old woman! Where's your pass?

> *This stops the woman, but in his haste to check the pass,
> the* GATEKEEPER *falls over the staff, which gets tangled
> in his feet.*

Ooop! [*Grasping the staff and resignedly crawling over to the
woman.*] It's safer this way.

OLD WOMAN [*gazing down at* GATEKEEPER]: Having trouble,
young man?

GATEKEEPER: Never mind about me. Where's your pass?

OLD WOMAN [*grumbling*]: All of a sudden we need passes. I
was going in and out of these gates when you weren't half as
big as that staff you've got.

GATEKEEPER: I can't help it. It's the King's law.

OLD WOMAN [*mimicking*]: King's law! All of a sudden the
King passes all kinds of new laws. What was wrong with the
old ones?

GATEKEEPER: I'm sorry, old woman, I don't know anything about the new laws. I just want a gate pass.

OLD WOMAN [*finally finding a piece of paper which she hands to the* GATEKEEPER]: Here's your pass. Lot of foolishness if you ask me. I'm not going to steal the palace.

GATEKEEPER [*ignoring her and looking over the pass*]: Seems to be all right. You can go, old woman.

OLD WOMAN: Thank you. [*Leaving.*] Tell me, do you do all your gatekeeping on your knees? [*She is out.*]

GATEKEEPER [*looking down*]: What–? Oh——

> As he rises, a well-dressed, portly, middle-aged man enters and walks briskly to the gate. The keeper looks up and immediately takes off his cap and bows to the man, indicating he has recognized the gentleman, who carries a mass of disorganized papers under his arm.

Good morning, sir.

MAN: Good morning.

GATEKEEPER: Nice morning, sir.

MAN: Yes, nice.

GATEKEEPER [*rather nervous*]: Find everything to your liking, sir? I hope you had a good trip, sir. Everything in order all over–everywhere–everyone–everybody?

MAN [*puzzled*]: Yes, yes, everything was excellent. Here's my pass. [*Extends piece of paper.*]

GATEKEEPER [*with a nervous laugh*]: Oh, I know you! Everyone knows you! I don't need to check your pass.

MAN [*putting it away*]: Well, all right, but I thought you had to check all——[*Leaving.*]

GATEKEEPER: Oh, not you, sir. [*In great relief.*] Phew! I don't know why, but every time the Royal Tax Collector comes along I think he's after me.

> Now a ragged PEDDLER enters. He carries his wares upon his back which bend him over. He wears a hood. The combination of posture and hood prevent the audience from seeing the man's face.

GATEKEEPER [*as the* PEDDLER *approaches*]: Whoa now, peddler. On your way to sell some of your junk to the cook, eh?

> The PEDDLER *grunts.*

Well, you seem to have quite a load there.

The PEDDLER *grunts.*

Now then, if you have a pass, I'll let you in.

PEDDLER *hands him a pass.*

[*Before looking at pass.*] What wares have you in your packet?

P E D D L E R [*nastily; in harsh voice*]: You are too nosey, Gate-keeper. Go about your duty or I'll report you.

G A T E K E E P E R [*insulted*]: Report me! [*Looks at pass and thrusts it back to* PEDDLER.] Here!

P E D D L E R [*entering through the gate*]: Next time mind your own business!

G A T E K E E P E R [*pacing again before gate*]: What a disagree-able old man!

> *As he is pacing, a dark-complexioned man comes out through the gate.*

P R I M E   M I N I S T E R [*with authority*]: You, there, Gatekeeper! Come here!

G A T E K E E P E R [*looking up; crossing to man*]: Yes, sir, Mr. Minister. Can I be of some service?

P R I M E   M I N I S T E R : Has anyone passed out of this gate since yesterday carrying a large book?

G A T E K E E P E R : Large book, sir? [*Pauses to think.*] No sir, not that I recall. What's happened?

P R I M E   M I N I S T E R : The Royal Record Book is missing. It's very old and very valuable. It contains a record of all the King's family for hundreds and hundreds of years. If the King finds it's gone, my job may be gone.

G A T E K E E P E R : When did you discover it was missing?

P R I M E   M I N I S T E R : Only a few minutes ago. I saw it early yesterday morning. So it's been taken during the last day.

G A T E K E E P E R : I wish I could help, but the only people I've allowed in and out have been an old woman who visits the cook, the peddler who sells odds and ends, and the Royal Tax Col-lector who just returned.

P R I M E   M I N I S T E R : The Royal Tax Collector! Did he have books with him?

G A T E K E E P E R : I don't believe so. He had some papers.

PRIME MINISTER: Perhaps he got the Royal Record Book mixed with his papers. I'll go see. [*Exits.*]

> GATEKEEPER *resumes pacing. As he has his back to stage left,* ETHAN *enters and heads right for the gate. He is at the gate before the* GATEKEEPER *turns and sees him.*

GATEKEEPER: You, Boy! I'll have a look at your pass first! [*Crosses to* ETHAN.]

ETHAN: What pass?

GATEKEEPER: The gate pass!

ETHAN: What gate?

GATEKEEPER: This gate, of course!

ETHAN: I didn't know you had to have a pass. I was here a month ago——

GATEKEEPER: A month ago you didn't need a pass. The King passed the law three weeks ago.

ETHAN: I don't have a pass.

GATEKEEPER: Then you'll not get into the city.

ETHAN: But I have to get in.

GATEKEEPER: No one gets in without a pass!

ETHAN: I have to see the King on urgent business.

GATEKEEPER: No one gets in!

ETHAN: I've been sent by a most powerful sorceress!

GATEKEEPER: No one!

ETHAN: I have proof. [*Reaches for ring.*] I have a——

GATEKEEPER: No!!

ETHAN: But the sorceress gave me——

GATEKEEPER: Sorceress! Sorceress! Go tell your wild tales to the birds; I don't have time to listen to them!

> ETHAN *dejectedly crosses left and sits down on whatever has been provided. If there is nothing, he sits on the stage. Then an attractive young lady comes out through the gate. The* GATEKEEPER *sees and recognizes her.*

GATEKEEPER: Good morning, Lady Alison. Can I be of some help?

LADY ALISON: Gatekeeper, have you seen the Princess?

GATEKEEPER: No ma'am, I haven't. Is she missing again?

LADY ALISON [*heaving a sigh*]: I'm afraid so. She is the most impossible twelve-year-old I've ever seen.

GATEKEEPER : What a blessing if she'd have been a boy.

LADY ALISON : You don't know how many times I've said that to myself. Oh well, thank you, anyway. If you see her, just yell. I'm going around to check the back gate.

> *She exits right. ETHAN has been too far away to have heard this conversation. A young girl, the PRINCESS slowly emerges from stage left on tiptoe. She appears to be concentrating on the GATEKEEPER who has his back turned to her. She passes in back of ETHAN and continues for a very short distance and then, stopping in mid tiptoe, turns to look at the dejected figure of ETHAN. She studies him briefly and then crosses to him and sits beside him.*

KATHLEEN : What's the matter?

ETHAN [*still deeply concerned with his troubles*]: Wh—what?

KATHLEEN : I said, what's the matter?

ETHAN : Nothing.

KATHLEEN : There is too; I can tell.

ETHAN : Little girl, go away and don't bother me!

KATHLEEN : If you'll tell me, maybe——

ETHAN : Will you go away and leave me alone!

KATHLEEN [*angrily*]: If you don't stop being so impolite and tell me what's wrong, I'll see that you get in more trouble than you're in already. Besides, how can I help you if I don't know what the trouble is?

ETHAN [*coming to his senses*]: Help me?

KATHLEEN : Yes, help you.

ETHAN : How can a girl help me?

KATHLEEN : I might be able.

ETHAN : It's very simple. I've got to get into the palace and I don't have a pass for the gate, and I don't know any way to get one.

KATHLEEN : Is it important that you get in?

ETHAN : Very important.

KATHLEEN : That's wonderful. Now I can do what I was going to do before I stopped to talk to you and I'll end up doing a good deed. Watch me and when I give you a signal, go in through the gate.

ETHAN : I don't know what you're going to do, but thank you for helping. I—I'm sorry I was rude to you just now.

KATHLEEN: In return for the fun I'm going to have, I've already forgiven you.

> *She rises and continues on her tiptoeing way toward the* GATEKEEPER, *who has his back to her. When she gets behind him, she steps to his side and gives him a swift kick in the shins. There's an immediate howl from the* GATEKEEPER, *who bends over to minister his injured ankle. When he bends over* KATHLEEN *grabs his glasses and jumps out of his reach. The* GATEKEEPER *puts up a howl.*

GATEKEEPER: My glasses! Give me back my glasses! Wait till I get hold of you! I don't care who you are!

> *He continues shouting at her as she signals* ETHAN *to enter the gate, which he does. The* GATEKEEPER *is stumbling around looking for* KATHLEEN. *She dashes stage right as if to exit. Just as she gets to the exit* LADY ALISON *enters and* KATHLEEN *runs into her. Before she can get away,* LADY ALISON *has a firm grip on her.*

LADY ALISON [*crossing with* KATHLEEN *to* GATEKEEPER]: Gatekeeper! Gatekeeper, please stop yelling. I've got your glasses for you.

GATEKEEPER [*blindly*]: Lady Alison?

LADY ALISON: Yes. Here they are. [*Hands glasses to him.*] It appears I got back here in time. [*To* KATHLEEN.] Well, young lady, do you have anything to say for yourself? [*Silence.*] I think you have an apology to give the Gatekeeper. [*Silence.*] I suggest that you apologize, say you're sorry, and assure him that it won't happen again.

KATHLEEN [*hastily*]: I apologize; I'm sorry; it won't happen again.

LADY ALISON: That's much better. Now let's go and get you cleaned up.

> *She drags the protesting girl toward the gate. As the* PRINCESS *passes in front of the* GATEKEEPER *she stamps heavily on his foot bringing a howl of pain from him. As he hops about grasping his injured foot, there is a black-out ending the scene.*

Act One

Setting for the Throne Room of the Palace

Scene 3

SCENE: *The scene is the King's throne room about an hour later. The setting is made up of a combination of drapes; the side walls are flats. These side walls are each decorated with three shields and other weapons.*

AT RISE: *The stage is deserted. After a moment the well-dressed man who entered the gate in scene 2 comes into the throne room. He is followed immediately by his two sisters,* HILDA *and* MATILDA. *Both are amazon types.* HILDA *is affected; she attempts to be ladylike, but is not quite successful. She can be quite clumsy at times.* MATILDA *is the first-sergeant type. She talks loudly and walks heavily. As they enter they are berating the poor man who is with them.*

HILDA : Where have you been, Cecil? We've been waiting and waiting for you to come back.

CECIL : I told you I had business that had to be done.

MATILDA : Well, you've got business to be done right here and now. No two girls ever had such a lazy, undependable oaf for a brother.

HILDA : Other brothers do things for their sisters. They buy them nice big jewels, and summer homes, and winter homes——

MATILDA : And spring homes and fall homes and beautiful horses and fine carriages. You're the Royal Tax Collector, Cecil. And who ever heard of a tax collector that didn't take advantage of his position to borrow a dollar here and there from the King. Why, why do you have to be such an old fool? Most of all, why do you have to be so honest?

HILDA : Besides sweet, darling, thoughtful Cecil, we don't want jewels or big homes or fine carriages. We don't want you to take one cent from the treasury to buy us anything.

MATILDA : That's right. All we want you to do is to make sure one of us marries the King. He can marry again. His first wife is dead!

HILDA: He does need companionship.

MATILDA : We'll even overlook that brat of a daughter he has.

HILDA : We don't even care which of us gets the King. Although I do feel more qualified for the honor.

MATILDA [*angrily*]: Now just a minute! We agreed to let Cecil decide. We'd do nothing to influence his decision. You do that once more and I'll—I'll——

HILDA : You'll do what?

> At this point the dark-complexioned man enters and stops to listen.

Just remember what happened last time you tried to get the best of me.

MATILDA : I slipped! You'd never have gotten me down if I hadn't slipped.

HILDA : Slipped my foot! Why, you've never——

PRIME MINISTER : Don't you two ever do anything but fight? May I remind you that we've been called here by the King and he does not approve of your constant arguments. [*With authority.*] Now will you please stop this immediately.

HILDA [*huffily*]: Just a disagreement. Come, we'll go elsewhere. [*They move away from the* PRIME MINISTER.]

CECIL [*remaining behind*]: I'm terribly sorry. We didn't mean——

MATILDA [*jerking him with them*]: How dare you apologize to him! How dare you!

PRIME MINISTER: Just a moment please. I want——[*They stop.*]

HILDA: To apologize. Well, we accept your——

PRIME MINISTER [*persisting*]: I want to ask you a question.

MATILDA [*disappointed*]: Oh!

PRIME MINISTER: Have any of you see the Royal Record Book?

> *In the middle of the speech* LADY ALISON *enters. The words Record Book bring her to an abrupt halt. She stands, unnoticed and listens to the following conversation.*

CECIL: Is it lost?

PRIME MINISTER: It's not in the library.

MATILDA: I don't know where it is. I do know I don't have it.

HILDA: Are you accusing us of——

PRIME MINISTER: I'm not accusing you of anything. Just forget it. [*He turns away in disgust and sees* LADY ALISON.] Good morning, Lady Alison. I didn't know you were here. Perhaps you've seen the Royal Record Book.

LADY ALISON [*a bit flustered*]: Why—why no. I haven't the slightest idea of its whereabouts. [*Crosses past him to* MATILDA, HILDA, *and* CECIL.] Good morning.

> *The sisters ignore her, but* CECIL *seems willing to speak to her.*

CECIL: Good morning——

MATILDA [*cutting him off*]: Cecil, since when do we speak to common palace help?

CECIL: Yes, Matilda. [*When she turns away he gives* LADY ALISON *a little wave which she graciously acknowledges.*]

HILDA: Why do you suppose we've been called together by the King this morning?

MATILDA: Probably to hear some more of those new laws he's passed. Every week there are new ones. I can't keep up anymore. Why he's passed more laws in the last three weeks than he passed in three years.

> *During the following dialogue,* LADY ALISON *and the*

PRIME MINISTER, *both on opposite sides, sidle down to eavesdrop on this conversation.*

MATILDA: And grouchy! The man absolutely lost his sense of humor. He certainly has changed. He used to smile all the time but now he never smiles. The palace used to be such a pleasant place with balls and games. Now's there's nothing.

At this point the PRIME MINISTER *and* LADY ALISON *see each other and quickly pull back. An instant later* KING JUSTIN III *enters the room. He is in his late thirties and he gives the appearance of being both nervous and deeply troubled by the cares of state. He strides directly to his throne. As he moves to his throne the five bow to him, a gesture he chooses to completely ignore. Once in front of his regal resting place, and without sitting, he immediately gets to the reason for the meeting.*

KING: I've called you here today to see if anything can be done to control the Princess. To me, she has become absolutely impossible. If none of you are able to offer anything better, I plan to send her away.

MATILDA: I wouldn't send her away, I'd lock her away. The little monster!

PRIME MINISTER [*stepping forward*]: Your Majesty, as your Prime Minister I think it would be a grave mistake for you to send your own daughter away from her home. In the past, Your Highness, the girl's pranks have never seemed to bother you.

HILDA [*to her brother and sister*]: Well, they've bothered me. Do you remember the time she put glue in my toothpaste. I couldn't talk for three days. [CECIL *laughs*.] Cecil, that is not funny.

CECIL: Yes, Hilda. [*When she turns away, he laughs and nods his head as if to say, "yes it was," pantomiming her past efforts to open her stuck jaws.*]

LADY ALISON [*stepping out*]: Your Majesty, I agree with your Prime Minister. If I may, Sir, I would like to call to your attention the fact that many of her past pranks were your idea.

PRIME MINISTER: That's right, sire—— [*He continues speaking in the background.*]

MATILDA : If we don't do something right away those two will talk the King into keeping that brat here and increasing her allowance on top of it.

HILDA : Don't just stand there, Cecil, say something.

CECIL : Say what?

HILDA : Anything! Just make sure you agree with the King.

MATILDA : He'd better agree or I'll break both of his arms. [*Pushing* CECIL *out.*] Now do as we've told you!

KING [*seeing* CECIL *move out*]: You wanted to speak, Cecil?

MATILDA [*as* CECIL *hesitates*]: If you want to stay in good health, you'd better speak up.

CECIL : Yes, sire, we—that is—I think that——

> At this moment ETHAN *bursts into the room and before he can halt runs full tilt into* CECIL *knocking him flat. His forward progress arrested, he gazes down at the prone figure at his feet.*

ETHAN : Oh—I—I'm sorry, sir. Please let me help you.

CECIL : What—what hit me?

ETHAN : Here, sir, I'll get you up.

KING [*bellowing*]: Who is this boy? How did he get past the guards?

ETHAN : Now, sir, just give me your arm and—— [*Helping* CECIL *rise, but he is standing on the latter's robe; as* CECIL *rises there is a ripping noise. At the sound of the noise,* ETHAN *lets go of* CECIL, *who falls flat again.*]

KING : Guards! Guards!

MATILDA [*attempting to push* ETHAN *away*]: Young man, get out of the way! I'll help my brother get up.

> *Stops to help* CECIL, *but* ETHAN, *on the other side, persists in assisting. Both bend over at the same time and their heads bump.*

My head! [*Moaning, she staggers back holding her head.*]

> *At this point two guards,* LESTER *and* LEROY *by name, both attempt to enter at once. Because the entrance is too small, they succeed in getting in each other's way to the extent that they tumble in not in the manner recommended for guards entering a throne room. They do get in, even though they end up in an unsightly heap on the floor.*

LESTER : You called, Your Majesty?

KING : Called? I hollered, yelled, shouted, and bellowed! Will you two get on your feet and get this boy out of here!

LESTER : At once, Your Majesty.

> *They hastily rise and grab for* ETHAN, *who by now has gotten* CECIL *to his feet. In grabbing, however, both get hold of the same arm.*

ETHAN : Wait, sire, I must see you on a most urgent matter!

KING : Get him out of here!

LESTER [*looking down; realizing that they both have the same arm. To* LEROY]: Leroy, his other arm! Take his other arm!

LEROY : Huh? Oh, yeah! [*Changes hold to other arm.*]

ETHAN [LESTER *and* LEROY *are dragging him out*]: But, Your Majesty, I was sent by the sorceress to——

> LESTER *and* LEROY *exit with* ETHAN.

MATILDA : Of all the nerve, bursting unannounced into the throne room.

HILDA : What are today's youth coming to?

KING : Enough of this, let's get back to the question of what to do with my daughter.

> *He finally settles down on the soft pillows that make up the seat of his throne. However, he does not sit on the throne, but right through it. This places him in a most absurd position, one that will be most difficult to get him free of.*

KING : Help! [*Struggling.*] Get me out of this thing!

> *The* PRIME MINISTER *rushes to help him. At this point the figure of the* PRINCESS *emerges from behind the throne. She is almost doubled with laughter and it is not difficult to determine who is responsible for the* KING's *predicament.* LADY ALISON *is the first to see her. She rushes up to the girl.*

KING : Help me out of here!

MATILDA [*shoving* CECIL]: Don't just stand there, idiot, help them!

LADY ALISON *is hustling* KATHLEEN, *who is almost hysterical with laughter, out of the throne room.* CECIL *and the* PRIME MINISTER *are tugging on the* KING *and the whole throne tumbles over knocking them down. As the two sisters rush to the rescue the curtain mercifully closes.*

Scene 4

SCENE: *This scene starts as soon as the curtains close on scene 3. It is set before the palace gate as scene 2.* THE GATEKEEPER *is not present.*

AT RISE: *The gate opens and* ETHAN *is rudely tossed out into the street.*

E T H A N [*as he is being thrown into the street*]: I tell you I must see the King!

L E S T E R [*he and* LEROY *are standing in front of the gate*]: Do you hear that, Leroy? He has to see the King. What about? Did your rocking horse break a leg? [*Both laugh.*]

L E R O Y : Maybe—maybe, he's lost his toy soldiers and can't find them?

L E S T E R : Or—or his toy boat went down a sewer and he wants the King to go after it.

E T H A N : I do have important business with the King! I've been sent here by the sorceress! Here's her ring to prove it!

He pulls out the ring and thrusts it at LESTER *and* LEROY. *They stop laughing almost simultaneously, look at the ring, then look at each other.*

L E S T E R [*impressed by the value of the ring*]: Well, now, why didn't you say so in the first place. This ring makes things entirely different, doesn't it, Leroy?

L E R O Y [*drooling over ring*]: Yeah! Different!

L E S T E R [*faking earnestness*]: We'll take this ring to the King right away. Won't we, Leroy?

L E R O Y [*taking* LESTER *at face value*]: Are you crazy; this ring is worth——

LESTER *gives him a swift kick.*

Ouch! I—ah—that is—yes, sir, we'll take it to him right away.

During LESTER's *speech the* OLD WOMAN *of scene 2 enters from stage left. She crosses to left center and halts to listen. The two guards are about to leave when* LESTER *sees the woman.*

L E S T E R : What are you doing here, old woman. You know the King has forbidden begging in the city without a permit. Do you have one?

O L D   W O M A N [*to herself*]: Another of the King's new laws.

L E S T E R [*crossing to her*]: I said do you have a permit to beg!

O L D   W O M A N : No, I don't! I'm not a beggar; I'm a fortune teller.

L E R O Y [*crossing to her*]: Well, they're almost the same. Do you have a fortune-teller permit?

O L D   W O M A N [*pulling out piece of paper; annoyed*]: Yes, here it is. Would you like for me to tell your fortunes?

L E S T E R [*laughing*]: Our fortune! No, old woman. [*Holding up ring to* LEROY.] We've already got our fortune. Come on, Leroy, we've more important things to do. [*Exit, laughing.*]

O L D   W O M A N : Would the young laddie like to have his fortune told?

E T H A N : I'm sorry, old woman, I am not interested in having my fortune told.

O L D   W O M A N : How's this? Surely you are curious to know what the future holds for you—every young man is.

E T H A N : Oh, I—I'm interested, but—ah—I have no money.

O L D   W O M A N : If I give you a free sample of your fortune, would you let me finish and give me a piece of silver for my labors?

E T H A N [*trapped*]: Yes, ma'am.

O L D   W O M A N : So be it. Now keep still so that I can think. [*Pauses as if concentrating; then goes on slowly.*] First your present comes to me. You are on a most secret and important mission. You must recover a very valuable object.

E T H A N [*definitely impressed*]: That's—that's right. [*Taking out coin.*] Here, old woman, take this coin. Is there anything more you can tell me?

O L D   W O M A N [*she continues slowly again*]: I see your past. You are an orphan lad who has been given, by royal decree,

into the care of a kind, elderly woman. She is the possessor of
great power. Someday you will take this woman's place. You
have been sent by her to recover a most valuable possession.
However, your luck has been bad, so far. [*She pauses, then
frowns and shakes her head.*] I cannot go on. Your future is
clouded; I am unable to see it clearly. I see only that you must
be very careful for your life is in danger. That is all. Don't ask
me for more. There is no more. [*She leaves.*] Now I must leave
in order to earn a few more coins.

E T H A N : Wait, old woman! You say my life is in danger. Who
wants to harm me?

O L D W O M A N : I told you not to ask. Your future is blank beyond what I've told you. [*Exits.*]

E T H A N : My life is in danger and I don't know what to do. If
the guards would only let me see the King! [*Realizes that the
guards have never returned.*] The guards! They never came
back! What happened to them?

> *Crosses to the gate and knocks on it; after a moment it
> opens and* LESTER *comes out.*

L E S T E R [*giving no sign of recognition*]: I'm sorry young man.
The palace is closed for the day. Come back tomorrow, or the
next day, or, better still, next week. [*Goes in and closes the gate.*]

E T H A N [*momentarily stunned, then realizing what has happened*]: Hey, open this gate! [*He raps on the gate a good deal
harder this time; now the gate is opened by* LEROY.]

L E R O Y [*also giving no sign of recognition*]: We just told you
the palace is closed. Besides we don't want any of whatever
you're selling. So be on your way. And if you bother us again,
I'll call the guards and have you thrown in jail. [*Turns to reenter gate and stops; looks down at his uniform, then turns back
to* ETHAN.] What am I saying? I'm a guard! If you bother us I'll
personally throw you in jail. [*Reenters gate and closes it.*]

E T H A N [*very angry now*]: You! Open up!

> *Now he pounds on the gate. The gate is opened once
> more and both* LESTER *and* LEROY *try to look through it,
> but it is not wide enough for them. So, after a bit of a
> struggle,* LEROY *stoops down and* LESTER *peers over* LE-
> ROY's *back at* ETHAN.

ETHAN : Where's my ring? I want it back!

LESTER [*looking down at* LEROY]: Leroy, have you taken a ring away from this poor boy?

LEROY : I certainly have not. I haven't even met the lad. Lester, did you take this boy's ring?

LESTER : Are you accusing me of being dishonest?

LEROY : Goodness no, you have the most honest face of anyone I know.

LESTER : Then how can you have the nerve to ask if I would do anything as mean as taking a ring from this young lad?

LEROY [*hanging head*]: I'm—I'm sorry, Lester, I wasn't thinking.

ETHAN [*angry*]: I demand you return my ring right now!

LESTER [*calmly*]: Young man, we have been very patient with you. You have been most impolite to us. Lunch is now being served in the palace kitchen; we're hungry; and [*getting louder*] if you don't mind, you're wasting our time!

> *The gate slams.* ETHAN *pounds again, but it remains shut. Completely defeated, the boy sits down centerstage. As he sits trying to hold back the tears, the palace gate slowly opens and a* MASKED FIGURE, *grasping a dagger, emerges from the door. This figure is dressed in the clothes seen on the* PEDDLER *in scene 2. The boy is too deeply engrossed in his own problems to be aware of the step-by-step approach of the silent assassin. Closer and closer to the boy the would-be murderer creeps until he is directly behind him. He raises his knife to strike and then suddenly lets out a howl of pain. In one movement he drops the knife and clutches his rear end. Then* ETHAN *whirls, but the sight of the masked man freezes him motionless for a moment. The figure dashes back to the gate, opens it, and disappears inside the palace, closing the gate after him. As the figure is escaping, the* PRINCESS, *carrying a slingshot in one hand, rushes onstage.*

KATHLEEN : Don't just stand there, stop him! [*It is too late.*] Can't you do anything for yourself? First, I get you through the gate and now I have to save your life. If I hadn't seen him sneaking up behind you and stopped him, you'd have a dagger sticking in you right now.

ETHAN [*still stunned*]: You stopped him? How?

KATHLEEN: With this, silly. [*Holds up slingshot.*] Boy, did he jump! Good shot, huh? Whoever it was doesn't like you very much.

ETHAN: No, I guess not. [*Picks up dagger.*]

KATHLEEN: Why?

ETHAN [*puzzled*]: Why? Oh, you mean why doesn't he like me. I–I guess because of the mask.

KATHLEEN: Mask?

ETHAN: The sorceress's mask. [ETHAN *sits on edge of stage with feet dangling over the apron's edge.*]

KATHLEEN: I still don't understand. [*She joins him.*]

ETHAN: Well, you see, I'm an apprentice to a very powerful sorceress, only the golden mask she owns was stolen and I have to get it back.

KATHLEEN: Is it valuable?

ETHAN: Yes, but, more than that, it has great power. Whoever has it could destroy all of us if that's what he wanted.

KATHLEEN [*indicating door*]: That–that was the thief; I bet you!

ETHAN: I'm sure you're right. I only wish I knew who it was.

KATHLEEN: He looked like a beggar, or a peddler, maybe.

ETHAN: He could have been either, but what if the clothes were just a disguise? We have the knife. Maybe that will help.

KATHLEEN: That's just a knife from the palace kitchen. The only way to learn anything is to find out if the guards spotted anyone.

ETHAN: That won't do us any good. Whoever does answer won't tell you anything. You'll get a gate slammed in your face. Two guards by the names of Lester and Leroy have done it to me three times already.

KATHLEEN: Well, I'm going to try the gate and I bet I have better luck than you. [*She rises and crosses to gate; she knocks.*]

LESTER [*opening the gate almost immediately*]: I thought I told you–Your Highness! I'm sorry. I didn't mean any disrespect. Please don't report me, Princess Kathleen, I won't do it again. [ETHAN *is visibly startled by the revelation that this is the Princess.*]

KATHLEEN: Oh, be quiet!

LESTER *stops babbling.*

Tell me, did a masked figure pass you while you were on duty?

LESTER: I haven't been here, Your Highness. I've been eating lunch. My partner, Leroy, has been on duty though. Maybe he saw someone. [*Calling.*] Leroy! [*No answer.*] Leroy!

LEROY [*finally appearing at gate; listlessly*]: Huh!

LESTER [*to him out of the corner of his mouth*]: The Princess, you fool! [*Indicating the Princess.*]

LEROY: Oh! [*Bowing as he speaks.*] I'm sorry, Your Majesty.

LESTER: Has a masked man passed by here lately?

LEROY: I–I don't know. Your shout just woke me up.

LESTER: Oh, no!

KATHLEEN: If I were king you'd lose your heads for this. It may be hard, but try to stay awake from now on and if you see anyone, tell me. [*Turns to* ETHAN, *who is still standing with his mouth slightly agape.*] I haven't had much influence with my father lately, but I'll try to get you in to see him. In the meantime, I'll hide you in the palace. If the thief knows you're here, he might try to hurt you again.

ETHAN [*still stunned*]: I–I didn't know——

KATHLEEN: Don't try to say anything, just come on.

> *Pushes* ETHAN *into palace.* LESTER *and* LEROY *have come out of the palace in order to speak with the Princess. Now she dashes past them through the gate.*

See how it feels to have a door slammed in your face! [*Closing the gate, leaving the two guards alone out on the apron.*]

LEROY: Now what do we do?

LESTER: You go up and reach through the gate and unlock it, stupid!

LEROY [*blankly*]: Oh! [*Crosses up to gate and reaches through to turn key which is on inside of gate, but without success.*]

LESTER [*impatiently*]: What's the matter? Can't you even do that right? [*Crosses to* LEROY.] Here let me do it!

> *Pushes* LEROY *aside; the key which* LEROY *has been hanging onto snaps in two when he is pushed.*]

LEROY [*holding broken end of key*]: Now look what you did!

LESTER: What I did! Did I make the Gatekeeper quit so that we had to watch the gate? No! Did I take the ring from the kid all by myself? No! Did I have trouble turning a key? No! Don't go blaming me for being locked out. It's just as much your fault as mine!

L E R O Y : Oh, yeah!

L E S T E R : Yeah!

L E R O Y : It's your fault! This entire, complete mess is all your fault!

L E S T E R : I don't have to take that kind of talk from you or anybody else!

> *Both swing sweeping haymakers simultaneously, they land simultaneously, the two tumble to the stage simultaneously. After a pause* ETHAN *and* KATHLEEN *reappear at gate.*

K A T H L E E N : I'll get the ring back for you. I'll just—— [*Sees unconscious guards.*] Well, what happened to them?

E T H A N : They're unconscious! That's great! All we have to do is go out and get the ring.

K A T H L E E N : No, we can't!

E T H A N : Why not?

K A T H L E E N : Because the key is broken off in the lock and there's no other key.

E T H A N : Now what do we do?

K A T H L E E N : You wait here and I'll go get a locksmith. [*Exits.*]

E T H A N [*building*]: Kathleen, come back! That'll take too long! What if they come to and get away? I've got to have the ring! I'll never find the mask without it! [*Blackout.*]

Act Two

Scene 1

SCENE: *The scene is the throne room several nights later. The set is the same as act 1, scene 3, except that a small table has been placed near the throne.*

AT RISE: *As the curtain rises, the* PRIME MINISTER *enters with a medium-size piece of paper rolled up and tucked under his arm. He briskly heads across stage. At center he has a sudden thought and stops dead, then snaps his fingers.*

PRIME MINISTER: Of course! I know who can help me! If I describe [*turns to audience*] it, maybe *you* can find the Royal Record Book for me! It's about so big—— [*describes size with hands*] and it's black, and it has metal dodads on the side, —and—— [*desperately*] and I'll get fired if I don't find it! [*Remembers rolled paper.*] Look! Look what I've got here! [*Unrolls paper; it is a sign offering a reward for the return of the Record Book.*] See! It says that I'll give a huge reward to anyone who returns the Record Book. I'm on my way to put this up by the palace gate. [*Starts to leave; turns when almost out.*] Please, if any of you find that Record Book return it right away or I'll lose my job and I don't want to lose my job. [*Exits crying.*]

As soon as the PRIME MINISTER *is out, the* KING *enters. He is reading from a long piece of paper which reaches the floor and drags behind him. Following the* KING *while trying to avoid stepping on the paper, is* CECIL.

KING [*disgustedly laying aside the list*]: Promises, promises, promises! Cecil, has anyone on this list paid all his taxes?

CECIL: No, sire, but they all promise——

KING: Cecil, you're too softhearted. You shouldn't be so easy on the people—they take advantage of you.

CECIL: But they all do pay their taxes eventually.

KING [*begrudgingly*]: Yes—you're right. You know, Cecil, you're about the only honest man I've ever found.

He picks up the list and is about to resume reading from it, when HILDA *and* MATILDA *are heard noisily arguing offstage. Their impending entrance has a noticeable effect on both men.*

KING [*hastily*]: I—I just remembered I've completely forgotten an appointment I had with a man about patching a leak in the palace roof. Please excuse me.

He rushes off. CECIL *rises to follow, but in his haste, he drops the large book he has and must stoop to recover it and some papers that fall out. He then heads for the exit, but he has lost his chance.*

HILDA [*entering*]: Oh, there you are, Cecil. We've been looking all over for you. We've been having a little argument. We know you can settle it for us.

MATILDA: All you have to do is decide which one of us should be the first to try to win the King.

CECIL: Really, dear sisters, I don't think——

HILDA: We'll tell you when to think. And don't try to wiggle out. You should have no difficulty in choosing me. After all, I'm the most attractive, and the most intelligent, and the most talented, and if you don't agree with me I'll stretch your arms out so long you'll be able to touch your fingers to the floor without even bending over.

MATILDA: Cecil, you see, I don't agree with Hilda. I say that since I'm the elder, I should get first chance. Besides, if you don't pick me I'll twist your head around so far you'll have to look where you've been instead of where you're going.

HILDA: You see how simple it is. Just choose one of us.

CECIL [*hesitates a moment, then goes on*]: I wouldn't pick either of you; the King deserves a better fate! [*There is a deadly pause.*]

MATILDA: What! Why you weasel!

The two sisters converge on CECIL. *Each from one side and grab for him, but he ducks and they grab each other. He races for the exit, but as he gets to it, he stumbles over his long robes and falls in a heap.*

HILDA: He's down, after him!

They rush for him, but he rolls away and scrambles to

*his feet. He retreats to the dais upon which the throne
rests and hides behind the latter.*

MATILDA : I'll go this way!

She goes one way as HILDA *goes the other.*

PRIME MINISTER [*entering hastily and stopping*]: Ladies,
please, I ask you to be quiet. [*He is drowned out by the sisters.*]

HILDA : Watch him! Don't let him get away.

MATILDA : You think you're smart, don't you, Cecil? Just wait!

PRIME MINISTER [*louder*]: Ladies, be quiet!

*They advance on him and it seems they will capture him,
but he pulls the throne back and races around behind
MATILDA toward the exit in which the PRIME MINISTER
is standing.*

HILDA [*yelling*]: Come back here!

MATILDA [*yelling*]: I'll break his neck!

PRIME MINISTER [*yelling*]: Be quiet!

*CECIL is headed full tilt for the PRIME MINISTER. He sees
him just in time to avert a crash, but his sisters can't stop,
and crash into CECIL almost knocking him down. They
fall silent as they see the PRIME MINISTER.*

[*still yelling*]: Quiet!

MATILDA [*quiet and with great dignity*]: We are quiet. You're
the only one making noise.

PRIME MINISTER [*yelling*]: What? [*Quietly.*] Oh—yes.
[*With a degree of patience.*] I've told you time and time again
you must control the noise at these family fights. [*Losing patience.*] Every time you fight, the guards think that we're being
invaded and rush to their posts ready for battle. The guards are
so nervous that most of them are quitting to get nice peaceful
jobs like taming lions!

HILDA : You don't have to shout; none of us is hard of hearing.
We're sorry. We promise it won't happen again. Come, sister.

She and MATILDA *start to leave;* CECIL *heads in the opposite direction, but doesn't make it.*

And you too, Cecil.

CECIL *retraces his steps and exits with his sisters.*

The PRIME MINISTER *is about to leave when noises of another argument are heard offstage right. The* MINISTER *hastily crosses up and hides behind the drapes to the left of the throne dais. He will peek out from time to time during the following scene.* LESTER *and* LEROY *enter arguing.*

L E S T E R : I tell you we've got to sell the ring as soon as possible. The kid almost got it the other day. If I hadn't come to before they got the locksmith, he would have taken it back. We'll sell it and split what we get for it.

L E R O Y : But what if the ring does belong to a sorceress. She might change us into frogs or something if we sell it.

L E S T E R : I've told you a dozen times the kid was lying to us. No sorceress would just give him a ring this valuable. [*Takes out ring.*] Look at it. Why, do you know how much this is worth?

L E R O Y : No, and that's another thing, if you sell it how do I know I'll get half of the money?

L E S T E R : What's the matter? Don't you trust me?

L E R O Y : No.

L E S T E R : All right, we'll both go together. That way I can't cheat you.

L E R O Y : Well, that might be okay.

L E S T E R : Come on, we'll sell it right now.

P R I M E   M I N I S T E R [*coming out of hiding and crossing down*]: Just a minute. Let's see that ring. [*Puts out his hand.* LESTER *just stands.*] The ring!

Now LESTER *puts it into the* PRIME MINISTER'S *hand. The* MINISTER *looks at it and is visibly shaken.*

Where did you get this?

L E S T E R and L E R O Y [*pointing at each other*]: It was his idea.

P R I M E   M I N I S T E R : I want to know where this came from!

L E S T E R and L E R O Y [*pointing again*]: It's his.

P R I M E   M I N I S T E R : I'll ask you once more—where did you get this? Answer me or I'll tell the headsman to sharpen his ax.

L E S T E R : We got it from that boy that broke into the throne room the other day.

LEROY : He said it was given to him by a sorceress who sent him here.

PRIME MINISTER : Where is this boy now?

LESTER : In the palace kitchen, sir.

PRIME MINISTER : What's he doing there?

LEROY : He's the cook's new assistant. Honestly, we didn't know it was a sorceress's ring; we thought the boy was lying.

PRIME MINISTER : Don't think! Bring that boy to me and if you so much as breath a word of this to anyone, I'll have your heads.

LESTER : Y—y—yes, sir. [*They start to leave.*]

PRIME MINISTER : Wait!

They stop dead.

Have you two been stealing other things from the palace to sell for your own profit? A rare black book that has been in the King's family for years is now missing. Do you know anything about it?

LESTER : Oh no, sir! Not us! Nothing! We've taken nothing!

PRIME MINISTER : Very well. Get that boy and bring him to me in my quarters.

> *They leave left in a hurry. The* PRIME MINISTER *looks at the ring, then shoves it in his pocket and hastily leaves right. He's no sooner off when the rear drapes to the right of the throne part and* LADY ALISON *comes onstage, carrying the Royal Record Book. She crosses down and gazes after the* PRIME MINISTER, *then she turns and quickly exits stage left. The stage is deserted again and then from stage right* ETHAN *enters. Right behind him is the* COOK. *She is a middle-aged woman who would be an excellent member of her profession if she weren't always complaining about something.*

COOK : I've had all kinds of helpers: lazy ones, clumsy ones, stupid ones, but you're the first one that has his mind on seeing the King more than on doing the cooking. You're the best assistant I've had and you don't want to do anything but talk to the King. I could train you to become a fine royal cook, if you'd let me.

Boy is not listening.

You haven't heard a word I've said. [*Silence.*] Are you determined to wait for the King?

E T H A N : I'm sorry. I must stay until he gets here.

C O O K : How do you know he'll talk to you when he gets here?

E T H A N : He must talk to me.

C O O K : That's nice. Are you going to tell the King he must listen to you? If you do, you'll spend the rest of your days in the dungeons under the palace.

E T H A N : I'll just have to risk that.

C O O K : I give up! I get one good assistant and what happens— he's crazy! [*Leaving.*] Other people have nice comfortable, easy jobs. I have to be a cook!

> *The boy stands waiting for the* KING. *As he does so, the* MASKED FIGURE *emerges from behind the drapes left, but* ETHAN *has his back to him and doesn't see him. The presence of the apprentice startles the villain, for he stops short as soon as he sees the boy and then hastily retreats behind the drapes.* ETHAN *wanders closer to the shields on the right wall. As he does so, the figure appears carrying a large cloth sack. He comes up behind the boy without* ETHAN *becoming aware of his presence. As the figure seems about to raise the sack,* ETHAN *moves. Now the figure moves behind* ETHAN, *who is looking at another shield. This time the villain actually raises the sack high above his head and starts the downward movement of his arms when* ETHAN *moves forward to examine one of the swords hanging by a shield. The figure tries to stop the downward movement of his arms and succeeds after almost falling off balance. Now* ETHAN *replaces the sword and backs up, almost backing right into the figure. The villain must hastily back up. He raises the sack and brings it down over the boy's head. The boy struggles, but to no avail. As the figure drags* ETHAN *off through the drapes, the scene ends.*

Act Two

Setting for a Chamber in the Palace

Scene 2

SCENE: *The scene is a chamber in the palace. The apron can be used for this scene. The lights rise to reveal the chamber. The furnishings are slight: there is a chair facing the entrance to the room. No door is visible; the imaginary door is just an entrance stage right. In front of the chair, but not under it, is a rug, approximately 3' x 5'. There may be a small table placed on the upstage side of the chair.*

AT RISE: *After a pause, the villain drags in the struggling boy.*

MASKED FIGURE [*in a disguised voice*]: It's useless to struggle, boy. There's no way you can escape. Besides, you'll use up what little air there is in the sack if you keep struggling this way. [*He drags* ETHAN *to the chair and pushes him down. The boy's struggles subside.*] That's much better. [*Produces length of rope.*] Now, we'll just tie your hands behind you so that you can't use them—— [*Does so and then pulls another length of rope from pocket.*] and your feet together so that you won't walk away before I'm done with you. [*Ties them together, but not to the legs of the chair.* ETHAN's *head slumps over. The villain notes this.*] Here, here, we can't have you dying like this. I've other plans for your death, young man. [*Removes the sack. Slowly, the boy revives.*] Your only fault is that you know too much. For this you must be removed. I'm not in favor of this sort of thing. I cannot personally, bring myself to do away with you. So I must depend upon my assistant to do the job for me. [*Undoes a bag he has hanging from his belt, crosses to the exit, and stops.*] I'm leaving now, but my helper will be in in a moment. [*Exits.*]

> *A moment later a medium-sized snake slithers slowly through the entrance. The snake must be large enough to be seen by the audience. It is pulled through from stage left to stage right by means of a black cord. If it seems desirable for the snake to be upright at any point in its approach, the cord will have to be rigged through the flies.* ETHAN *struggles as soon as he sees the snake. The movement attracts the reptile which moves toward him across the floor. Realizing he can't free himself,* ETHAN *stops his attempts to get loose. As he becomes still the snake stops.*

ETHAN : It's stopped, thank goodness. Well, what do I do now? [*Pause.*] I wonder why it's stopped. [*Renews his struggle against the ropes and, once again, the snake moves toward him. Seeing this,* ETHAN *stops and the snake stops.*] It only moves when I move! [*Loudly.*] If I talk does it move? [*No movement.*] No. Then I can try yelling. Maybe someone will hear me. Help! Help! [*Silence.*] Help! [*More silence.*] No one heard. I—I guess the walls are too thick. I can't sit here forever, but when I move, it comes closer. The only way out is through the door and the snake is in the way. I must destroy the snake so I can get to the door and pound on it to make some noise out in the hall. But how can I get rid of the snake? [*He looks at the table.*] Nothing there that's any good and if there was how could I get hold of it. My feet are partially free, but there's only the rug. The rug— I wonder——

*His feet are tied, but he is able to swing them forward.
Slowly, but obviously, he starts to wiggle his feet under
the edge of the rug. The snake sensing the movement,
starts forward. The boy continues to move about until
the snake is almost to the middle of the rug, then he flips
the portion of rug on his feet over onto it. Quickly by
means of his feet, he scoots the chair over to the snake
and by simply raising and lowering his feet violently
several times crushes his foe. This task finished, he scoots
his chair to the door and kicks at it. Since there is no door,
obviously, this must be pantomimed. At first nothing
happens.*

ETHAN [*discouraged*]: They still don't hear me. [*He kicks
again.*] Someone's outside! They're trying to unlock the door!
Help! Get me out of here!

KATHLEEN [*in a moment* KATHLEEN *has entered the room*]:
Ethan, what's happened?

ETHAN: Kathleen! Am I glad to see you! Please get me loose.

KATHLEEN: I don't know what you'd do without me. This is
the third time I've helped you. [*Untying him.*] How did you get
here?

ETHAN: The masked man caught me in the throne room and
brought me here. He put a snake in the room. It was supposed
to kill me, but I trapped it in the rug and killed it instead. [*He
is free.*]

KATHLEEN: At least try to stay out of trouble, Ethan. Suppose
I couldn't help you the next time.

ETHAN: Next time! Kathleen, I've got to see your father so that
there won't be a next time!

He hustles KATHLEEN *out of the chamber as a blackout
ends the scene.*

Scene 3

SCENE: *The scene is the throne room next morning. The table of scene 1 has been removed. A piece of paper lies conspicuously on the floor.*

AT RISE: *At rise the* KING *is alone. He is seated on his throne reviewing the list we have seen him going over with* CECIL *in the first scene. He is deeply immersed in his perusal of this list. So immersed is he that he does not observe the head that peeks into the throne room, or the body that follows the head, attached of course, as* HILDA *enters the throne room. The* KING *is still too occupied to note her as she coquettishly skitters across the stage and out the other side. There is a pause, then the head pokes out again as she peers at His Highness. Slowly she tiptoes on stage. Considering her size, this is a rather ludicrous action. Matters are further complicated by the fact that she steps upon the edge of the long gown she wears. After doing this twice, she tiptoes holding her skirt aloft, which gives her somewhat the appearance of an overweight ballet dancer.* HILDA *tiptoes up to the dais upon which the throne is set, then carefully climbs up on it. We still do not know what her aim is. As she reaches a point directly behind the Monarch, who is turned so that his back is partially toward her, she restrains a giggle and then reaches her hands around to cover the* KING's *eyes in a "guess who" game. However, in typical* HILDA *clumsiness, she manages to poke a finger in the* KING's *eye.*

KING [*jumping up, clutching at his eye*]: Ooow! My eye! [*Turning.*] It's you! Are you trying to blind me?

HILDA [*tremendously apologetic*]: I'm terribly sorry, Your Majesty. I didn't mean to hurt you. I just meant——

KING: Tell me, please, just what did you mean! Do you or your sister ever behave like normal intelligent human beings?

HILDA: Oh, yes, Your Majesty. It's just that—well—I peeked in and saw you sitting on your throne and you looked so solemn and so sad and I just said to myself, [*As a Florence Nightingale.*] Hilda, here's your chance to bring a ray of light into this man's dull existence, make his day a bit brighter——

KING [*sits*]: My dear woman, would you please brighten things up elsewhere before you cripple me for life.

HILDA [*pouting*]: Now that's not nice. I was trying to make your day a happier one. You just don't appreciate me, that's all.

KING: I'd appreciate you if you'd just go away and leave me alone.

HILDA [*changing her approach*]: You don't know the real me. If you did, you'd think differently. Why Cecil says I'm the best cook in the palace. He swears by my cakes. I bake them for him all the time. In fact, I just finished one not ten minutes ago. I'd be glad to let you have the first slice.

KING: That's really very nice of you, Hilda, but I never eat between meals.

HILDA: Now I won't take "no" for an answer. You just wait right here and I'll be back in a minute. [*She crosses to exit.*]

KING: Can't you understand that——

HILDA [*coy little wave*]: Now don't go away. I'll be right back. Byeee.

KING: I've got to get out of here before she tries to poison me with that cake.

> *Moves to the opposite exit; as he reaches it,* MATILDA *enters and completely blocks his avenue of escape.*

MATILDA [*making no attempt to be tactful or diplomatic, she operates like a high pressure salesman*]: You're just the man I'm looking for. Your Highness, have you ever considered getting remarried? [*She emphasizes each of her points with a poking, pushing motion to the* KING's *shoulder, which tends to move him backward from the exit to down center.*] Have you ever considered the advantages of married life? Just think of having someone around to mend the holes in your robes, someone to help you out of your armor after a hard day at the battlefield, someone you can practice giving royal decrees to. [*She backs him around so that her back is opposite the exit through which her sister left.*] And the companionship! Are you tired of going to royal balls and having everyone whisper: there goes that King Justin III all by himself, poor man? Tell you what I'm going to do.

> *At this moment* HILDA *enters carrying a plate upon which is a generous slice of cake. The cake is one that is laden with a heavy, rich icing. The scene that meets her eye brings her to a sudden halt.*

I'm prepared to make you an offer you can't afford to pass up.

> HILDA *straightens herself up and, cake in hand, crosses to her sister, who is still talking.* HILDA *starts to tap her on the shoulder and it looks like* MATILDA *is going to get a cake in the face. However* HILDA *reconsiders at the last moment, crosses to the throne and puts the cake on the dais in front of the throne.* MATILDA *is still going strong.*

M A T I L D A : I can cook, I can bake, I can put your armor on you, I can shoe your horse.

H I L D A [*crossing between her sister and the* KING]: Just what do you think you're doing, sister dear?

M A T I L D A : What does it look like, [*Mimicking.*] "sister dear"?

> *The* KING *is now completely forgotten and takes the opportunity to get out of the immediate vicinity. Just as it looks like he's going to sneak out, the two sisters still talking, move toward the same exit. He pulls back out of their way and they go right by him without even looking at him.*

H I L D A : We agreed that we'd each get a chance. Cecil said he'd tell us who would go first! I waited! Why couldn't you?

M A T I L D A : I got tired of waiting for Cecil. That weasel probably didn't even intend telling us.

H I L D A [*they start to move to the exit*]: I bet you're right, Matilda. Just wait until I get my hands on him. He'll look like a jigsaw puzzle.

M A T I L D A : I'll go along just to make sure none of the pieces you leave are too big.

> *They are gone.*

K I N G [*relieved*]: I've got to sit down.

> *He staggers back toward his throne. He does not notice the piece of cake that is lying on the dais in front of his throne until, in mounting the dais, he steps in the cake. At first he seems too stunned even to look down, then he finally gazes down into the mess into which he has stepped.*

[*Enraged.*] This does it! This is the last straw! [*Turns and starts hopping to an exit.*] When I get this mess cleaned off, out go Cecil and those two nuts. I don't care how honest he is. [*Exits.*]

> *As soon as the* KING *is out, the* PRIME MINISTER *enters agitatedly; he looks about.*

PRIME MINISTER : Where are those two empty heads! How many brains do you need to get a boy out of the kitchen!

> *At this moment,* LESTER *and* LEROY *enter the room. From somewhere* LEROY *has picked up a spear which he carries on his shoulder. As he and* LESTER *stand before the* PRIME MINISTER *the spear should be on the shoulder near* LESTER.

PRIME MINISTER : Oh, here you are! Where have you been and where is the boy?

LESTER : We couldn't find him.

PRIME MINISTER : What!

LEROY : That's right. He wasn't in the kitchen.

LESTER : We did find the cook there.

PRIME MINISTER : Where else, pray tell, did you expect to find the cook?

LEROY : Oh, I don't know, she could have been——

PRIME MINISTER [*totally exasperated*]: Be quiet! [*Louder.*] Quiet, I say! [*They are silent. Gathering himself and speaking slowly as if to three-year olds.*] Now listen carefully, so that you get this right. Go to the kitchen and get the cook and bring her here. Maybe she knows where the boy is.

LESTER : At once, sir. Come on, Leroy.

> *They turn to leave. In the normal procedure of turning to leave, the two guards should turn the same way, but* LEROY *is not so adept at things like turns. As a result he turns the wrong way and the spear smacks* LESTER.

LESTER : Will you be careful with that thing! I don't know who told you that you had to carry a spear, but if I did I'd sock him right in the snoot! Now be careful and come on!

PRIME MINISTER : I hope I never have to depend on those two to save my life.

> *The* KING *enters, apparently bent on discharging* CECIL; *seeing* PRIME MINISTER.

KING : Oh, here you are. Have you seen Cecil anywhere?

PRIME MINISTER : Your Majesty, I was about to go looking for you. I have a most important bit of news to tell you.

KING : I asked if you've seen Cecil.

PRIME MINISTER : What? Oh—Cecil? No, sir, I haven't seen him yet today. Your Highness, please, what I have to tell you is much more important than Cecil.

KING [impatiently]: Well, what is it?

PRIME MINISTER [showing him the ring]: Do you know what this is?

KING : Certainly, that's the sorceress's ring, but how did you get it?

PRIME MINISTER : That's what I'm trying to tell you. This ring was brought here by the lad you gave to the sorceress a number of years ago. That lad is her apprentice.

KING : Why does the boy have the ring?

PRIME MINISTER : That's what I want to know. I have two guards out now looking for him.

> LESTER and LEROY enter with the COOK; LEROY still has the spear.

LESTER : Here she is, sir.

KING : I thought they were looking for the boy?

LESTER : We were, sire, but couldn't find him. So we brought the Cook.

KING [not understanding at all]: Oh, I see.

PRIME MINISTER : The boy we're seeking works as your assistant in the kitchen. Do you know where he is?

COOK : No, sir. The last time I saw him was right in this room. I left him here waiting to see the King.

KING : I never saw the boy while I was here last night.

PRIME MINISTER : Then where is he?

LESTER [acting the hero]: Leroy and I will find him. Just leave everything to us.

COOK : You two couldn't find a whale in a fish pond.

PRIME MINISTER [seeking to avoid a possible argument]: That will be all, Cook. You may leave.

COOK : Yes, sir. [Leaving.] Gets me all the way up here and asks me one ridiculous question. Lunch is probably ruined. [She is out.]

Until this moment the piece of paper that has been lying in a most conspicuous place onstage has gone unnoticed by those in the scene. Now the paper catches LEROY's *attention.*

KING [*to the guards*]: All right, you two, go see if you can find the boy.

During this speech, LEROY *has shifted the spear and now has it cradled under his arm, the business end pointing in back of him. Now he bends over to pick up paper. At the same instant* LESTER *is saying his line.*

LESTER: At once, Your Majesty. [*He bows as* LEROY *is bending over picking up paper and bows right into the point of the spear.*] Yow! [*Grasping seat; turning.*] Didn't I tell you to be careful with that spear! Give it to me! [*Jerks it away.*] We'll leave it outside the door, where it can't hurt anyone. Come on. [*Drags* LEROY *off.*]

PRIME MINISTER: Why do you put up with those two, Your Majesty?

Before he can answer, "those two" return dragging LADY ALISON.

Now what!

KING: What are you doing with Lady Alison? Don't you know a young boy when you see one?

LESTER: Oh yes, sir. We were going to look for him, but we opened the throne room door and found Lady Alison eavesdropping.

KING: Is this man right?

LADY ALISON: Yes and no, sir.

KING: That makes no sense.

LADY ALISON: Well, you see, Your Majesty, I'm looking for Princess Kathleen. I thought perhaps you had seen her, but I had no wish to disturb anything important that was happening in here. So I paused a moment outside the door to see what I would be interrupting. That's when these two came along.

KING: I consider this very thoughtful on your part, Lady Alison.

LADY ALISON: Thank you, sire.

PRIME MINISTER: Tell me, do you know of this boy we're seeking and his reason for being here?

LADY ALISON : I don't, but I'm sure the Princess does.

PRIME MINISTER : Then bring her here at once.

LADY ALISON : May I remind you that I don't know her where-abouts, so it would be most difficult to bring her here "at once."

LESTER : We'll find her, Your Highness. [*Starts to leave.*]

PRIME MINISTER : You stay right where you are! You two have caused enough trouble already.

> At this moment KATHLEEN and ETHAN burst into the throne room.

KATHLEEN : Father, Father!

KING : Where have you been?

PRIME MINISTER : Your Majesty, this is the lad.

KING [*startled by the appearance of* ETHAN]: Why this boy is— ah—— [*Catches self.*] This boy is—the lad who broke into the throne room a few days ago!

PRIME MINISTER [*shoving ring at* ETHAN]: Did you bring this to the palace?

ETHAN : Yes, sir, but those two took it away from me. [LESTER *and* LEROY *shuffle uncomfortably.*]

PRIME MINISTER : I know that! I want to know why you had the ring!

ETHAN : I was to use it to identify myself to the King as an of-ficial representative of the sorceress.

KING : Why should you need to see me?

ETHAN : A golden mask that hangs in the sorceress's cave has been stolen. It has great magical powers. I was sent to try to find it.

KING : I know of this mask. It's a dangerous weapon in the hands of an evil man.

KATHLEEN : And Father, the thief is someone right here in the palace.

PRIME MINISTER : Someone here! How do you know that?

KATHLEEN : The person who stole the mask has tried to kill Ethan two different times. The first time was outside the palace and the second time was last night when he was inside the palace.

KING : It certainly seems that the person responsible is someone here. If the thief is in the palace, then so is the mask. We haven't had any magic spells so maybe the thief hasn't had time to use the mask. We must find it before it's too late. [*To* LESTER *and* LEROY.] Guards, I command you to start a stone-by-stone search of the palace at once.

LESTER LEROY: Yes, sire. [*They rush off in a state of confusion.*]

PRIME MINISTER: Something tells me they'll need all the help they can get. I'll join them. [*He leaves.*]

LADY ALISON: Your Majesty, as long as the mask hasn't been found, I'm afraid the thief will make another attempt to hurt Ethan.

KATHLEEN: That's right, he might try.

KING: Would it be possible to find an empty chamber and lock the boy in it. Of course, it would be up to him not to leave the room or let anyone in.

LADY ALISON: That's exactly what we'll do, Your Majesty. We'll find Ethan a room, put him in it, and not let him out until we find the mask. Come on, you two!

> *They exit.*

KING: I might as well give them a hand with the search. [*Exits, leaving the throne room empty.*]

> LESTER *hurries on from one side and* LEROY *hurries on from the other.*

LESTER LEROY [*as they pass*]: Any luck? No.

> *They exit. A moment later the process is reversed; they pass.*

Any luck? No.

> *Before they are out, they turn almost simultaneously and cross to meet center.*

Where have you looked?

LEROY: Everywhere!

LESTER: Everywhere?

LEROY: Well, almost everywhere!

LESTER: How about the kitchen?

LEROY: Haven't looked there.

LESTER: Shall we?

LEROY: After you, Lester.

They bow to each other and exit. There is a pause, then a violent noise is heard in the direction in which the two have exited. Then the two race back in.

LEROY : How did I know she had a cake in the oven?

LESTER : Well, she did and you ruined it.

COOK [*entering with pot in hand*]: Here you are, you—you fools! [*Approaching menacingly.*] I'll teach you not to burst into my kitchen like two elephants.

LESTER [LESTER *and* LEROY *retreat; to* LEROY]: Don't just stand there! Get something to hold her off or she'll crown both of us!

LEROY : Right away [*He races off.*]

COOK : Come back here, you coward! [*The* KING *rushes in.*]

KING : What's going on here?

COOK : These two barged into the kitchen and completely ruined a cake I had in the oven.

PRIME MINISTER [*entering*]: Have you found the mask?

KING : No, but the Cook has lost a cake.

LEROY [*enters brandishing his spear which has a piece of paper stuck on the point*]: Let me at her. I'll teach her not to bother us when we're on official business.

KING : This has gone far enough. Kindly put that spear down.

LEROY : Yes, Your Majesty.

He bangs down the spear on LESTER's *foot.* LESTER *howls and is about to grab the spear when he notices the paper impaled on it.*

LESTER : What is that on the end of your spear?

LEROY : I don't know. [*Takes paper off, opens it, and reads it.*] Oh, my!

LESTER : Well, what is it? [*No answer.*] Have you lost your voice? Give it here! [*Takes it, reads it.*] Oh, my!

PRIME MINISTER : Let's have a look at this paper! [*Takes it from* LESTER *and reads it.*] Oh, my!

KING : For goodness sake, what does it say?

PRIME MINISTER [*reading*]: No matter where you hide the boy, he shall die!

BLACKOUT

Scene 4

SCENE: *The scene is once again the throne room. It is the night of the same day and the stage is dimly lighted.*

AT RISE: *The stage is empty. Almost immediately the figure of the* OLD WOMAN *of act 1 emerges through the rear drapes. She heads toward the down right exit. When she reaches it, she halts suddenly, then whirls and heads for the down left exit. As she reaches this exit her flight is again arrested. She turns again and hastily retraces her steps out through the rear drapes. As soon as she exits* ETHAN *backs on from right, simultaneously* KATHLEEN *backs on from left. The two back toward each other until they meet center stage.*

KATHLEEN and ETHAN : Yow!!

KATHLEEN : Help!

ETHAN [*recognizing her; grasping her by the shoulders*]: Kathleen!

KATHLEEN : Help! He's got me!

ETHAN [*shaking her, but not hard*]: Shhh! Kathleen, stop it! It's Ethan.

KATHLEEN [*coming to her senses*]: What? Ethan! What are you doing here! You're supposed to be locked in your room.

ETHAN : You're supposed to be asleep. What are you doing out of your room?

KATHLEEN : I got hungry! I was on my way to the kitchen for a midnight snack. But why are you here?

ETHAN : I was too nervous to sleep, so I got up to look for the mask.

KATHLEEN : We looked all over the palace this afternoon and couldn't find it. I wonder where it is.

ETHAN : I wish I knew.

KATHLEEN : Don't you think you ought to go back to your room?

ETHAN : I was on my way when I bumped into you. I've got all the stuff for the warning.

KATHLEEN : What warning?

ETHAN : I'm going to put a warning in the hall outside my door, just in case I have a visitor tonight.

KATHLEEN : Will it work in here?

ETHAN: I guess so. Do you think I ought to put it in here?

KATHLEEN: Why not? We can set it up just to see what we catch. We might not get anyone, but you can't tell.

ETHAN: All right. I've got the stuff right outside the door. Come on, let's get it.

> *They leave and return in a moment carrying a length of cord with assorted pots and pans. ETHAN also has a lantern.*

KATHLEEN [*putting cord, pots and pans down centerstage*]: What are you going to do with this?

ETHAN: Just watch and you'll see. [*Takes the twine and unravels a part of it; to this he ties a pot.*]

KATHLEEN: Why are the pots and pans being tied to the string?

ETHAN: You'll see.

KATHLEEN: May I help?

ETHAN: Sure.

> *They tie five or six pots and pans to the twine. He takes out a small knife and drives it into the floor at DC; and then ties one end of the twine to the knife and the other to the base of the throne. KATHLEEN helps him. The actors may ad lib their actions as they do them. The results of their efforts should be a twine tied with pots and pans stretching from the throne straight down to the front of the stage.*

Now when someone hits the cord, we'll hear it for sure.

KATHLEEN: Say, that's pretty good.

ETHAN: Now let's turn the lantern off and hide behind the drapes to see if we catch anyone. You hide on one side and I'll hide on the other so that we can stop him.

KATHLEEN: Or her!

ETHAN: If he or she starts to run.

KATHLEEN: All right.

> *They split up. It is not long before a figure enters and heads across stage and succeeds in setting off the warning system.*

CECIL: Don't hit me, Hilda! I didn't mean it!

ETHAN and KATHLEEN come down from their hiding places. ETHAN turns up the lamp as he comes down. In the light we see that a frightened CECIL has been caught by the warning system and now stands centerstage.

KATHLEEN: Cecil, what are you doing up at this hour?

CECIL [*in relief*]: Oh, it's you, Your Highness. I thought it was my sisters.

ETHAN: Why are you up?

CECIL: Well, you see it's this way. My sisters have been arguing all day and all night. They've been at it so long that I've got a headache. I'm on my way to the palace medical supplies to get a sleeping powder for my head and some cotton for my ears so that I can get some sleep.

KATHLEEN [*to ETHAN*]: He sounds as if he's telling the truth. We did hear his sisters yelling at him today.

ETHAN: Okay. Go on, but don't come back this way or you'll set the things off again.

CECIL: I won't; believe me, I won't. [*He hurries off.*]

ETHAN: I'll reset the warning. We certainly didn't catch much did we? [*He resets it.*] There. Now, let's try again.

The lamp goes down and they hide again. Again the wait is not a very long one. Once again a figure enters and crosses the stage, setting off the warning.

LADY ALISON: Oh! What's happening!

Again the two come out of hiding. ETHAN is turning up the lamp. In the light we see LADY ALISON has tripped the warning system.

ETHAN: Lady Alison! We didn't mean to startle you with our warning system.

LADY ALISON [*seeing KATHLEEN*]: So here you are! I've been looking for you, young lady! Don't you realize that it's dangerous to wander around the palace tonight!

KATHLEEN: I'm helping Ethan. Maybe we'll catch the thief.

PRIME MINISTER [*entering*]: What on earth are you doing to make so much racket at this ungodly hour of night? All three of you get to bed at once and stop whatever it is you're doing.

KATHLEEN: I was just getting——

PRIME MINISTER: I don't care! Lady Alison, please take the Princess to bed.

LADY ALISON: Yes, sir. [*Regally.*] Come, Princess, your bed awaits you. [*She hustles* KATHLEEN *off.*]

PRIME MINISTER: And you, boy, aren't you supposed to be locked in your room? Do you want to get hurt?

ETHAN: No, sir.

PRIME MINISTER: Well, then, get back to bed where you belong. [*Turns and leaves.*]

ETHAN [*to himself*]: Well, I guess I'd better do as he says. I think I'll reset the warning. [*Does it.*] Will I be able to hear it if it goes off? I'd better not take a chance. I know—I'll sleep over there for a little while and *then* go back to my room.

> *He lies down upstage and goes to sleep. The throne room once again settles itself in shadows. Then, from behind the drapes emerges the* MASKED FIGURE. *It is not possible at first to understand exactly what he is doing. He pauses to see if the palace is quiet; then he heads downstage. He does not cross the trip wire to get to his destination. He reaches the wall and stands absently at one of the shields. As he stands there,* ETHAN *rises on the opposite side of the stage, stops for a moment when he sees the* FIGURE, *and then starts to sneak up on the villain. The figure meanwhile, reaches up and removes one of the shields from its place. As he does so,* ETHAN *hits the trip line, which he has forgotten and sets off the racket of the tumbling pans. The* FIGURE *drops the shield and whirls around to find that* ETHAN's *feet have become entangled in the rope and he is struggling to free himself.*

MASKED FIGURE: Caught in your own trap, eh? Things couldn't be better. Now I can do what I failed to do twice before.

> *He grabs a sword from the wall, removes it from scabbard, drops scabbard, and crosses to the boy. He takes a swing at him, but misses as the boy scrambles up and runs behind the* MASKED FIGURE.

Come back here!

The assassin turns to strike again. As he is about to bring the sword down, he is hit squarely in the back by a hurtling human projectile in the person of PRINCESS KATHLEEN, *who, hearing the warning go off, has rushed to the throne room.*

Ooof!

The force of the impact jars the sword out of the villain's grasp so that it drops in easy grabbing distance of the boy's hand.

KATHLEEN : The sword! Get the sword!

ETHAN *seizes the sword.*

MASKED FIGURE : Oh, no, you don't. It's not that easy!

Whirls and grabs hold of KATHLEEN *and, using her for a shield, backs to the other wall where he takes down another sword.*

Now boy, if you know what's good for the Princess, you'll throw down that sword. If you don't there won't be any Princess.

Holds the blade of the sword to KATHLEEN'S *throat;* ETHAN *is forced to throw his sword down.*

That's very wise of you, my boy. I'll just leave you to enjoy the presence of the Princess. I hope you will excuse me for not staying longer.

Just as it seems that he will make good his escape, the PRINCESS *sinks her teeth into the hand that the culprit has been holding over her mouth.*

Ow! You bit my hand!

Lets go of her only to receive a swift kick in the shins.

My ankle! Oh, my ankle! My hand!

Bellowing in double pain, he hops about bending over to grasp his painful ankle. As he does so, ETHAN *grabs the scabbard lying by him and brings it down upon the villain's head knocking him senseless.*

ETHAN [*looking down at* FIGURE]: Well, I guess that does it.

I might as well take off his mask. [*Stoops to do so.*]

> *Before* ETHAN *can do so, the* PRIME MINISTER *enters.*

PRIME MINISTER : What is going on here? I thought I told you—— [*Sees the unconscious form of the* MASKED FIGURE.] Who's this?

KATHLEEN : It's the thief! Ethan knocked him out!

PRIME MINISTER : So it is. Now, at last, we can get to the bottom of this whole mystery.

> *Strides to the prone figure. As he does so,* LADY ALISON *appears in the other entrance and stops short.*

We'll just remove this mask. [*Tears off the mask and we see the man is the* KING.] The—the King!

ETHAN : I—I can't believe it!

KATHLEEN : Father!

LADY ALISON [*crossing to them*]: No, you're wrong! This is not the King!

> CECIL, HILDA, *and* MATILDA *enter.*

HILDA : What is all the noise!

MATILDA : Can't people sleep in peace and quiet?

HILDA [*seeing the Monarch*]: The King! Oh, poor man, what happened? Here let me help him. [*Starts for him.*]

PRIME MINISTER : Stay where you are, please. Lady Alison, repeat the statement you just made.

LADY ALISON : I said, this is not the King.

MATILDA : Not the King! You're crazy!

LADY ALISON : I should know if this is the King or not! After all, I'm the Queen!

CECIL PRIME MINISTER [*in unison*]: What!

ETHAN KATHLEEN [*in unison*]: The Queen!

HILDA MATILDA [*in unison*]: Who's the Queen?

PRIME MINISTER : You have proof of this?

LADY ALISON : Certainly I have. [*Takes out a document which she hands to the* PRIME MINISTER.] That is a marriage permit. King Justin and I were married in secret because I'm not of royal blood. He feared too many members of the court would object if he made it public right away.

HILDA : I, for one, certainly would have.

LADY ALISON : One morning not long after our marriage, the

King suddenly failed to recognize me as anything but a lady-in-waiting. I felt something was wrong; I watched him carefully and after a few days I became convinced this was not the real King.

KATHLEEN : How did you find out who he really is?

LADY ALISON : Well, I watched him carefully. I disguised myself as an old woman so that I could follow him. He always disguised himself as a peddler. One day he left here carrying a large book from the Royal Library. I followed him out of the city. In a clearing, he set the book on fire, but left before it finished burning. This allowed me to get the book before it was destroyed. It was the Royal Record Book.

MATILDA [*to* PRIME MINISTER]: And you accused my sister and me of taking that book.

LADY ALISON : The Record Book showed that King Justin was the first of royal twins. His brother was supposed to have been put to death because there is a law in this land that says the second of royal twins must be killed. However, somehow the law was not obeyed and this is the real King's twin brother.

PRIME MINISTER : His twin brother! Yes, he does look like the real King! But, Lady Alison, why didn't you tell me this sooner!

LADY ALISON : Because I don't know where the real King is hidden. I couldn't put his life in danger. I couldn't even protect Ethan and I knew the identity of the thief. I did try to warn him though while I was in disguise.

ETHAN : The fortune teller!

HILDA : Have you found the real King?

LADY ALISON : No.

PRIME MINISTER : That shouldn't be difficult. [*He drags up the imposter, who is now reviving.*] Come on, you. We know you're not the King. For your own good, you'd better tell us where he is.

IMPOSTER [*still groggy*]: In the dungeons—he's in the dungeons.

PRIME MINISTER [*pushing him out*]: Take me to him! Move!

The IMPOSTER *stumbles through the drapes and exits with the* PRIME MINISTER.

HILDA: Oh, dear, and I wanted to marry that—that person!

MATILDA: To think I tried to get him to marry me!

> CECIL *starts to chuckle.*

What's so funny?

CECIL: I was just thinking what would happen if either of you had married him.

HILDA [*shocked*]: What! Why you heartless weasel! You'd better start running because if I catch you, all the King's horses and all the King's men won't find enough of you to put together again.

> CECIL *starts out with* HILDA *and* MATILDA *in hot pursuit.*

MATILDA [*exiting*]: Let me do it, sister. It's my turn.

KATHLEEN: There they go again!

ETHAN [*suddenly*]: The mask! I didn't ask him where he hid the mask!

LADY ALISON: You can ask him when they bring him back.

COOK [*entering in stormy mood*]: Where are my pots and pans? How can I can cook without them!

ETHAN: They're by the throne.

COOK: What are they doing there?

LADY ALISON: Never mind, they've served their purpose. You may have them.

COOK [*crossing to throne grumbling*]: The minute my back's turned they come in and take half my pots and pans. [*Grabbing hold of the pots and pans, and dragging them noisily over the dais.*] For goodness sakes, what were you doing with them? [*Stringing them over her back, marching to the exit, then turning.*] Come on, breakfast is ready. I cooked it without these pots and pans. [*She leaves.*]

> *The* PRIME MINISTER *returns with the real* KING. *There is a warm welcome between* LADY ALISON, PRINCESS KATHLEEN, *and the* KING.

ETHAN [*not concerned with welcomes*]: Where's your brother? Bring him here. I must find out where he hid the mask.

KING JUSTIN: My Prime Minister has told me all you did. I'm sorry to tell you this—my brother is dead.

ETHAN: Dead! But he was just here!

PRIME MINISTER: He tried to escape from us as we returned

and in the struggle he fell, struck his head, and was killed.

ETHAN : Now, I'll never get the mask. How can I go back? That mask is dangerous if it falls into the wrong hands. I must get it.

PRIME MINISTER : How did this get here? [*Points to shield.*]

ETHAN : The fake king took it down while I was trying to sneak up on him.

PRIME MINISTER : Why should he want to do that?

KING JUSTIN [*suddenly*]: Let me see that! [*Crosses and takes shield and looks at it.*] Just as I thought. Look here! [*He turns the shield around and hidden inside is the golden mask.*]

KATHLEEN : The mask!

LADY ALISON : That's why the shield was taken down! He wanted the mask!

ETHAN [*taking mask*]: Now I can go back to the sorceress.

KING JUSTIN [*surprised*]: Right away?

PRIME MINISTER : At least stay for breakfast. Whoever heard of traveling on an empty stomach!

LADY ALISON : Please do. The cook just told us that the breakfast is ready.

KING JUSTIN [*to the* PRIME MINISTER]: Go tell the others breakfast is being served. [*To* ETHAN *and* KATHLEEN.] These two will help you. We don't want to get the cook angry.

PRIME MINISTER : Yes, sire. [*Exits with* ETHAN *and* KATHLEEN.]

KING JUSTIN : Come, we'll wait for the others in the dining hall. [*Links arms with* LADY ALISON *and they leave.*]

> *The stage is deserted a moment and then* LESTER *enters with* MATILDA *alongside. They walk across the stage and exit on the opposite side.*

MATILDA : Have you considered how wonderful it would be to have someone polish your armor, to darn the holes in your socks, to sharpen your sword? I'm prepared to make you an offer—— [*They are off.*]

> *As soon as they are out* HILDA *and* LEROY *enter.* HILDA *is hanging on* LEROY'S *arm.*

HILDA : I simply love big, strong men and you're so big and so strong. And I'm so little and weak I need a big strong man to protect me. [*They are out.*]

As soon as they are out the PRIME MINISTER *enters helping* CECIL *who has one arm in a sling, his head bandaged and he is limping.*

PRIME MINISTER : Careful now! Take it easy! That'a boy!

Amid a combination of groans from CECIL *and admonitions from the* PRIME MINISTER *the two make their way across the stage. As soon as they are out,* ETHAN *and* KATHLEEN *hurry on.* ETHAN *is carrying a crutch.*

ETHAN : Mr. Tax Collector, here's your crutch!

KATHLEEN [*stopping center*]: He didn't hear you.

ETHAN : I guess he doesn't need it.

KATHLEEN : Well, there's only one thing left to do.

ETHAN : What's that?

KATHLEEN [*indicating audience*]: Say good-bye to them.

ETHAN : Oh! All right.

ETHAN and KATHLEEN [*turning to audience*]: Good-bye, everyone.

If there is a reaction from audience here, wait until reaction dies.

KATHLEEN : Come on, I'll race you to the dining room. Last one there is a rotten goose egg!

They race off as curtain closes.

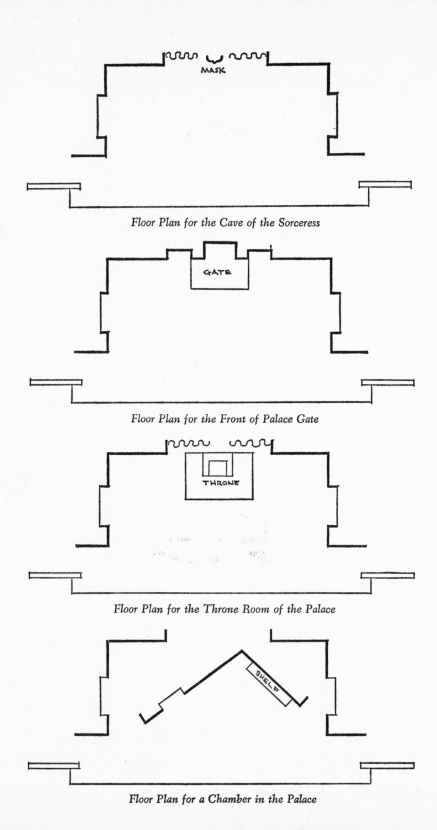

Floor Plan for the Cave of the Sorceress

Floor Plan for the Front of Palace Gate

Floor Plan for the Throne Room of the Palace

Floor Plan for a Chamber in the Palace

Huck Finn

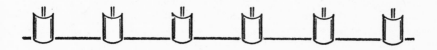

AN ADAPTATION OF

MARK TWAIN'S

The Adventures of Huckleberry Finn

BY

Paul Brady

Cast of Characters

JIM	DOCTOR PARSONS
HUCK	THE TRAVELER
OLD FINN	AUNT SALLY
THE KING	UNCLE SILAS
THE DUKE	TOM SAWYER
SUSAN WILKS	TOWNSPEOPLE
MARY JANE WILKS	

Synopsis of Scenes

Act One   Scene 1:   A woodland thicket.

             Scene 2:   The same, a short time later.

Act Two   Scene 1:   The Wilks's home.

Act Three Scene 1:   The Phelps's farm.

PROPERTY LIST

Act One

A man's belt
A red bandanna with all Huck's things in it
A suitcase (carpetbag) with posters and costumes inside
Two saplings

Act Two

Three blankets
Money bills (forty)

Act Three

A note
A bedsheet
A white shirt
A needle

Act One

Setting for a Woodland Thicket

Scene 1

SCENE: *A woodland thicket.* AT RISE: JIM *enters running and hides.*

H U C K : There ought to be some place to hide around here.

Enters running.

J I M : Over here Massa Huck.

H U C K : Jim, what're you doing here?

F I N N : Huck, you good for nothing no good lazy whelp, where are you?

H U C K : Oh Lord, it's paw.

J I M : Is he lookin' for you?

H U C K : It ain't the devil that he is lookin' for. I got to hide somewhere.

J I M : Behind that barrel.

F I N N : That little rat is some place around here. I seen him come this way. I'll show him that he can't treat his old man that-a-way.

HUCK *sneezes.*
What was that?

HUCK *sneezes again.*

FINN : There it is again. It came from this direction.

HUCK *sneezes again. He scrambles out from behind the barrel and runs from his father.*

FINN : Oh no, you don't, you little rapscallion. You're not going to get away from me this time. I want the money.

HUCK : I ain't got it.

FINN : I said I want that money.

JIM *crosses to cabin—unseen.*

HUCK : I ain't got it.

FINN : I'm going to beat you within an inch of your life if you don't tell where you hid it.

HUCK : I gave it to Judge Thatcher.

FINN : I told you not to give that money to anybody but me. Now how the devil am I going to get my hands on it?

HUCK : That's just why I did it so you couldn't touch it.

FINN : You good for nothing, I'm going to teach you a lesson that you will never forget.

He takes off his belt and proceeds to beat HUCK.

JIM [*still hiding*]: Massa Finn.

FINN : Who is that?

JIM : This is the Devil speaking.

FINN : The Devil?

JIM : That's who it is.

FINN : The Devil from down there?

Points down.

JIM : That's the only place that the Devil lives.

FINN : What do you want?

JIM : Set that boy free and don't pester him again do you hear?

FINN : But he is my son, I can do anything that I want to to him.

JIM : Not this time. Let him go.

FINN : But he stole some money from me. I just want to get it back.

JIM : He didn't steal it from you; it was his reward for capturing Injun-Joe.

FINN : I have heard your voice before.

JIM : More than likely and you'll hear it again unless you be good. If you don't straighten out you will spend the rest of forever in my everlasting fire.

FINN : Anything but that.

JIM : Let the boy go.

FINN : But my money.

JIM : The fire.

FINN : All right. I'll let him go.

JIM : Now get out of here before I lose my temper and send you down there right away.

FINN : I'm going. Don't get in a rush.

JIM : Get.

FINN : I'm going—I'm going.

Exits and JIM *comes out of hiding.*

JIM : Worked pretty good, didn't it?

HUCK : It sure did. Thanks Jim, I was getting sore—here.

JIM : I kinda thought so.

HUCK : I'm owen to you Jim.

JIM : It twarn't nothing.

HUCK : Jim, why ain't you over to old Mis' Watson's?

JIM : I ain't 'gwin to stay there any more.

HUCK : But you belong to her; she can do anything to you she pleases.

JIM : I know, that's why I ran away. Huck, I don't want to be sold down the river.

HUCK : That makes you a runaway slave.

JIM : I guess it does.

HUCK : I ought to turn you in.

JIM : Oh! Don't do that Massa Huck.

HUCK : You know it is against the law to help a runaway slave.

JIM : I know, but please don't turn me in. I never did nothing to you.

HUCK : That's right, in fact, you just helped me a lot, so I'm goin' to help you get away, Jim.

JIM : Why thank you Massa Huck but iffen you do that it will make you a slave stealer.

HUCK: I know, but you did me a good turn so I can do the same for you.

JIM: It ain't necessary Massa Huck.

HUCK: I got a boat hidden down by the river. We'll wait till dark and then I'll take you over to Illinois.

JIM: That's mighty kind of you Massa Huck.

HUCK: We just stay hid here 'till Tom comes.

JIM: Tom? What's he comin' here for?

HUCK: He's bringin' me some stuff—I'm goin' down river. Mis' Watson wants to civilize me.

JIM: That's bad.

HUCK: I'll say it is. She thinks that I should go to school every day and I have to wear shoes and a necktie and all kinds of other things. Well I don't have to sit there and take it so I'm goin' down river.

JIM: That's what I'd do too.

TOM [offstage]: Hello.

JIM *jumps up.*

HUCK: There's Tom, now.

TOM [*entering with a red bandanna with all* HUCK's *things in it*]: I got your stuff, Huck. What's he doin' here?

HUCK: Jim's runnin' away and I'm goin' to help him get to Illinois!

TOM: Whoa, that makes you a slave thief. That's worsin' a horse thief.

HUCK: I know, but he did me a good turn so I'm gonna do him one.

TOM: But it is agin' the law.

HUCK: It won't be the first time I done stuff that was agin' the law.

TOM: I won't let you do it; they hang people for stealin' slaves.

HUCK: Don't you say nothing you hear, or I'll tell Aunt Polly who put the snake in her bed.

TOM: You wouldn't do that. You don't snitch on your friends.

HUCK: This time I would. Old Mis' Watson is goin' to sell Jim down river. You don't know who might buy him.

TOM: I didn't know she was goin' to do that. Then I guess it is all right to help him escape.

HUCK: You better hightail it for home now, Tom, before people miss you.

T O M : You're right, I'll be seein' you. Good luck.

H U C K : Thanks, Tom.

J I M : Bye, Massa Tom.

T O M : Bye, Jim.

J I M : What we going to do 'till dark?

H U C K : I don't know. You got anything to eat?

J I M : Nope. Not a thing.

H U C K : That's too bad. I got the hungries.

J I M : I do too.

H U C K : I could sneak back into town and smouch some grub.

J I M : I wouldn't do that, you might get caught.

H U C K : That's true.

J I M : We can just lazy around here for a while. This is a good
safe place.

H U C K : I guess this is as good a place as any.

J I M : What you goin' to do after you gets rid of me?

H U C K : I guess I'll just float down the river.

J I M : How you goin' to live?

H U C K : Offen what I can steal I guess.

J I M : You don't got to do that, Massa Huck! You gonna be rich
some day, I knows.

H U C K : I ain't ever gonna be rich and you ain't neither.

J I M : I was once.

H U C K : You was?

J I M : Yep. Once I had two dollars saved up for when I got free.

H U C K : What did you do with it?

J I M : I invested it in stock.

H U C K : You mean like on the New York stock exchange.

J I M : What air you talkin' about? I mean stock.

H U C K : That's what I'm talkin' about.

J I M : Do you mean pigs and cows?

H U C K : No, I mean stock like business sell when they need
money to buy somethin'.

J I M : Well I's talkin' 'bout a cow I bought oncet.

H U C K : You bought a cow for two dollars?

J I M : No, I bought it from a friend of mine for a dollar and a half.

H U C K : It must have been some cow.

J I M : It was, even if she up and died on my hands.

H U C K : So you lost your dollar and a half.

J I M : Not all of it. I sold the hide to some feller for fifty cents.

H U C K : Then that left you a dollar.

JIM : Dats right. Dis time I didn't buy no stock. I was smart. I put it in the bank.

HUCK : Which bank?

JIM : The one dat's run by Sam, Massa Bradish's slave. He say dat everybody dat puts a dollar in de bank gets four mor' back at the end of the year. Well all the slaves in de neighborhood went together and put der money in de bank. Since I had more money dan all of dem I held out for more money.

HUCK : That was smart.

JIM : I thought so. I told dat Sam dat iffen I didn't get more den de rest of dem slaves I would start my own bank. Sam he say dat der whern't enough business for two banks so he agreed to give me thirty-five dollars at the end of the year.

HUCK : That sure made you a rich man.

JIM : Dats what I thought. So I thought dat I should spend some of my money. You know dat one-legged slave lives over by Free-port; well he have a big skinin knife dat I want. I tell him dat he ken have my thirty-five dollars for the knife.

HUCK : That must have been a good knife.

JIM : It was, so I take the knife and start to do a little whittlin' and you know what happens? Dat knife breaks in two.

HUCK : It looks like he got the best of that deal.

JIM : No he didn't. Sam told me the next day dat the bank went broke, so de one-legged slave didn't get nothing either.

HUCK : But you was broke.

JIM : No I wasn't. I kept a dime of dat money for good luck so as that wouldn't happen.

HUCK : That was smart.

JIM : I thought so, because the very next day a feller named Balaum comes by and tells me how the preacher tells him dat iffen you invest in the Lawd you gets your money back a hun-dred times. Well I tell you I didn't want to miss dat chance, so I do.

HUCK : Sure, I'm glad to hear that you're going to be rich at sometime or other, Jim.

JIM : So am I.

Noise is heard offstage.

HUCK : What's that? Hide Jim, it may be people looking for runaway slaves to sell into the Deep South.

J I M : You right.

> DUKE *and* KING *enter, running.* HUCK *hides when he sees the two.*

K I N G : This looks like a good place to stop.

D U K E : That it does.

K I N G : What got you into trouble?

D U K E : Well I had been selling an article to take the tartar off the teeth, and it does take it off, too, and generally the enamel along with it. I stayed about one night longer than I ought to, and was in the act of slidin' out when I ran into you. What happened to you?

K I N G : 'Bout the same as happened to you.

D U K E : What's your line?

K I N G : Journeyman printer by trade; do a little in patent medicines; theatre actor, mostly tragedy; and now and then take a turn to mesmerism and phrenology when there's a chance; teach singing, geography, school for a change. I do lots of things just so as it ain't work. What's your lay?

D U K E : I've done considerable in the doctoring way in my time. Layin' on o' hands is my best holt for cancer and paralysis, and sich things. I k'n tell fortune pretty good when I've got somebody along to find out the facts for me.

K I N G : How about you and me hitchin' up and see what we can do together?

D U K E : I ain't undisposed to that, iffen it means that I can get some money and don't have to work.

K I N G : That's just how I feel.

H U C K [*comes out of hiding*]: You gents lookin' for something?

K I N G : Why yes, we happen to be lookin for lodgin' for the night.

H U C K : This here is the only place unless you want to go into town.

D U K E : I don't think that we want to do that.

K I N G : Nor do I.

H U C K : Then you're welcome to stay here. Come on out, Jim.

J I M [*entering*]: Is it safe Massa Huck?

H U C K : I reckon it is. Where do you gentlemen hail from?

K I N G : Alas! Alas!

D U K E : What are you alassin' about?

K I N G : To think that I should have lived to be leading such a life, and be degraded down into such company. [*Begins to cry.*]

D U K E : Darn your skin, ain't the company good enough for you?

K I N G : Yes it is good enough for me; it's as good as I deserve; for who fetched me as low when I was so high? I did myself. I don't blame you gentlemen—far from it; I don't blame anybody, I deserve all I got. Let the old world do its worst; one thing I know—there's a grave somewhere for me. [*Bawls.*]

D U K E : We hain't done nothing to you.

K I N G : I know you haven't. I did it to myself. It's perfectly right that I should suffer. I brought myself down. [*Cries.*]

H U C K : Brought yourself down from where?

K I N G : You wouldn't believe me if I told you the secret of my birth. [*Cries louder.*]

J I M : The secret of your birth?

D U K E : The secret of your birth——

K I N G : Gentlemen, I will reveal it to you, for I feel I may have confidence in you. By rights I am a king.

D U K E : No! You don't mean it.

K I N G : It is true. My father was the King of Scandinavia. He was murdered by his brother who seized all the lands and estates of my father and drove me from the country.

J I M : Lawd almighty, is that true?

K I N G : It is, so help me.

D U K E : Looky here, I'm powerful sorry for you, but you ain't the only person that's had troubles like that.

K I N G : No?

D U K E : No you ain't. You ain't the only person that's been snaked down wrongfully out'n a high place.

K I N G : Alas—Hold! What do you mean?

D U K E : Kin I trust you?

K I N G : Till the bitter death. That secret of yours being——

D U K E : I am the late Duke of Orleans and the Dauphin.

K I N G : You are what?

D U K E : Yes, my friend, you are lookin' at the Dauphin. The son of the late Duke of Orleans and Marry Antonette.

K I N G : At your age—you mean King Arthur.

D U K E : Trouble has done it. It has brung these gray hairs and this premature balditude. You see before you in blue jeans and misery, the wanderin' exiled, trampled on, and sufferin' rightful Duke of Orleans and Dauphin.

JIM : Poor old man. I mean Dukeship, Your Highness, what do I call you?

DUKE : Your Majesty will do.

JIM : Your Majesty.

KING : You can call me Your Majesty, too.

JIM : Your Majesty too.

KING : Just Your Majesty.

JIM : Your Majesty. How can you be Your Majesty if he is?

HUCK : Because they are both of royal birth.

JIM : What has their birth got to do with it?

HUCK : They was born kings and dukes so that makes them majesties and that means that you call them Your Majesty.

JIM : Oh?

KING : You boys have a mighty fine place here.

HUCK : We like it.

KING : I was thinkin' that it would be good enough to stay in for a week or two.

JIM : We would be pleased to have your company.

HUCK : Course we 'hain't got no food and no money to buy any.

DUKE : That does present a problem.

KING : Not at all.

DUKE : How do you figure that?

KING : I will give one of my stellar performances to which we will charge admission.

DUKE : I call that using the old head Your Majesty.

KING : Thank you for the compliment.

DUKE : I have done some acting in my time. Is there a part for me?

KING : I don't know, let me hear you recite something.

DUKE : Four score and seven year ago our fathers brought forth a new younker conseved in liberty and I knew him well. Good night sweet prince and flights of angles sing thee to thy rest.

JIM : Dats good.

KING : Not bad. Think that there is a place for you in this stellar company. Here is a copy of the show; go and learn your part.

HUCK : I'd like to try my hand at actin'.

KING : What can you do?

HUCK : I know the pledge of allegiance.

KING : Let's hear it.

HUCK : I pledge allegiance to the flag of the United States of

America, and to the republic for which it stands, one nation indivisible——

KING: I don't think that you will make an actor.

HUCK: What can I do?

KING: You can take the money.

JIM: Can I do something?

KING: You can be a side attraction.

JIM: What is that?

HUCK: That means that people look at you before the play starts.

JIM: Oh dat sounds like fun.

HUCK: It is.

KING [going through his suitcase]: I think that I have a costume that will do.

HUCK: What are these posters from?

KING: From the last performance that I gave.

HUCK [reading]: Shakesperean Revival—wonderful attraction for one night only the world-renowned tragedians, David Garrick the younger of Drury Lane Theatre, London, and Edmun Kean the elder of the Royal Haymarket Theatre, Whitechapel, Pudding Lane, Piccadilly London, and the Royal Continental Theatres in the sublime Shakesperean Spectacle entitled the Balcony Scene in Romeo and Juliet—Romeo—Mr. Garrick, Juliet—Mr. Kean. Also the thrilling masterly and blood-curdling broadsword conflict in Richard the III—Richard III—Mr. Garrick, Richmond—Mr. Kean—Who are these people?

KING: Famous actors from England.

JIM: Are they going to be here?

KING: That's us.

JIM: I thought that you were Royality.

KING: Ah——

HUCK: They are. See here, the Royal Continental Theatre.

JIM: Are you going to do that sword fight?

KING: We are.

JIM: With real swords? I hain't never seen a broadsword.

KING: We won't use real swords—but wooden ones so as nobody won't get hurt.

HUCK: Ah, heck!

JIM: That's a good idea.

KING: Now if you go to the woods and get two sturdy saplings I will make the swords. Put some of these posters around while you are there.

JIM [*exits*]: Yes sir.

KING: Young man is that a runaway slave?

HUCK: No sir. He is mine.

KING: What is a boy like you doing with a slave?

HUCK: If he were a runaway slave, why is he going south?

KING: Good question. I guess that he is yours.

DUKE: I think that I am ready.

KING: Let me hear it.

DUKE: To be, or not to be; that is the bare bodkin
That makes clamity of so long life;
For who would fardel bear, till Birnam Wood do come to
Dunsinane, but that the fear something after death
Murders the innocent sleep,
Great Nature's second course,
And makes us rather along the arrows of outrageous for-
tune
Than fly to other that we know not of.

HUCK: Ooh, my.

KING: That's fine. I think that we are ready.

HUCK: Where are the people going to sit?

DUKE: In chairs. Where else?

HUCK: We don't have but one.

DUKE: That creates a problem.

KING: They can stand just as they did in Shakespeare's time. I think that we are ready.

JIM: I done everything that you told me to, Your Majesty. Here is them saplings.

DUKE: What are these for?

KING: You shall soon see my friend. Have you ever done any fencing?

JIM: I have, I put up fences all over Mis' Watson's farm.

HUCK: That was the lady that owned Jim afor I did.

DUKE: I reckon that I put up as many fences as the next man.

KING: Fencing doesn't mean putting up fences; it means fighting with swords.

DUKE: Well why didn't you say so. I done as much of that as the next man, too.

KING: Good! Shall we have a go at it?

DUKE: With real swords?

KING: No, with these saplings.

DUKE: Oh!

KING : Let us rehearse.

DUKE : I'm for that.

KING : Engard.

> *They fight over the stage. The DUKE obviously has never held a sword in his hand. The KING is the better although not much.*

DUKE : How am I doing? Ouch! Watch the point of that thing.

KING : You need a little practice. Watch me. Now you lunge like this——

> *He lunges after assuming the proper position.*

and you parry like this. And you advance like this.

> *He does.*

DUKE : I got you; how is this?

HUCK : Look out.

> *The DUKE gets tangled up in his own feet and trips.*

DUKE : Tarnation.

KING : Let us get ready for the performance. Huckleberry, get me my carpet bag.

HUCK : All right. Here it is.

KING : And this is your costume my good man.

> *He hands the DUKE a dress.*

DUKE : What is this for?

KING : That, my good man, is your costume.

DUKE : This?

KING : That.

DUKE : You won't get me into that thing. I ain't no sissy.

KING : That is your costume. I can see that you ain't no actor.

DUKE : Ain't no actor? I'll show you, gimmy that dress.

JIM : Do I get one of them costumes?

KING : Of course you do. And here it is.

JIM : That is a mighty fine costume. What is it?

HUCK : That is your king robe.

KING : That is right.

JIM : It looks like something that the undertaker at home would wear.

KING : That my good man was worn by the late King Arthur.

JIM : Really?

HUCK: More like the early King Arthur.

KING: Put it on and let us see how you look.

JIM: How do I look?

DUKE: You look ridiculous.

JIM: What dat mean?

HUCK: That means that you look fine.

JIM: What am I 'posed to do?

KING: You just walk around and look fierce.

JIM: Like dis?

KING: That will do fine.

JIM: Excuse me I gots to go and rehearse lookin' fierce.

DUKE: Quit complainin'. You don't have to wear this silly dress.

The DUKE *and* KING *go into the shack.*

CURTAIN

Scene 2

SCENE: *The same, a short time later.*

AT RISE: *Townspeople begin to enter.*

HUCK: We're almost ready folks.

FIRST TOWNSPERSON: Is this the place that them play actor fellers are goin' to be?

HUCK: This is the place. Just find a place to stand.

SECOND TOWNSPERSON: How come you ain't got no chairs?

HUCK: Because——

SECOND TOWNSPERSON: I don't like to have to stand around, I wants to sit.

HUCK: It was good enough for the people of Shakespeare's time, so as it ought to be good enough for you all.

THIRD TOWNSPERSON: Shakespeare. Who's he?

HUCK: Just the fellow that wrote the plays that is bein' performed.

SECOND TOWNSPERSON: I ain't never heard of the fellow.

HUCK: He's the great English playwright.

During the sequence more of the people have entered.

HUCK: Well I guess we are all here and we can start. If you

don't mind, I will pass among you and you can put your money in the hat.

FIRST TOWNSPERSON: You mean we got to pay to see this here play? I don't think that I am goin' to stay. Come on fellers, lets git.

HUCK: Don't you want to see Edmun Garrick the younger and David Kean the elder.

SECOND TOWNSPERSON: Who is they?

HUCK: The English actors that is playin' the play.

FIRST TOWNSPERSON: Feriners huh! What is they doin' so far away from home?

HUCK: They ise just passin' through on their way to St. Louis.

SECOND TOWNSPERSON: Well tell 'em to get busy actin'. They better be good. You tell 'em that too.

HUCK: No need to tell 'em that. They is.

SECOND TOWNSPERSON: They'ed better be.

HUCK: I guess they is ready. Come on fellers, begin the play.

> *The KING and DUKE enter. The DUKE is dressed in the dress. The KING in an old cape that looks like it had gone through a hammer mill.*

KING: Engard, you fool.

DUKE: Don't call me a fool. You old goat.

> *They begin to fight. The KING gets very serious and forgets himself.*

DUKE: Hey don't do that—it ain't in the play.

KING: I'll teach you to call me an old goat.

> *He starts to beat the DUKE, using the sword as a club.*

DUKE: Look out, that ain't nice.

FIRST TOWNSPERSON: That-a-way, old man, get 'em.

DUKE: Hey, that ain't in the script.

KING: I don't care. I am not an old goat.

> *By this time the KING is clubbing the DUKE vigorously.*

DUKE: Somebody stop him.

SECOND TOWNSPERSON: Hey fellers, that old codger really means what he is doin'. Somebody better stop 'em.

FIRST TOWNSPERSON: What for?

HUCK : Your Majesty, that ain't in the play—you had better get on with the next part.

KING : I must have forgotten myself, come along, we will do the next part. My lad get the chair and we will use it for the balcony.

JIM : I get it for you.

KING : Thank you, Your Majesty. That, my dear friends, is the King of Africa.

FIRST TOWNSPERSON : He looks more like a runaway slave making faces.

KING : Not at all he is merely askin' help for you all from his leader.

FIRST TOWNSPERSON : I still think that he is a runaway slave.

THIRD TOWNSPERSON : He sure looks like one.

KING : Gentlemen, please let me finish.

FIRST TOWNSPERSON : You are finished, my friend. Git that slave!

HUCK : Hide, Jim.

FIRST TOWNSPERSON : Simpson, get that slave, and hold him.

JIM : I ain't no slave, I is a freeman.

SECOND TOWNSPERSON : We'll soon see about that, you're coming with me.

FIRST TOWNSPERSON : I'm goin' too—you ain't get no reward without splitin' it with me.

SECOND TOWNSPERSON : Come along then.

The rest of the crew exits after them.

KING [*entering*]: Have they gone?

DUKE : I think so.

HUCK : They took Jim.

KING : They won't harm him because he is worth money, but they would have skinned us alive. I can't understand what happened.

HUCK : I got news for you. They didn't like you.

KING: Nonsense. They love me.

DUKE : That is a funny way to show love.

HUCK : Somebody is coming.

Whistling offstage.

DUKE: They're coming back.

    He hides.

KING: I think that you're right.

    TRAVELER *enters.*

HUCK: Howdy stranger.

TRAVELER: And the same to you.

HUCK: Where you goin'?

TRAVELER: To St. Louis to get an undertaker.

HUCK: An undertaker?

TRAVELER: That's right, old Peter Wilks died over by North Platte leven all kinds of money and two young daughters and nobody to look after them 'cept two uncles in England.

    DUKE *and* KING *enter at the mention of money.*

KING: Did you say that Peter Wilks died?

TRAVELER: I did.

KING: Alas.

DUKE: Huh?

KING [*poking him in the ribs*]: Alas we are too late.

DUKE: Huh?

TRAVELER: Are you Uncle Harvey Wilks?

KING: That I am.

TRAVELER: Then he must be Uncle Will the one who can't talk.

KING: That he is.

DUKE: Huh?

KING: That is all he can say, except for some strange noises.

DUKE: Huh?

TRAVELER: That is a shame. Then I suppose that you will be officiatin' at the funeral and I won't have to bring back the Preacher.

DUKE: Huh?

KING: I reckon that we will.

TRAVELELR: That's good, it's a hard journey for the Preacher.

KING: Could you tell me how to get to the town.

TRAVELER: Just keep headin' south and run right smak dab into it. Mary Jane and Susan will be glad to see you.

KING: I'm sure they will and we will be glad to see them too. It has been a long time?

T R A V E L E R : About fourteen years as I hear tell.

K I N G : That is right.

T R A V E L E R : I hope that your trip hasn't been too hard on you.

D U K E : No—oooffff.

The KING *hits him in the ribs with his elbow.*

K I N G : You see what I mean, only I can understand him. He says that the trip was very hard.

H U C K : Did you see any men along the road?

K I N G : We heard tales of highwaymen in St. Louis when we were there.

T R A V E L E R : They are around these parts. But I didn't see none. I only saw some men taken a runaway slave to Silas Phelps's place.

H U C K : Who is that?

T R A V E L E R : A farmer that lives just south of South Platte.

K I N G : If you will excuse us we are anxious to see our nieces before the day is out.

K I N G : Good-bye my friend and thank you for all the information.

T R A V E L E R : You're welcome and good luck to you all. [*Exits.*]

K I N G : Come on we got to go.

D U K E : Where?

K I N G: To get that money.

D U K E : How much money?

K I N G : I don't know but I bet it is plenty.

H U C K : I heard about old man Wilks, they say that he has money enough to light his cigars with five-dollar bills.

D U K E : I ain't never seen anybody with that much money.

K I N G : Come along and it will be ours.

D U K E : What do I got to do?

K I N G : Don't say nothin' remember you can't talk.

H U C K : Are we goin' to get Jim back?

K I N G : After we get the money.

H U C K : I'm with you if you promise to help me get Jim back.

K I N G : That is fair enough. Come along boys.

CURTAIN

Act Two

Setting for the Wilks's Farm

SCENE: *The* WILKS's *home.*

AT RISE: *A knocking is heard at the door.* MARY JANE *enters.*

M A R Y   J A N E : I'm coming, I'm coming. [*Opens the door.*] Oh it's you, Doctor. Come in, won't you?
D O C : Thank you, Mary Jane.

> DOC *enters with* KING *and* DUKE *in hand. There are three or four other men with him.*

D O C : These men say that they are your uncles from England.
M A R Y   J A N E : They could be, as I haven't seen them for many years.
K I N G : Mary Jane, I am your Uncle Harvey and this is your Uncle Will. We were so sorry to hear about Peter——
M A R Y   J A N E [*sobs*]: He wanted so much to see you.
K I N G : I know.
M A R Y   J A N E : Thank you, Doctor.
D O C : But Mary Jane, you don't know nothin' about them.
M A R Y   J A N E : They can't do anything to me as long as you're here.

D O C : That is true.

M A R Y   J A N E : We can question them and see if they are my real uncles.

D O C : I suppose that we can.

M A R Y   J A N E [to KING]: Now Uncle Will——

K I N G : Uncle Harvey. Uncle Will can't talk, and this is my servant, Huckleberry.

M A R Y   J A N E : That is right. How was the trip?

K I N G : Sea travel from England at this time of year is terrible.

M A R Y   J A N E : What do you do for a living?

K I N G : I am a preacher, you know that, Mary Jane.

M A R Y   J A N E : That is enough proof for me. Welcome Uncle Will and Uncle Harvey. Susan!

S U S A N [offstage]: What is it, Mary Jane?

M A R Y   J A N E : Come and meet your Uncles.

D O C : Mary Jane, you don't know if these are your uncles or not.

M A R Y   J A N E : I have enough proof.

S U S A N [entering]: Uncle Will.

D U K E : Huh——

S U S A N : Uncle Harvey. We are glad that you got here in time for father's funeral.

K I N G : So are we. May he rest in peace.

M A R Y   J A N E : We miss him so. I am glad that you are here now so that you can preach the sermon at the funeral.

D O C : Mary Jane, you don't know enough about these men.

M A R Y   J A N E : Doctor, I am tired of your accusations. As proof of my belief of them I shall give them father's money.

K I N G : May he rest in peace.

D O C : But look how they are dressed.

K I N G : I can explain that, my good man. On the highway from St. Louis, we were robbed of all our personal belongings. As we were traveling along the road two kind men gave us these old clothes.

D O C : How do I know that you are tellin' the truth?

K I N G : Would a preacher from England be dressed this poorly?

D O C : I guess not, but I still don't believe you. Don't worry I will be back with proof. [Exits.]

M A R Y   J A N E : Susan, this is Huckleberry—Uncle Will and Uncle Harvey's servant. Now I want you to go upstairs and get some of father's suits; we can't have them looking like a couple of tramps.

SUSAN: Yes, Mary Jane. [*Exits.*]

MARY JANE: I'll get father's money for you.

KING: Thank you, Mary Jane. We have to settle the estate as quickly as possible as we are due back in England soon.

MARY JANE: I understand. I'll be back in a minute.

KING: Everything is going smoothly.

DUKE: It is a good thing that you got rid of the Doctor.

KING: You are so right, my friend. He is going to cause us some trouble.

DUKE: Let us get the money and leave tonight.

KING: I want more than just the money that is in the house.

DUKE: How you goin' to get more than that money?

KING: I shall sell the house.

DUKE: You will what?

KING: Sell the house.

DUKE: You can't do that.

KING: And why not?

DUKE: Because it ain't legal.

KING: Oh, but it is. You see we as their uncles are the girls' legal guardians, and that means we can do anything with the girls' money that we want.

DUKE: But those poor little girls! Have a heart.

KING: I am without one where property is concerned.

DUKE: But what will they do when we go?

KING: The town will take care of them.

DUKE: I still don't like taking the money from them.

HUCK: Ssh—they're coming.

SUSAN [*entering*]: Who were you talking to Uncle Harvey?

KING: I was just praying to your father.

SUSAN: About money?

KING: I just told him not to worry about money, that we would take care of his two loving daughters.

SUSAN: Dear Father——

> She begins to cry.

KING: There, there, Susan.

> He begins to cry.

DUKE: Huh!

> He begins to cry.

MARY JANE [*entering*]: What is all the crying about?

KING: We were just thinking of your dear departed father.

MARY JANE [*begins to sniffle*]: Dear Father.

KING: To think that he is gone forever. My dear brother is no more.

Cries even louder.

MARY JANE: I brought his money for you to count, but I can see that this is no time to be counting money.

KING [*stops crying*]: Oh yes, the money.

MARY JANE: I can't ask you to do it now.

KING: That is all right, my dear, I will make the sacrifice for my dear departed brother.

MARY JANE: Not now, Uncle. It can wait.

KING: No, I insist that we get this unpleasant business done with and then we will be off to England.

MARY JANE: To England?

KING: That is right, you don't expect me to leave you here with no one to look after you do you?

MARY JANE: I didn't realize that we would go to England.

KING: But, my work is in England.

MARY JANE: I know, but this is my home, I don't know what to do with it.

KING: Don't worry your pretty little head about that, just leave everything to your Uncle Harvey.

MARY JANE: We can discuss our plans over supper, come Uncle Harvey.

They all exit except HUCK *and* SUSAN.

SUSAN: Did you ever see the King?

HUCK: Who? William the Fourth, you bet, I have—he goes to our church.

SUSAN: What—regular?

HUCK: Yes—regular. His pew's right over opposite ourn.

SUSAN: I thought that he lived in London.

HUCK: Well he does. Where would he live?

SUSAN: But I thought that you lived in Sheffield?

HUCK: Ah—I mean he goes to our church regular when he's in Sheffield. That is only in the summertime when he comes to take sea baths.

SUSAN : Sheffield ain't on the sea.

HUCK : Who said it was?

SUSAN : You did.

HUCK : I didn't neither.

SUSAN : You did too.

HUCK : I didn't.

SUSAN : You did.

HUCK : I never said nothin' of the kind.

SUSAN : Well, what did you say then?

HUCK : I said that the comes to Sheffield to take sea baths.

SUSAN : Well, how is he goin' to take sea baths if it ain't on the sea?

HUCK : Did you ever see any congress water?

SUSAN : Yes.

HUCK : Well, did you have to go to congress to see it?

SUSAN : Why no.

HUCK : Well, neither does William Fourth have to go to the sea to get a sea bath.

SUSAN : Well, how does he get it then?

HUCK : The way people here get congress water—in barrels. There in the palace in Sheffield they've got furnaces, and he wants his water hot. They can't bile that amount of water away off there at the sea. They haven't got no conveniences for it.

SUSAN : Well, why didn't you say so in the first place? Do you go to church regular too?

HUCK : Yes—regular.

SUSAN : Where do you set?

HUCK : In our pew.

SUSAN : Whose pew?

HUCK : Ourn—your Uncle Harvey's.

SUSAN : His'n—what does he want with a pew?

HUCK : Wants it to set in. What did you recon he want with it?

SUSAN : Why, I thought he'd be in the pulpit a preachin'.

HUCK : Ah—Why, blame it, do you suppose that there is only one preacher in that church?

SUSAN : What do they want with more?

HUCK : Why—to preach before the King. I never did see such a girl. They have no less than seventeen preachers.

SUSAN : Seventeen! My land! I'd never set out such a string— not if I never did get to glory. It must take 'em a week.

HUCK : Shucks, they don't all of 'em preach the same day—only one of 'em.

SUSAN : What do the rest of 'em do?

HUCK : Nothin' much. Loll around, pass the plate—and one thing or another. But mainly they don't do nothin'.

SUSAN : Then what are they for?

HUCK : Why they are for style. Don't you know nothin'?

SUSAN : I don't want to know such foolishness as that.

MARY JANE [entering]: Such foolishness as what?

SUSAN : He has been tellin me a pack of lies.

MARY JANE : Susan, that is no way to talk about our guests. You apologize to the young man.

SUSAN : Why?

MARY JANE : Because I said so. How would you feel if someone treated you like that when you were in a strange country?

SUSAN : I suppose I'm sorry, boy.

HUCK : You can call me Huck.

MARY JANE : What a strange name.

HUCK : It is short for Huckleberry.

SUSAN : That is a silly name.

HUCK : I know but I didn't have no choice in the matter.

MARY JANE : Very well. It is time for bed, Susan.

SUSAN : Aw, do I have to?

MARY JANE : I'll get you some blankets. Come along, Susan.

They exit.

HUCK : I'll be a flapdoodle if I'm going to let these old reptiles get that money from those nice girls.

KING [offstage]: Good night, girls.

DUKE : Let us count that money.

KING : An excellent idea.

MARY JANE : Here are some blankets for you. I'm sorry that we don't have a room for you to sleep in.

KING : That is all right.

MARY JANE : I wish that you would take my room.

KING : We wouldn't hear of it. Would we, Will?

DUKE : Huh.

MARY JANE : Very well, as you say.

KING : Now off to bed with you.

MARY JANE : Yes, Uncle. [Exits.]

KING : We will have to be careful. Keep your voice down or we will be found out.

DUKE : Let's take the money and get out of here.

HUCK : Let's get Jim.

KING : But, my friend, there are bigger stakes.

DUKE : Sometimes it is better not to be greedy and settle for the small stuff.

KING : Nonsense, my friend. Let us count the money.

DUKE : Holy pazausas!

KING : Ah, what lovely little pieces of paper. They can do so much.

DUKE : Quit the talk and count.

HUCK : Are we going to free Jim?

KING : Excellent. One for you and one for me.

DUKE : Hey, you only get one of those.

KING : Sorry, I forgot myself.

DUKE : Don't let it happen again.

KING : One for you and one for me.
　　　Two for you and two for me.
　　　Three for you and three for me.
　　　Four for me and four for me.
　　　Five for you and five for me.

DUKE : You did it again.

KING : You are too fast for me.

DUKE : Once more and I spill the beans to Mary Jane.

KING : Oh don't do that. I'll try to curb my natural instincts.

DUKE : You'd better. Count.

KING : Six for you and six for me.

DUKE : That makes six thousand dollars.

KING : That is right, my friend. We are rich men.

HUCK : Now can we get Jim.

DUKE : Something that I have been after all my life.

KING : Later, my boy.

DUKE : We'd better hide this stuff someplace.

KING : Right.

DUKE : How about under the chair?

KING : What happens if someone sits on the chair?

DUKE : I never thought of that.

KING : The only safe place is to sleep with it.

DUKE : Right. Hand it here.

KING : I had thought that I would keep it with me.

DUKE : I don't trust you. Hand it here.

KING : What, you don't trust me?

DUKE : Right, hand it here.

KING : Very well, here you are.

DUKE : Thank you my friend. Sleep tight.

KING : And don't let the bedbugs bite.

DUKE : Huh.

KING : Nothing my friend, good night.

> HUCK *waits until they are snoring loudly and then creeps out and reaches for the money. The* DUKE *almost wakes up.* HUCK *tries again, the same thing happens. Again with the same result. Finally,* HUCK *gets the money. He doesn't know where to hide it. The* KING *about wakes up, causing* HUCK *to hide the money under the hat.* HUCK *flops on a blanket. The* DUKE *reaches for the money in his sleep, not finding it, he wakes up.*

DUKE : Wake up, you thief.

KING : Huh—What——

DUKE : Don't pretend to be asleep with me. Where is that money you thief?

KING : What money?

DUKE : Don't play stupid, you know what I am talkin' about.

KING : I haven't the slightest idea what you are talkin' about.

DUKE : You don't, huh? Well let me refresh your memory for you. We counted the money that Mary Jane gave us. You gave it to me, after trying to cheat me out of my share. I didn't say nothin' and then I went to sleep with it under my bed. Then you waited for me to fall asleep and then you took it from me.

KING : I did no such thing.

DUKE : You did.

KING : I did not.

DUKE : Don't lie to me. I know that you did it.

KING : Are you questioning my honesty?

DUKE : You might say that, since I called you a liar.

KING : No one calls me that and gets away with it.

> *He takes a swing at the* DUKE *and misses.*

DUKE : Oh you want to fight do you, well you had better learn to do better than that. I will be glad to give you a few lessons without charge.

> He and the KING get into a good fight, knocking over chairs, lamps, etc.

HUCK : Help! Help!

MARY JANE [entering]: What is going on here.

KING : Your Uncle Will was just having a nightmare.

MARY JANE : Oh the poor man. There, there, Uncle Will, no one is going to hurt you.

DUKE : Huh . . .

MARY JANE : You just go back to sleep. Mary Jane will take care of you.

> She leads him over to his bed and puts his head in her lap.

KING : That is kind of you, Mary Jane. He gets so frightened when he has these dreams. He almost goes out of his head.

DUKE : Ummmm–huh.

KING : You see what I mean. He doesn't even recognize his own kin.

MARY JANE : The poor man.

KING : I just don't know what to do with him. I think that I should put him in an insane asylum.

DUKE : Huh–ummhumm [mumbling incoherently].

KING : But he is my own kin.

MARY JANE : I wouldn't do that if I were you, Uncle Harvey.

KING : I just don't know what to do.

> There is a violent knocking at the door.

MARY JANE : Now who could be calling at this hour? Who is it?

DOC : It's me, Doctor Parsons.

MARY JANE : I'm coming.

> She opens the door. In comes the DOC and several other men, including the TRAVELER.

DOC : Are they still here?

MARY JANE : If you mean my uncles, they are.

DOC : Good, they are frauds and so is that boy that they have with 'em.

MARY JANE : Doctor, we went through all this once this afternoon.

DOC : I know, and I said that I would be back if I found out anything and I have.

MARY JANE : Nonsense. I won't listen to anything that you have to say.

DOC : You will, Mary Jane Wilks. It was me who brought you into this world and I feel responsible toward you now that your father is dead, rest his soul.

KING : Amen.

DOC : You be quiet, you fraud.

MARY JANE : How do you know that they are frauds?

DOC : You know Jud Lewis don't you?

MARY JANE : I know him and I know of his reputation as a drunk.

KING : Please, Mary Jane, such words from your lips?

MARY JANE : I'm sorry but it is true.

DOC : That may be so but I'd believe him over these two strangers.

MARY JANE : They aren't strangers—they are my uncles.

DOC : They ain't neither.

KING : Let him show his proof that comes from a drunk.

DOC : Go ahead, Jud.

TRAVELER : Well I seen these two fellers and a kid just after I seen you fellers takin' that runaway slave over to Silas Phelps's place.

KING : The man speaks the truth. We did meet him on the road and asked him for directions.

TRAVELER : They did ask me for directions and a lot of other things too, like all about your dad. May he rest in peace.

KING : Amen.

MARY JANE : Is this true, Uncle?

KING : It is, every word of it, but wouldn't you expect me to ask about my relative who I have not seen in fourteen years?

MARY JANE : I would have thought you to be unhuman if you didn't.

DOC : I don't believe you.

KING : You mean that you don't believe a man of the cloth?

> *Crosses to* DOC *and picks up hat and the money falls out.*
> SUSAN *begins to pick up the money.*

What is this?

MARY JANE: This is my money.

DOC: What is it doin' there?

DUKE: So that is——

DOC: What did you say?

DUKE: Huh—ummhumm [*mumbling incoherently*].

KING: Nothing.

DOC: I heard him say "so that is."

MARY JANE: Uncle Will, you can talk.

DOC: Mary Jane, no man who has been dumb from birth can talk like that.

MARY JANE: Maybe it was a miracle.

DOC: Miracles like that don't happen.

DUKE: It was all his idea.

DOC: What do you mean?

DUKE: It was his idea that we should come here and take the girls' money.

DOC: What kind of monsters are you? Taking girls' money.

KING: Don't believe him. He stole the money and put it in here.

DUKE: I didn't—you stole it from me.

KING: He is lying to save his own skin.

DUKE: You call me a liar.

> *He makes a break for the* KING *and gets in one good punch.*

DOC: Stop him.

SUSAN: Where is Huck?

DUKE: He is the one who stole it and you let him get away.

DOC: He won't get far. Come along to the sheriff.

DUKE: You'd better find that boy.

DOC: Don't worry about the boy. If you're smart you will worry 'bout yourself. You know what we do to people who try and fool us?

KING: What?

DOC: Did you ever hear of tar and feathers? Off to the sheriff's.

MARY JANE: Oh thank you, Doctor.

DOC: Good night, girls.

KING, DUKE, DOC, *and* TRAVELER *exit.*

MARY JANE : Well, all our money is here. Thank goodness.

SUSAN : I wonder where that boy is?

HUCK [*putting his head through the window*]: I'm here.

MARY JANE : You! Susan, get the sheriff.

HUCK : The sheriff? Why?

MARY JANE : That's right, for trying to steal our money.

HUCK : But I was the one who hid it where you could find it.

SUSAN : You did?

HUCK : Yes.

MARY JANE : Thank you, Huck.

HUCK : You're welcome. I just didn't want those two old reptiles to hurt you.

MARY JANE : What are you going to do now?

HUCK : Free Jim.

SUSAN : Jim?

HUCK : My friend who was captured.

MARY JANE : Captured? By who?

HUCK : By someone named Phelps.

MARY JANE : Silas Phelps? That nice man.

HUCK : That's right. Where does he live?

SUSAN : Take the north road out of town and you run right into his farm.

HUCK : Thanks, bye. [*Exits.*]

CURTAIN

Act Three

Setting for the Phelps's Farm

SCENE: *The PHELPS'S farm.*

H U C K : Pssst—Tom.

T O M : How's that? Who are you?

H U C K : It's me, Huck Finn.

T O M : You're dead.

H U C K : I ain't neither.

T O M : I know you is. You was murdered.

H U C K : I was?

T O M : That's right.

H U C K : But I ain't dead.

T O M : You is.

H U C K : I ain't neither—if I was how could I talk to you?

T O M : Maybe you is a ghost.

H U C K : I hain't no ghost.

T O M : Honest Injun?

H U C K : Honest Injun.

T O M : I don't believe you.

H U C K : You can pinch me and you'll see that I ain't.

T O M : Can I?

Crosses and pinches HUCK.

H U C K : Yow! There! You see I ain't dead.

T O M : Back home we all thought that you was dead. I thought that your paw done it 'cause he disappeared right after you left and ain't been seen since.

H U C K : Well I ain't—I just been on a trip.

T O M : What you doin' at my Uncle Silas's?

H U C K : I come to get Jim.

T O M : Jim who?

H U C K : Mis' Watson's Jim.

T O M : But he run away.

H U C K : I know, he was with me till he up and got caught.

T O M : And he is here?

H U C K : This is where I heard that he was took. I aim to get him back.

T O M : How you goin' to do that?

H U C K : Don't rightly know yet. I suppose that I will have to steal him.

T O M : But he is free.

H U C K : What you say?

T O M : You want some help?

H U C K : You mean to say that you would help me steal Jim back?

T O M : That's what I said.

H U C K : Then you are no better than a slave thief and that is worser'n a horse thief.

T O M : I know but I wants to do it on a count of our friendship. Now here's what we do——

A U N T   S A L L Y : Who's that out there?

T O M : Run——

A U N T   S A L L Y : That you, Tom?

H U C K : Yes, mam.

A U N T   S A L L Y : You don't look as much like your mother as I expected.

H U C K : Yes, mam.

A U N T   S A L L Y : I am so glad to see you, it do seem that I could eat you up.

H U C K : Yes, mam.

A U N T   S A L L Y : You had breakfast?

H U C K : Yes, mam. I had it on the boat.

A U N T   S A L L Y : Now sit down and tell me all about the folks.

H U C K : Well, they is——

U N C L E : What happened to the boat.

H U C K : She blowed——

A U N T S A L L Y : How's your maw?

H U C K : She is——

U N C L E : The boat blowed what?

H U C K : A cylinder head.

A U N T S A L L Y : How is your paw?

H U C K : He is——

U N C L E : Blowed a cylinder head?

H U C K : That's right.

A U N T S A L L Y : And your sis, how is she?

H U C K : She is——

U N C L E : Anybody killed?

H U C K : No, nobody that amounted to much.

A U N T S A L L Y : Will you give the boy a chance to talk.

U N C L E : He is talkin'. It's you that is askin' all the questions.

A U N T S A L L Y : Well don't you want to find all the news about the family? Lawd, I never did see such a man.

U N C L E : Hesh up woman an' give the boy a chance to talk.

They wait for HUCK *to say something but nothing comes.*

U N C L E : About the accident, boy?

H U C K : Well, she blowed a cylinder head and we had to get towed into the wharf.

U N C L E : That was lucky because sometimes when them things blow, people get hurt.

A U N T S A L L Y : Where's your suitcase, boy?

H U C K : I hid it down by the wharf.

S I L A S : What in tarnation for?

H U C K : Didn't want to carry it.

A U N T S A L L Y : Hitch up the wagon and go and get it.

H U C K : No need to do that. I know a short cut. I can be back before you get hitched up.

S I L A S : I can take you boy.

H U C K : I can go by myself.

S I L A S : All right—come on Sally let's go finish the dishes.

They exit.

H U C K : Tom—Tom.

T O M : Here, Huck.

HUCK : Boy was that close.

TOM : I don't know.

HUCK : I had to tell some pretty fancy stories.

TOM : Come on, let's go to the house and get somethin' to eat.

HUCK : There's just one hitch.

TOM : What's that?

HUCK : Your Aunt and Uncle think that I am you.

TOM : They do?

HUCK : That's right.

TOM : Now ain't that the stupidest thing that you ever heard?

HUCK : Yep, but they think that I'm you. You got to be someone that they haven't seen for a long time.

TOM : I'll be my brother Sid.

HUCK : That is a good idea.

TOM : Come on, let's go.

HUCK : Hold on. What you doin' here?

TOM : I come to see them.

HUCK : Does they know you was comin'?

TOM : Huck Finn, have you gone off your head?

HUCK : I'm just trying to make you think of some lies to tell your Aunt and Uncle.

TOM : Don't worry about me. I won't get caught.

HUCK : Just see that you don't—I don't want nobody to bungle gettin' Jim out.

TOM : Don't worry about me. We'll get Jim all right.

AUNT : Tom is that you?

TOM : That is just——

HUCK *kicks* TOM *to make him shut up.*

HUCK : It's me, Aunt Sally.

AUNT : Who you got with you?

TOM : It's me, Aunt Sally.

AUNT : Who is me?

TOM : Sid Sawyer.

AUNT : Really I didn't know you were comin' too. Silas, come here, we got more company.

UNCLE : Who's here?

AUNT : Sid.

UNCLE : Well, I'll be a tadpole. We didn't know that you was comin'.

T O M : I didn't neither 'till after Tom left. Then I carried on so that maw said I could come just to shut me up.

U N C L E : We is mighty glad to have you all here. Come in and set a spell and tell us about the trip.

T O M : Hain't much to tell, it was uneventful as you might say.

U N C L E : Tom here had quite a trip.

T O M : What happened to him?

H U C K : I'll tell you about it sometime.

A U N T : Would you like somethin' to eat?

T O M : I guess I would. I ain't et since supper last night.

AUNT SALLY *exits.*

H U C K : You got a runaway slave, Uncle Silas?

U N C L E : Yep, caught him with some actor fellers. How did you know?

H U C K : Heard it in town.

T O M : What you goin' to do with him?

U N C L E : Hold him until his rightful owners come.

H U C K : Can I see him?

U N C L E : What you want to do that for?

H U C K : I ain't never seen a runaway slave.

U N C L E : I guess it won't do no harm. He's in here. [*Points to shack.*] I'll just go up to the house and see what happened to the food. [*Exits.*]

H U C K : How we goin' to free Jim?

T O M : Let me think.

H U C K : How 'bout stealin' the key from Uncle Silas and runnin'.

T O M : That is too simple. We got to think of somethin' better than that.

H U C K : Maybe there is a loose board on the shed that iffen we pulled it off Jim could crawl through.

T O M : It's as simple as tit-tat-toe, three in a row, and playin' hooky from school. I should hope that we can think of somethin' harder than that.

H U C K : Maybe we can saw him out.

T O M : That's better—it's real mysterious and troublesome, and good. I bet we can find a way that's twice as long. There ain't no hurry. Jim ain't goin' no place.

H U C K : What do you mean, we ain't in no hurry?

T O M : I know! We will dig him out.

H U C K : What?

T O M : We will dig him out, that ought to take about a week. Too bad there ain't a night watchman.

H U C K : What do you want a night watchman for?

T O M : Because, so as we can give him a sleeping mixture. Look for a file.

H U C K : What do you want a file for?

T O M : To saw the chain offen Jim's leg.

H U C K : Why don't you just lift the leg of the bed and slip the chain offen it?

T O M : You can get up the infant-schooliest ways of goin' at a thing. Why hain't you ever read any books at all?—Who ever heard of getting a prisoner loose in such an old-maidy way as that? No, the way all the best authorities does is to saw the bed-leg in two and leave it just so and swallow the sawdust, so it can't be found, and put some dirt and grease around the sawed place so the very keenest can see no sign. Then the night you're ready, fetch the leg a kick, down she goes; slip off the chain, and there you are. Nothin' to do but hitch your rope ladder to the battlements, shin down——

H U C K : Rope ladder, what the nation does Jim need a rope ladder for?

T O M : To get down the battlements to the moat.

H U C K : Moat?

T O M : I wish we had time to dig one of them. Maybe if things go good we can dig one.

H U C K : What do we want with a moat when we is goin' to snake Jim out under the cabin?

T O M : I suppose you're right. Take too much time anyway.

H U C K : How is we goin' to get a rope ladder?

T O M : Make it from one of Aunt Sally's sheets.

H U C K : Oh, no, we ain't goin' to do that. I ain't goin' to steal nothin' from her.

T O M : We ought to have some spoons to dig with. Get them when you steal the sheet. Better get three.

H U C K : I ain't stealin' nothin' from Aunt Sally.

T O M : We can smuggle the spoons in with the rope ladder.

H U C K : I see that the only way that we is goin' to get Jim free is to do it your way.

T O M : I'm going to send Uncle Silas this warnin' note that a band of thieves is goin' to steal Jim.

UNCLE *enters unseen by* TOM.

H U C K : Umph. Umph.

T O M : Uncle Silas, Uncle Silas, here is a note we found on the shack door.

U N C L E : Listen to this. Don't betray me, I wish to be your friend. There is a desperate gang of cutthroats from over in Indian Territory going to steal your runaway slave tonight. They will sneak down from the north, along the fence at midnight exact. I am to be off a piece and blow a tin horn iffen anybody comes; instead of that I will be like a sheep to let you know that they are here. If they do suspect something will raise a whoopjamboree-hoo to let you know that the plan is off. Unknown friend. Well, what do you make of that?

A U N T : What is the matter?

U N C L E : This note, so help me I don't know how it got there. There is somethin' mighty strange goin' on around this place. I'm goin' to get the neighbors.

H U C K : I already got a ladder made and a shirt too.

T O M : Now to get them to Jim.

H U C K : What are you goin' to do with a shirt?

T O M : It is for Jim to write his journal on.

H U C K : Don't you know that Jim can't write?

T O M : I know but that don't make no difference, prisoners got to have a journal. 'Sides who ever heard of readin' a prisoner's journal?

H U C K : What does they write them for?

T O M : So as people know what happened to the prisoner.

H U C K : It do seem like a waste of time.

T O M : Do you want me to help you get Jim free or not?

H U C K : I do, but there ought to be a simpler way.

T O M : Of course there is, but they ain't mysterious enough. I got some snakes and spiders and maybe a few rats for Jim to make friends with.

H U C K : What did you do with them?

Scream is heard from the house.

T O M : We is in for it now. I had them under the bed in our room.

H U C K : That was a fool thing to do.

AUNT SALLY *enters running.*

A U N T : There is a snake in your room.

T O M : I know, I put him there.

A U N T : What in tarnation for?

T O M : He is a pet of mine I take him every place I go.

A U N T : He can't sleep in the house.

T O M : Where then?

A U N T : In the barn. Now you march right up there and get him.

T O M : Yes, Aunt Sally.

TOM *and* AUNT SALLY *exit to the house.*

H U C K : Jim.

J I M : Over here, Huck.

H U C K : Tom and me's goin' to free you.

J I M : What took you so long?

H U C K : Tonight at midnight.

J I M : You is?

H U C K : Yep, I brought this sheet for the rope ladder and this shirt
for you to write your journal on.

J I M : I can't write—you know that.

H U C K : I figured as much but Tom thinks that it's important for
you to keep a journal.

J I M : What for?

H U C K : Dinged if I know. He seems to think that you got to have
a journal because all famous prisoners had one.

J I M : But I ain't a famous prisoner.

H U C K : That don't make no difference to Tom.

T O M : Huck.

H U C K : I got to go.

T O M : Where you been?

H U C K : Talkin' to Jim and I gave him the shirt.

T O M : He got anything to write with?

H U C K : I don't guess.

T O M : Well how is he goin' to keep a journal if he don't got
nothin' to write with?

H U C K : That ain't my problem.

T O M : Are you goin' to start complainin' again?

H U C K : Nope I wasn't complainin', ole buddy.

T O M : Come on, I got somethin' that Jim can use.

HUCK : What?

TOM : I got a needle from Aunt Sally.

HUCK : How's he goin' to use a needle?

TOM : Come on and see. Hey, Jim.

JIM : Hi ya, Massa Huck. You back, Huck?

HUCK : I forgot to give you somethin' to write your journal with.

TOM : Here, use this needle, Jim.

JIM : How?

TOM : Poke your finger and use the blood on the shirt.

JIM : You boys is sure goin' to a lot of trouble to get me out.

TOM : It ain't nothin'.

JIM : I wish you wouldn't do all this for me.

TOM : We want to.

JIM : That is mighty nice of you.

TOM : Well aren't you goin' to start on your journal?

JIM : Not just now.

TOM : Come on Jim, you got to do it.

JIM : Not just now, but I will. I promise.

TOM : Okay, come on, Huck, we got to get ready for tonight. We got to do something.

HUCK : What we goin' to do?

TOM : Free Jim right now.

HUCK : But the plan don't call for that until midnight.

TOM : I know but I didn't figure on all those neighbors.

HUCK : Come on Jim, let's go.

JIM : You back again?

TOM : Come on Jim, let's go. I'll get the chain.

JIM : Is it midnight already?

HUCK : No, but Uncle Silas called in all the neighbors so we got to change our plans.

TOM : Just let me get the chain off the bed.

JIM : Just bring the bedpost.

TOM : Come on Jim, let's go.

UNCLE : There they go. After 'em.

> *Shouts offstage.* TOM *and* HUCK *and* JIM *running across the stage.*

TOM : They went the other way. Come on, let's head for the river.

JIM : I's with you Massa Tom.

UNCLE : There they go. I'll stop them.

Offstage a shot rings out. TOM *falls.*

TOM : Oh, they got me. I'm dyin'.
JIM : This here nonsense has gone too far. Missy Phelps!
AUNT [*entering*]: Who called me?
JIM : I did.
AUNT : What you want?

Seeing TOM.

Sid, what is the matter?
JIM : He was shot and is dying.
AUNT : Shot! Gracious. Oh Sid!
HUCK : He ain't neither dying, he was only shot in the leg.
TOM : I am too dying.
AUNT : Sid, you ain't goin' to die. Tom is right.
UNCLE : What is the matter?
TOM : I been shot.
UNCLE : What?
TOM : I was tryin' to help Jim escape and I got shot. I'm dying
and I want to confess.
UNCLE : Confess?
TOM : Yes, Old Mis' Watson died and in her will she made Jim a
freeman.
UNCLE : You mean this here slave is a freeman?
TOM : That's right. His owner died and felt so bad about threatin'
to sell him down river that she set him free.
JIM : You mean I's free?
TOM : That's right, Jim.
JIM : Glory be!
HUCK : Then he ain't a runaway slave.
TOM : That's right.
HUCK : Why didn't you tell us before, Tom?
TOM : Ain't nobody goin' to get me a doctor? I'm dyin'.
UNCLE : Let me have a look at that wound.

Crosses to TOM *and looks.*

There ain't nothin' wrong with you. You will just be a little sore
for a while.
HUCK : Then you knowed all along that Jim was free?

T O M : Somebody get me a doctor. Yes, I knowed.

A U N T : And you didn't tell 'em, then it serves you right gettin' shot.

H U C K : Aunt Sally, do I have to go back and——

U N C L E : If Mis' Watson died, there is no place for you to stay.

A U N T : Then he can stay here with us.

U N C L E : That is a good idea. The school is just down the road. It'll do him good.

H U C K : No, I ain't goin' to stay here. I don't want to go to school. I don't want to be civilized. [*Exits.*]

J I M : I get him. Don't worry, when I gets through with him, he'll be glad to go to school.

H U C K : Aw right, aw right. Aunt Sally, I reckon I'll be happy to stay.

U N C L E : That's a good boy.

A U N T : Good, sit down, let's get started.

H U C K : Do I have to?

A U N T : Yes. Now spell cat.

H U C K : K–a–t!

T O M : You'll never teach him anything.

A U N T : Now, Huck, spell school.

H U C K : S–c–h–o–o–l.

CURTAIN

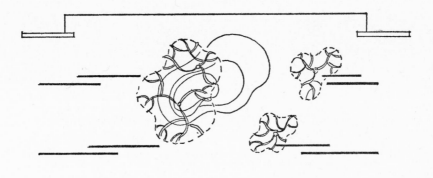

Floor Plan for a Woodland Thicket

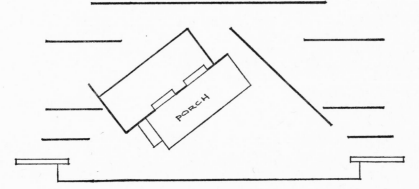

Floor Plan for the Wilks's Farm

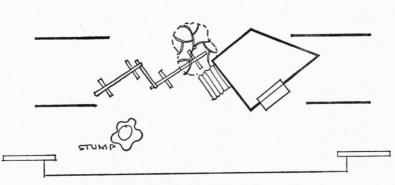

Floor Plan for the Phelps's Farm

The Strolling Players

A PLAY FOR CHILDREN
BASED ON THE TRADITIONAL
CHARACTERS OF THE
COMMEDIA DELL' ARTE

BY

Darwin Reid Payne

AND

Christian Moe

Cast of Characters

PANTALONE *Master of the House*

COLOMBINA *Serving maid to Pantalone*

ARLECCHINO *Servant to Pantalone*

THE DOCTOR *A foolish pedant*

CAPTAIN BOMBASTO *A boasting soldier*

MISTRESS LOVAJESTA *Keeper of a wayside inn*

1ST MUSICIAN (Also 1ST GYPSY)

2ND MUSICIAN (Also 2ND GYPSY)

MAYOR OF THE TOWN

TOWNSPEOPLE

TIME : The 17th century

PLACE : A town square someplace in Europe

The action of the play is continuous

PROPERTY LIST

Handbell
Ornate walking staff
Large purse of gold on belt
Lantern
Nightcap and nightgown
Feather duster
Tray with wine bottle and
glasses
Young boy's costume for dis-
guise
Apple tree branches with ap-
ples attached
Wooden staff
Small rug
Basket of apples
Cart with troupe's equipment
Swat stick
Long straw
Bundles and large picnic bas-
ket, prop food inside

A number of large books
Map which unfolds to about 4
feet by 6 feet
Nightcap and nightgown
Rapier-type sword
Floppy soft hat with floppy
feather
Recorder
Various simple percussive in-
struments
Property rock, large enough
for two people to stand
Cloaks with hoods
Cutout of sun on long stick
with SUN written on it
Cutout of new moon on long
stick

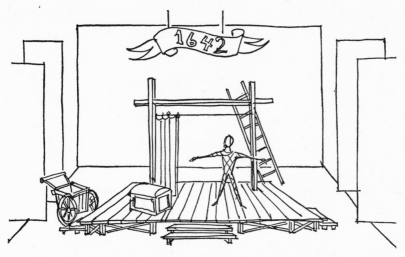

Setting for a Wooden Stage in the City Square

SCENE: *A town square in 17th-century Europe around which can be seen the suggestive outlines of local dwellings. In the center of the square stands a large crude wooden scaffold backed by four tall wooden posts connected by a crossbar. There is a set of steps on both sides and the front of the platform. The platform serves to support the city fathers during town meetings and also doubles as a makeshift stage whenever troupes of strolling players come to town.*

AT RISE: *The curtain opens on an empty stage. A moment later the* MAYOR *enters and goes to the platform. He rings a bell that he carries in his hand.*

MAYOR: Here ye, all citizens of the town. Come from your houses for the news I have to tell! Hear ye, all citizens of the town!

From various parts of the stage the citizens enter. The MAYOR *steps down from the platform and advances to the front of the stage.*

And for you who are visitors to our city in this happy month of May of the year 1642, I bid you a most cordial welcome. [*To all.*] My news is this: Every year at this time, a band of strolling players passes through our city. For only one day they stay with us before they continue their journey through the world.

1 ST CIT : But on that day, such things you have never seen!

2 ND CIT : Songs . . .

3 RD CIT : Dances . . .

1 ST CIT : And plays filled with bright laughter.

2 ND CIT : So that all the town and countryside around rocks with happy sounds.

MAYOR : Yes, all this the strolling players bring with them, for this is their life—traveling from small village to great city, stopping wherever a group of people meet and setting up their little stage.

1 ST CIT : There's Arlecchino who plays such pranks and jokes.

2 ND CIT : And Columbina who tries to catch him.

3 RD CIT : And Master Pantalone who tries to catch them both!

The townspeople laugh.

MAYOR : And today, here in our city square, they will perform.

The people cheer the news.

[*To the audience.*] Will you wait here with us till they come?

1 ST CIT : Shhh! Listen!

There is a distant sound of drum and recorder.

2 ND CIT : I hear them now!

3 RD CIT : And I can see them! They are coming through the city gate!

MAYOR : My friends, make way! Make way all! The strolling players are . . . HERE!

The troupe marches onto the stage led by the Master of the Players, PANTALONE. Behind him comes a drummer and a boy playing a recorder. Then comes the troupe's cart pushed by ARLECCHINO. After him walks the DOCTOR, COLOMBINA, the MISTRESS, and the CAPTAIN. The troupe marches completely around the platform leaving the cart behind. The musicians quickly begin the task of setting up the makeshift stage and putting out the various pieces of equipment necessary to the performance. While this is being done, the MAYOR *welcomes the Master of the Players.*

MAYOR : Good sir, we of this town welcome you with great joy.

He makes a courtly bow.

PANT : It is with pleasure that we once more play before you and your gracious citizens.

He also makes a grand bow to all. The townspeople applaud and cheer.

But I see many strangers among you this year.

MAYOR : Oh, yes, all these people have never been to our town before today, nor have ever seen your company play.

PANT : Ah, then, I must introduce our troupe of players before we start our play.

He claps his hands and the players quickly range themselves across the platform and on both side steps leading to it.

First, may I introduce myself.

[*Sings.*] I am Pantalone and my greatest love is gold.
    But happiness it will not seem to buy.
    For as my wealth grows larger, my sadness does grow too.
    I'm rich yet all I seem to do is cry.
    Boo-hoo-hoo.

He bows.

This gentleman is the Doctor of our play.

DOCTOR [*sings*]:
    Here stands a learned Doctor, long words are my delight.
    Still, I cannot seem to ever get things straight.
    And when it comes to problems like how much is 2 and 2,
    My brain will never ever calculate.

He bows.

PANT : And this is Captain Bombasto.

CAPT [*sings*]:
    A gallant captain I, Bombasto is my name.
    I'm brave and strong and handsome as you see.

I love to tell tall stories of my deeds of derring-do.
But the truth is I am rather cowardly.

He bows.

P A N T : And this is our famous Colombina.

C O L O M [*sings*]:
My name is Colombina, I serve my master well.
My duties are to keep the household neat.
But though I pay attention to all my household chores,
I must confess I'd rather play than eat.

She bows.

P A N T : And this . . .

M I S T R E S S :
Is Auntie Lovajesta, I'm the Mistress of the inn.
A better inn you'll not find on this earth.
And just like Colombina who also is my niece,
My life is filled with jokes and tricks and mirth.

She bows.

P A N T : And, of course, no play would be complete without that greatest of all rascals, ARLECCHINO! [*He looks around.*] But where is the rogue?

From over the top of the curtain pops up ARLECCHINO.

A R L E : Here! Always where you least expect him! That is where you'll always find me! [*Sings.*]
Here is Arlecchino, the master of all rogues.
Beware when I begin to make a jest.
My brain's so filled with mischief that I have to laugh out loud.
At making jokes you must admit I'm best.

At this the townspeople laugh and applaud.

P A N T : So that is all our troupe. . . .

I S T M U S C : But Master Pantalone! You've forgotten us.

2 N D M U S C : You always do, you know.

P A N T : So I have! These, good people [*he puts his arms around the musicians' shoulders*], are most important persons in our troupe. [*The musicians beam.*] They make our music. . . .

I S T M U S C [*eagerly*]: And sometimes play a part or two.

2 N D M U S C : That's what I like most, to put a mask on my face and a cloak about my shoulders.

1 s t   m u s c : Then, in a twinkle of an eye, we're anyone we choose to be!

They bow; the audience applauds.

m a y o r [*to the townspeople*]: Quickly, take your seats in the square [*indicating offstage right and left*] so that the play may begin without further delay.

The townspeople exit.

p a n t : Now we are ready! And may our play bring you all great delight.

> *He bows and then retires behind a side curtain. The musicians play a sprightly little tune by way of an overture.* colombina *comes through the center curtain and begins dusting with her feather duster.*

c o l o m [*sighs*]: Work, work, work! I never seem to finish. And it's twice as hard in Master Pantalone's house because he is always so sad. [*She pulls a long face.*] It is much easier to work in a happy house. But morning, noon, and night, glum, glum, glum. And try as I can, I can't seem to make him happy or laugh. I dance for him [*she does a step*] and sometimes sing a song or two—and I dearly love to pull a good joke. Nothing seems to work. [*Sighs.*] Ah, well, no matter what, I'll not let him keep my spirits down.

> *She sings as she resumes her work.* arlecchino *pokes his head through the center curtain and puts his finger to his lips for the audience to keep silence about his presence. Quietly he tiptoes through the curtain and secretly steals behind* colombina. *Then, with his slapstick, he swats her. Her surprise sends him into gales of laughter.*

c o l o m : Oh! . . .

a r l e : How do you do, my Colombina?

c o l o m : You rascal! How dare you pull your tricks on me. I'll give you something you aren't looking for.

a r l e : Come, come—that's just my way of saying "Good morning."

c o l o m [*winds up her arm and brings the feather duster down on top of his head, sending him sprawling on the floor*]: And that is my way of saying "Good night."

ARLE: Ohhh . . . you've broken my head!

COLOM: Then mind you don't get sawdust all over my clean floor.

ARLE: Ohhh . . . help me. . . .

COLOM: I'll help you with the end of my foot.

ARLE [*getting up*]: Well, while you are busy kicking people about, why don't you give that Captain Bombasto a little help out the door—

He mimes a kick.

COLOM [*coquettishly*]: Captain Bombasto? Why, what ever do you mean?

ARLE: You know very well what I mean! Feeding him in the kitchen—flirting with him in the pantry. And him, strutting about like a prize game rooster. [*He imitates the* CAPTAIN.] "It reminds me of this—it reminds me of that." I know all about it, don't think I don't.

COLOM [*teasing*]: But Captain Bombasto is such a gallant soldier—so brave—so . . . so. . . .

ARLE: So stupid? Is that the word you are looking for?

COLOM: Not at all! I rather fancy the Captain.

ARLE: I'll fancy him—with my paddle!

He begins to make fencing motions.

COLOM: Your paddle would make a poor match for the Captain's sword. Why, I could beat you with my feather duster. On guard, Arlecchino!

ARLE: On guard, Colombina!

They fence. Whenever COLOMBINA *touches* ARLECCHINO, *he is tickled and begins to dance.*

Ho! Ho! Oh, stop, you are tickling me to death! Oh, stop.

COLOM: Do you give up? Braggard!

ARLE: Never! [*She resumes.*] Oh, stop, please! Ho! Ho!

Behind the curtain PANTALONE *calls.*

PANT [*off*]: What is going on out there? What is that laughter? You are disturbing me.

COLOM: Now, you zany! You've upset the master with your silly pranks and laughing.

A R L E : And who was tickling who, might I ask. Vixen!

He swats at her. She ducks and tickles him again.

Ho! Ho! Oh, you wildcat!

He swats at her again but misses and hits PANTALONE *as he enters through the center curtain.*

P A N T : Oooof! What do you mean, rascal, hitting your master?

COLOMBINA *is dusting again as though nothing had happened.*

A R L E : Master, she is the one who I was trying to hit.

C O L O M [*innocently*]: Why, Arlecchino, what ever for?

A R L E : Oh, you . . . you . . . WOMAN!

C O L O M : Dear master, poor Arlecchino sometimes suffers from these fits and you really shouldn't beat him—much—for something he cannot help.

P A N T : A good whipping might do wonders for this scoundrel.

A R L E [*almost weeping*]: But she is the one. . . .

C O L O M : No, indeed. He is not to blame. It is a kind of sickness that can only be cured by NOT letting him have any FOOD for a day or so.

A R L E : No food? I'd sooner die! I'd sooner take a hundred beatings than that. Oh, the very thought of missing a single meal makes me weak! Ohhh. . . .

P A N T : Hush, or I'll beat you anyway! Colombina, finish your dusting. My friend, the good Doctor, is coming to see me today.

C O L O M : Are you ill?

P A N T : Sick! Sick of being sad. And I'm so much sadder and unhappy today than usual. . . .

C O L O M [*aside*]: How sad can one man be, I'd like to know?

P A N T : That I have called for him to come.

C O L O M : Well, I have tried everything to make you happy, master.

A R L E : And I.

P A N T : I simply cannot go on being sad a day longer. It is very hard to be happy when one is sad.

C O L O M : Very true. I have noticed that every time I am sad, I am not happy.

A R L E : But, master, I have a sure cure for sadness.

P A N T : You do?

ARLE: Certainly! Whenever you are sad, just be happy and the sadness will go away.

PANT: Fool, it is not so easy as that.

DOCTOR [off]: Holla—hey! Someone come to the door. I've got my arms full of wonderful books.

PANT: Quick, Colombina! It's the Doctor. Let him in at once.

She goes through the center curtain.

PANT: And you, you rascal, no tricks while the Doctor is here!

ARLE: Oh, master, you know I never play tricks!

PANT: Rogue! Go hide yourself some place till I call.

ARLECCHINO darts out a side curtain. COLOMBINA shows the DOCTOR in. He is loaded with books. He dumps them on the floor.

DOCTOR: My dear friend Pantalone. I am so happy that you are so sad to see me.

They embrace and pat one another on the back.

PANT: Colombina, quick, bring some wine for the good Doctor.

She goes out one of the side curtains.

DOCTOR: Many thanks. I am greatly in need of a thirst-quenching beverage. The carrying of books is an arduous task, and as the most learned and ancient philosophers have often pointed out, when one drinks one relieves one's thirst.

PANT: Most true, most true! I have a wine which is very light and dry. A wonderful wine—you'd hardly know you'd drunk it it's so light. Very good!

DOCTOR: Oh, marvelous, marvelous! I can hardly wait to try this wonderful vintage.

COLOMBINA enters with a bottle and two goblets.

PANT: Ah, here we are. [*He pours a glass.*] For you, good Doctor.

DOCTOR: A thousand thanks. I propose a toast:
He raises his goblet above his head. At this moment ARLECCHINO appears above the center curtain with a long straw. While the goblets are being held up, ARLECCHINO drains the DOCTOR's goblet.

With the aid of my vast and superior knowledge of all things great and small and with the help of my many various and beautifully bound books, may we soon find the nature of your malady and soon dispel the cause thereof.

They drink. The DOCTOR *looks puzzled.*

You are right, my dear Pantalone, a very dry wine indeed.

P A N T : The very best, you must agree. Very light.

D O C T O R [*a little dubious*]: Yes, quite light indeed. [*Aside.*] Hardly tasted like anything, if you ask me.

P A N T : Another glass?

D O C T O R : Yes, I don't mind if I do. [*Aside.*] I can't see what harm it would do.

PANTALONE *pours again.*

P A N T : A toast: [*They raise their glasses.*] To my dear friend and medical advisor whose great knowledge of small things and many various and ill-bound books will, I most sincerely hope, aid him in the search and happy resolution of my sad malady.

During this time ARLECCHINO *has drained the glass again. The* DOCTOR *and* PANTALONE *drink.*

P A N T : A truly delicious wine.

D O C T O R : Ummmm . . . A very strange one to be sure.

P A N T : One more glass, my good friend?

D O C T O R : Dear Pantalone, may I pour the last glass of this marvelous wine. I would like to examine it more closely at first hand.

The DOCTOR *takes the bottle and looks at it for a long moment, then peers down into the goblet. As he does,* ARLECCHINO *reaches down and lifts the bottle out of the* DOCTOR's *hand. Not noticing this the* DOCTOR *begins to pour and is completely taken aback to find nothing in his hand.*

Gracious galaxies! The wine was so light it flew right out of my hand.

They look up and around. By this time ARLECCHINO *has drained the bottle. Giving a mighty "Hic," he disappears behind the curtain.*

But never mind, I really feel quite full already.

PANT: Then to business, good Doctor, I am not well. . . .

DOCTOR: In that case, I would say you are sick.

PANT: And because I am not happy. . . .

DOCTOR: You are therefore sad.

PANT [amazed]: How wonderfully quick you are, dear Doctor!

DOCTOR: How right you are, dear Pantalone. I suppose I am about the best doctor in the world.

PANT: But do you think you might cure me of my sadness? I am so unhappy being sad all the time.

DOCTOR: Of course I can cure you.

PANT: But how?

DOCTOR [secretly]: Here in these books.

PANT: But which one? There are so many.

DOCTOR: Well, as a matter of fact, I did have the page marked, but I lost it. However, it is in one of these books, I do remember that much.

PANT: Oh, then do let us look!

They kneel and begin to open the books.

DOCTOR: Ummm . . . nothing much in this. Only how to make blackbird pie. Do you like blackbird pie?

PANT: Can't stand it!

DOCTOR: Then that would not make you very happy and if you are not made happy you will remain sad. [Discards it.]

PANT: This is a strange book.

DOCTOR: Let me see. Oh, that is my stamp album. Of no use to us in the present situation. [Discards it.]

PANT: Oh, Doctor, are you sure there is something to make me happy in these books. I've looked and looked.

DOCTOR: Chin up! Chin up! We'll come across something soon. Ah! What's this? A tree that grows happy apples!

PANT: Apples? Happy apples?

DOCTOR: Wait. Listen. [Reads.]

> There is a tree which bears a fruit.
> An apple for the sad.
> And whomsoever eats this fruit
> Will be forever glad.
> And smile too.

PANT [almost in tears]: Oh, hooray!

PANTALONE *dances about the stage.*

We've found the answer! We've found the answer! Oh boo hoo!
How sad it makes me.

COLOMBINA *sticks her head through the curtain.*

C O L O M : Here now! What's all the noise. I have a cake baking
and you are going to make it fall.

P A N T : Oh, bother the cake! The good Doctor has found a cure
for my sadness. Tell her.

D O C T O R : Indeed the possibility seems most favorable, for by my
vast knowledge of all things and with the aid of my beautifully
bound and illustrated books. . . .

C O L O M : I'm glad to hear it! Now maybe the house won't be so
glum all the time.

D O C T O R : But a moment, sir. If I read this book aright we must
seek this wonderful tree where it grows.

C O L O M : And where might that be?

D O C T O R : Nothing simpler! I have a map.

P A N T : A map?

C O L O M : A map?

D O C T O R : A map! And here it is. You see, we begin here.

*He proceeds to unfold the map as they trace the route.
As they unfold it, it becomes larger and larger until it is
necessary for all three to help hold it.*

D O C T O R : To find the tree we must go from here to here and
from there to there and from there to here. And from here to
there and from here to here to here to there to here to there then
to there . . .

ARLECCHINO *comes through the curtain*

A R L E : Hey! Are we going to wallpaper the wall?

C O L O M : Fool! Help us here. We're looking for apples.

A R L E : Why don't you look in the backyard. There's plenty out
there.

P A N T : Nitwit! We want special apples.

A R L E : These are special. I eat them all the time.

C O L O M : Help me hold this map, you zany.

ARLECCHINO *reluctantly picks up one end of the map
which has now become enormous.*

DOCTOR : And from there to there to here to here and so to here.

The DOCTOR *has traced a route that makes a complete circle.*

And that, my dear friend, is where you will find the apples which will make you happy. Exactly at the spot marked with a big X.

ARLE [*aside*]: It looks to me as if they were going in a circle. Ah, well, never tell a fool his business.

PANT : That is a very long trip, and very long trips make me very unhappy.

DOCTOR : And a journey beset with many dangers, if I read the map correctly.

ARLE : Danger is something I can do without.

COLOM : How well I know that.

DOCTOR : Dear sir, if I am to sure you, as I trust you wish, we must undertake this journey.

PANT : Anything to regain my happiness again.

DOCTOR : And I would also suggest we take with us some brave and courageous person to protect us on our way.

COLOM : Well, here I am.

DOCTOR : A woman!

PANT : A woman!

ARLE : You! A woman!

This sends him into fits of laughter.

COLOM : I'm as good as ten men like you, Arlecchino.

ARLE : Take care I do not beat you with my paddle.

COLOM : Take care I do not beat YOU with your paddle.

She jumps at him. ARLECCHINO *hides behind* PANTALONE.

PANT : Well, it is certain you are not the man we want.

COLOM [*aside*]: Ah, I know just the man they want. In truth the biggest coward in the world, but the bravest man that ever lived, if you hear him tell it. [*To* PANTALONE.] Sir, I know just the man you need.

ARLE : You do?

COLOM : Of course! Captain Bombasto.

ARLE : Arg! That boasting, bragging bag of wind!

COLOM : You are one to talk of windbags.

PANT : Do you think he would undertake this journey?

COLOM : Nothing more likely. [*Aside.*] If you stuff him with food night and day.

PANT : Where is this man?

COLOM : I can have him here in the smallest part of a minute.

PANT : Then by all means let us see him.

COLOM : I'll be but a moment. [*Exits.*]

ARLE : Master, I tell you this man is . . .

PANT : Peace, or I'll have you paddled.

ARLE : But . . .

PANT : Mind, rascal. I will keep my word to have you whipped.

ARLECCHINO shrugs. COLOMBINA enters.

COLOM : Here is the mighty Captain Bombasto!

CAPTAIN BOMBASTO enters through the curtain. He is tall and gaunt and wearing the uniform of a Spanish Captain. An enormously long plume protrudes from his hat and an equally enormously long sword without a sheath hangs tightly at his side, the point up. Twirling his pointed black mustache, he crosses to PANTALONE and makes a sweeping bow. At the same time the DOCTOR has leaned over to pick up one of his books. He and the CAP-TAIN bend over in opposite directions. The sharp point of the CAPTAIN's sword jabs the DOCTOR's posterior.

CAPT : An honor, sir!

DOCTOR : Yow!

All turn to look at the DOCTOR in surprise. Not seeing the sword as the CAPTAIN turns, the DOCTOR sheepishly rubs his affected part.

Something stung me.

PANT : It must have been a bee.

The CAPTAIN turns to PANTALONE and bows again and the same action with the DOCTOR is repeated.

CAPT : Your gracious invitation . . .

DOCTOR : Yow!

Since ARLECCHINO is standing close by, the DOCTOR glares at him and swats him with his hat.

CAPT [*again bowing*]: Permit me to say . . .

DOCTOR: Yipe!

> *This last thrust of the sword sends the* DOCTOR *several*
> *feet in the air. When he lands he glares at a surprised*
> ARLECCHINO. *All glare at the* DOCTOR *and then glare at*
> ARLECCHINO *who shrugs helplessly and takes himself a*
> *good distance from the* DOCTOR.

PANT: Let us get down to the business at hand. I have been told, sir, of your brave exploits. And I have asked you here to . . .

CAPT: Brave hardly describes my deeds, sir. When only a boy of twelve, I was captured by Barbary pirates and pressed into service as a galley slave at the oar. After six months I was forced to walk the plank. Fortunately I landed on the back of a monstrous whale who stove the ship in two, gobbled up all the pirates, and, doubtless, impressed with my courage, politely took me back to shore. There I promptly enlisted in the army, for I had lost both my parents . . .

ARLE: That was careless of him.

CAPT: And fought in the Spanish wars.

DOCTOR [*searching through his books*]: The Spanish wars?

PANT [*to the* CAPTAIN]: That's very interesting. Now we are planning a journey and we want . . .

CAPT: Talk you of journeys, sir? Why, as a mere boy in the Spanish wars I journeyed up and down Europe for five years without stopping, slaying armies right and left as David slew Goliath . . .

DOCTOR [*searching through his books*]: David? Goliath?

CAPT: With a small sword which I still wear today and taken from the Turks in Istanbul.

DOCTOR [*searching through his books*]: Turks? Is—Stan— What?

CAPT: After I killed fifty men with one blow, I was put in command of an entire army, for my industry and love of work was noted. Then . . .

COLOM [*aside*]: If he can mow men down as fast as he can blow words out, he's a mighty fighter indeed.

CAPT: Why, I'm so ferocious I eat armies for breakfast, giants for lunch, and dragons I barbecue. Furthermore, I have rescued more damsels in distress from cutthroat castles, dangerous dragons, and gruesome giants than I can count.

COLOM [*aside*]: How does a maiden get rescued from his lies, I wonder?

CAPT [*twirling his mustache*]: Ah, the ladies they adore me. I am sorry for them for there isn't enough of me to go round.

COLOM [*aside*]: Who would want any of him!

CAPT: You wished to say something to me, sir?

PANT: Now that you mention it, I did. In brief, we need a brave man to lead us to an apple tree.

CAPT [*aside*]: That doesn't sound very dangerous. [*To* PANTALONE.] There is only one little thing.

PANT: I can't afford to pay you money but I'll give you all the food you can eat.

CAPT: That was the "little thing" I had in mind. I am your man.

PANT: Good. So now let us prepare for the trip. Arlecchino, make ready. Good Doctor, let us get our things together necessary for the journey.

ARLECCHINO *exits.*

CAPT: And by all means let us carry a picnic basket filled with all manner of tasty morsels, such as cake, pie, tarts, cookies, sausages, chickens roasted to a turn, watermelon preserves, figs, grapes, prunes, puddings of all flavors, cheese. For, as you doubtless know, one must be fit to face all the great dangers that lie before us.

COLOM: What should I pack in the way of clothes, master?

PANT: Why, pack nothing and you will pack enough, for you are staying here.

COLOM: But master . . .

PANT: No words. You are a woman and would only be in the way. This is work for men.

COLOM [*aside*]: We'll see who stays behind.

PANT: And now, good friends and comrades all, prepare for the journey.

DOCTOR: I shall gather all my books.

All exit but the CAPTAIN *and* COLOMBINA.

CAPT [*pinches her cheek*]: Ah, my pretty pancake. Do not weep too much when I am gone.

COLOM: It will be hard, but somehow I will manage.

CAPT: And when you pack the food, pray don't forget a few little things to nibble on such as a ham or two, a slab of good fat bacon, and a pleasing plump goose stuffed with chestnuts.

COLOM: Have no fear. You'll be well taken care of. Oh, dear Captain, there is something I want to tell you.

CAPT: Ah, do not waste a moment more. Tell me.

COLOM: Do you really think I should?

CAPT: By all means, my little watermelon seed.

COLOM: It is this—there is a mouse standing just behind you, and he has a wicked look in his eye.

The CAPTAIN *is frozen for a moment. He then jumps a foot off the floor.*

CAPT: A mouse! How they do afright me. Ohhhh . . .

He quickly rushes through the center curtain.

COLOM [*to the audience*]: And there you have the BRAVE Captain Bombasto. I would be a bad servant if I let my master start on a journey with such fools and cowards as those. And since he will not let me come along as Colombina, I will disguise myself as a boy and offer my services to Master Pantalone as a guide. In that way I can keep my eye on them all and steer them out of danger as only I can. Perhaps there might be time for a little joke or two along the road. But I waste time here when I should be halfway there. Here I'll not stay. Colombina's on her way!

The musicians bring on a property rock and set it on the stage. Both exit through back curtain. The travelers enter with the CAPTAIN *strutting at the head of the column, while* PANTALONE *and the* DOCTOR *slowly follow behind.* ARLECCHINO *brings up the rear, loaded with bundles and a huge picnic basket.*

DOCTOR [*holding up a book*]: My good Pantalone, you need have no fear. For science tells us the world is round. And thus if we walk straight, we are sure to end up where we begin. Of course, when man passes the other side of the world he is forced to walk upside down and he must be careful so as not to fall off the earth, but he becomes rightside up again when he comes to where he started.

ARLE: Upside down or rightside up, I shall fall bottomside flat if I have to climb one more hill.

PANT: Oh, unhappy day! How tired I am. Let us rest for a moment.

DOCTOR: An excellent idea. Bene Bono Burp, as the ancient philosophers were wont to say, which is to say "An excellent idea."

CAPT: What! Tired already! Why, in the war against the Turks, I led an army for 40 days and 47 nights without food or drink.

ARLE [aside]: If he ever missed one day without food and drink, his feather would brush the ground. That dumb block!

CAPT: What did you say?

ARLE: I said I see a rock. [Then, actually spying a rock ahead.] I do see a rock—a shady rock on the path ahead. Look!

CAPT [quickly]: Then by all means let us rest. I'm exhausted.

Arriving at the rock, the party stops.

ARLE [aside]: There's a hardy soldier for you.

PANT: Doctor, where in the name of unhappiness are we?

ARLE: Six leagues past lost, that's where we are.

PANT: Lost! Oh, most unhappy day! Oh . . .

He begins to weep.

DOCTOR: Now old friend, never fear. I'll just take another peek at this map.

He pulls open the huge map and turns it in every direction.

ARLE: I doubt if he could find the nose on his face with that map.

CAPT: Lost! In the middle of the day?

DOCTOR: It is the middle of the night.

CAPT: The day!

DOCTOR: The night!

A cutout of the sun appears above the curtain with "SUN" written on it and the FIRST MUSICIAN puts his head over the top of the curtain.

1ST MUSC: It's the middle of the day.

ARLE: And that settles that.

COLOMBINA enters disguised as a young country boy. Upon seeing her, the CAPTAIN jumps to his feet and draws his sword.

CAPT : Not a step closer or I'll run you through, vicious varlet!

COLOM : Oh, don't be silly.

She pushes his sword aside with a finger and goes directly to PANTALONE.

Please, good sir, let me join your company.

PANT : Oh my, no. You're just a boy.

ARLE : Not dry behind the ears yet. But . . . [*walking around* COLOMBINA] a pretty boy to be sure. You remind me of someone but I can't remember who. Why do you want to join us?

COLOM : My home is a goodly piece down the road. I would like to join you for protection from the many dangers that lie along the way. I can be very helpful, I promise you. I know where all the best inns lie. You'll never be lost with me along.

ARLE : Let's take him with us. He looks like a likeable lad.

PANT : You say you know of a good inn? Very well then, you may join us.

PANTALONE rejoins the DOCTOR who is still investigating the map.

COLOM : Oh, good. [*To the* CAPTAIN.] It will be an honor to serve with the great Captain Bombasto.

ARLE [*surprised*]: You've heard of him? That proves that bad news travels fastest.

CAPT : And who hasn't heard of me? Why, my praises are sung by all fair maidens and brave men from here to the shores of Arabia. I must withdraw to meditate upon my greatness.

Before the CAPTAIN leaves the group, ARLE swats him with his stick, then ducks behind rock. The CAPTAIN turns, sword in hand, but seeing no one retires to far side of stage. The DOCTOR and PANTALONE huddle over the map.

ARLE : Nobody ever sang his praises except himself. Don't be fooled by him, boy.

C O L O M [*teasingly*]: But he's so brave and so handsome!

A R L E : Yes, if a mouse is brave and a pickled herring handsome.

C O L O M : You're just jealous.

A R L E : Jealous of that nincompoop! Ooooh, you are making me angry—just like Colombina. That's who you remind me of! Colombina.

C O L O M : And who is Colombina?

A R L E : Oh, just a hot-tempered little serving maid who hopelessly loves me.

C O L O M [*winking at the audience*]: Oh? Tell me more about this Colombina.

A R L E : When she's mad she spits like a cat and has the temper of a stepped-on snake. Her eyes are flaming coals, her ears are great and long and pick up every little word they shouldn't. She has legs like a bull, teeth like a whale, and a tongue like a ten-foot whip that lashes out at the drop of a word.

C O L O M : She doesn't sound so pretty.

A R L E : Perhaps I exaggerate a bit. [*Wistfully.*] She's quite pretty really . . . sometimes.

C O L O M : And she likes you.

A R L E : She can't help herself. She waits on me more than the master. She brings me all the food I want from the kitchen.

C O L O M [*aside*]: He's lucky if I ever give him so much as a cold sausage again.

A R L E : Yes, she dotes on me like a lovesick puppy dog.

C O L O M [*aside*]: That is about to bite. [*To* ARLECCHINO.] And how do you treat her?

A R L E : Why, like a servant, of course, for she is only a woman.

C O L O M [*aside*]: And the master of any man, you can bet your best boots!

A R L E : And when she fails to obey me, I spank her with my swat stick.

C O L O M [*aside*]: But I always spank him first. [*To* ARLECCHINO.] What do you think of her?

A R L E : That is a secret I will never tell. But I can tell you since you are a boy. Even though she makes me as mad as a running rhinoceros . . .

C O L O M : Yes?

A R L E : The truth is, I like her very much and someday would like to make her my wife.

COLOM [*aside*]: If she'll have you. And that's a secret that may do me some good some day. [*To* ARLECCHINO.] How can you be so mad at her and like her at the same time?

ARLE : When you're a man, you'll understand such things.

COLOM : That day I'd like to see.

PANT [*looking up from the map*]: Arlecchino, set the picnic basket here. It's time to eat.

ARLE [*to* COLOMBINA]: Here boy, give me a hand.

> *During the remainder of the last speeches, the two musicians have donned the cloaks and masks of gypsies. They come up onto the platform.*

PANT : Here come two gypsies. Maybe they can give us the right direction.

DOCTOR : I know the right way. But ask them if you wish.

PANT : Excuse me, ladies.

IST GYPSY : What did you do wrong, sir?

PANT : Perhaps you can help us. We are looking for a certain kind of tree that grows apples which make you happy when you eat them.

> ARLECCHINO *and* COLOMBINA *set down the huge picnic basket in front of* PANTALONE *and the* DOCTOR. *The gypsies eye the basket hungrily.*

IST GYPSY : We can help you. If you will but listen to our tale, you will learn how to get anywhere.

ARLE : Masters, I wouldn't trust them. Two gypsies tell more fibs than one gypsy and one gypsy can tell a tale taller than the neck of a giraffe.

DOCTOR : Balderdash, boy. Perhaps the knowledge of these colorful natives can quicken our quest.

PANT : I do hope so. Let us talk to them alone. [*To* ARLECCHINO.] Off with you, Arlecchino and bring some water from a nearby stream. [*To* COLOMBINA.] Go with him, boy.

CAPT : I'll go with you too. You'll need my protection.

ARLE [*aside*]: He couldn't protect us from a rabbit!

> ARLECCHINO *and* COLOMBINA *exit with the* CAPTAIN. *The gypsies sit down on either side of the picnic basket behind which sits the* DOCTOR *and* PANTALONE.

P A N T : Tell us your tale. It may help in our search for the happy apple tree.

1 S T G Y P S Y : I shall begin. [PANTALONE *and the* DOCTOR *turn to the* FIRST GYPSY. *During his speech, the* SECOND GYPSY, *without being noticed, removes from the basket a long string of sausage links, bananas, a ham, grapes, etc.*]
Once my fellow gypsy and I borrow a chicken from a farmer's barnyard. I have hold of one leg of the chicken and he the other. Suddenly a chicken hawk swoops out of the sky and carries off the chicken with each of us holding on. The chicken hawk flies higher and higher until we can no longer see the peaks of the highest mountains. Then a vulture flies by and grabs the chicken hawk who grabbed the chicken. And the vulture and the chicken hawk and we go even higher. Then a giant eagle passes by and seizes the vulture who seized the chicken hawk who seized the chicken. And he flaps his wings and up and up goes the eagle and the vulture and chicken hawk and the chicken and gypsies. [*Noticing that the* SECOND GYPSY *has finished taking all the food from one side of the basket.*]

D O C T O R : Yes, yes, go on.

1 S T G Y P S Y : But let my friend tell you the rest.

> PANTALONE *and the* DOCTOR *turn their attention to the* SECOND GYPSY. *During the following speech the* FIRST GYPSY *removes food from his end of the picnic basket without being noticed.*

2 N D G Y P S Y : Suddenly the eagle bumps into a small star and drops the vulture and the vulture drops the chicken hawk and the chicken hawk drops the chicken and the chicken shakes us free and we land—on the moon. Kerplop! Once on the moon we see it is not made of green cheese but yellow. Yellow cheese we do not like, so we decide to get back to earth. But we have no way to do so. Using our gypsy wits, we merely wait until the night has fallen and the long moonbeams are shining straight to earth. Then we climb on a nice fat moonbeam and slide down the beam like a child down a banister. And we land right in our own backyard.

> *By this time, the* FIRST GYPSY *has finished taking all the food from the other side of the basket. The gypsies rise quickly and prepare to go.*

P A N T : But you haven't told us how to get to where we are going!

1 S T G Y P S Y : Oh, that!

2 N D G Y P S Y : Simple!

I S T G Y P S Y [*starting to exit*]: Just fly to the moon first.

2 N D G Y P S Y [*also starting to exit*]: And take a telescope. When you're on the moon——

I S T G Y P S Y : Look at the earth below through the telescope——

2 N D G Y P S Y : And it will be right under your nose. [*Both exit laughing. They resume their places as musicians.*]

D O C T O R [*meditating*]: We go to the moon. And we take a telescope. And we look at the earth. Yes, it sounds quite logical to me.

P A N T [*looking at the* DOCTOR *with some annoyance*]: I'm feeling unhappier every minute.

The CAPTAIN, ARLECCHINO *and* COLOMBINA *enter.*

A R L E : Did they tell us the way?

P A N T : No. I know no more than I did before.

C A P T : Bother the gypsies. My stomach says it's time to eat.

PANTALONE *opens the picnic basket. He puts in his hand expectantly, but his expression quickly changes.*

P A N T : Why, the food is—— [*His hand searches further and brings up nothing.*] gone. Not a bite left to eat. [*Starting to cry.*]

A R L E [*unable to keep from laughing*]: You'll just have to eat your words. Ha, ha.

C O L O M : Why are you laughing, donkey. It means no food for you, either. [ARLECCHINO *stops laughing.*]

P A N T : Varlet!

D O C T O R : Dunderhead. [*Raises his hand to strike the servant. However,* ARLECCHINO *ducks and the two old men hit each other and fall to the ground simultaneously.*]

C O L O M : Oh, master, I can lead you to some food. I know an inn nearby. I will run ahead and tell the mistress of the inn we are coming. Follow the road that way and you'll be there in the twinkle of an eyebrow. [*Exits.*]

P A N T : Thank goodness at least those gypsies didn't get my gold.

C A P T : Let me guard your purse of gold. It shall be as safe with me as if in the treasure house of the king of France. [*Takes purse.*]

ARLE [*aside*]: We shall see about that.

CAPT: Company, forward march.

>All rise and move off the platform to below it, making a half revolution to the other side of the stage, COLOMBINA enters from the side, turns rock around to reveal tree stump, and walks up to the rear curtain. The musicians supply a musical accompaniment to the action.

COLOM: This looks like my Aunt's inn, but no one seems to be about. [*She mimes knocking on the curtain. The musicians underscore the action with their instruments.*] No answer. Holla. Mistress of the inn! Answer your door. Holla!

MISTRESS [*offstage*]: Who's calling? Who's there?

COLOM: That's my Aunt's voice all right! I wonder if she will recognize me in my disguise. [*Calling.*] Hey! Come and look after your guests.

>The MISTRESS of the inn looks over the top of the curtain.

MISTRESS: What's your business? I'm up to my arms in dirty dishes.

COLOM: I hear you give free food here.

MISTRESS: What? Who told you that?

COLOM [*supressing a laugh*]: Why, it's known all up and down the road. And since I have no money——

MISTRESS: No money! Then you have come to the wrong inn. I'm a poor woman. I can't feed every beggar that comes to my door. Now be off.

COLOM: No, I think I'll just stay till you give me some food.

MISTRESS [*coming down*]: Oh, we'll see about that.

>She enters with a broom.

And now, will you leave by yourself or must I beat you with this broom?

COLOM: In order to beat me you must first catch me.

MISTRESS: You saucy knave! I'll give you something to run about. Take that! [*She misses the elusive* COLOMBINA.] And that!

>And she misses her again. Being older and heavier than COLOMBINA, the MISTRESS soon tires. The musicians' instruments have underscored the chase.

Ohhh, I'm out of breath.

>COLOMBINA is overcome with laughter.

Why are you laughing, scoundrel. If I catch you with this broom, you'll not be laughing long.

COLOM : I'm laughing because you don't recognize me, Auntie.

MISTRESS : Auntie? You call me Auntie? But I have no nephew. Only a niece.

COLOM [taking off her cap]: And here she is!

MISTRESS : Colombina, you little minx! Have you nothing better to do with your time than run over the countryside playing tricks on your old Auntie.

COLOM : You're not the one I want to trick but someone else. And I need your help to do it.

MISTRESS : Me? What can I do? I have my hands full with the inn.

COLOM : It's as an innkeeper that I need your help.

MISTRESS : Say on. You know I'll do what I can. But I'm certain there is mischief afoot if you have any part of it.

COLOM : To be brief, my master Pantalone is coming this way. I have persuaded him to stay the night here.

MISTRESS : And he could do no better on any highway, I'll have you know.

COLOM : With him are some prize fools. There's his friend, a foolish Doctor who talks big words and walks in circles.

MISTRESS : I never met a doctor who didn't.

COLOM : And a bragging Captain who's frightened of his own shadow.

MISTRESS : They're all the same. And is that rascal Arlecchino with them?

COLOM : He'll be here too. But wait, I see them down the road. Make them welcome first, and I'll tell you of my plans when they are settled.

MISTRESS : Good. I've been looking for a little excitement and now it appears there might be some.

COLOM : But don't let on you know me so that no one will be suspicious.

MISTRESS : Leave all to me. Quiet, though, they're almost here.

PANTALONE, *the* DOCTOR, *the* CAPTAIN, *and* ARLECCHINO *enter.*

COLOM [loudly]: Yes, good mistress, I'm sure that will please my master. Oh, in good time, these are my masters. Master

Pantalone, the Doctor, Captain Bombasto, may I present the mistress of the inn.

MISTRESS [*coyly*]: Oh, good masters, you do my humble inn an honor by staying in it.

CAPT: Nay, good woman, rise. I understand you have good food hereabouts such as pies and cakes and tarts——

MISTRESS: And cookies of my own baking, and grapes, figs, and chickens roasted to a turn, watermelons, puddings of every kind.

CAPT: This is the place for us to stop.

DOCTOR: Indeed, it has a favorable aspect to it. A very nice inn.

PANT: I'm so tired I could sleep on a bed of nails.

MISTRESS: Anything you wish, Master Pantalone. I'll have my servant boy make you a bed of nails right away.

PANT [*flustered*]: No, no. That's just a saying.

MISTRESS: But if you really want a bed of nails, it would be no trouble.

PANT: An ordinary bed will do, madam.

MISTRESS: If you will all come this way, I'll show you to your rooms. I'm sure you'd like to rest awhile before supper.

DOCTOR: A delightful suggestion, my good woman.

The men exit.

COLOM [*to the* MISTRESS]: Psst. Come back as soon as you can. I'll tell my plan then.

ARLECCHINO, *having gone around the side, overhears this.*

ARLE [*aside*]: Aha! A plan. I smell some fun brewing. Perhaps I should keep my big ears open.

COLOMBINA *looks off to one side and then to the other, making sure no one is about. The* MISTRESS *reenters.*

MISTRESS [*secretly*]: They are all in their rooms. Now, what is your plan?

COLOM: Very simply, it is this. When the clock strikes midnight and all my masters are in bed, you will tiptoe to Master Pantalone's bedroom window——

MISTRESS: Yes?

COLOM: Then——

> *She whispers in the* MISTRESS's *ear. The old lady nods, then smiles, then bursts into laughter.*

MISTRESS : I can hardly wait to see their faces.
COLOM : And then——

> *She whispers again.*

MISTRESS : Ho! What a joke that will be!
COLON : But not a word to a soul.
CAPT [*within*]: Ho! Mistress of the inn! We want our supper. Bring out those pies and cakes and tarts.
MISTRESS : Coming! Coming! [*To* COLOMBINA.] Till midnight.
COLOM : Till midnight.

> *They both put their fingers to their lips and exit. After they are gone,* ARLECCHINO *steps out of hiding.*

ARLE : So that's their game! Well, three can play as well as two. And Arlecchino is a match for anyone when it comes to making jokes.

> *He exits. The lights dim. A half-moon is thrust over the top of the curtain. A moment later the* MISTRESS *secretly steals through one of the side curtains. A chime strikes. The following action is underscored when appropriate by the musicians.*

MISTRESS : One, two, three, four, five, six, seven, eight, nine, ten, eleven— Midnight! Ooooo. It's scary out here in the night.

> *An owl hoots.*

[*Jumps.*] What's that. Oh, just an old hoot owl. Well, to business.

> *She looks both ways to see if the way is clear. Satisfied, she tiptoes to the curtain and calls up in a loud whisper.*

Master Pantalone! Master Pantalone!
PANT [*within, waking*]: Ump ahh, what! Who calls?
MISTRESS : Master Pantalone. Come to your window.

> PANTALONE *appears over the top of the curtain. He is wearing a nightgown and a long nightcap. In his hand he holds a lantern.*

PANT: What do you want? Who's there?

MISTRESS: The mistress of the inn.

PANT: What's wrong? Is the house on fire?

MISTRESS: Not at all. But I have something to tell you.

PANT: But I was sound asleep. Can't it wait until morning?

MISTRESS: This is something important.

The DOCTOR *appears next to* PANTALONE, *rubbing his eyes.*

DOCTOR: Dear sir, what means this nightly watch. You know it is a well-known fact that night air is bad for the health. It fills the lungs with dark air, which, as the ancient learned philosophers tells us is——

MISTRESS: Sshhh.

DOCTOR: Egad! What kind of bird is that I hear?

MISTRESS: Masters, listen to me. I have some news of the apples you seek. The apples which make one happy.

PANT: What! Do you hear that, good Doctor?

DOCTOR: Yes, a very strange bird indeed—one that talks.

MISTRESS: No, no. I'm not a bird. Good sirs, listen, for time is short.

PANT: I'm listening.

MISTRESS: I know you are seeking a strange apple tree.

PANT: Indeed we are. Do you know of such a tree?

MISTRESS: Yes. And if you will come with me, I will take you to it now.

PANT: Do you think we should go?

DOCTOR: By all means, it may be just the tree we're looking for.

MISTRESS: Hurry, masters.

The two men disappear from sight. The MISTRESS *motions to the hidden* COLOMBINA.

Colombina, come quickly. They will be here in a moment.

COLOMBINA *enters with branches bearing apples.*

COLOM: I'm here.

MISTRESS: Now what is your plan?

COLOM: I am going to be an apple tree. And those are my branches. If they are seeking a strange apple tree, I'll show them a tree so strange that they will never need seek another.

MISTRESS: A good joke to be sure.

ARLE [*jumping out of hiding*]: The joke's on you. For I know your plot. And unless you let me join you, it will be a poor joke indeed.

COLOM: Join us then, and we'll play the joke together. But quickly take these branches and do as I do.

MISTRESS: Listen, they are almost here! Stand on this.

> COLOMBINA *and* ARLECCHINO *step up on the tree stump. Standing back to back, they raise the branches up in a treelike attitude.* PANTALONE *and the* DOCTOR *appear through the curtain.*

Here masters! This way.

DOCTOR: It's so dark I cannot see an inch beyond my nose.

PANT: Nor I! Are you there?

MISTRESS: Take my hand, and Doctor, you take Master Pantalone's. But first, I must tell you that this is an exceedingly strange tree. It may do some surprising things.

PANT: Are you sure the apples of this tree will make one happy, for such a tree we seek.

DOCTOR: Indeed, we seek no other.

MISTRESS: Come, that you must learn for yourselves.

> *She leads the two men around the box on which* COLOMBINA *and* ARLECCHINO *stand. When they have come full circle, she stops. The musicians accompany the march.*

DOCTOR: Is this the place?

MISTRESS: Not yet. Ssssh!

> *They encircle the box once more.*

PANT: Here?

MISTRESS: Just a few steps more.

> *They encircle the box for the third time.*

Here is the tree.

> *She withdraws from the men and exits through the curtains.* PANTALONE *stands on one side of the "tree" and the* DOCTOR *on the other. The characters' movements are underscored by the musicians.*

PANT: Can you see the tree, Doctor?

DOCTOR: Just barely [*Reaching out and grasping* COLOMBINA's *leg.*] Ah. here it is.

> PANTALONE *reaches out and touches* ARLECCHINO's *ribs.*
> ARLECCHINO *giggles.*

Pantalone, my friend, this is no time for laughing.

PANT: I can't laugh.

DOCTOR: To be sure, I forgot. Who giggled then?

PANT: It must have been you.

DOCTOR: You are imagining things.

> *They both reach out for the tree with their other hands. Simultaneously* ARLECCHINO *drops one arm hitting* PANTALONE *and* COLOMBINA *drops one arm hitting the* DOCTOR. *The "hits" are underscored by the musicians.*

PANT DOCTOR [*in unison*]: Oof!

> *Simultaneously reaching above their heads, they both grasp an apple hanging from the branches above them.*

It is an apple tree!

PANT: Quickly, let us pick one.

DOCTOR: It may be the apple that will cure your sadness.

> PANTALONE *reaches for his apple but* ARLECCHINO *raises his arm, putting the apple out of reach.*

PANT: I can't reach it.

DOCTOR: Never mind. I'll pluck this one. Oops!

> COLOMBINA *raises her arm, taking the apple out of the* DOCTOR's *reach. Then* ARLECCHINO *drops one arm and* COLOMBINA *drops one of her arms.*

PANT: Here is one down here.

DOCTOR: And one down here.

> *They both reach for an apple. Simultaneously* ARLECCHINO *and* COLOMBINA *raise the apples out of the men's grasp. Then, simultaneously,* PANTALONE *and the* DOCTOR *reach to one side and then the other. Every time their branches move out of reach.*

PANT: My apple is always out of reach.

DOCTOR: So is mine.

PANT: Doctor, let me climb up on your shoulders. Perhaps I can reach it from there.

The DOCTOR *hoists* PANTALONE *up on his shoulders.*

Now a little closer.

The DOCTOR *takes a step.*

A little closer.

The DOCTOR *moves one step closer.* PANTALONE *finds himself directly opposite* ARLECCHINO's *nose. He looks at the tree then at the audience.*

I think I've seen this tree before.

DOCTOR: Quickly, good Pantalone. I cannot hold you up there all night, you know.

PANT: I'll have it in a moment. It's almost in my grasp. Gracious.

The apples move out of his reach. He continues to reach for the apple and in doing so, he and the DOCTOR *are forced to circle the tree three times, moving faster all the while.*

DOCTOR [*out of breath*]: My dear friend, I cannot move an inch more.

PANTALONE *gets down.*

PANT: Nor can I get hold of a single apple!

ARLE [*in a ghostlike voice*]: Why don't you ask me for an apple.

DOCTOR: Pa-Pa-Pan-talone! The tree spoke!

PANT: Ohhh, I knew that was not an ordinary tree. It's bewitched.

DOCTOR: A haunted tree! Ohhhh!

They begin to dance for fear.

ARLE: But if you have come to steal my apples, I'll make you wish you had never heard of apples or apple trees again.

PANT: Fly, good Doctor!

DOCTOR: Good tree, we meant no harm. In truth we did not intend to steal your apples, for as the ancient learned philosophers have often said——

Both ARLECCHINO *and* COLOMBINA *begin to make ghostly moans.*

PANT : Quickly, Doctor. Let us find our way from this haunted place. Our very lives are in danger.

DOCTOR : A marvelously sound idea. Let us flee by all means. But which way is the road? I cannot see a thing in the dark.

ARLECCHINO *and* COLOMBINA *begin to moan louder. Slowly they begin to step off the box.*

PANT : Ohhhh! The tree is coming toward us. Ahhhh!

They both take to their heels and run down the steps to behind the platform.

COLOM [*to* ARLECCHINO]: Quickly! Let's give a good chase!

ARLE : Good! I'm right behind you.

They run offstage after the DOCTOR *and* PANTALONE *moaning more loudly than ever and shaking their branches. The two reenter in a moment.*

Now to play a trick of my own making.

COLOM : On whom?

ARLE : Captain Bombasto, of course. I'll show that lying windbag up for what he's worth. All the company shall see his true colors. And perhaps Colombina won't think so highly of him when news of this night's work reaches her.

COLOM [*aside*]: It may reach her sooner than you think. [*To* ARLECCHINO.] I let you in on my trick. Now you must let me in on yours.

ARLE : Promise not to speak a word of it?

COLOM : I promise. What is it?

ARLE : You know how the Captain carries Pantalone's gold wherever he goes and boasts it is always safe with him.

COLOM : But if something should happen to it——

ARLE : Like a robber stealing it——

COLOM : Then the Captain would be in disgrace. I see!

ARLE : You're quick to catch my meaning. Listen, I'll disguise myself as a bandit and steal the gold from the Captain.

COLOM : You'll give it back to the master, won't you?

ARLE : This very morning.

COLOM : How can I help?

A R L E : First, get the Mistress to lure him outside. All she has to mention is food. He's always wanting to fill that bottomless belly of his. Then once he's outside, you hide in the dark and frighten him before I enter. Oh, it will be sport to watch our brave Captain shake.

C O L O M : I'll do it to a turn. [*Aside.*] And turn the trickster Arlecchino upside down with his own trick.

A R L E : You're a prankster after my own heart. Now tell the Mistress our plan, and I'll get ready. [*Exits.*]

C O L O M [*calling*]: Auntie! [*The* MISTRESS *steps from behind the back curtain.*]

M I S T R E S S : What is it, Colombina? Another trick, I hope.

C O L O M : Of course. Listen! [*She whispers the plan to her Aunt who enjoys what she hears.*]

M I S T R E S S : Consider it done; off you go.

COLOMBINA *exits. The* MISTRESS *calls upstage.*

Captain Bombasto!

The CAPTAIN *looks sleepily over the top of the back curtain.*

C A P T : Who calls me at this unearthly hour of the night?

M I S T R E S S : It is I, Captain, the Mistress of the inn. I have some tasty goodies here for you—pastries and sweets and fried chicken from the kitchen and——

C A P T : Say no more, good woman. My stomach answers your call.

M I S T R E S S : Wait for me in the innyard. I'll be just a moment.

C A P T : My stomach and I will be right down.

M I S T R E S S [*aside*]: He'll be *down* all right when Colombina and Arlecchino get through with him.

Exits through the center curtains as the CAPTAIN *enters from the side curtains. He wears his uniform and sword; the bag of gold hangs from his belt. The following scene is underscored with music and sound effects.*

C A P T : Here I am. A leg of fried chicken first, please. [*Noticing that no one is there.*] Where is the woman? Oh, I shall have to wait, I suppose. [*Peering into the dark.*] It is a fearfully dark night. [*Taking one step downstage, he jumps in terror.*] Yipe! What is that? [*Looking at the ground.*] Oh, only an ant. [*Jump-*

ing.] What was that? I thought I heard a noise. Oh, I wish that woman would hurry. I'm afraid of the dark. [*As he backs across the stage, he bumps into the box used in the previous action.*] Help! [*He pulls out his sword. It trembles in his hand almost as much as his knees shake. Suddenly he hears all manner of imaginary enemies. Terrified, he jabs at the air with his sword.*] I see you hiding there. Take that. And that. [*Whirling around.*] Oh no, you don't. En garde! [*He dashes his sword into the ground where it becomes stuck.*] Let go of my sword, villain. [*After several pulls, he retrieves it.*] I must have run the scoundrel through.

C O L O M [*hiding behind the curtain*]: Whoo! Whoo! Whoo!

C A P T : Who's that?

> COLOMBINA *creeps downstage.*

C O L O M [*aside*]: One more noise to frighten the Captain, and then I'm off to outtrick a bigger fool than this one—named Arlecchino.

> *She lets out a blood-curdling moan and exits. The* CAPTAIN *falls to his knees, petrified with fear.*

C A P T : Ooooh!

> *Disguised as a bandit with a kerchief over his face,* ARLECCHINO *enters, unnoticed by the* CAPTAIN.

A R L E [*in a ghostly voice*]: Captain Bom-bas-to. Your time has come.

C A P T : Who said that?

A R L E [*raising his swat stick and stepping out behind the* CAPTAIN]: 'Tis I, Black Bart, the horrible highway robber, and his cutthroat band.

> *The* CAPTAIN *collapses on his back, his sword sticking upright.*

C A P T : Have mercy!

> *Running around the* CAPTAIN, ARLECCHINO *clashes his stick several times against the soldier's upraised sword.*

An army and every man a sword.

A R L E [*looking down at the* CAPTAIN]: Where are you, *captain* of the long feather and the black mustache? Ah, there you are. [*Pokes him with his stick.*] Are you dead?

C A P T [*raising his head for a moment*]: Yes. Dead as a doorbell.

A R L E : But not dead enough to quiet your tongue. Are you the great, the brave, the valiant Captain Bombasto, conqueror of armies and nations?

C A P T [*in a meek voice*]: No, not me. A relative perhaps.

A R L E : Liar. No more of this. Give me the gold at your side.

C A P T : It doesn't belong to me.

A R L E [*sternly*]: At once.

C A P T [*still flat on his back, he holds up the bag of gold*]: Here it is.

A R L E [*taking it*]: Oh now you have proved yourself a brave keeper of your master's gold indeed, Captain Mouse!

C O L O M [*appearing disguised as a bandit and carrying a staff, she sneaks close to* ARLECCHINO *and swats him; in a muffled voice*]: Hand me the gold or it will be the worse for you.

A R L E [*falling to his knees*]: Ooooh! Who are you?

C O L O M : One who wants your gold.

A R L E [*terrified*]: But it doesn't belong to me.

C O L O M : At once!

A R L E [*on his knees*]: Here it is.

C O L O M [*aside*]: What is more fun than tricking a trickster.

> *Exits, laughing. The* MISTRESS *of the inn runs onstage.*

M I S T R E S S : Why, Arlecchino, you look like you have seen a ghost.

A R L E : Who, me?

> *He quickly rises.*

Madam, pray don't be silly. I merely saw a bandit stealing Pantalone's gold from the Captain. There lies the Captain, poor fellow.

M I S T R E S S : Master Pantalone, good Doctor, come down quickly!

> *The heads of* PANTALONE *and the* DOCTOR *slowly appear over the top of the back curtain. They are now completely dressed.*

P A N T : We're not coming down as long as that haunted tree is there.

DOCTOR : I should say not.

ARLE : There is no tree here now.

MISTRESS : Masters, come quickly. There has been a robbery. Your gold has been taken.

PANT : Oh my, my gold taken!

MISTRESS : And Captain Bombasto lies dead at our feet.

PANT : My gold taken. My poor gold!

DOCTOR : Pantalone's precious gold gone? We'll be right down.

> ARLECCHINO *and the* MISTRESS *look at the prone figure of the* CAPTAIN.

MISTRESS : Oh, the poor Captain. So noisy in life and so quiet in death.

ARLE [*aside*]: A better actor than a soldier. He plays dead better than any possum could.

> PANTALONE *and the* DOCTOR *enter.*

DOCTOR : Is this the body of Captain Bombasto? How peaceful he looks.

PANT : But he let a thief steal my gold.

ARLE : That he did, master, for I saw it all. But I shall speak no ill of the dead.

> ARLECCHINO *tickles the* CAPTAIN *with his swat stick. The* CAPTAIN *giggles.* PANTALONE *and the* DOCTOR *jump in surprise.* ARLECCHINO *jabs the* CAPTAIN *with his stick causing him to sit up quickly.*

CAPT : Yow!

PANT [*angrily*]: So, Captain Bombasto, you are not so dead after all! Where is my gold?

CAPT : Sir, I have just been attacked by fifty men, all armed with swords and cudgels. Throwing up me sword, I parried with twenty to the right of me and twenty to the left.

> *He stabs the air with his sword.*

DOCTOR : How many men did you say there were?

ARLE : Twenty and twenty make forty.

CAPT [*hesitating a moment*]: Perhaps there were only forty. [*Quickly.*] Then I felled all thirty with one sweep of me sword.

PANT : Thirty men, Captain?

CAPT: Er . . . thirty men I meant. It was very dark you understand. [*Continuing and amply illustrating the actions he described.*] Yes, ten attacked me from the front and ten at the back. I held them all off.

MISTRESS: Ten and ten make twenty, Captain.

CAPT [*hesitating, then forging ahead*]: Twenty it was. I held them off with a thrust here and a thrust there. The odds were ten to one.

ARLE: So, only ten men!

CAPT: Perhaps ten, now that you mention it—but with the strength of a hundred. Finally they cried for mercy and ran from the field.

PANT: Carrying my gold with them!

CAPT: They stole it while I wasn't looking.

ARLE [*stepping forward*]: One man stole it and here he is! I did it for a joke to show what a cowardly windbag this Captain Bombasto is.

PANT [*furious*]: I hire you to guard my gold and you let my own servant steal it from you. Out of my sight, you Captain of Cowards!

> PANTALONE *beats him with his hat and* ARLECCHINO *swats him with his stick. The* CAPTAIN *runs off one side as* COLOMBINA *enters from the other.*

ARLE: And that's the last we'll see of him.

PANT [*holding out his hand*]: Now, where is my gold?

ARLE: The gold? Oh yes, the gold. Master, strange as it may sound, five fierce bandits robbed it from me just as I robbed it from the Captain.

COLOM: How many men did you say?

PANT: Villain, you lost my gold.

> *Grabbing* ARLECCHINO's *stick, he begins to beat him.*

COLOM [*taking the bag of gold from her cloak*]: Wait, I played a trick on Arlecchino. I am the five bandits that took the gold and here it is.

PANT: My gold is safe.

ARLE: But not my reputation.

PANT: I'm not staying in this place a moment more. Doctor, either you take me to the place where the tree with the happy apples grows, or I'm turning back for home this very day.

COLOM [*aside*]: I've had my fun. Now to return to Pantalone's house before I'm discovered. [*To* PANTALONE.] And now I must take my leave of you for my home is close by. Good-bye to all. [*To* ARLECCHINO.] And to you too, Master Trickster. [*Exits.*]

PANT: There's something strange about that boy. I have a feeling we shall see him again.

ARLE: I hope not.

PANT: Arlecchino, gather the bundles. Doctor, your map had better lead us to the tree this day or else . . .

DOCTOR: According to my map the tree that we seek lies straight as an arrow down this very road.

ARLE [*aside*]: That map couldn't lead him from the front yard to the back.

PANT: Doctor, I am getting more unhappy by the minute. If I get any more unhappier, I shall take your map and make you eat it.

MISTRESS: I know nothing of maps, but if you eat any more of my food my pantry will be empty. So be off with you before I become unhappy myself. And luck go with you. [*Aside.*] These fools will need it aplenty.

> The MISTRESS *exits. The three men with the* DOCTOR *in the lead move down the side steps and make a complete revolution around the stage, going behind the curtain and coming on from the opposite side of the stage. This march is accompanied by music. Having circled the stage, the group comes back onto the platform.*

ARLE: Master, I cannot drag myself a step farther. Let us stop!

PANT: And if I ever find my way home again, I'll never step more than two feet from my front door!

DOCTOR: Hold, my friends. For if I read the map correctly we are very near our destination. Yes, I am most certain that we cannot be far from that we seek. For here you see is the point marked with an X and, if you will look closely, there is the X which marks the spot.

> *A placard bearing a large black X is thrust through the curtain.*

PANT: An X! Then we are here! We have arrived.

> *The card is withdrawn.*

ARLE : At last! [*He collapses on the ground.*] I'll never be able to walk another step.

DOCTOR : Yes. This is the very spot beyond the smallest shadow of the smallest doubt.

PANT [*looking around*]: Doctor, do you notice anything strange about this place.

DOCTOR : It looks quite ordinary to me.

ARLE : I don't care what it looks like, I'm going to sleep. Wake me up sometime next month.

PANT : That house . . . this street . . . that tree . . . it seems to me I've seen them before.

DOCTOR : A trick of the mind, dear sir, for as the ancient learned philosophers say . . .

> COLOMBINA *appears over the top of the curtain shaking a rug. Seeing* PANTALONE, *she drops the rug on his head in surprise.*

COLOM : Why, Master Pantalone! What are you doing down there?

PANT : Colombina! What are you doing up there?

COLOM : What am I doing? Why, I was shaking a rug.

PANT : But how did you get here? We must be near the end of the world. I'm certain we've walked that far at least.

COLOM : But, master. This is your own house.

PANT : What? My own house! But we have been following the Doctor's map. How could we be back where we started?

DOCTOR : It is very simple, my good friend. We walked here.

ARLE [*realizing what has happened*]: Ohhhh! My poor feet!

> COLOMBINA *has come down and has come out the center curtain. She is carrying a basket of apples.*

COLOM : Good master, it is quite clear you have been walking in a circle and have simply ended up where you started from.

DOCTOR [*elated*]: Which simply proves the world is round! Astounding.

PANT [*to the* DOCTOR]: Which proves that though the world may be round your head is flat. Oh, what a fool I've been.

COLOM : So, welcome home. Here, have an apple. I just picked them off our tree in the backyard.

PANT [*taking the apple*]: To think I wasted all my time and money looking for happy apples in the most unlikely places. [*He bites the apple.*] Why, nothing we ate the whole trip tastes as good as this apple. Oh, how happy I am to be back at my own little home eating apples from my own little tree.

COLOM: Master, do you know what you said?

PANT: That I am . . . HAPPY . . . to be home. [*Realizing the import of his statement.*] Why, I am HAPPY! Did you hear!! I'm happy!!!

ARLE: And look! You are smiling! The master is smiling!

COLOM: You have a smile as wide as any I have ever seen.

PANT: How foolish of me to go the whole world round and not realize that happiness was in my own backyard right under my nose.

DOCTOR: Indeed, for the learned ancient Chinese philosopher has said . . .

PANT: Oh, poo, Doctor. Talk less and eat more apples. Here!

> *He takes an apple and stuffs it in the* DOCTOR'S *mouth. The* DOCTOR *tries to talk but can only make sounds.*

DOCTOR: Eh . . . umph . . . ooph . . .

COLOM [*aside*]: That's the wisest thing I ever heard the Doctor say.

> *They all laugh at the* DOCTOR.

ARLE: Here, Colombina, give me one of those apples. I'm starved.

COLOM: Are you sure you want to take anything from a woman who has legs like a bull, teeth like a whale, long ears that hear everything they shouldn't?

ARLE [*hand to mouth*]: How in the world did you . . . [*the truth dawns on him*] Colombina, it was you who . . .

COLOM [*she puts her finger to her lips*]: Shhhh! Not a word. Let this be our little secret. And don't forget I know your secret too.

ARLE: You! You were . . . [*he begins to see the great joke*]: ho—ho—ho!

> *He doubles over with laughter, and then quickly swats the unsuspecting* COLOMBINA. *She starts to throw an apple at him.*

PANT : What's so funny Arlecchino? What's the matter, Colombina?

COLOM : It's the apples, master. The happy apples! Here, let's all have another! And another, and another!

> *Music begins as they all begin eating apples furiously. Laughing, all the characters dance down off the platform as the MAYOR and the townspeople enter from the wings applauding. The characters bow to the townspeople and to the audience as the curtain closes.*

CURTAIN

NOTES

The Strolling Players was expressly written for two reasons, the most important of the two being that it was felt the traditional characters of the *commedia dell'arte* still have much fascinating magic in them. That they have become subjects of scholarly research does not essentially change the fact that they were created for all audiences, untutored and sophisticated alike. Such was the charm of the *commedia's* performances that only the most priggish and straightlaced did not succumb to the inspired foolishness of the numerous individual characters the *commedia* engendered. But how often are these characters, still so full of life, allowed back on the stage? Certainly not often enough. And so the prime reason for creating such a play was to introduce to children some of the figures which have become the very touchstones of the theatrical art and to allow them to enjoy the simple magic of an actor who, by his actions as a *commedia* character, shows us just how much fun there is in living and just how funny living can be.

The second reason for this play's existence is more specific. How often are young actors given the opportunity to inspect at such close range the actual problems and practices of the historical *commedia* companies? A written history can at best only begin to give an insight into what this sort of theatre was really like. But, since this play is based on traditional "lazzi" or skits, it is expected that the actor taking part in it will wish to embroider on the script much as the actual *commedia* actors did on their somewhat less developed scenarios. While the action of this play is more detailed (and this was done to acquaint present-day actors with information their predecessors attained from years of actual experience) it is in no way complete in its present form. Like most plays of this type, plot is an excuse for the actors to perform. What is most important is the vitality of the present moment. If an audience does not enjoy each moment as it arrives, then the play can hardly be expected to succeed. But therein lies the challenge to the performer. It is certainly one he can consider worthy of accepting in order to provide the true enchantment of the *commedia dell'arte*.

Costumes

Granting their variations throughout theatre history, the salient features of the individual costume of each separate character in the *commedia dell'arte* have become sufficiently so particular to that character that it would be a mistake not to use them in the dress of the characters in this play. Arlecchino's traditional outfit is perhaps the best example of how a costume can accurately reflect the character and actions of the performer wearing it. This is not to say the costumes need to be slavishly copied from contemporary prints and drawings. Even when the *commedia* was in full flower there was much variation in costume, however each of the individual characters was clearly identifiable as known characters as well as types. But aside from this, the same principles of costuming hold true as with any other children's play; bright shiny materials are used for young active people, darker heavier materials for older, more sedate characters. Particular emphasis should be paid to the cut and silhouette of the costumes since the characters themselves must be able to form interesting visual images without the aid of an elaborate background.

Masks and Makeup

Most of the traditional characters in the *commedia dell'arte* wore half masks which gave the audience a very good clue as to the nature of the character being portrayed. It would be a mistake, however, to have all the characters in this particular play in masks. It is quite possible, in fact, for stylized makeup to take the place of masks altogether. But if masks are used they should be such that they do not impair the speech of the wearer or "come between" the actor and his audience. That is, they should be natural to the extent that they do not continually call attention to themselves as masks. Perhaps the following individual notes will be helpful in preparation of masks or makeup:

MAYOR   Straight makeup for a middle-aged man.

PANTALONE   Mask, if desired. Features of face: sad eyes, long pointed nose, pale droopy moustache, sallow complexion with deep lines on forehead, around eyes and at the sides of the mouth.

COLOMBINA   Straight ingénue makeup with fresh complexion, bright eyes, and a beauty mark.

ARLECCHINO   Young man, an obvious match for Colombina.

The traditional leering mask of Arlequin would be inappropriate to the character as presented in this play.

THE DOCTOR   Mask, if desired. Features of face: little eyes behind oversized black glasses. Full face with ruddy coloring and plump rosy cheeks; scraggly gray hair coming out from under his tall hat.

CAPTAIN BOMBASTO   Mask, if desired. Features of face: large eyes under bushy black eyebrows; long pointed nose turning slightly up; big black moustache waxed to fine points which point up; swarthy out-of-doors complexion.

MISTRESS   Straight middle-aged makeup. Features of face: bright eyes set in a rather heavy face; slightly overly made up with large beauty mark like Colombina's; some lines of age beginning to show.

MUSICIANS   Straight juvenile or white makeup if such stylization is so desired. Gypsy masks should be sallow in color, with very large noses, white bushy eyebrows set over small eyes. Heavy lines in forehead and around nose and mouth.

TOWNSPEOPLE   Straight makeup.

The Setting and Properties

The setting for *The Strolling Players* need not be any more elaborate than was its actual historical counterpart which generally was a simple booth stage. For this reason the play may be presented under conditions which would severely limit many plays and completely rule out others altogether. Most definitely it is not confined to the proscenium stage and would work just as well, quite possibly better, on the open stage. Special lighting is not required and there are no trick effects which will not allow an audience to be too close. But such a simple setting makes it imperative that the actor is always of great interest to the audience. Two things can greatly help him in this regard: properties that are both useful to the action and are interesting objects in themselves, and a potentially useful scenic structure which furnishes him with places to hide, things to climb on, etc. All properties should be made to correspond to the style of the production. For example, the Doctor's books should not be two or three pocket-sized volumes. Rather, they should be of such a size and number that the Doctor is staggered —or should seem to be—by them. Naturally, actual books of that size would not be possible to carry. But it is not a difficult task to make prop books which, while they are large and bulky, are extremely light and manageable. Whenever possible a property should be as large in concept as the characters who use them.

While it is not necessary, some producers may wish to suggest the city square and the buildings surrounding it in order to more specifically identify the location. It is also quite possible to have the setting in full view as the audience enters the theatre; even a curtain is not really necessary.

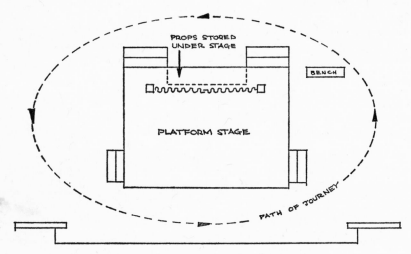

Floor Plan for a Wooden Stage in the City Square